Praise for Leo Dark's *Lucifer Sam*!

"Leo Darke has created a heavy metal nightmare made of hard-driving prose, a dark sense of humor, and a jovial nod to 1980s horror fiction. There's sex, gore, and suspense to spare, and it all unfolds to a heavy metal beat. An enjoyable read."

—Ray Garton, author of *Crucifax* and *Ravenous*

"Just like the punk rock era that it so finely evokes, Darke's tale is edgy, dangerous, thrilling, unpredictable, and scary. Lucifer Sam rocks. Hard."

—Stuart R. West, author of *Twisted Tales from Tornado Alley* and *Ghosts of Gannaway*

"Death Metal has a new vanguard band—and a literal meaning. This band's music is truly Killer."

—Mallory A. Haws, The Haunted Reading Room

THEY HAD A HELL OF
A BAND

LUCIFER SAM

LEO DARKE

Leo Darke

A
Grinning Skull Press
Publication
PO Box 67, Bridgewater, MA 02324

Lucifer Sam
Copyright © 2019 Mickey Lewis

The Skull logo with stylized lettering was created for Grinning Skull Press by Dan Moran, http://dan-moran-art.com/.
Cover designed by Jeffrey Kosh, http://jeffreykosh.wix.com/jeffreykoshgraphics.

Published by Grinning Skull Press, P.O. Box 67, Bridgewater, MA 02324

ISBN: 1-947227-26-2 (paperback)
ISBN-13: 978-1-947227-26-2 (paperback)
ISBN: 978-1-947227-27-9 (ebook)

DEDICATION

I guess I should dedicate this book to those dead rock stars who inspired it. Sidney Vicious, Stiv Bators, Brian Jones, Lemmy, Philthy, Fast Eddie, and, of course, Syd Barrett. But also to those thankfully still very much alive and well: Johnny Lydon, Steve Jones, Captain Sensible, Rat Scabies, Dave Vanian, Micky Geggus, Jeff Turner, and Paul Di'Anno. Without these legends, there would certainly be no Lucifer Sam…

CONTENTS

ACKNOWLEDGMENTS

Big thanks to Micky Geggus and Jeff Turner. Micky once put me on a guest list for one of their gigs when they'd sold out. I intended to buy him a drink to thank him and never did. This will have to do instead! Check out the Rejects' latest albums, Unforgiven and East End Babylon. They've never sounded better.

And to Andy Heinz of The Men That Will Not be Blamed for Nothing for free band CDs and t-shirts! And for being a decent bloody human being.

And to anyone else who picks this up and gives it a "spin." Thank you. Just make sure you wear your plugs.

Promo Single

I'm old now, but once upon a time, I used to be the front man for Lucifer Sam.

Never heard of 'em? Probably reasons for that. Ugly reasons. Nasty reasons. We died to save your souls, you suckers, and you never even heard of us...

Of course, we didn't all die, or I for one wouldn't be here to tell you the tale (Kirk Stammers, if it means anything to you). But we'd certainly gone through a lot of band members and in only a fairly short time, too. And, of course, the reasons for that are those same ugly, nasty ones that are responsible for us being well off the mainstream radar. But I'm sure some people on the underground remember us. Remember the wild gigs, the blood, the horror...the fornication and the fury.

Did I say we were good people? I don't think I promised that; just that we saved your asses. Didn't make us saints. Did I say we were good *musicians?* Don't think I did, but on both counts we weren't really bad. See here, I can remember us playing our best gigs, when we were at the top of our game, like it was last week. A place like the Ten Bells in Whitechapel, maybe, with the crowd pushing forward, sweat stinkin' em up, excitement gluin' their eyes to the stage, exhausted from plunging and slammin', takin' a break through a slow song, maybe "Bones of My Dreams."

Out there on my right, there's Johnny Diesel; that was never his real name, of course, but who gave a shit about real names? He thought he was Keith Richards, but he was closer to Brian James, the demented, wild-eyed, original geetarist from the Damned, but then I don't expect you to remember *him* either. Our Johnny didn't so much play, as burn. The notes sparked from his fretboard, ignited into a bushfire licking out and consuming the audience so they flamed with him. It wasn't technical excellence; it was demonic fury.

Behind me, the bummed-out, empty bottle that was the Clown—but don't make the mistake that he was funny just cos he dressed in circus clobber. If he hadn't been in a band, he would've been in maximum security, and I'd seen him kill, so I should know. I'm sorry, I'm sure I told you earlier that we weren't bad people. Sometimes I lie. In fact, I'm lying now, or at least my memory is: the Clown wasn't our first drummer, just our nastiest. Ned, the original skins man, was much nicer. He used his Tourette's Syndrome like a weapon. Funny as fuck. Best stand-up comic I ever saw, even if he was a shit drummer.

Where was I? Did I say I'm old? You might say so. I feel old, and I get a little confused. Ned? Was I talking about him? Still, I don't remember him staying with us for long, or Clown for that matter. You see, I'm talkin' about the original line up, the mad, motley bunch of fuckers that kick-started the Sam and were there when it really mattered—at that fateful Wembley gig when the world was all set to end. Lucifer Sam's origin story if you like, Marvel fans. It was the gig that made us what we are.

I'm going too fast, aren't I? I nearly told you about how we were cursed, how our fuckin' songs could save people's lives cos of what got into our instruments. Okay, they weren't strictly *our* instruments to begin with… And I haven't even finished my roll call…

Over there you'll find Davey, tangled up in the cable from his bass, spitting and snarling, a mock werewolf in leathers that would meet the genuine article one day and leave the band suddenly, leaving his entrails all over a bookshop floor as he did so… But right now I'm talking about this gig in the grimy, old Ten Bells. What was it, our fourth, our fifth? Who knows. All I *do* know is, it was before we got the demons in our souls, before we changed from just another desperate and filthy band—albeit talented, hey, our songs were *magnetic*—into the most important act in the world. Yeah, you heard that right. Don't believe me, do you? You're thinkin', "Well, if they was that fuckin' great, why ain't I heard of 'em?" Yeah, an' I refer the honorable gentlemen and ladies to my previous statement, so fuck you.

Where did I get to...? Did I tell you I was old? I did. I know I did. But here's the catch: I'm only thirty-seven. And last time I checked, thirty-seven wasn't old. But that's not how it feels to me. That's certainly not how it feels *inside*... In my heart, I feel closer to sixty-five. That's what being in Lucifer Sam done for me. They say being in a band can be bad for your health, but shit...

Back to the here and now, and look at this place. What a shithole. These are the only venues we can get now. I'm standing in front of the urinal, waiting for a piss before we hit the stage (like a proper old man, I wait a lot for that as well these days), watching the cockroaches come out to play, and there's more here than I ever saw on our "tour" in Java—that time we played the haunted hill.

Here we go. Wash one of them fuckers down the porcelain wall. Teach you, ya bastard. Is this what my life has culminated in? Waiting to play in front of twenty old drunks in a Wetherspoons and pissing on a cockroach? Hell of an achievement.

But I was talkin' about something, wasn't I? Oh yeah, Dave the bass player...wolfish and sullen, smelled a little bad sometimes. We called him Davey Crooked on account of his yellow snaggleteeth. Had a personality disorder: thought he was Sid Vicious most days, the rest of the time he was convinced he was Steve Jones, except he played bass instead of guitar. On good days he got almost witty. We called those his Johnny Rotten coffee mornings. We quite liked him then. But really, the only thing he had in common with Sid was that he was shit on bass. So why did we keep him? Probably because he swore better than any trooper I ever heard of. Real inventive with his profanities. He made cussing a fucking art form. Still smelled bad, though.

Have I forgotten anybody? One more I think, and if you was in that audience at the Ten Bells back in 2011 or whatever year it was, you'd a bin lookin' straight at him. You're listening to him now. The good-lookin' one: the devil in a black highwayman jacket and biker boots. Messy, black spider hair, nose big and predatory. Yeah, the girls used to like me. They said I frightened them (have you *seen* my eyes?), but my vulnerability drew 'em in, too. Had a lost expression, they said. Aaaahhh. Are you feeling sick enough yet? I ain't makin' this shit up. Cheekbones to die for, I believe is the expression, and believe me, I nearly did die for 'em once, when Slick Nick wanted to steal 'em right out of the flesh of my face and make stew with 'em. That was about the time the skulls turned up, bobbing in East-ville Park Lake. Ducks didn't know what the fuck to make of it... But I'm doing it again, aren't I? Getting ahead...

Was I telling you how attractive I was to the ladies? Better not let Johnny hear that. He'd cut me down to size, reveal me to be the liar I some-times am, but there's no chance of that anymore, of course, Mr. Diesel no longer being with us. Alright, *some* girls liked me. Most of 'em liked Diesel, the bastard, on account of him being the cool, thoughtful one, with chick-trap eyes (yeah, yeah, okay, okay—*he* was the one with the razor-blade cheekbones) and perfectly coiffed '50s hair. Twat. But don't worry, I still got enough chicks...the fucked up ones, mostly. And Rose... Better not talk about Rose right now. Not good for me. Even after all these years...

So what was I... Oh yeah, chicks... Maybe they were drawn to the vac-uum inside me, sensed I was as lost as they were. But then we were *all* lost, every last, damned member of Lucifer Sam. You could see it in our eyes, and if you looked deeper, you'd see it in our souls. The ones we sold, to quote Black Sabbath, for rock 'n'... alright, I'll save on the cheese and leave it there.

I know it was a quick introduction to our band, but it's gonna have to do for now cos I'm drifting back a few years to that makeshift stage at the Ten Bells, and it's around about June, and this is the biggest crowd we've pulled so far—oooh, all of thirty—so let me enjoy the memories. I can remember us launching into "Night of the Crabs" a good few years be-fore Guy N. Smith reappeared on the literary scene and brought all the horrible characters from the pages of his pulp books out into the light of day with him. Sorry, gotta stop that…

So we're playing to our first really enthusiastic crowd, and they're livin' it, juices are flowing, blood and sex are in the air. We're playing tight for once, and they've cottoned onto the fact that our sound is unique. Voodoo Punk, we call it, all evil fuzz tone guitar and spooky sound effects, along with my haunted vocals, and murder melodies that dig right into your soul and paint it black. In short, the catchiest, weirdest, motherfuckin' punk music you ever heard. Devil got all the best choons? You ain't heard of Lucifer Sam.

So let me drift back a whiles, at least as long as it takes me to finish this piss, and let me be that young killer rocker I once was and…

And I'll tell you all about that gig at Wembley Arena that changed our lives forever, and all about the Adventures of Lucifer Sam…

But hang on. I'm not really here to tell you Lucifer Sam's potted history, am I? Maybe you don't wanna hear about us. I kinda forgot it's that *other* band you want to know about, ain't it? Admit it. You don't give a fuck about us, what we did for you. You just want to hear about *them*. And if you never heard of Lucifer Sam, I can bet you a million guitar picks you heard of these boys. Do I really have to name them? Maybe we should've nicked that name as well as their instruments… And if you said it was taking their gear that got us in all this trouble in the first place, you'd definitely be right. But it wasn't really the instruments, was it? More like what got inside 'em. A haunted backline? Yeah, if you like. What's that you say? We should've dumped the lot? Yeah, that'd be right. But that was never our way. We always took the dangerous path. If we hadn't snatched that kit, a lot of crazy shit—good and bad—wouldn't have happened. But there's no turning back the Rolex. And look, see where it got us: three o'clock in the p.m., playing to a bunch of old pissheads with stains down their strides and seven days a week of free time.

Yeah, yeah, I get the picture. You've heard enough of my crazy dribbling. Time to zip up and get out there and join the boys. Hmm? Oh yeah. I was gonna tell you about Cat O' Nine Tails first, wasn't I? The biggest fuckin' rock band on the planet. Like I said, everybody heard of Cat O' Nine.

And now, at last, you'll find out what really happened to 'em.

To start with, it was all about their singer, Ray. Former Portobello Road barrow boy. Right proper cockney. Maybe he should have stuck to shouting "Apples and Pears" than banging out vocals for the biggest metal band in the universe. Would certainly have been better for his health.

Ray Starling was mad, in both senses of the word—he knew that more than anybody. Anger boiled in him constantly from the day he was fired from the band after only appearing on the first of Cat O' Nine's mega-selling series of albums. He was mad as the proverbial geezer at the tea party, and I don't mean the dormouse. Here he is, young and desirable on stage at a festival in Germany with Cat O' Nine Tails. The rest of the line-up includes Motörhead and a whole load of other New Wave of British Heavy Metal acts. We're talking a good few years back now. Shall we be polite and say twenty? Alright, twenty-five... So here's Ray, standing on stage, shirtless, body glistening with sweat, his punky hairstyle a slap in the face for the rest of the conventional rockers in the band and in the audience. Ray didn't give a fuck about that. Ray was, as we said, pretty damn mad. Bad and dangerous, too. To himself and others.

But you don't really need me to tell you what Ray Starling was like. You'll have read all the headlines. So forget the tabloid shit for now and picture this instead: Cat O' Nine Tails savoring their first massive festival success.

Take it away, Ray...

CD 1

FLIGHT TO ETERNITY

Chapter One

1989

Barra boy no more, my son...

Ray was staring at 15,000 upturned faces. And they were all staring at *him*.

The realization didn't hit him at first. He stood on the lip of the stage, struggling to take it all in. Proper head-fucked, as Barney, the drummer, would have put it. He was half naked, his slim torso slick with sweat. Two songs in and he still couldn't accept the enormity of it all. He stood still in the few moments grace between songs, hand unconsciously brushing at his spiky mop as he tried to get his head around it. Jezza, the guitarist, was busy tuning, head down as he concentrated so Ray couldn't see his expression. Probably thinking about playing *Dungeons and Dragons* with his Tolkien-obsessed mates, the nerdy twat. He only got hard for prog rock solos. Ray was sure his guitar mags were all very sticky. Phil, the bass player and band leader, was staring at the audience, too, a dumb grin on his square face, long, curly hair matted with sweat. Ray beamed over at him, shaking his head numbly, sharing a WTF moment. They had never been close, but this was a moment even enemies could share. This was momentous. The crowd was roaring for more, and distinct above the colossal noise, Ray could hear his name in a rising chant. He felt electrified. The vestiges of coke left in his system buzzed through his veins, boosted by his euphoria.

Then the truth of it smashed him like a hammer. This was it. He had made it. No more getting up at 5:00 a.m. to look after his old man's fruit and veg stall on Portobello Road. No more skimping on beer money to feed the electricity meter in his dingy flat off Brick Lane. No more borrowing a sub off his surly old man to take a bird to the flicks. No more scrapping outside the Ten Bells on a Friday, Saturday night cos some bastard looked at him wrong. There was gonna be no more of that shit! From now on there would be chauffeurs to every venue, drinking champers like water at top London clubs with big-breasted tarts falling all over him. He was *big time, baby!* He sucked it all in, standing on the lip of the stage. This was a fuckin' epiphany! He felt joy orgasm through his body. He spread his arms, tilted his head to one side to take in the adoration of the crowd. His name was a massive chant that would shame the rest of the band: "Starling, Starling… STARLING!!!"

Ray Starling, twenty-one years old and at the top of the world. Headlining the Frankfurt Rock Festival to 15,000 punters all screaming his name was his Mount Everest scaled. He had the voice, he had the look. He certainly had the attitude to achieve—he took no bullshit, and the desire to make it had driven him through a poverty-stricken childhood and teenage years that had seen him punch and struggle every step of the way to this moment. But it wasn't just his sheer brute willpower. His voice was unforgettable. It could chisel stars and make the Gods roar. Ray had a vocal range that allowed him pinnacle-ascending falsettos one minute and punky, thunderous growls the next. His voice had a quality that transcended the puerile subject matter Phil insisted the band concentrate on: all fantasy imagery, torture implements, and dodgy war films. It reached your soul and your gut at the same time. And not only was Ray's voice pretty damn unique, but he was also young and eminently shaggable. The first album had gone platinum across the globe, and things really couldn't get better than this.

Within two months he would lose it all.

Chapter Two

2014

The punch took Ray in his left eye, and for a moment he could only see in mono.

The blow took him clean off his bar stool, dumped him on the floor of the boozer like the sack of shit the geezer who hit him obviously thought he was.

"Fuckin' rock star? More like a used-up tissue that everyone's spunked in, mate. Ain't nuffin' sadder than a pathetic Has Been who still thinks he's got what it takes. Fuckin' loser." The big man took a step back as if to deliver a kick to the fallen idol. Ray saw it coming but was too pissed to dodge it. The toe of the geezer's boot caught him on his left cheekbone, just below his foggy eye. The pain was sickening. He rolled over on his back, and the dingy pub revolved around him, darkening.

He could see a couple of faces hanging over him, repeating his name in anxious tones—certainly not the 15,000 that once roared it in exuberance. Michelle's face was tear-streaked as she knelt down next to him, her sister, Bella, turning away to scream at the man who had kicked him.

He peered up at Michelle as if wondering who she was. Was she still his bird? The last in a looooong fuckin' line of 'em. But this one had been a keeper. Before Michelle, none of 'em had meant much to him. Not really.

Apart from Michelle, *nothing* meant much to him anymore.

He stared up at the cracked ceiling of the Victorian-era boozer and wondered where it had all gone wrong.

Now it was Phil Carter's face looming into vision. But Cat O' Nine Tails' bass player certainly wasn't in this back-street boozer. Nah, he'd be drinking champers on a jet somewhere on the latest leg of a world fuckin' tour no doubt…

It was just a memory. Just the same old memory that had rolled through his mind throughout the last twenty-five years like a mossy stone that could not be stopped. Phil's face was young again, just a couple years older than Ray's had been on that fateful day in October 1989 when Phil finally called time on Ray's Cat O' Nine career.

He was sitting in the EMI office again, the shades partly pulled down over the gorgeous autumn day that filled the Kensington street outside. He'd been summoned to the meeting the day before, his manager sounding curt and evasive on the blower. "Tell ya what it's all about when we see ya, Ray, old son. Gotta go."

But his manager was late. Ray had always been punctual. That was something you learned in the East End. Certainly on the fruit market. Be on time or lose your fuckin' place. Well, here he was on time…

Doug, the manager, finally showed his face, ten minutes late, and Phil was with him. They entered the office quietly, shook his hand formally, and Ray knew why he had been called before they even opened their mouths.

"Sit down, Ray, son." Doug was a tough, no-shit businessman from Essex. The band looked up to him like a father figure. He was tight as a hamster's ass with their money, but he always looked out for them and had got them where they were today. Phil might have written most of the songs, and Ray sung the fuck out of 'em, but it was Doug who had the unerring business sense to broker the deals that had sent them into metal orbit. Ray had always respected him. Which was why looking at him now and reading his fate in that boxer's mug of a manager's expression, Ray felt even more betrayed. Doug was avoiding his gaze. Something he'd never done before.

Ray dropped into a leather swing seat like he'd been felled. He stared at Doug and knew his mouth was opening to say something, but there was no breath. He coughed violently, clearing his throat, but Doug was already speaking as Phil and the manager took seats across the oval table from him.

"Ray..." Doug began, flicking a quick look at the singer, then directing his gaze to a pen he'd fished from his pocket. "I think you know why we've called you."

Ray swung his gaze to the bass player. Phil was studying the blind over the window, his stolid face expressionless.

"No," Ray said. He stood up slowly. The world had suddenly grown very small in his head. "No," he said again. "You ain't gonna—"

"Mate, you've really left us no choice!" Phil had his hands wide, and his eyes were all wide, too, in "I'm the real victim here" innocence.

Ray started to shake. He felt sicker than ever before in his life, the evilest hangover was nothing on it. His mouth wouldn't let any more words out.

Doug took over, rising from his chair to grab Ray's arm in a consoling fashion, trying to ease him back into his seat. "Ray, you know I love you like a son. You know how much it fuckin' hurts to do this to you?"

Ray looked into his eyes, and at last Doug met his gaze. The forty-one-year-old looked genuinely sad. Was that a glint of a tear in his eyes? Crocodiles cried, too... Ray began to feel the familiar anger building, replacing the shock, the hurt, the desolation. The anger that had carried him through childhood and beyond, made him the tough fucker he was today. He shook Doug's grip away and rounded on Phil.

"You cunt," he said slowly, his voice trembling with rage. "You never fuckin' liked me. I *made* this band. Without me, you're fuckin' nothin'!"

Phil sighed heavily, studied his fingers for a minute—the stubby fingers that Ray had always thought too short for a bass player—and then sat back in the swivel seat. "You did it to yourself, mate. We can't control you. We can't take it anymore. We have to look to the future and take this seriously. Me an' Jez are always experimenting with the music. We want to push it further, but you don't give a fuck. You're just here for a ride, not to take it to the next step. And you're ruining your voice. You're always fucked out of your nut on coke or speed. And that's when you're not pouring Jack Daniels down your throat like there's no tomorrow."

Ray took that in. That was a major speech for the usually laconic band leader. He sat down again. His anger, tipped nearly to the boiling point, curdled, miraculously stalled. Phil was right; he was diametrically opposed to the bass player in literally everything. Phil very rarely drank, certainly never took drugs. He was a family man, with two babies—twins—to look after, and even when he was on tour, he would stay in his hotel room reading a Sven Hassell novel rather than boozing and shagging like Ray and whoever was brave enough to accompany him on one of his blitzes. And Phil was right about the other thing as well: they thought he didn't know about their stupid experimental sessions, but he did, and it wasn't for him—the three of them jamming together secretly without Ray, fixated on Jimmy Page, Aleister Crowley bollocks, tryin' to add some quasi-mystical, arcane nonsense to the music. He'd always just let 'em get on with it. His job was to sing, not fuck around pretendin' to be into Black Magic when they was just four ordinary blokes from the East End. To Ray, it was only Rock 'n' Roll, and he liked it. He should've seen this coming. He really should.

"But there is no tomorrow," he finally answered Phil, his voice slow and empty.

Phil looked at Doug, and then both of them looked at the table.

"We're offering you a deal, son." Doug said eventually. "Sixty grand for signing off rights to the songs you wrote for the album. It's a good deal, son. You should take it."

Ray took it.

He walked out of the office on shaky legs, but he took it. Suddenly the future didn't seem so bright, the birds wouldn't be so fit or so numerous, and the champers and the clubs would be a lot cheaper.

But there is no tomorrow...

The haze began to clear, the dingy décor of the back-street boozer swam back into focus. Michelle was still bending over him, tears streaking her pretty face. Ray shook his head to clear it. The five-inch metal sword on a chain around his neck jangled. He remembered the fans who'd forged it for him, gave it to him after he'd been fired, when they told him he was the best singer the band would ever have. He saw their faces now. He began to push himself up from the grubby floorboards.

"Comin' back for more, old timer?" The muscle-bound bastard who'd slugged him was grinning from ear to ear.

Ray had always been a scrapper. Outside his local down Canning Town, impressing the birds by being the hardest, the mouthiest, the meanest. Top Dog. Leader of the pack. He'd filled many a chick's panties on that rep. You had to fight to prove who you were, and Ray had instinctively understood that. He understood it now, twenty-five years older than that slim, sexy Rock God who had stood on the stage at Frankfurt and surveyed all that he owned. Except he was a bit slower now, a lot fatter, and that punky barnet had fallen to the winds. But he was still Ray Fuckin' Starling, and he'd been proving that just about every night he hit the boozers. Been fighting that memory of the office in Kensington for twenty-five long years, fighting anyone who got mouthy and called him out. Because people *always* wanted to take him on so they could tell their mates they put one over on the ex-Cat O' Nine singer. And now here was another one itching to get his bedpost notch. Ray's head began to buzz the way it always did when the Beast was coming out. Couldn't they ever let it lie…? *Couldn't HE ever let it lie?*

No. If he had to prove he was still Ray Starling, badass lead singer of the biggest rock band in the world, then a twenty-five-year-old Best Before Date wasn't gonna stall him. Ray had always been the mad one in the band. The others were boring pussies. But did he really have to point that out to every cunt in a bar who wanted some of him?

So be it.

Ray blinked to clear the haze in his left eye. He felt the rage surge through his veins, the way euphoria had done once upon a long time ago in Frankfurt.

He focused on the big man who'd started on him for no reason other than he'd once been famous. The big lug was still grinning, still waiting for Ray to get up. *Latest in a long line, son.* All the years of regret, despair, smashed dreams, oceans of booze, and mountains of drugs had led to this. Had led to every other night just like it.

Ray was on one knee now. The pain in his head was like a pile driver battering away at his skull. His left eye was half closed.

He faced the big man, swaying slightly. Then he let the anger take him.

When Ray got really mad, wise men knew to duck for cover. All hell was there, all ready for the breaking. Unfortunately, tonight's assailant wasn't too wise. "Reckon I got one more Comeback in me..." Ray said.

And suddenly everything got *very* messy.

Ray Starling had always been a scrapper.

Chapter Three

Rose said, "I don't believe it."

Kirk said, "Fuck-ing *hell!*"

They were both watching the news in Kirk's ropey Stoke Newington flat. The TV screen showed stills of four long-haired musicians, then a video clip from one of their colossal stadium gigs. The caption beneath rolled across in the Breaking News red banner:

PRIVATE JET CARRYING FAMOUS ROCK BAND DISAPPEARS OVER INDIAN OCEAN

Kirk started to speak again, but Rose shushed him urgently. Cat O' Nine Tails had always been her favorite band.

The newsreader was short on facts. Kirk and Rose watched breathlessly as he delivered all he had, then Rose flicked to another news channel with the same headline news and tried to pick scraps from the slight variation of detail. But there was nothing more. The facts were very minimal: the band was on the last leg of their world tour, taking them to Asia with dates in Jakarta and Japan before finally climaxing the tour in Sydney. Somewhere high above the Indian Ocean at approximately midnight GMT, Air Control had lost contact with the private jet. It had simply and inexplicably disappeared from airspace. Australian and Indonesian maritime rescue patrols were already covering the area where contact had been lost, expanding to allow for wreckage drift patterns. So far, absolutely nothing had been discovered, although, as all newscasters on all channels kept repeating, it was a vast area of empty ocean to cover. A spokesperson from EMI, the band's record label, was rolled out to completely insipid effect— Kirk wondered if he'd ever even met the band. One channel scooped Phil Carter's distraught wife and his teenage son (a younger copy of his Dad), red-eyed and devastated, trying not to fear the worst despite the words the news anchor seemed determined to put in their mouths. Baz Cropper's wife, a still-glamorous blonde with a sensitive face in her early forties, looked broken as she eulogized on how attentive and kind her husband was. And there was Jez Tweed's girlfriend, who looked remarkably like the guitarist, equally as sensible and thoughtful in appearance as her missing lover. She looked a little shell-shocked but was keeping it real. She dismissed the anchor's suggestion of terrorist hijacking as absurd. It was a private jet with the same pilot and aircrew they always used. There was no question of anybody suspicious being on board. Besides the pilot, co-pilot, and two air stewards who had been flying with the band for the last ten years, the only other occupants of the jet were the manager, Doug Roscoe, the four members of the band themselves, and a handful of road crew who, again, were loyal and trusted members of the band's entourage. Besides, she pointed out patiently, rebuffing the anchor's interruptions, Air Traffic Control had reported conversations with the pilot for the first two hours of the flight since leaving Kuala Lumpur, and there had been nothing out of order reported.

Speculation continued to fly on all the channels. Had the jet crashed, or had it indeed been hijacked, despite protestations from family members of the band? Engine failure or terrorist activity? More experts and spokespersons were rolled out. Aircraft engineers who had checked over the jet before the flight and found absolutely nothing amiss. "This craft was exhaustively and extensively serviced since the last flight," one engineer stressed somewhat defensively as the headlines unspooled on a strip beneath his strained expression. "And the service records speak for themselves. This jet was good to go." But where *did* it go, that was the question that was on all news anchors' lips.

In between footage of Cat playing Wembley Arena and happy, smiley interviews with the four musicians that constituted the band (Barney cracking fart jokes, Baz beaming in his Sherlock Holmes titfer), there were more family members dredged up. Rose was close to tears when Barney's parents appeared, looking fragile and utterly overcome with grief. The old couple clung to the hope that their drummer son would be returned safely to them at any minute. Kirk had his doubts but said nothing; he could see how increasingly upset Rose was becoming with each revelation.

Finally, the news channels appeared to have exhausted all avenues, exploited all potential resources. When they had seen the same clips of the band laughing and joking on a previous jet tour and touching down in Japan the year before three times in a row, even Rose was tiring of the repetition. Kirk took the remote from her and switched off the TV. He pulled her against him on the sofa, stroking her long brown hair, saying nothing for a while, and if he felt she was maybe wallowing, being a little *too* melodramatic in her grief (after all, it wasn't as if she knew any of the band personally), he certainly wasn't going to mention it. She was a sensitive soul, which is why he loved her.

She had dragged him to see them twice on the European leg of the tour. Once at the London O2, and again at the not-so-accessible Birmingham Arena. She had all their albums—all fifteen of them!—and while Kirk liked the band's first album well enough, the rest left him cold. While Cat O' Nine's music was undeniably appealing in a mass-market fashion with riffs and melodies as catchy as a docker's billhook, Kirk had always found their lyrics a little naff and the subject matter a trifle undergrad. Hell, that was being polite; sixth form nerd metal would be more accurate. Cat O' Nine had made themselves accessible on such a huge scale by ostensibly not being offensive to anyone, something Kirk had always struggled with. Surely, the true appeal of a band lay in their ability to challenge. To outrage as well as excite. And in his opinion, Cat O' Nine Tails (again, with the honorable exception of their first album, which, grounded by the ferocious vocal abilities and punk-rock attitude of their original singer, Ray Starling, had been vital and blistering) was anything but exciting. They had forged a career in safe, melodic metal. Pleasing to the ear, easy on the mind. Nothing wrong with that, of course, but metal had never really been Kirk's cup of tea. The genre was way too conservative despite its obsession with imagery the practitioners obviously deemed shocking. No offense, Cat O' Nine, but horror movie covers and references to stranglers and gibbets steeped in chiming guitars and twinkling solos was as far removed from shocking as you could get.

Crypt Metal was how he'd described them to Rose once, and it seemed accurate enough. The band floundered in adolescent obsessions with fantasy gore and Hammer Horror chic while lyrical howlers decimated grammar left, right, and all over the show.

It had always struck Kirk that Cat O' Nine had dabbled in pretend Crowley Satanism and dark imagery, but in a comic book fashion without ever seeming to really believe in it. He was pretty sure they didn't subscribe to the Black Arts. He'd once attended a Cat O' Nine signing with Rose, and Phil Carter had chuckled dismissively when Kirk asked him if they really believed in the Horned One as the guitarist signed a copy of *Fear Stalkers* for Rose. "Nah, mate. The missus would kill me. She banks with the other side, know what I mean?" Jez Twist had confirmed the bass player's statement in a couple of subsequent interviews, and the band's jolly drummer, Barney Smolt, had once joked on a chat show a few years back about "riding bronco with the Devil, just for a laugh like" in a mock oafish accent. It was all a piss take, window dressing. Cat O' Nine Tails were four down-to-earth geezers, cheery, a little middle-of-the-road, not to mention middle-aged; a little *conservative* with the collective imaginative powers of a squad of road menders. Long-haired, good-natured Brit rockers up for a hearty chuckle, but as boring as accountants in their private lives. In fact, Baz had been an accountant when he first left university, a fact that didn't go unnoticed by the music press eager to spotlight the new guy in town who had replaced the infamous headline bagger, Ray Starling. They wouldn't get any booze and whore stories out of Baz; no threesomes in a Premier Inn coffee lounge there. Baz was a fine vocalist, but he was dull as Dutch cheese. Then there was Barney Smolt, who had retained a hobby most boys grew out of when they were fourteen—he spent a lot of his adult pocket money buying and assembling model airplane kits. Jez

Twist did role playing! Phil Carter played golf. R.I.P. rock 'n' roll. Sid and Elvis died for *this*?

But for all that, Kirk didn't exactly hate them; he'd listen to them if he had to, say on long drives with Rose or while doing the gardening at his Mum's little bungalow. Mostly only if Rose asked him to, though.

But it hadn't always been that way. He would never forget the first time he saw Cat O' Nine Tails when he was barely ten years old and visiting his big brother who lived in Germany. He had never heard of most of the bands, but his bruv was a metal fan and dragged him along to the open-air festival at Frankfurt.

What was more eye-opening than any of the raucous and wild hair bands was the sight of his brother smoking a joint with his mates as they sat in the sun watching the festival. He appreciated the way his bruv had trusted Kirk enough not to say anything to his parents. That had been mutually understood. He'd even offered Kirk a toke for a joke. And then Cat O' Nine Tails had come on stage...

It had only been about one man for Kirk; the others were just background to Ray Starling's barnstorming performance. Kirk would never forget one moment that had burned itself into his mind and chased him through childhood to the present day—an instant influence: Ray, standing on stage between songs, legs slightly apart, his shirt stripped away, chest heaving from his exertions, hair bushy and semi spiked. He was surveying the audience as if he wasn't quite sure he was really there, a "This is It" moment unlike any other Kirk had witnessed before or since (Kirk had certainly not experienced it with his own band up to this point). Then Ray had flung out his arms, head tilted to one side, Jesus on the Rock Cross, and the chanting had lifted into the sunny skies, rising, deafening: "Cat O' Nine, Cat O' Nine... CAT O' NINE!!!"

The first album was an indispensable rock classic, burning with Starling's barely contained fury and a handful of compositions that blew away Carter's songs in terms of intensity and unleashed craziness. But it had been evident then that Ray was too much of a loose cannon for his more staid fellow band members, and the signs were there that he wouldn't last if you really looked for them. After Starling's departure, the band racked up a truly impressive amount of albums and went interstellar in terms of sales. The music became less fierce, less punky and in your face. A thoughtfulness and lyricism replaced the fury (at least in the music, the lyrics themselves remained as dodgy and English teacher-baiting as ever). Cat O' Nine settled themselves into almost cozy respectability to accompany their newfound massive wealth, despite the playful gore of their cover imagery and bellicose pretense of their song titles.

As for Ray Starling…?

He had dropped out of the public arena completely. He had taken the sixty thousand pounds for the rights to the songs he had written for the band and disappeared for all intents and purposes. Although "disappeared" was not entirely true. Kirk was vaguely aware he had started up a couple of bands, attempted a solo career, and attempted comeback after comeback over the years. But all this was just stuff he'd heard down the pub; Kirk had never heard any examples of Ray's non-Cat stuff, and there was probably a good reason for that. As one of his mates had told him, "It sounds like his heart wasn't in it." And that made sense to Kirk. After seeing Ray live when he was ten and witnessing the absolute euphoria burning out from him, how could he ever truly replicate that in any other band? Cat O' Nine had been his life, even if it had only been for a short moment in time…

"I don't want to hear any more, Kirk…" Rose said, turning away from the TV.

Kirk switched off the news and pulled Rose against him.

"You don't have to, Rosie," he said and kissed her cheek fondly.

She turned to him, her dark brown eyes troubled. "Do you think they're really dead?" She sucked in a breath, and when it came out again, it trembled. "Baz is one of the nicest musicians ever. He kissed my cheek last time we saw them, remember? Such a true, kind gentleman… This just isn't right. It isn't *fair*…"

He stroked the red stripe that grew from her crown and snaked through her thick brown hair. He loved that stripe; his very own Bride of Frankenstein dipped in blood. Kirk shrugged, then leaned in to kiss her, and knowing she was sorrowful, he felt a little ashamed of his instant arousal. She always did that to him, though, and he hoped she would continue to turn him on for a long time to come. Her face was a sexy contrast of strength and vulnerability; her finely chiseled cheekbones guarded eyes that were sensual and soft, yet her lips were stubbornly firm, her nose curved, forceful. She had a temper you wouldn't want to unleash (and Kirk had set it free a few more times than he would have liked), and she was tall and imposing, maybe with half an inch on Kirk. But right now, she was bare, confused, and had never looked sexier.

So Kirk forgave himself and kissed her again, pushing her gently back on the sofa and getting to work caressing her right breast through the material of her tee. He was pulling her shirt up over her head to get at her purple bra when she stopped him.

"What the fuck!?" She pushed his hands away and sat up. "I don't fucking believe you..."

Kirk sat back against the sofa cushions, his mouth dropping, hands wide and adopting what he hoped was his best look of bewildered innocence. "What?"

"You can really be an unfeeling bastard, d'you know that?"

He shrugged again. "Thought you wanted consoling, hun."

"Do you normally console people with a hard-on? Hate to see you at a funeral."

He smirked at that, which didn't help his case. But that was another thing he really liked about Rose; she could always make him laugh.

"Sorry, Rosie." He gave her a quick kiss on the forehead. "Forgiven?"

"No. Fuck off and make me a cup of tea."

He did as he was told. He was no fool.

As he bustled around in the kitchen of the small flat, he heard the first bars of "The Stranger" start up from the living room. She'd slipped on Cat O' Nine's second album. She had always preferred the band post Starling, something Kirk could never quite understand. The volume rose as she adjusted the remote on the stereo, and he smiled. *Rosie's little tribute*, he thought fondly and put the kettle on.

"Best rock band on the planet, my arse! A fuckin' metal Genesis is all they are. *Were.* Tweed jackets and plus fours be more suitable for 'em than leathers, the phony bastards. 'Bout fuckin' time they took their last encore, if you ask me." Davey Crooked finished his tirade and took a hefty gulp of lager.

"Well, I'm not asking you. Show some fucking respect, they're dead," Kirk told the bassist before Rose could rise from the pub table and lamp him one. She could take him, too; Kirk was sure of that. Davey was a lanky streak of piss, and all the leathers in the world couldn't make him any good in a scrap. Kirk had seen him go down too many times in rucks both before and after gigs. He remembered one particularly funny moment when Davey had decided to get involved in a post-gig punch-up in a dodgy pub they'd just been playing in Cardiff. The brawl between two huge Welsh women was getting increasingly nearer the table where the members of Lucifer Sam were sitting. Davey had no idea what they were fighting about, and Kirk had no idea what made him stand up and get involved. Maybe he fancied one of the big tattooed lasses—Davey was never renowned for his refined taste in females. But there he was anyway, jumping up to part them, and he succeeded in doing so, even if only for the second it took for one of them to turn round and chin him with one meaty fist. The time between Davey rising from his feet and landing on his ass couldn't have been more than five seconds. The two Welsh gals ignored him as soon as he hit the deck and turned back to slapping the hell out of each other. Kirk and the rest left him underneath the table where he'd landed, stunned as a felled calf. Let him rot, was their motto.

"Why the fuck should I show respect? We're better off without 'em. They'd become an embarrassment. Silly old bastards pretending to worship the Devil while playing golf and selling afternoon teas to the middle class." Davey pointed a long finger at Kirk. "You do know Baz Cropper bought a cream tea shop for his Missus to run down in Devon during the Summer Season, don't ya? They're about as rock 'n' roll as my old Nan. Fuck no, she's got way more attitude and rhythm in her mobility scooter than those twats ever showed. They've been pedaling the same cartoon shit for way too long."

Even if Kirk agreed with him, he wasn't going to say so for fear of upsetting Rose again. But Rose didn't need Kirk to protect her—not when she had her own Sir Galahad in the form of Johnny Diesel (nee John Dover). The slick-haired guitarist had always been a little too quick to step in on Rose's behalf for Kirk's liking. It was probably his paranoia, but were the little conversations and smiles they seemed to be sharing all the more frequently of late entirely as innocent as Rose would have him believe? She had been furious with him the one time he'd broached it, but the paranoia remained, the little pricks of jealousy kept coming, and here was one now.

"Because they're Rose's favorite band, you dick. And if you don't respect your mates' feelings, what kind of twat does that make you?" The guitarist glared at Davey with his blue eyes (dreamy blue? Is that what Rose thought of them?), and the bass player dropped his gaze and took another gulp of lager.

Rose didn't need a knight with a gleaming Gibson right now, however. "I'll tell you why you should show respect," she said, eyes flashing with real anger. "Because not only were they a great band—yes, a *great* band, not everyone thinks *Sid Sings* is the best album ever recorded you twat—but also because they've left loved ones behind who will be in a very bad place right now. Loved ones, Davey. I know you're not familiar with the term. But you mentioned Baz's wife. Do you think she gives a shit about how musically diverse or challenging they are? She just wants her kind, lovely husband back, her childhood sweetheart who stuck by her all these years. These are *real* people who lived *real* lives. *Moron!*" She took a furious sip of her vodka, and Kirk felt his love for her swell more than ever. He put his arm around her (before Johnny could?), but she was too angry and prickly now and shrugged it off.

"Bollocks to it," Crooked muttered. "Just sharing my opinion around. No need to climb on my ass for that."

"Your ass is the last anyone would wanna climb on, cabbage head," Ned assured him. The drummer emphasized the statement with a minor twitch. His arm rose half-heartedly, as if his Tourette's couldn't really be bothered to play with him today.

"Fuck you, Brain Crack," Davey responded defensively. He never knew quite how far he could go with insulting Ned on account of his disability, no matter how minimal it was. But today he was feeling the pressure and would take on any comer. "Gonna take my head off with that tic in a minute, retard. Get your straitjacket on."

"Doesn't take a guy with Tourette's to take your head off, not when we can find any five-year-old girl to do the job."

"Fuck you all. I got better things to do than chat to a bunch of wank-cocks like you lot. Stickin' my prick in a mouse hole would be more productive."

"Way too roomy for you, mate." Ned was straight in.

Kirk could tell the bassist was feeling outnumbered, and tiring of the banter, he shut them all up with a slam of his pint glass on the table. He hadn't failed to notice the grateful smile Rose had flashed at Johnny either.

"We're not here to talk about how Davey achieves his pleasure. Or even to discuss Cat O' Nine Tails…"

"R.I.P. Rockin' in the Pacific."

"Shut the fuck up, Davey. And it was the Indian Ocean, you moron. This is supposed to be a band meeting. We need to discuss what we're actually working toward because it seems to me one or two of you seem to be losing interest." That was aimed at Diesel, though it could equally apply to Ned. Both of them had missed the last rehearsal, and Diesel had missed the one before that as well. He could feel the entire band beginning to crack at the seams, and he wasn't sure how he could reverse the situation, especially with everyone seemingly at each other's throats. Still, maybe it would be a good thing if Johnny decided to quit…

Kirk glanced at the handsome guitarist and felt guilty for even wishing it. He couldn't let himself give in to his own insecurities. Diesel was a good guitarist. Johnny blinked back at him over his beer. Even so, the man was just *way* too good looking. The bastard.

Johnny tipped him a little grin. Had he read Kirk's mind?

"Lucifer Fuckin' Sham, faggots…" Davey brought everyone's attention right back to him. Did it make him happy irritating them all the time? It seemed like it.

Kirk sighed. "Got something useful to say, Davey?"

"Yeah. Just this: you're all a bunch of pussy wipes, and I'm not sure I can be arsed pluckin' my strings for you anymore. And why the fuck does the Bride have to be at every band meeting anyway? She don't fuckin' contribute musically." He sat back in his chair, folding his arms, screwing Rose with his narrow eyes. His hair was more messy than usual. It looked like it hadn't been washed for a week or more, a spiky hay rack the color of sewage. Stubble lined his face like smeared mud. His sneer took them all in, well-practiced.

Rose yawned at him, and once again Johnny beat Kirk to the defense. "She's here to provide the elegance and intelligence you so obviously lack, Numbhead. And the only string you're good at plucking is the one between your thighs."

Kirk tensed when Rose gave Johnny that sweet smile again. The smile hurt. And it shouldn't, cos it meant nothing, surely? Kirk lost his thread, self-confidence slipping away. He stood up as if about to give a speech, but he'd forgotten the script. They were all watching him now, waiting for him to say whatever he had been about to say. Even Johnny managed to take his eyes off Rose for a second to focus on the singer.

The singer. The frontman. Leader of the band… Yeah, right. This band was a shambles. Did any of them *really* like each other? At this moment in time, that seemed a little doubtful, which was very sad, as they had all been close once. Even the slightly tubby Ned—one of Kirk's oldest and best friends whom he'd met at school alongside Johnny, and besides Rose, one of the only people he knew who could genuinely make Kirk laugh, and whom he admired greatly for not being beaten by his condition—could push the wrong buttons with his humor sometimes. And he was very critical of Kirk's songs, too. Kirk had a growing suspicion the multi-talented drummer was going to drop the band soon anyway and pursue either his stand-up ambitions or the less-stressful career of sound design. While he had a knack for twiddling knobs on a mixing board, Kirk felt the drummer was drawn more to comedy. Ned was hilarious on stage, where his firmly held belief in not trying to suppress his TS but manage it instead, and indeed use it as a comedy tool, really came to the fore. Whichever route he chose to eventually move down, Ned's boredom of the band was becoming more evident, as was his increasing indifference to Kirk's vision.

Kirk opened his mouth to speak, then paused. Why the fuck bother? He suddenly wanted to call it a day. He was getting too old for his dreams for the band to come true anyway. Thirty-three was practically geriatric in rock terms. If he—if *they*—hadn't made it by now, it was obvious they never would. He wavered on his feet, momentarily defeated.

Rose came to his rescue. "Kirk's written some new songs. Stuff you won't believe, it's that good." She beamed at him encouragingly. *That's* why he invited her to band meetings. He smiled gratefully and opened his mouth to elaborate, to tell them exactly why his new songs would go down so well live, why they should make a great new demo that would attract a manager, a deal. He was going to tell them how they would soon be playing to 200 people at their gigs instead of twenty, how they would soon be able to afford decent equipment, go on tour, hell, maybe even have a crack at America if the new album he had in his mind went according to plan, if only they could all pull together and make it work. He was going to tell them all this and more. And then just as he was about to start, Ned broke in instead with the mother of all Tourette's outbursts, his extremely loud shout of "NHS!" turning heads all around the pub, the drummer looking as completely bewildered by what was coming out of his mouth as the rest of them, and then they were all falling about laughing—all except Kirk.

His moment was gone. Rose had given him the stage, and Ned had taken it. Kirk wasn't even convinced the cry was a genuine TS tic (and felt ashamed to even think it).

"Whoah!" Johnny was clapping his hands. "Where the fuck did *that* one come from, Ned, old son?"

The drummer put his hands wide. His shaved head shone under the pub lights. "Fuck knows. New material to me, too!"

Davey was still guffawing, truly back in his comfort zone—he hated talking about the future of the band's music; he just wanted to play bass, fuck women, talk shit, and drink lots of beer. And now Ned was moving the conversation on to one of Davey's own pet topics, the state of today's music industry, and he and the bass player were almost in agreement for once, although it wouldn't last.

"That cunt responsible for the Z Factor should be hanged outside HMV for a start," Davey was proclaiming loudly, so loudly that some rock girls at the next table were smiling in agreement, which was dangerous. You should never encourage Davey Crooked. "He's turned music into puppy food for the brain-dead. Get a tramp to roast his fuckin' nuts in a brazier and sell 'em for 50 pence. Then he'd finally be contributing to society, the cum-bucket."

Ned nodded. "Set the music industry back thirty years. It's like punk never happened." When he got riled, the drummer's arm tics became a little more aggressive, which just made him madder. He could control them in the confines of a comedy routine when he was on stage, using his Tourette's to provide extremely refreshing and self-deprecating humor. But when he was angry, it became his enemy. "And as for Rap, don't even get me fuckin' started! Sexism with all the fun taken out. Calling girls bitches and lyrics about guns and gangstas…is that what kids should aspire to?" Ned's round face was getting redder by the minute. But now he had lost Davey, as the bassist liked lyrics about slapping bitches and fucking hoes. When he pointed this out to Ned, the drummer produced a physical tic that startled them both for a minute. Ned's arm tilted in a parody of a Nazi salute, while his head twitched manically.

"Cocks in orbit, man, that was a wild one!" Davey responded with his usual sensitivity.

Ned ignored both the drummer's remark and his own tic. "What do you know about music anyway, Davey? It's like talking to an eight-year-old. You've as much musical ability as a tapir. Hell, I'm sure a woodlouse knows more chords than you."

Davey's only answer was a belch that could peel the top off a beer can. It was at this point that Kirk walked away, heading for the toilet and a breath of fresh air.

By the time he'd returned, some idiot had put Cat O' Nine Tails on the jukebox and Johnny was chatting quietly to Rose while the other two argued with increasing ferocity.

He left the pub quietly and didn't turn back.

Chapter Four

Ray thought he heard a giggle as he stepped out of the lift and walked toward his room on the third floor of the Holiday Inn.

He halted outside his door, searching for the key, before realizing the door was slightly ajar. The chuckle came again, feminine, drunk sounding. He didn't pause for long; he knew what to expect. One of the groupies from the party below had fished his room keys as well as groped his cock. *Shit, man. Can't a rocker ever get a moment's peace? I need to sleep...*

So he pushed the door open, half prepared to get snappy and irritable, to kick the tart out so he could get some kip. He certainly hadn't expected to find *two* of them, both already tucked up in bed and, from the looks of it, completely naked.

He swung the door shut behind him and stepped forward, checking them out. A brunette, the top half of her small, pert breasts revealed by the sheet draped over both girls. She was sexy in a slutty way, all pout and lipstick. His eyes flicked to the blonde beside her. This one caught his attention more. Eyes glittered like blue ice, cheekbones that carved sophistication into her face, and thin, sensual lips. Her hair was a natural dusky blonde. He found himself wondering what her pussy would be like, whether her beaver was a sun-kissed tawny, too...

Ray stopped at the foot of the bed. He was tired. So tired. He had been drinking most of the day, even before the Cat O' Nine gig at the Mermaid Casino. Phil had not been happy when he turned up at the sound check already a little worse for wear. Ray didn't give a fuck; it was their first American tour. Every gig had sold out, and the Mermaid was the last stop in L.A. The gig had been a wild success, even by Cat's standards, and Ray had sucked up every euphoric moment of it. He'd been in top form despite consuming enough glasses of JD and lines of coke to fell a giant. And despite singing his fucking guts out, Ray had not been oblivious to the resentful glances Carter had been giving him onstage. *Live a fuckin' little, ya boring prick.*

Bringing the party back to the Holiday Inn had been the final straw for the bass player. He'd stormed off to his room when all the groupies piled in and the coke started piling *up* on the Holiday Inn's dinky lounge tables. Jez had soon followed, no doubt to toss one off to *Guitar Techniques Monthly*, the sad fuck. Only Barney had remained to sample the delights only a rock group at the peak of their popularity could expect.

That had been three hours ago, though. Barney had long since succumbed. *It's four thirty in the goddam morning, my yank friends*, Ray thought as he swayed slightly, looking down at the two girls. He was conflicted; he'd already received a blow job on the lounge sofa from one of the other groupies. The same one who had eventually dragged the bleary-eyed Barney away to bed. Ray had been the last one standing, suffering an onslaught of groping, snogging, licking, sucking, and generally being manhandled in just about every conceivable way a woman of wanton sexual appetites could devise. On top of that, he had snorted the equivalent of the Sahara desert in coke. He was wired as fuck and still buzzing. But his fatigue was winning the fight now. His brain wanted more; his body was telling it to fuck the hell off.

But now the two girls were slowly pulling down the sheet that covered them, first revealing their breasts, then finally flicking it off the bed altogether, and Ray's qualms began to fade.

The blonde especially was really starting to hold his attention. Her eyes were magnetic, and her breasts were large and full, the pink aureoles circling erect nipples. When her long, shapely legs were bared, what lay between them revealed, he felt the last of his resolve begin to slip away. The brunette was stroking her pussy with one hand, the other caressing her petite breasts. What red-blooded male could resist? *Not fair*, Ray thought as he stripped off his t-shirt and unbuckled his leather trousers.

He watched them for a bit longer, enjoying the view. He was completely naked now, erect and throbbing. The brunette had turned her attention to the blonde's pussy, stroking the tawny landing strip above the moist lips, then letting two delicate fingers ease down and between them. The blonde kept her eyes on Ray as she gasped slightly at the entry, mouth parted. The brunette moved closer to her companion, leaned across to flick her tongue gently over the blonde's right nipple, closing her mouth over it to suck gently, her fingers still probing between the blonde's parted thighs.

Ray stared at the brunette's pert ass as she raised herself up on her knees and realized he had to be the luckiest man alive. Twenty-one-years-old, touring the USA with the greatest rock band on the scene, staying in the swankiest hotels while fucking the hottest girls on the planet. *God Bless America...*

"Are you going to join in, or just stand there with your cock saluting us?"

Ray grinned. It was the blonde who had spoken, and with a cheeky Lincolnshire accent.

"Fuck me, lass," he chuckled. "You're a long way from home."

"I didn't follow Cat O' Nine on tour just to watch you wave your dick at me. This lady's getting all the action."

The brunette turned to smile at him, sliding her fingers out of her companion's pussy and into her own mouth, sucking the juices slowly while watching Ray's reaction with lascivious, smiling eyes. She stopped licking long enough to say in a valley girl accent, "Do as the chick says, man. Come get dirrrrty."

Ray didn't have to be told twice.

He got in, and he got dirty.

Ray woke to big, big pain.

His head hurt like it had been used as a football. Then he remembered it *had* been. His eye was still half closed, and he knew without looking in the mirror he would be sporting a shiner as black as a lump of coal. But it wasn't just the physical abuse that made his skull ache like some bastard was revving up a jackhammer inside it; he'd swallowed enough alcohol to drown a battleship. When he moved his arm under the sheet, the raw skin on the knuckles of his right fist stung maddeningly, reminding him of just how much damage he'd inflicted the night before. That was some satisfaction at least. There was one prick who would never challenge him again. Not that that was much consolation right now. He groaned as his own pain rocked him. The bedroom ceiling swung a little, like he was at sea.

"You're finally awake then." Michelle's soft Lincolnshire accent was colder than he'd ever heard it. There was rebuke and disappointment mixed in with the cold elements that had been creeping into her voice a lot more frequently of late. And that hurt, too. He couldn't lose Michelle as well.

Along with everything else he'd lost in his life.

He tried to sit up, but the pain knocked him back down on the pillow.

Michelle sat down on the edge of the bed. She was already dressed, had probably been up for hours. She looked as good as ever. Didn't she ever age? So she'd lost the smooth sheen of youth she had when he had first met her, but her face was practically unlined, her jawline firm, her breasts firmer still. She looked bloody good for forty-three. What the hell did she see in this bald, lost-eyed degenerate who was gaining all the wrong pounds after losing all the right ones?

Michelle's kind blue eyes held his for a moment until he looked away, groaning and touching his head gingerly.

"You're forty-six years old, Ray. You're body just can't take this anymore."

He knew that. Of course, he did. Didn't mean he could do anything about it. He had demons, didn't he? Didn't she know fuck all about the demons? 'Course she didn't. She just lived her normal, safe, caring, considerate, blessed life while he...

While he did his best to fuck it up for both of them.

Guilt, too, huh? Hey, come join the party, jive along with Pain, Depression, and Hangover, my most loyal buddies.

"Oh, snap out of it, Ray," Michelle said when he closed his eyes and rolled over on his side. "I'm tired of this. Of all of this."

Of course, she was. Who could blame her? She'd been by his side faithfully for the last ten years, since he'd met her for the second time that fateful night at the *Kerrang* record awards event he'd attended as a hopeful nominee along with his latest doomed band venture, Hellside. He hadn't won the award (of course, he hadn't), but he'd recognized the eighteen-year-old with the magnetic eyes he'd spent forty-eight hours straight fucking at the Holiday Inn on that glorious last night of the Cat O' Nine US tour. In the long years spent senselessly shagging anyone who would have him between that night and the *Kerrang* event, he'd often thought about her, wished he'd got her number or address before waving her off almost without thinking as she climbed into a taxi to fly home to England again. He couldn't even remember the brunette's name, but he'd never forgotten the blonde. When he saw her again at the *Kerrang* bar, when she turned and gave him that cheeky little smile, her soft blue eyes warming instantly, he knew he couldn't let her slip through his fingers this time, the way he had with everything else.

Would he let her slip away now, like he'd done back in 1989 when he kissed her goodbye outside the Holiday Inn and watched the taxi take her away?

"Love you, Michelle," he said through his pain. And he knew she would believe him. It was the one thing he'd never bullshitted about. The one constant in an ever-changing, shitty world.

She sighed and got off the bed. "Is that enough anymore, Ray? I'm beginning to wonder…"

He heard her leave the room, and a few seconds later the TV was on. The One O'clock News signature jingle just about audible.

He opened his eyes and waited for the pain to subside. He thought about calling Michelle back and asking for a cup of tea and some aspirin but wisely thought better of it. Then he heard the sound of the TV increase in volume and realized she had opened the door again. He swiveled round to look up at her, and her expression made him immediately forget his discomfort.

"What is it?" Her evident alarm jolted him. His first thought was she'd just had a phone call. His parents? They were very old now.

"You'd better come see this."

That got him out of bed. He ignored the pain that dragged at him and followed her through to the lounge. The 55" Sony dominated the small room. A clip from a recent Cat O' Nine gig was playing, and for a moment he was angry that she would be insensitive enough to drag him out of bed just to rub salt in the oldest wound he had. But then he saw the scrolling Breaking News banner beneath the screen and the music clip was fading to be replaced by the news anchor telling the world that Cat O' Nine's jet had disappeared from airspace thirteen hours before with all contact lost.

Ray sat down slowly, eyes glued to the screen.

After a while, after he'd listened to the news report in its entirety and the anchor had moved on to the next story, he leaned back in the armchair and said, "They're gone."

Michelle watched him from where she sat isolated on the settee, waiting for…. Waiting for *what?* What the fuck did she expect him to feel? Sadness? Grief? A sense of loss? What the fuck for? He'd had all those feelings and a million more twenty-five years ago when the fuckers kicked him out of the band. And one thing he was quite sure of, they had never felt those things about doing it to him. Apart from maybe Barney, who had always been a mate to him; even long after the band had dropped him, when it became a little embarrassing for him to do so, Barney had still tried to stay in touch. Even though Ray never returned his calls.

So yeah, okay, he felt sorry for Barney. If they really had crashed in the Indian Ocean somewhere, then, of course, there would be no survivors. So there was a pang of regret that the cheerful drummer was under the waves along with the other three… But too much fucking water had gone under the bridge (no pun intended) for him to give too much of a shit about any of it anymore. Did that make him an unfeeling bastard? Having the only thing he'd ever really cherished ripped away from him, and twenty-five years of trying to dull the pain with implausible amounts of drink and drugs tended to do that to you.

"That's that, then," he said to Michelle impassively as he got up to make himself a cup of tea.

He took a few sips of the brew, his mind ticking over sluggishly. The tea wasn't hitting the spot, but he knew the gram of Goodtimes he had in his jacket pocket certainly would. A line or two (fuck, maybe three) would hit that spot right good and proper. He placed the mug in the sink and was already fishing out his credit card and a twenty-pound note to roll before he'd even left the kitchen.

CD 2

RETURN FROM NOWHERE

Chapter Five

Rose said, "I don't believe it."

Kirk said, "Fuck-ing *hell!!*"

The news anchor had rather more to say on the subject.

"The missing private jet carrying four musicians from the band Cat O' Nine Tails has been picked up by Air Traffic Control over the Indian Ocean six months after dramatically disappearing from airspace, fueling fears the aircraft had crashed into the sea."

Rose seized Kirk's hand and squeezed it. Hard. The expression on the normally prosaic face of the news anchor looked like he was struggling to believe it himself as he continued. "Reports from ATC suggest that the band, along with their manager, various members of the road crew, pilots, and flight attendants are all in good health, although details of what happened to them have not as yet been divulged to the world's press."

The report cut to a hastily organized and conducted press conference and a spokesperson from Air Traffic Control in Kuala Lumpur, a harassed-looking Malaysian official who seemed at a loss how to answer the flurry of questions being fired at him from excited international journalists. Beside him sat a rather more stoic suit from the British Embassy and a controller from Sydney Airport, although it looked like they had failed to dredge up any spokespeople for the band itself.

The Malaysian was fielding requests for personal details about the musicians, able to offer only the slightest of scraps in return. He told the crowd how they picked up the jet on radar in the early hours of the morning in the exact same position from which it had disappeared half a year earlier, and after sending a flurry of calls to the craft, finally received a response that was all was well with everybody on board. The jet had since landed at Sydney, and the previously missing passengers were all resting in exclusive quarters provided for them. The Australian Controller took up the reins in typically antipodean laid-back fashion to request a plea for some privacy on behalf of the musicians and their entourage while they recuperated from their six-month flight. He finished by apologizing that there was no more information available at present and asking for cooperation and patience from the world's media. The rest of his words were drowned by the series of ecstatic screams from Rose, who was up and dancing around the room in front of the TV like an eight-year-old on Christmas morning.

"Fat chance he's gonna get that," Kirk grunted as the report went on to repeat all the facts about the bizarre case that were already in the public domain.

Rose finally found words, but only very limited ones as she finished her jubilant pogoing and returned to her seat. "What... what...?" Her face was a picture of confusion, joy, and disbelief.

"What the hell is going on? That what you're trying to say?" Kirk muted the TV. "If I were at all cynical, I would be tempted to scream Publicity Stunt."

Rose looked at him like he'd just grown a breast from his forehead. "Prick!" she managed at last. "Is that the most insightful observation you can make? This is... Well, it's a miracle, isn't it?"

"Exactly. And I don't believe in miracles. Or Father Christmas. Okay, bad example: I do still believe in the big, bearded geezer. Easter Bunny, then. He's far less credible. A bit like Cat O' Nine in general."

"But this is different! Cat don't go in for cheap publicity gimmicks! You can't seriously believe the shit coming from your own mouth? You've been hanging 'round that brain-dead, beer-head Davey for too long. Starting to sound like him."

"Their career is one big gimmick, Rosie. Giant animatronic Devils in their stage act and sham Satan imagery on all their CD covers!! Come on! I wouldn't put this shit past them. Clever though, I'll give them that. Though I don't know how they managed it, evading contact and hiding an aircraft for six months. Pretty ingenious. I'd go as far as saying their best stunt ever."

Rose snorted in disbelief. "Listen to yourself. How the hell could an aircraft hide for six months without being spotted somewhere? That's a really stupid thing to suggest. Didn't realize quite what a cynical twat you could be." She snatched the remote and freed the news anchor from his silence. But there was nothing more on Cat O' Nine Tails. Some sick fuck had suffocated his step sister in a Bristol flat, then dismembered her with a power saw. Kirk made a mental note not to visit Bristol in a hurry. Rose sighed. "I feel like crying. This is THE best news! Cat O' Nine is alive!! Just one thing killing that joy. You."

"What else could it be but a PR stunt? Boeing jet planes can't disappear and then reappear in exactly the same airspace six months later without something really fishy going on. Think about it. And by the way— sorry you think I'm turning into Davey Crooked. Maybe you'd prefer it if I was more like Johnny—"

Rose was getting up to switch the TV off. She stopped in her tracks, standing over Kirk with an exasperated look on her angular face. "You really are doing your best to piss on my parade, aren't you? Why can't you celebrate with me? You know how much this band means to me. Oh, and just for the record… No idea what that Johnny crack was all about. Are you going to be happy and celebrate with me, or do I have to go out shopping on my own?"

He let it go. She was a bundle of energy, all fizzing with excitement (and not a little irritation on account of his tactlessness), and he didn't want to be the one who pooed on her party. *Oops! Already done that.*

"Sorry, Rose. I really am. I just can't take it in, I guess. A natural skeptic. I'll buy you a Spiced Pumpkin Latte if you fancy it."

But Rose looked like she was thinking better of her invitation now. "On second thought, think I'll go out on my own. You'd only drag me down." She disappeared into the bedroom to apply some makeup, and ten minutes later she was gone.

Kirk regretted the remark about Johnny; he didn't want to sound like the jealous boyfriend, insecure and possessive. What girl was ever turned on by that?

The flat seemed yawningly empty without her. He sat on the sofa wondering what to do. He plopped an Uncle Acid CD into the player, but the horror sleaze tones depressed him. He wandered around the flat, pulled out a can of Mulligatawny soup, cooked it, and ate it desultorily while sitting at the table in the kitchen and looking out at the terraced street beyond. No sign of Rose. An hour became two. He played another CD, The Men That Will Not Be Blamed For Nothing. That depressed him, too, but for a different reason; Lucifer Sam was supposed to be supporting the steampunk Oi band next month, and Kirk knew they really weren't ready for it. It would be a good platform for them, but not if they were a shambles, which is pretty much what they were. They were going to disappoint the Blamed For Nothing vocalist, who had been kind enough to suggest them for the slot after bumping into Kirk and Ned at a pub off Charing Cross Road a while back. Kirk ejected the CD. It was too good. Lucifer Sam was not.

He'd run out of things to do. He pulled out his phone, called Ned.

"Yo, esteemed bandleader," the drummer answered. *Was that a piss take*, Kirk wondered? Another thing he decided to let go today. He could hear traffic in the background. "Fat bastard!" Ned yelled suddenly before Kirk could speak.

"Me?"

"No, not you, ya prick. Just some poor bastard who didn't deserve that. I'm out and about, abusing the general public. It's part of my charm."

"You heard? Flight seven fourteen's back."

"Seven fourteen?"

"Name of a Tintin Book. Aircraft abducted by aliens. Scrambled my mind as a kid."

"We gonna talk about children's books? That why you phoned me up?" Ned's voice suddenly went up a few octaves as he delivered a cleverly managed Tourette's outburst to some hapless passerby: "CUNT-ry walks!! Sorry, mate, I'm back in the room," he resumed, returning his attention to the phone. "As I was saying, I could've been doing something important."

"Ned, the only important thing you consider doing at this time of day is choosing which girl on Myfreecams to wank over."

"Know me too well."

"Wish I didn't."

"You gonna tell me now?"

"What?"

"We really doing this?"

"Doing what?" Kirk chuckled, despite his anxiety over Rose. Ned always cheered him up.

"Hangin' up in five, four, three—"

"Nob! I'm trying to tell you Cat O' Nine is back."

"Back? From the grave?"

"Don't you ever watch the news?"

"Only when that Nancy Nannar or whatever the fuck she's called is on. Her eyes are dark, limpid pools. She has a really cool and intelligent way of arching her eyebrows. And she always has one button more than necessary undone on her blouse."

"You're a dick."

"That's a fact. So what about Cat?"

Kirk told him the latest, expecting Ned to react the same as him. But he discovered after a moment's silence that Ned wasn't even listening. It sounded like he'd put the phone down while he did something else. "That's rude, dude," he told the silent line.

Then the drummer was back. "You got the TV on now?"

"Why?"

"Just turn it on. I just got a breaking news notification on my iPhone with a live feed. This is fucking unbelievable."

"I know. That's exactly what I told Rose. Gotta be a stunt."

"No. This is something weirder. Turn the telly on, ya big-nosed twat."

"You gonna try telling me that was the Tourette's as well?" Kirk retorted fondly. He picked up the remote, and a second later a news bulletin was on. No Nancy Nannar or whatever her name was. This was a live press conference, only this time without the harassed-looking air officials and Embassy bods. This time it was all 100% Cat.

They were sitting at a raised table in front of a horde of seated journalists. The caption read LIVE FROM SYDNEY. Cameras flashed, microphones were extended, the faces of the congregated media were flushed with excitement and urgency. Kirk got that before he even looked at the musicians properly.

And when he looked, when the camera closed in on a medium shot of all four men sitting stiffly behind the long table, he knew exactly what Ned had meant.

Cat O' Nine Tails had come back.

And they all looked ten years younger.

Baz Cropper, the singer, his hair still in the same shorter style he'd adopted of late after conceding he was now in his mid-forties with the first alarums of a graying, retreating hairline. But now the hair looked thicker, fuller, not receding at all, and the gray had vanished. Kirk could have put that down to a good dye (apart from the receding bit) if it wasn't for Baz's face. Where there should have been a nest of crow's feet around each eye, there was nothing. His jawline, previously beginning to sag, had tautened, the pouches under his eyes lifted.

Kirk turned his gaze to Phil Carter sitting next to Baz. The same result: younger, fresher, more vital. Jez Tweed, who was next to Phil, had also lost the threads of gray in his long, wavy hair; his cheeks unpuckered by advancing age. Barney, at the far end of the table, had lost his double chin, along with a good decade of overindulging in fast food and real ale that had caused his genial features to sag noticeably on his last TV interview.

But the new, invigorated look wasn't the only difference.

There was something else that took a moment or two for Kirk to pick up on. And when it did, a creeping cold flooded his veins.

He'd forgotten the phone in his hand until he heard Ned squawk his name as loud as he could. "Kirk!! You still there? Kirk, ya deaf wanker!"

Kirk lifted the cell to his ear slowly, eyes still glued to the TV screen.

It was an effort to speak. He couldn't look away from the four musicians sitting at the podium before the flashing cameras.

"I see them," he said ever so slowly. He could see them alright. The way they sat in their chairs, bodies rigid, expressions even more rigid, eyes that had never been this dark fixed ahead of them without the slightest glimmer of emotion or interest, their mouths set stoically, not the ghost of a smile for the congregated press. He saw them, yes, but—

"They're not right, Ned. They've come back. They've come back, and they're all *wrong.*"

Chapter Six

He watched the same interview with Rose again later in the evening. She had come back laden with shopping bags (one of which contained a new Cat O' Nine Tails t-shirt to top off her celebration nicely) and a fresh smile, which he had promptly stolen right off her face as he told her about the latest press conference.

He'd told her how they were different, how they'd apparently regressed in age, about their lack of any emotional engagement with the barrage of questions the journalists had thrown at them. He'd told her about their eyes.

Of course, she'd refused to believe any of it.

So he sat her down to watch the news, and she had watched in a state of barely contained excitement as they answered the pleas for information about their bizarre disappearing and reappearing act with calm, banal statements that gave little away.

"You see?" he said after a few minutes.

"See what? Yes, they look younger. So what? They've obviously been taking care of themselves while they've been away. I don't know what you're getting at."

He felt stifled by his own frustration. Was he the only one to see it? Even Ned had laughed it off after his initial bafflement, joking about in-flight facelifts. A few of the journalists had commented on their "refreshed appearance" but had received nothing satisfactory in return by way of explanation. And then there was the rather more important matter of their whereabouts for the past six months. Everybody wanted an answer to this one, along with how the jet had reappeared in exactly the same airspace from which it had vanished. And what answer did they get?

As usual, Phil Carter was the spokesperson for the band. Phil had never been renowned for being a loquacious fellow; he was shy, a homebody with a devoted wife and four teenage kids. He always let his music do the talking. But now, pressed by the media representing the frenzied interest of the entire world (and it would get even more frenzied over the coming days as newspapers continued to call for answers as well as spreading crazy speculation at an ever-escalating rate), he was more tight-lipped than ever.

He stared into the camera, the lens focusing on his new smooth complexion, on his thicker, luxuriant hair that tumbled over his shoulders, and on his eyes that were sharper, darker than they had been six months ago, and said simply in a voice that was dry and deep:

"We were lost. But now we are back."

Of course, that would never do. The media hammered him with questions, a wave of shouted pleas that were becoming increasingly desperate as it looked like they were going to be thrown mere bewildering and cryptic scraps. *But where??* the press wanted to know. *WHERE have you been exactly?*

If Phil Carter was experiencing any alarm at the barely suppressed hysteria from the accumulated press, then his face did not betray it. Phil had always been a reluctant and nervous interviewee. Not so now.

"We were lost," he repeated, his voice parched, like he'd swallowed a mouthful of crickets. "We don't know where. Or how. All we remember is the call."

"What call was that, Phil?" a journalist from the *National Enquirer* beat out the competition to ask.

Phil paused a moment. Baz answered for him, sounding like he was talking from a long distance away. "From Flight Control last night. They asked if we were receiving them. We told them we were coming home."

A *Mojo* journalist got the next question in, and it was a good one: "You say you don't remember where you've been, but could that just be a euphemism for hiding away on a remote desert isle somewhere to write new material undisturbed?"

Phil swiveled his head to gaze at the music journalist. His face was utterly blank as he said, "There *is* new material. It will be recorded imminently. Expect an album. Expect it very soon. We're back."

And that was it. No matter how much the press bombarded them with requests for more information, they always got the same response. *We were lost. But now we are back.*

And why was it only Kirk seemed to find that prospect so chilling?

Rose refused to find anything unduly strange in their behavior, however. "They're jet lagged. What do you expect?"

Kirk snorted. "Not surprised. It's been a long flight. Six months long, in fact. Bullshit! Something's not right. They're different. Can't you see? Couldn't you hear their voices?"

Rose got up to leave the room, then turned to fire a parting shot. "You just hate me liking any other band than yours, don't you? That's what this is all about."

"Don't be stupid!" he called after her as she left, slamming the door. "That's complete bollocks!" He heard the outer door of the flat close, too. She'd left him alone again. He rubbed his face with both hands, confused by his own suspicions and her inability to accept them.

The next day brought another deluge of news stories, one of them echoing Rose's comments of the evening before. Kirk stood in the kiosk across the road from his flat and read them all. First, there was a rational recording of facts from *The Independent:*

THE BAND THAT RETURNED FROM NOWHERE

Following the dramatic and still-unexplained reappearance in airspace over the Indian Ocean in the exact same coordinates in which they abruptly vanished six months before, the rock band Cat O' Nine Tails revealed they had no idea where they had been during the period of their absence. With this claim mocked by some as a rather ingenious publicity trick—the band managed, however, to remember to announce that they would be starting work on a new album imminently—others have commented on the rather strange appearance of the four musicians, who, judging by their rejuvenated looks, all seem to have undergone rather effective health-restorative treatments. Fans and the press have bombarded the offices of EMI for more information on the band's rather odd hiatus and for more details on the promised new album. A spokesperson for the band revealed the musicians were preparing to enter studios very shortly, but there was nothing further to announce at present.

The *Sun*, meanwhile, had a different slant:

ROCKING TO HEAVEN AND BACK

If their appearances at last night's Sydney press conference was anything to go by, the metal band Cat O' Nine Tails has discovered the secret of Eternal Youth!

After singing about corpses coming back to life and Satan worship for the last twenty-five years, the prodigal rockers seem to have hit on a recipe that will bring the cosmetic industry to its knees and make people have a lot more Sympathy for the Devil—at least, if they want to get rid of those stubborn traces of gray. It seems that in order to restore youth and beauty you just need to disappear in a jet plane for half a year and then make like rock 'n' roll rabbits miraculously popping out of magicians' hats with brand new fur and whiskers. These Cats are now blessed with the virtually unlined complexions and full growth of hair you would expect from men at least ten years younger. The tongue-in-cheek, cheeky chappies have always played at being mean in their lyrics and on their album covers, but the truth has always been very apparent that these four boys to men to boys again are actually very much very down-to-earth, cheerful types in real life. Until last night, that is, when their appearance before the cameras of the assembled worlds' press left people criticizing their strained, uncharismatic performance—a world away from the exuberant theatrical sense of fun exhibited at one of their popular gigs during the last Cat O' Nine tour. Some fans have hit back, stating their unforthcoming, restrained public appearance was only to be expected after their still-unexplained ordeal, while various media pundits (among them, Jonathan Ross, a prominent fan) have commented on the band seeking a new change of direction away from the sometimes-buffoonish metal image they upheld for more than twenty-five years and opting for cool, rather than fool. Jet Lag or Jaded Publicity Stunt. In the words of Big Brother... you decide...

Kirk scanned some other papers, but none of them hinted at that sense of subtle menace he'd picked up on himself until he stumbled upon a brief piece on Mrs. Baz Cropper on page three of *The Daily Mail.* For a moment, he forgot all about the hostile stares of the Indian kiosk owner, who was becoming increasingly indignant about this wild-haired young man reading papers for free in his shop.

Kirk read the article, and the cold trickle returned, rolling slowly down his back. There was nothing overtly damning in the piece to account for his reaction, but it tied in with his own feelings regarding the band exactly.

Sheila Cropper had been door-stepped at her home in Surrey repeatedly over the last twenty-four hours since the news of the band's return had been announced (along with members of the other musicians' families), but she had refused to comment until now. No, she had not heard from her husband. She had tried to contact him on numerous occasions but had received the same response from the band's PR in Sydney and from the EMI office: Baz Cropper was unavailable to comment. Incredulous retorts of "But I'm his wife" gained her no ground whatsoever, it seemed. She went on to clarify that she had tried her husband's mobile, which seemed to be working again after a six-month hiatus, during which she had only reached voicemail, and twice she had heard somebody breathing on the other end. "It was extremely odd," she elaborated. "I knew it was him. I just *knew* it. You know how your husband's breathing sounds after fifteen years of marriage. But he would not speak. It was very distressing. But he's due home soon with the rest of the band. I shall get to the bottom of it all then, no doubt."

Kirk tucked the paper back in the rack and waved goodbye to the shop owner, whose scowl followed him onto the street.

He considered telling Rose about these latest revelations as he retraced his steps toward his flat in the mid-terraced house on Clissold Crescent and dismissed the idea pretty rapidly. He wanted to rebuild his relationship with his beautiful girlfriend, not destroy it completely as he'd been apparently doing his best to achieve over the last day or so. *Ever since that fucking band turned up again, like a bad smell, like a piece of rotting dog turd on his shoe.*

He had to admit he was becoming fascinated by the band, albeit in a rather unhealthy manner. He was beginning to hate Cat O' Nine Tails, too, and he did not know the reason for that either.

He would grow to hate them a lot more over the coming months.

Chapter Seven

His cell ring tone roused him from sleep. He blinked at the caller ID, reluctant to answer at first. Then he remembered he was striving for a new sense of band camaraderie and thumbed the answer button.

"Yes, Davey."

"Got news."

He peered blearily at the bedside clock. 10:00 a.m. He should have been up by now. Beside him, Rose continued to sleep, which was probably what had kept him here, too. She had got in late last night, waking him up. Remembering the argument they had on her returning at 2:00 a.m. over where she had been, the same sense of despair returned. He wasn't in the mood for Davey Crooked, that was for sure.

"Good, I hope," he managed to keep his voice on an even level. Beside him, Rose stirred, turning to face him. He felt her thigh, naked below the brief negligee, warm against his own, and lust rose in him, beating away his anxieties. A good, old hard-on worked wonders for depression.

"Depends. But thought you might be interested, being the nosy cunt that you are."

From any of his other friends, the "C" word was used in a term of twisted affection that was quintessentially English. Except when Davey used it.

Kirk sighed. "You gonna make this brief? If it's anything to do with pulling out of the gig in two weeks, you'd better start looking for a new band."

"Why the fuck would I do that? When this band worships me sooo fuckin' much. Feel the love, brother. I do."

Rosie opened her eyes and looked at him. God, she was beautiful. He wanted to apologize for the paranoid accusations he'd thrown at her, wanted to stroke her wicked cheekbones and kiss those sensual lips, but Davey wouldn't give him the chance.

"It's that twatty comic strip band your bitch is so fond of."

That brought him to attention, and his stiffy soon began to wilt.

"What about them? And don't call Rose a bitch again or you'll be practicing bass from the morgue."

"Chill your panties, loser. It's a term of respect."

"The only thing you respect is cheap whiskey and cheaper whores."

"Banter. Don't you just fuckin' love it. Love *you*, maaan." He managed to sound like a combination of Johnny Rotten and a grizzly bear, and as disingenuous as a quiz show host praising the career of a Z list celebrity guest nobody had heard of.

"Spit it, or fuck off. I've got things to take care of." And he did. He had to take care of Rose. Or at least his relationship with her, before it broke completely.

"Cat O' Nine Twats are doing a 'secret' signing at HMV Oxford Street on Friday."

Davey let that register for a moment. The bass player was aware of Kirk's new and unhealthy obsession with the band and had known this news would appeal to him—for all the wrong reasons.

"What's the point of a secret signing? Nobody will turn up," Kirk pointed out. He was fully aware that Rose was listening to the conversation now, up on one elbow, fully awake. "And that's fucking fast; they've only been back in Britain a week or so."

"Could you not hear the sarcasm in the word 'secret,' fool?" Davey sighed in mock exasperation. "It's a low-key job, not publicized anywhere apart from word of mouth. I guess they don't want millions of cunts turning up ruining their day. 'Nother publicity stunt, I reckon. Probably the only thing we've ever agreed on is how fuckin' lame this band is."

That made a kind of skewed logic, Kirk thought. A low-profile signing in front of only a couple hundred or so lucky fans "in the know" was a lot more manageable than the horde that would descend on the band if word got out too soon, especially after all the press interest in them over the week or so since their return. This way, they could get headlines about their signing after the fact, reap the same publicity but avoid the headache of major queues. It smacked of cynical self-promotion: let the public know we're back on track with minimum hassle. They would wrap up the signing before the word spread too far and the masses started turning up. They would be pushing the forthcoming new album, no doubt. Yeah, it made sense.

"So how did word spread as far as your gutter, Davey?"

"Harsh. Vindictive, even. I'm the best bass player Lucifer Sam ever had, ya cunt."

"You're the only one. Do you want me to ask again?"

Davey snorted back some mucus, and Kirk heard him flob it out somewhere—and Kirk hoped he wasn't in public, although that was very naïve of him—and then Davey's mouth was directed at his phone again. "Got a mate works at the HMV store. He's under orders not to put anything on Facebook or anywhere shit like that. Sucker will lose his job if he does. But he told me."

"That was brave of him," Kirk answered. Then, already planning: "What time Friday?"

"Eleven. Reckon it'll be all done by one. They ain't gonna hang around. Then sit back and let the internet go crazy afterward. Clever fuckers."

"Gonna be a lot of disappointed fans," Kirk said and hung up. Friday was still three days away. Did he have anything planned for that particular day? Was he struggling to think of some prior engagement? And what the hell made him feel so uneasy about seeing the band anyway? *Pussy.*

Rose said, "I'm coming."

He thought of arguing but couldn't think of a good reason. The fact the newly returned band disturbed him in some unfathomable fashion just wouldn't cut it with Rose. He shrugged and stroked her naked shoulder. She let him, her eyes ringed with dark shadow. He let his hand trace the line of her jaw, then her neck. When his hand wandered under her negligee to cup her small left breast, she pulled it away.

"I'm tired," she said, and then lay back down and turned away from him again.

"Yeah," said Kirk quietly. *But what are you tired of, Rosie girl?*

He pulled himself reluctantly from the bed and went to take a shower.

Chapter Eight

Nick James tipped the cab driver and looked up at the EMI office building. He'd been here before during his fifteen-year stint as a rock journalist, had interviewed a couple of bands belonging to the high-profile label, although he had no taste for their commercial, middle-of-the-road mentality. Still, this was Cat O' Nine Tails, one of the biggest dinosaurs—ahem, groups—on the planet, and thanks to their recent magical disappearing and reappearing Jet Act, extremely high-profile right now.

So he swallowed his pessimism—at least for the time it took him to get inside the lobby and to the reception area, only to be confronted with a framed picture of the band placed prominently (and probably very recently) above the pretty young thing manning the desk.

He told her his reason for visiting, then nodded at the picture. It showed all four musicians smiling and relaxed. It was a fairly recent photograph and didn't show any signs of being photoshopped (unlike the band itself), and Nick could see plenty of gray flecks, receding hairlines, and wrinkles scattered amongst the four middle-aged men.

"Your cup of tea?"

The petite blonde couldn't have been more than twenty-two. Her white blouse was packed to bursting, though, Nick noticed appreciatively. She turned to follow his gaze, a bewildered look on her pretty face. Nick suddenly had an image of that same sex-doll face pressed against his crotch, those blow-job lips getting to work on him, and felt his loins tense with lust. Such images visited him a lot, with seeming more frequency as he got older.

He could see his own reflection in the glass of the picture: curly hair that fell to just above his shoulder, his own rebellious hints of gray rebutted by Just For Men, his ever-present shades masking the beginnings of crows nests around his weak gray eyes.

The blonde was turning back now. "Sorry?" she said. And he wanted to thrust his length into that half-open mouth, pump her head good until he had blasted every drop of middle-aged muck inside her mouth. His eyes were fastened on the taut blouse as he explained, "Cat O' Nine. They rock your gorgeous boat?"

She smiled politely. "They're waiting for you. Room 314, third floor."

He took the hint and fucked off, passing a couple of suited execs as he did. He thumbed the lift button for the third floor and hummed a little tune to himself as he rose, and it wasn't a Cat tune. He had mixed feelings about this job. When the editor of *Rock!!* asked him to do it (after the band's management had specifically requested Nick for the assignment), he had been reluctant to accept immediately. He'd never been a metal fan, and CONT seemed to him to display all the worst possible attributes of that woeful genre. They dressed like twats for a start—*leathers and long hair was sooo eighties, maaan.* And the endless guitar solos and wailing falsettos that Jez Tweed and Baz Cropper indulged in were cringe-worthy, and resoundingly, conservatively AOR (and Nick could think of no more damning indictment). As for their predilection for horror imagery, zombies and demons on their cover artwork, well… Nick remembered sixth formers reveling in a myriad of sound-the-same hair metal bands with exactly those sort of album covers at school, remembered those silly boys as maladjusted, social misanthropes who would cum on themselves if a girl even spoke to them. And that summed CONT perfectly for Nick, a Sixth Form band for teen nerds with dandruff problems. Hell, this bunch of good-natured and dreary-minded (Conservative voting, too, no doubt) musicians didn't even do the time-honored Rock thang of shagging groupies like they were an endangered species. These Dullard pretend Cock Rockers preferred to stay home with their wives and girlfriends and watched History documentaries or played golf, for fuck's sake! Nick had always felt slightly betrayed when he discovered Alice Cooper could regularly be found on an eighteen hole course as well, positioning his ball on a tee with all the rock 'n' roll pizzazz of a retired stockbroker. But Cat O' Nine had never been in Alice's league, who had been genuinely demented in his day.

And it wasn't just Nick who found the metalers from Bethnall Green a bit of a joke; they were widely ignored or patronized by the trendier rock mags, which had no time for their low-brow theatrics and music to dig graves to. *But what the fuck do I know*, Nick thought as the lift arrived at the third floor and the doors opened smoothly. They had millions of faithful fans, and each record (which sounded exactly like the preceding one) sold in their gazillions. Puzzling, and dispiriting.

He stepped out of the lift and padded along the thickly carpeted corridor, shaking off the feeling the building's interior reminded him more of a hotel than an office block, and arrived at a varnished wooden door with a small plaque revealing the office as number 314.

There was no window. He paused. He had passed nobody in the corridor, and the entire floor was silent. Had he expected to hear twinkling guitar solos and screeching vocals awaiting him from the other side of the door? A pang of self-doubt (extremely unusual for this cocksure music journalist) assailed him briefly. He shook it away like a dog ridding itself of a flea. What the fuck was there to be worried about? He'd interviewed far bigger (according to his conception of the word "big") bands than these heavy metal numbnuts. He'd chatted to The Who for fuck's sake, hung with Oasis, even been on the receiving end of John Lydon's acerbic wit after negatively reviewing a new P.I.L release and lived to tell the tale. He certainly wasn't shy of meeting a band whose greatest lyrical achievement was rhyming *"The devil took her in the shower"* with *"and she was in his demonic power."* Dylan and Tom Waits need not look over their shoulders, not to mention Jim Morrison or Morrisey for that matter. His hesitation, therefore, puzzled him. The silence from beyond the door puzzled him, too, and he irrationally imagined the band sitting on the other side in absolute stillness, awaiting him...

Okay, freaking yourself, Nicko!

Maybe he'd got the wrong number… But no, he was sure the blonde cutie had said 314. Fuck it. He knocked. And waited.

And waited. He knocked again. He was about to turn away, convinced he had come to the wrong door after all, but it was opening now, and there was the manager standing in the doorway.

Doug Roscoe stared at the music journalist with a hard, level gaze. He did not smile, nor step immediately aside for Nick to enter. Nick recognized him from TV interviews but remembered a much older looking man (the manager must be in his mid-sixties) than the relatively smooth-faced man who confronted him. The hair was short and conservative, the corners of his eyes barely troubled by wrinkles. He still had a chewed-up boxer's face, but one less assailed by time's punches. Nick would have sworn this geezer was not a day over forty-five.

Nick felt a quip rise and just managed to contain it. The interview would not go well if he kick-started it with wisecracks about skin lotions, facelifts, and hair restoratives. Best keep on track with a bit of very minor ass licking—at least to begin with—before he weighed in with the meatier questions and more provocative statements.

"Doug Roscoe?" he asked unnecessarily. "Nick James from *Rock!!*"

The manager finally stepped to one side. Nick nodded his thanks and strode into the office.

It was large but dim. The blinds were down, only allowing chinks of London daylight to filter in. An Anglepoise lamp hovered over a long meeting table, the pool of orange light illuminating the teak surface not sufficient to pick out the four figures seated along the far side of it.

Nick paused in the middle of the room. *This is freaky*, he thought, and the frisson of unease he'd experienced outside the door returned. *Just playin' with me, the corny fucks…* He remembered with another unpleasant jolt that he'd dismissed them in the pages of *Rock!!* a couple of times. Would they hold that against him? He hadn't been that rude, though. He wracked his brains in the handful of seconds he waited for one of the four shadows to speak, and one phrase rocked into his mind: *"Cat O' Nine Tails return with another tedious album of mock rock balderdash: 'bald' being a key component of their look these days, as this middle-aged, middle-of-the-road outfit of Beano Comic oafs continue to play at being bad with all the inherent cool of dads dancing with their kids at a school disco. Buffoonish Rupert Bears trapped in a cycle of endless, mundane repetition. Their riffs are as exciting as a stroll through the park with Grandma, and just as sexy."*

He scanned the four dark shapes rather anxiously. So was that what this was about? Were they trying to put the frighteners on him 'cause he'd done a hatchet job on them? Which, of course, explained why they'd asked for him to interview them over all the Cat fans who worked for various rock mags and were far better suited for the job.

The manager had closed the door and was standing behind Nick, also silent. *These theatrics were typical of the band,* Nick decided and felt some of his pluck return. They wouldn't scare him so bloody easily. What did they think he was, some kind of rookie journo? He'd been writing about rock music for fifteen years. He'd argued with Lemmy about his musical direction; he'd confronted Liam Gallagher over being a twat (and nearly been chinned by the volatile Manc); verbally tussled with Hugh Cornwall over leaving the Stranglers. If those genuine icons of rock hadn't been able to intimidate him, then these tawdry hams certainly couldn't.

Nerving himself for what he expected to be another tussle of opinions, he pocketed his shades, stepped confidently up to the table, leaned over, and adjusted the knob on the Anglepoise a touch or two until the figures sitting along the far side of the long table became a little more visible. He could see their faces now, and they were all watching him with a complete lack of expression that made him falter again. More light would make them less intimidating he decided and was about to turn it all the way up when the manager's sharp, cold voice came from behind like a terse knife in his back.

"Sit!"

Nick turned, ready to retort, but the manager was advancing on him slowly, his prizefighter face as resolutely menacing as a clenched fist.

"Okay! Chill, man..." Nick pulled out a chair opposite the band and sat. The manager took up position behind him, still standing. That made Nick even edgier, and that, in turn, made him aggressive. He had intended to start the interview with a softly-softly approach. Fuck that now. He pulled his compact voice recorder from the pocket of his leather jacket (a stylish soft one, made in Italy—not the corny rocker ones habitually worn by CONT). He cleared his throat, waiting for the musicians to speak.

He glanced from one to the other in turn, but none seemed ready to begin the session. Baz Cropper, his conventionally handsome face more suited to being a Captain of the Queen's Horse Guards than the singer of a rock band, now looking better than ever with his Missing in Airspace Makeover. To his left, Phil Carter, thick, curly hair down below his shoulders, square face as stolid and practical as an electrician's. He looked good, too, but the latent hostility in his gaze belied the shyness Nick had witnessed on TV interviews in the past. Then there was Jez Tweed, his wavy, sandy locks lustrous, even in the dim light from the Anglepoise. Finally, Barney what-the-fuck-was-his-surname, shorter and dafter-looking than the others, a jovial prankster with a high-pitched voice. He didn't look daft or jovial right now.

Nick felt the cold emanating from them all. It was more than disgruntled antipathy; it was more like a kind of hate. Nick shifted in his chair. He wanted the fuck out of here, but he was not gonna let them rattle him. This was all an act, of course. He would have to play it out, like a kid's staring contest. He widened his smile to show he was ready for any and all shit. He decided their hate was cartoonish, too, and he could handle that. He'd pushed them too far when he slated their last album. Deal, guys. For fuck's sake.

They were all wearing leathers, of course, and while their complexions seemed shiny and new, the musicians' jackets seemed to have taken on the burden of the stolen years—battered and disheveled, as if the band were four Dorian Grays who stored their jackets in the attic. Apart from today.

All four sets of eyes were fixed on him. *Unblinking? Surely not. That would be stupid...* The coldness of their gaze that he could take for either real hostility or comic strip bullshit was beginning to piss him off. *This is getting tired, guys.*

Nick cleared his throat again. He hadn't bothered to rehearse an opening gambit to the interview. He never did. He preferred to wing it. Spontaneity was the key to a great interview. But right now he realized he had nothing to say.

They were doing a bloody good job putting him off after all, then.

Bollocks to them. He would kick it off.

"Good to see you, I guess." Not over friendly, not downright hostile. They could take that opening remark however the fuck they wanted to. If they'd brought him here to do their own hatchet job on him, they were going to be disappointed. He waited for an answer, an acknowledgment of any kind from the four men. Nothing.

"Oooookayyyy then…" He smiled with arrogant swag just to let them know it wasn't working; whatever they were trying to pull was not doing it for him.

"Got over your jet lag, boys? Must be the mother of all hangovers, am I right?" That fell into empty space, too. Bunch of melodramatic pricks. They'd obviously taken his journalistic barbs about being dull phoneys rather too much to heart and wanted to dish him shit, prove to him they were bad boys really so he could re-evaluate his opinion for this piece. Not gonna happen boys. This was the corny type of bollocks he should've expected from them.

"So I guess we dispense with the pleasantries, huh? Dive straight in? Fine by me, boys." He pulled his chair closer to the table and sat back, affecting nonchalance. "Mind if I smoke?" He didn't wait for an answer, pulling out his Marlboros and lighting one with the silver lighter shaped like a naked girl he'd brought back from a trip to Bali. The tits lit up when you flicked the wheel. It never failed to piss off the PC brigade. He was sure it would piss off these guys, too. Their wives probably did most of their thinking for them.

"So, no more messing, here comes the biggy, the one everybody wants an answer to. Where ya been, guys?"

Silence. Nada. Just four sets of eyes fixed on him. And as yet, unless their game really was beginning to throw him, he still hadn't seen them blink.

He took a deep pull on his Marlboro, then let a jet of smoke flow over the table at them. They were the kind of soft rockers who would have quit smoking decades before, if they'd ever started, of course.

"This is gonna be a dull interview if you're not gonna speak to me, boys."

He took another drag, looked at his watch pointedly. Sighed.

When Phil Carter finally spoke, it startled Nick so much he coughed on his fag.

"Ask."

Just the one word, but it was a start. Even though it was delivered in a deep rasp that left Nick unsure whether to giggle or flinch.

"Er, just did. You want me to repeat the question?"

The Cat O' Nine bass player did not reply.

Nick went for it again. "What happened, guys? What happened to you all for six months? How does a jet disappear from airspace without any trace and then reappear again six months later...*in the exact same position?* How did you do that, guys?"

He knew the answer to that one, of course. There had been much discussion of it in the media, and none of it refuted or confirmed by the band's PR. It was all one biiiiig publicity stunt. And it had worked. It had got the world interested in a bunch of boringly predictable rockers. One fucking brilliant rabbit out of a hat, one monster of a *Tadah!* Nick could appreciate the balls of it, even if he couldn't appreciate their music.

Phil Carter's cold, empty eyes burrowed through Nick's brain as if considering the question. *Blink, you fucker.* But he didn't blink, so Nick did it for him, several times.

"We did...nothing." The dry rasp sounded as if it were dragged from the musician's throat from a long, long way down. *Spooky. Give ya that, Phil. Not bad on the spook-o-meter. But still not freaked, okay? Just for the record, pal.*

Carter spoke again, "We flew, and we arrived. We were lost—"

"—And now you're back. Yeah, I got that bit from the TV. No change on that stance then?" Nick took another drag on his cigarette. He still felt a chill from them, but at least they were engaging now. Speaking was good. Words were Nick's job. Without them he was nothing.

"We remember...nothing..."

Get a new act, Phil. The silly fuck had obviously watched too many Vincent Price movies. Except...

Except the expression on the bass player's face, the hostile vacancy of the cold, gun-barrel eyes seemed unsettlingly genuine.

Bollocks. He was falling for their game, that was all. They wouldn't rattle him.

He decided to fight back. He mimicked Phil's deep rasp as he repeated the musician's words, "You remember…nothing. Cool. Helpful, dude." He searched for an ashtray, found none, then stubbed out his Marlboro inside an empty flower vase instead.

"So you're telling me one minute you were flying along like happy rock babies, swigging beer, telling dirty jokes, maybe watching some in-flight porn, then—*Bang!*—you've suddenly jumped six months into the future, and you have absolutely no recollection how you got there or what the fuck you did for that half a year you were hanging in…wherever the hell it was you were hanging. Come on, guys!!" He spread his hands wide in mock indignation. "I'm not a brain-dead hack from *The Sun.* Planes can't just vanish and reappear without somebody being aware of it and know where it's gone. Hello! Give me *some* cred!"

Phil Carter said nothing. His eyes did not move, his expression did not change.

Nick sighed. "Fair enough, David Copperfields of the airways, we'll leave it at that. All I gotta say is…nicely done. Takes balls. And a lot of fixing money, of course. But, moving on, as I'm sure you want me to, I suppose I'd better ask about what plans Cat O' Nine has for the future, now you've miraculously returned from an apparent watery grave?"

If they were angered by his blatant skepticism, they didn't show it. The musicians' faces remained as immobile and inscrutable as ever. Their bodies remained absolutely still, too. Nick was doing all the moving for them. They were genuinely starting to get to him despite all his efforts to resist their psychological warfare. He was aware, too, of the manager still standing silently behind him. All in all, not the best Tuesday afternoon he'd ever spent. And it wasn't turning out to be a belter of an interview either.

This time it was Baz Cropper who spoke. His well-educated tones were slurred, as if his voice were reaching Nick from an old and dirty tape recording made in the '70s.

"We are working..." he said, then paused. *As if the tape had clogged up,* thought Nick and felt the unease poking him in the small of the back again. There was something.... Not right about all of this.

"On a new album..." the singer finished, his eyes darker than Nick remembered them being—not that he'd ever paid much attention to them before, but a memory nagged at him about some article describing him as a blue-eyed heartbreaker. Certainly not one of his articles, that was for sure. Nick wouldn't be caught dead writing such sub-hack drivel.

"You guys don't hang around, do you? That six months was obviously very productive."

Baz ignored that. "We have recorded a demo...of one track only, so far..." He sounded as though he was having difficulty speaking. Like his mouth wasn't used to words and was fumbling over shaping them. What emerged was dry and dragging. *Sawdust vocals,* Nick thought and wrote a mental note to include that line in his write-up.

"But we...return to the studio...imminently...to record the new album."

Nick resisted the urge to glance behind him to see what the manager was doing. That would show weakness. Prove their ruse to unnerve him had worked. He would show them it hadn't by needling them with his next question.

"Will the new material be the same as the old? Can we expect the same cartoon Satan metal as on all the other albums?"

Again they ignored the mocking tone. Carter answered for the band. His dark, dark eyes didn't so much as bore into Nick as exert a strange pull, a tug he felt down in his gut.

"The new album will be...oh, so darker...than any before," he said with his bass rasp. *A jar of crickets being burned to death.* That was another one for the write-up. And how he was beginning to wish he could get away home to do that piece right now...

"This is the album...we were always fated to make..." Carter's dry scratch of a voice ratcheted up a notch. Nick felt the tidal pull of his black eyes increase (Were they *really* black or was it just the subdued lighting?)

and moved the chair back a little, then fumbled for his cigarettes again. His hand shook as he lit the ciggy; it was only a little but enough to betray his unease. *Get a grip! This is Cat O' Nine, for fuck's sake! The corniest, unscariest dickheads in the music industry. They play golf and assemble model airplanes…*

Yet his hand trembled. He inhaled smoke to calm his ridiculous nerves as Carter continued. And it was only now that Nick realized how damn cold the room was.

"There have been…embryonic elements…in previous albums…that foreshadowed the path our… music would take. Clumsy, blind gropings in the dark…minimal and barely noticeable at first, to us…or to our listeners. The odd note, or chord that…seemed to strike through to something…or someplace not in our experience." The bass player paused as if unable to vocalize an idea that was beyond words. Nick hid the fact he was surprised Carter could use words with more than two syllables and shifted in his seat again. This entire interview was so far from what he'd expected. He didn't like it. He should be controlling the chat, controlling the band, but they had him on the spot like a pinned insect. And what they were talking about, he had no idea, of course. Stoner shit, no doubt. But Nick had assumed these clean boys of rock had given up joints along with every other vice years before.

He blew smoke up at the ceiling, trying to think of some witty challenge, some way to bring this round. Some way of making himself feel better about the whole thing.

"These…anomaly notes…intensified with each new album…as we struggled to find our way… We were architects of…the unknown… oblivious ourselves to what doors we might be opening… Our earlier music, as naïve and cartoonish as some have claimed…paved the way for what we are…what we have become."

Okay, nice barbed attack there. But Nick took it as a safety line and ran with it. It afforded him the opportunity to ask what had been nagging at him all day.

"Why me?" He sucked the ciggy harshly, affecting nonchalance but feeling the cold; the cold of the room, the cold of four sets of eyes. Feeling *so* cold…

He let the nicotine calm him before continuing. "Why did you pick me for this job?"

For the first time, Jez Tweed spoke up, his voice as slurred and gravelly as the others. Either they were still suffering from extreme jet lag, or they'd been drinking some evil moonshine. The guitarist's eyes were black as beetles, and they scuttled over Nick's nerves as he spoke.

"Because you love us…"

Nick almost laughed, but the statement was matter of fact, chilling in its implied menace.

"I do?" The cigarette was shaking faster in his hand. He stubbed it out brutally. He began to rise from his seat, determined to get out of this dim room, get away from these shadowy weird fucks, but two firm hands alighted on his shoulders from behind, pushing him gently but firmly back in his seat. He turned his head around to confront the manager, but Doug Roscoe said nothing, face expressionless, eyes equally as dark as the four musicians'.

"You must not…leave yet," Carter rasped. "The interview…is *not* over." His voice dropped to a growl that was almost distorted, as if the tape had run into a swathe of dirt on the play heads.

Nick began to panic. He tried to push himself up, but the manager's hands restraining him were strong, remorseless.

"We haven't played you…our new demo…yet…" Carter reached for a remote that Nick hadn't noticed on the table near the bass player. The musician turned to one side and aimed it at a deck barely discernible in a shadowy corner. "We must warn you…this is pure…. Raw, unmixed… This is *real* Cat O' Nine Tails…" A soft click, a reptilian hiss of dead recording air, then the first note struck through the room.

Chapter Nine

Nick tensed under the grip of the manager, feeling his panic rise as the chords began to slink out of the speakers situated in all four corners of the room. He didn't like those chords. No sir. This was not how Cat O' Nine sounded. Not how they should *ever* sound. The band's music he'd been exposed to over the years had been nothing like this. The fantasy Prog sensibilities, formal middle-of-the-road tameness with lyrical, decorous guitar layers that had made their previous tracks almost opulent in structure had been shockingly discarded. Nick's hackles were not so much up as desperate to tear themselves free. This music was wrong. Music? This was evil concealed in acetate.

The tempo was slow, seductive, the creeping riffs calling to some lonely place in Nick's soul and painting it black with each note. The vocals were fouled from a larynx buried in coffin dirt. The bass insinuated itself heavily around the room, a killer anaconda ready to crush him with coiling rhythms. The drums were a triceratops canter as the song speeded up toward some hideous climax.

Nick listened, and his mind unmoored itself slowly from his surroundings. The fear continued to pump into him with each beat, but the terror began to be fucked by a savage and erotic joy, too, so that his bowels contracted even as his cock swelled. He had never felt so liberated. His scalp was electrified, heart in cardiac, his synapses shorting with the brutal horror/beauty of the sound.

And then it was over. Just a hiss of dead air again. The grip on his shoulders relaxed, too.

Nick sat in his seat and said nothing.

After a while, he got up, turned away from the four silent musicians, walked slowly past the manager to the door.

He stood in the corridor outside for a second, his hand still on the knob of the closed door. He could still hear the music. It was in his ears, his brain, his guts. It stayed with him in the lift down to the lobby, curdling up inside him like a cancer; it showed in his eyes as he passed the blonde without acknowledging her, it showed in his white face as he ignored the security man's polite nod.

The earworm rode the tube with him back to Camden Town.

It was there when he climbed the steps from the platform and walked out into the afternoon sun. He carried it close now, his private hell, his secret heaven. It burned, it consumed.

He let it take him home to his small flat not far from Camden Lock. He climbed the steps to his second-floor apartment, let himself in, ignored the greeting from one of his neighbors, a Rasta with a joint clasped between two fingers standing in the doorway to his flat. The Rasta snorted, dismissed him, stepped back inside, the heavy bass thud of Dreadzone vibrating the entire building.

Nick ignored the heavy vibrations, too; he had enough vibes to keep him going, in his skull.

He sat down at his laptop, waited for Microsoft Word to fire up, then hunched over the keyboard and punched out words, the earworm whispering to him, the music he had heard in that executive EMI office bleeding down through his fingers and into the keys, the words a rhapsody of ecstasy and death.

He didn't need to play back the recording of the interview. The band's words were all locked away safe inside him, along with their music. Their pure, undiluted music. Raw and unmixed.

He finished the write-up. It would be the best article ever written about Cat O' Nine Tails. A sea-change piece from Nick James that encapsulated the electric terror and euphoria he had experienced during the scant few moments in which the demo played, although his words concentrated on the mesmerizing majesty the track had inspired in him, eschewing the fear. He could see the eyes of the band watching him as he typed and knew they would approve. He had earned their respect at last. It was the finest work he had ever written.

When he had finished, he emailed the file to his editor at *Rock!!* and switched off his laptop. He stood up, looking out of his bird shit-smeared window at the grimy backs of houses opposite, then left his flat again. The house-shaking bass from his neighbor across the hall went unheeded. His own earworm provided all the vibes Nick needed.

He left the house, the slam of the door behind him sounding like a coffin lid falling, and determined to work that into one of his next pieces…until he remembered there would be no more pieces.

He strode along Camden High Street until he reached a hardware store and bought two items without replying to the shop assistant's pleasantries. The man flinched a little at Nick's unwavering gaze, his sweat-matted hair and blanched face, and watched him leave the shop.

Nick wasn't quite sure where he was going or what he was doing. He listened to the earworm and let it lead him wherever it wanted. It wanted Camden Markets, so he took it there.

He walked through the noisy throng, one item tucked inside his soft leather jacket, the other, a coil of rope, clutched in his left fist. Market stall speakers blared at him, the scents of exotic food impinged on his nostrils and were rebuffed without a second thought. Pushers, punks, and tourists shoved along in a constant river of disparate humanity, all after this deal or that victim; rhythm or rip off, everybody had a choice. He continued at a firm pace, eyes fixed ahead, knocking aside several people who got in his way. He ignored their insults and gestures, intent on his purpose.

And what is that, Nicholas James? What are you gonna do, son? Are you gonna make Rock!! *proud? You gonna embellish your last ever article with the biggest exclamation mark ever? Rock on, Nicky boy…*

He crossed the road to Camden Lock, the extensive complex of markets beside Regent's Canal. Here, there were more crowds, a cosmopolitan bustle of ethnicities, a dazzling variety of stalls selling art and crafts, clothes, books, jewelry, music, and a tongue-enticing selection of food. Whereas previously Nick might have paused to savor the smells and the sights, maybe pass the time of day with any familiar faces, today the earworm had other plans for him.

He passed stalls with exotic names such as the Black Giraffe, Fairytale Jungle, and Soulbird Art, ignoring the intricately handmade necklaces and painted craft items on display. He didn't look in at Wicked, with its cornucopia of colored candles; he didn't pause to admire Nana Fanny's traditional Jewish bagels or the quirky fabrics in Woozy.

He made his way to the Stables Market as the first drops of rain began to spit from a gravelly sky. He paused outside Cyber Hound as if momentarily confused by the techno rhythms chopping through the open doors. He didn't blink at the visual assault of garish colors adorning the mannequins inside but searched his jacket pockets mechanically with his free hand until he found his shades before heading in as if succumbing to the insistent beats.

While shoppers browsed past the Day-Glo t-shirts and neon-hued PVC costumes on display, Nick seemed more drawn to the two staff members, a statuesque girl with a rainbow-dyed fan of hair who resembled a plasma ball lamp and a tall, skinny man with locks teased into a Ziggy mane. Both were standing at the main counter, casually chatting over the pounding beat of techno, and both wore body-snug rubber outfits that squeezed every contour.

The girl saw Nick coming but continued flirting with her colleague, legs crossed, breasts jutting like PVC volcanoes at him in an unfettered display of BDSM body language. Her eyebrows were caterpillar green, her lips a fuck-me blue.

Nick waited patiently for her to face him.

What was he doing here? Nick looked decidedly out of place; a fortysomething in jeans, a denim shirt, and soft leather jacket. Everything about him screamed middle-of-the-road. When he started to reach into his jacket pocket, the boy finally acknowledged him, tilting his head back arrogantly, no customer service smile here, his stance all *What the fuck do YOU want, Dad?*

Nick showed him what he wanted. He was a music journalist, and while he was here, he might as well do a crit. Still clutching the rope in his left hand, he used the hatchet he pulled from his pocket, the shiny, brand-new item he'd bought from the hardware store, as his pen and wrote his opening statement across the cyber boy's forehead. The slam of electro smothered his scream, but the blood made up for it. It was Day-Glo, too, under the garish lighting. The Cyber Hound boy fell back against a display of candy-colored baseball caps, which buried him as he slipped behind the counter. Nick pushed past the girl, who was standing in frozen shock, to retrieve his hatchet. He had to kick the mound of hats aside to do so and nearly fell over himself as the shop assistant's death jerks unsettled his footing.

Armed once more, he turned on the girl. She was moving now. Her finely curved buttocks were in motion, creasing the tight rubber as she cantered across the store. Nick watched appreciatively and wondered what line of phrase his hatchet would use on them. When the Cybergirl barreled into a small group of shoppers halfway across the floor space, he decided he would have to find out.

She had fallen to the floor, and the shoppers had parted, either too bewildered or too afraid to help her up. Nick moved unhurriedly toward her. Her mouth was open in a silent O as the music carried away her shrieks, accentuating her similarity to a PVC blow-up doll. Nick moved in to burst her everywhere. The volcanic breasts erupted under his hatchet job, the blade a piston rising and falling in frantic time with the techno beat, and the shop was soon empty. Nick stepped over the rubber corpse, out into the market again, moving past the stalls, shades splashed with red, hatchet held stiffly by his side, the tool of his trade.

He found himself gravitating toward the Dark Rose. Word of his presence had begun to spread it seemed; the passageways between the original stables were rapidly emptying of shoppers. Nick saw several stall holders beginning to lock their doors, staring at him through the glass of their doors in terror as he stalked forward, some frantically prodding cell phones. He was running out of time, he knew that. He had to bring his career to an end swiftly. One final review perhaps.

Dark Rose was still open. They had missed all the action. Sisters of Mercy was blasting, which would probably explain it. Nick could almost have forgiven them, but while Goth music had never been top of his hate list, and Andrew Eldritch had made some damn fine records, he was running out of options now. Beggars couldn't be choosers and all that. Besides, there were no rap or hip hop stores nearby. So he listened to the vibe in his ear and strode up to the entrance just as the music changed to My Chemical Romance. *That'll do nicely*, he thought, then entered the shop. Now he could enjoy his work.

The store was dark inside (of course) and empty apart from three or four teen Goths (or were they Emos, nobody had ever really explained the difference to Nick) poring through the black skinny jeans and racks of massive boots. He waited just inside the entrance to see if anyone had appreciated his grand entrance. They hadn't, so he forced his opinion on two teenage boys with matching acne and long leather Nosferatu coats. They didn't seem to appreciate his style of writing, however, or even understand his viewpoint, which just made him more furious as he wrote clumsily on them with special red ink. The man in his early thirties (too old for Goth?) who manned the stall didn't have the heart to argue with Nick, so the *Rock!!* journalist took it away from him, pinning him squealing against a rack of frilled shirts while he messily dug it out from under his Cannibal Corpse t-shirt and plonked it down on top of a stack of Bone Orchard CDs. He paused only to imagine what the CDs might sound like with blood in the grooves and decided it would be most authentic.

When he was done, there were only dead Goths left in the shop, which seemed only right. He silenced the sound system, too, his final act of disapproval, and made his way out.

The passages were completely empty now. He would need to hurry. The cops would be on their way soon. He reached the Horse Tunnel Market entrance with the bronze statues of horses rearing above and to either side of the arch. This was it.

He didn't hesitate now. He dropped the hatchet and climbed up one of the plunging statues, balancing on its neck while he unraveled the rope. Rain was pattering gently around him, making his purchase on the horse even more precarious and slippery. He tied one end of the rope tightly around the neck, then forged a noose out of the other end. He paused a moment, swaying on top of the bronze horse, leaned against the stone wall beside him to restore his balance, and then flung the noose upwards until it snaked over the head and forequarters of a horse emerging above the tunnel entrance and dropped over the other side, dangling about eight feet above the ground. Reaching it required more balance and persistence, but he managed to grab it eventually, even as he heard the first sirens bleating and wailing down Camden High Street toward the Lock.

Too late, my friends. Way too late.

He put the noose over his head and slipped the knot tight, the hemp itchy and rough against the skin of his throat. Rain slicked his curly hair over his face.

Is that it? He scanned the almost-deserted market. A few terrified (or just brazenly curious) onlookers hovered on the perimeters, hiding behind clothing mannequins, statues of Goddesses, or the pillars that lined the covered markets, becoming braver in their rubbernecking once it became apparent what Nick was going to do. One of the faces he recognized as the proprietor of the vinyl stall Rock Me, one of his habitual haunts. When his friend realized he had been spotted, he made an effort to conceal himself more effectively behind a stone Hera.

So much for mates, eh? Nick remembered selling him the first issue of *Appetite for Destruction*, the Guns N' Roses debut LP with the controversial murdered woman cover. He'd always regretted that sale. The bastard had probably made a mint out of it. Petty concerns. Didn't matter now.

He wavered on the horse's neck, listening to the vibes in his head. He thought of Cat O' Nine Tails and wondered if they would approve.

He knew that they would.

Vive le rock, suckers…

Nick took a giant leap of faith.

Chapter Ten

"I hate this."

"I know." Johnny leaned back against the worn velvet cushions of the seat he shared with Rose.

"You're his friend. He trusts you. As for me... I *hate* this..."

He grunted wryly. "Do you, though?"

She darted him an angry bird look. "What does *that* mean?"

He raised a quizzical eyebrow, his cheekbones like shards of hard bone in the subdued lighting of the back-street pub.

"You think this is *fun* for me...? I love Kirk. I do."

"Yeah. You do. And yet you're fucking me."

She stared at him for a second. "And is that all it is I'm doing, in your opinion?"

He shrugged.

"I'm beginning to wonder if you know me at all."

Johnny glanced away across the half-empty pub. It was mid-afternoon on a Wednesday, in the arse of nowhere, or Peckham as it was better known. There was very little chance of anyone recognizing them here. "So what you saying, Rose Petal?"

"Please don't call me that. You know he uses it sometimes."

Johnny sighed. "Don't know what you want from me then..."

Rose started to pick up her bag. "Neither do I..."

He stopped her, placing a firm hand on her wrist and pulling her toward him. He pressed his mouth against hers insistently, teasing her tongue with his when she finally succumbed and opened her lips. Then she was turning away again. "This should...*must* stop. I didn't mean for any of this to happen."

"People never do."

"It's not *his* fault. I can't ever blame him."

"Just blame me. My James Dean good looks turned your head."

She sighed. "Don't be a prick, Johnny. You're not that good looking."

That shut him up. *Hit him where his heart was*, she thought, and guilt flushed her again. Why *was* she doing this? Things had been bumpy between herself and Kirk for a while, for—she searched her memories—for a couple of years really. They didn't communicate anymore. The flat they shared seemed to be the only thing they had in common now. She had always felt he was more obsessed with his band than he was with her, and while that had been exciting to start with, to see the passion he carried for his music, lately that had lost its glamour. And lately, too, the constant jabs at Cat O' Nine. He knew how much the metal band meant to her. She'd grown up loving them, although she'd been a bit too young to be aware of them during their early years. Something about the comforting structure of the music, the cozy horror themes, the combination of melodies and riffs always made her feel warm and happy.

Kirk saw none of that. He continually harped on about how the first album with the original singer was so much better. Rose didn't care. She liked how they sounded *now*. Fuck the past. Nostalgia was so overrated. And as for his growing, unhealthy preoccupation with the way they had vanished and "staged a comeback" as he put it. No wonder she had begun to distance herself from him a bit. And then there was Johnny.

Always there to defend her, a modern-day Sir Galahad who sported a Gibson guitar instead of a lance. Always there with his burning blue eyes and sleek cheekbones, the rocker hair and gentle voice. Could anyone blame her? Really?

She knew the answer to that. She turned her face toward him, ready to tell him it was done. He'd been a stop gap, a sticking plaster to heal her growing sense of loneliness, her growing sense of...growing old? *Was that what this was? She was only thirty-five, for fuck's sake. Thirty-five, unmarried, with no kids. Yeah, THAT thirty-five. But what was Johnny gonna do about that? Pout his lips, tilt his head so the lights shone on his cheekbones, and level those blue peepers at her...? Yeah. Bye, Johnny. I've been a twat.*

So she turned her face toward him, and he did all those things. And she ended up kissing him anyway.

Kirk rang the editor of *Rock!!* as soon as he read the story in the kiosk across the road. This time he bought the paper and carried it straight home. Rose was out (again) so he had the place to himself.

He was scared.

Which was crazy. So what if the music journalist had just interviewed Cat O' Nine Tails right before he went on a killing spree and then hanged himself? He was obviously unstable. Didn't have to be a connection, did there?

But he rang the magazine regardless.

He knew the editor, Bill Ticer, albeit on a very casual basis. They were on nodding terms at gigs, and once Bill had offered to highlight Lucifer Sam as an up-and-coming new band, although the piece had never got published, much to Kirk's chagrin. Not enough space in that issue, the editor had told him over the phone, and then in a pub near the 100 Club the following month when the subsequent issue had made the newsstands, again Lucifer Sam-less. Never one to hold a grudge, Kirk had bided his time. The Sam would come good one day...

The editor was reluctant to come to the phone at first. That was obvious from the way the receptionist took so damn long getting back to him while she told Ticer who was on the line. *Come on, you double-chinned prick...* Kirk felt a rising sense of urgency as the seconds tipped into minutes. When she finally returned and told him the Editor was busy, Kirk told her exactly why he wanted to talk to her boss. After he mentioned Nick James and the Cat O' Nine Tails interview, this time she wasn't away for more than a few minutes before Ticer's nasal voice replaced hers, greeting him abruptly.

"Kirk. How's it? Can I do you for?"

Thought that would get your attention.

"Cat O' Nine," he said slowly.

"What about them? Sally said you wanted to talk about Nick. You know anything 'bout what happened?"

"No more than what it says in *The Mirror*. But I think the two things are connected. Don't you think it strange he'd just been to chat with the band before he went psycho?"

"Do *you?*"

Kirk said nothing for a second or two, waiting for the editor to give him some clue that would mean he was either completely paranoid or that he was sniffing the wind.

"Come on, Bill. There's something very bad about all this? Can't you smell it?"

This time the editor remained quiet for a beat. Then, "He wrote the article. Sent it to me about half an hour before the police say he went on his killing spree."

"And?" Kirk's pulse was fast now. He somehow knew what was coming.

"Unpublishable. His mind had gone. Nick James's final piece of rock journalism, and it'll never see print."

Kirk rubbed his head and dropped in his armchair. "Fuck."

"Fuck is right. It's scary shit. Like his mind was unraveling as he wrote it. Gave me the creeps. We'd never be allowed to put it out…" A pause, then: "And why the fuck am I telling you all this?"

"Because maybe you owe me. Because Lucifer Sam is going to be huge one day and because I seem to be the only other person in the world who thinks something very wrong is going on with Cat O' Nine. Please don't insult my intelligence and tell me you think him interviewing the band and then going postal is a coincidence."

"You know what I think? I don't have a fucking clue what to think, that's what. His article was like an insane paean to Cat. Like he had turned into their biggest uberfan ever. And if you knew Nick like I knew Nick, you'd know something stinks, and it ain't my ass."

"Send it to me."

"What? Are you out of your mind, too? Is this a contagion? You don't wanna read that bollocks. It tipped my mind upside down, mate. Leave it alone. Gonna delete it. Best thing."

"No!" Kirk realized he had almost shouted and forced himself to relax. "Don't delete it. It could be vital evidence."

"What, are you the C.I.D now as well as a second-rate singer in a third-rate band?"

Kirk let that go. This was too important. "Have the police seen it?"

"Of course they have. But *I* don't want to ever again. They put it down to the deranged doodlings of a rock journo way past his sell by. Amazes me why the band even asked him to interview them in the first place. Common knowledge he thought they were bland shit."

And the prize for least insightful prick in the city goes to... "Send it to me." Of course, James had often slagged Cat O' Nine in the music press. How could Kirk have forgotten that? Which just made everything all the more creepy. "Send it to me, and I'll guarantee you an exclusive on The Men That Will Not Be Blamed For Nothing. We're supporting them in a couple of weeks. You know they're actually the hottest band in the UK now." *And didn't it hurt to say that?*

"Interview?"

"Whatever. You can snog the singer, too, if you fancy it. Pink bristles 'n' all."

"Fuck's sake..." Ticer sighed. "Look, if I send you the file, you have to promise—and I mean on-your-fucking-life, pinkiest promise you ever made, not to show it to anyone else."

"Deal." He hung up, then sat at his laptop and waited for the editor's email.

Chapter Eleven

"Again? Jesus fucked an acolyte, I *do* have a magazine to put out. I already told your uniform boys everything I know."

"Yes, but you haven't told *me...*"

The Detective Sergeant sat down on Bill Ticer's desk, fixing him with her vivid green eyes. Her short, dark brown hair was aggressively styled, as was her chocolate pinstripe suit. Her shirt was the only concession to femininity, undone maybe one button too many, it exposed a tease of purple bra and the slightest curve of her small breasts. She was in her early forties, attractive in a predatory way, thin-lipped, straight-nosed, with a sharp, triangular face like a sheriff's badge. Her eyes were anything but conservative, however. Narrow and wild, they sparked with mischief and latent sexual promise. Bewitched, Ticer felt his anger begin to slip; a thickness between his legs took its place.

She was accompanied by a detective constable. A little shorter than the regular copper (The Met had abandoned its height restriction policy, Ticer remembered), his face was slack and comical, and he looked too young to be in the CID. Ticer ignored him after his first glance.

He sighed, sipping noisily at his coffee. "You really want me to repeat everything?" He shifted in his chair, hoping his slight arousal was not noticeable through his tight jeans.

The DS leaned over him so he could smell her perfume; erotic and subtle, it did the job. "Just tell me all about your boy Nicholas," she purred.

The detective constable shuffled slightly, tilting his head back, trying to look authoritative and failing. *What is this, sexy cop, dopey cop...?* "What do you wanna know...?" He caught sight of Jim, his assistant editor, chatting up Sally the receptionist again and a flash of irritation interrupted the spell the DS had wrought. "Oi, James, less flirting and more subbing. This bastard mag needs to get to the presses somehow and what with you staring down Sally's top and this lady copper sprawling all over my desk, we got as much chance as a cat locked in a dog's home! Give me a fucking break."

The DS smiled thinly. "My, my... We are a trifle overexcited, aren't we?" She shifted her thigh enough to extract a copy of the previous issue of *Rock!!* she'd been sitting on. She flicked through it with a quizzical turn to her lips. "Quite a few articles by Nick James. You must have trusted his professionalism."

"Been with us ten years or more. He knew what he was doing. Good at his job. Could always rely on Nick for good copy."

She narrowed her eyes even further. "Did he know what he was doing yesterday? Was that good copy, too? Shouldn't hurt sales, I imagine." She dropped the mag and stroked her leg as if brushing a crumb from the material. Bill couldn't help following the caress of her fingers. And when he started to lift his gaze toward her face, he couldn't help stalling at the undone button and the tantalizing curves glimpsed beneath.

"Up here, fella," she told him abruptly, raising her hand toward her chin. "My tits ain't doing the talking." The DC sniggered, then flushed scarlet. She ignored him, still fixing Ticer with her gaze.

Ticer flushed, too, glaring around to make sure his staff hadn't heard the comment. They were all pretty busy at their desks, but Jim had a smirk on his chops.

He wiped his mouth with a pudgy hand and blinked up at the detective. "I don't know about that," he croaked, wondering how swiftly he had lost control of the conversation in his own office. "I didn't know he was gonna crack up, did I?"

"No signs of it beforehand? No provocation here in the office, or at home?"

"Nothing! He got on with everyone alright. Apart from arguing with Jacko over there about Cat O' Nine." He gestured over to a long-haired journalist leaning back in his swivel chair staring at a PC. "And he lived on his tod. Bit of a sad fuck, to be brutally honest. Didn't have many mates. No bird. Thought he was cool, but he was living out of time really. Still wrote well, but the stuff he wrote about, the bands he liked, well…they weren't that cool anymore, so…we were kinda surprised Cat O' Nine asked for him, and him only."

The DS was staring over at Jacko, who realized he was an object of interest and sat up at his desk, unsettled.

"Jacko…?" she asked, still watching the writer. Jacko was in his mid-thirties, balding under the long hair, albeit not at as great a rate as Ticer himself, who had already been tempted (though managed to resist so far) to do a comb-over with his hair.

"Jacko's a huge Cat fan. Thinks they're the Queen's Arse, if you'll excuse my treason, ma'am." He grinned. She did not return the grin as she faced him again. He coughed. "Er, he likes 'em. A lot. So he was pissed off when Nick got the job."

"Maybe I should talk to Jacko. But first, I need you to tell me why you think he did what he did yesterday. Did you hear from him at all before he sent you the piece?"

"Not a dickey. I think he said it all in the article, though, don't you? He'd completely changed his mind about the band. Gone from feeling contempt for them to thinking they were the hottest feces on the planet. I'm minding my language there, ma'am, you'll notice." Another feeble, ingratiating smirk, not returned. His hard-on had long since wilted. "And no, I ain't got a clue why he flipped. He was just fine when he left the office. Usual snarky self. Thought he was a Rock God himself, not just a hack who wrote purple prose about 'em." He scratched his ear. "I heard he done some Goths, among others. He never liked Emos, so maybe that's it."

"Maybe that's it," she aped him wryly. "But he never liked metal either. So why the sudden change of heart?"

"Dunno. You read the article, I presume. Your uniform boys printed off a copy yesterday. Maybe you should ask the band. You think they influenced him in some way?""

"Do you?"

"Fuck do I know. I'm just the editor of this rag. I never get to interview the bands anymore. Too *busy.*"

She didn't get the hint. "And yes, I've seen his article. Doesn't make for bedtime reading, does it?"

He shrugged. "Well, I told the uniforms, I ain't gonna print it. Made my spine creep." He thought for a minute. "But if you *are* gonna chat to the band, if you think they might have changed his mind about them in some drastic way—"

"Your words. Not mine."

"Just sayin' what you're making me think, that's all. But if you *do* think there's summat odd going on, you're not the only one. Just been on the phone to some twat...er, I mean, acquaintance...whose theories you really might be interested to hear."

"Is that so? Maybe I could have the twat's name and number?" She bared her strong teeth in a cheesy grin. "And while you're at it, give me the contact details for Cat O' Nine as well. And then I might just let you get on with your day."

Kirk felt sick.

And he really wanted Rose to come home.

Nick James's article had terrified him.

Kirk was aware of the writer's work, had read several pieces in *Rock!!*, and while the journalist's usual style was cloyingly self-important at the best of times, it was usually conventional and rational enough.

Not this piece. His final article was a horrifying peep into a fractured mess of a mind. Kirk had felt himself tottering into an abyss as he read the file. The fact it was all about Cat O' Nine just made it all the more troubling.

Something had happened to him at that interview. Something had turned him from a strutting, cocksure pseud into a gibbering mega fan drooling meaningless superlatives. The musicians' words were transcribed by James with obsessional adoration, accompanied by elaborations of how awed he was to be in their presence, worshipping every syllable they uttered. And judging by this interview, that wasn't many.

Because you love us...

Those words from Jez Tweed struck Kirk as particularly sinister.

He walked to the window, staring out at the gray street outside.

The new album will be oh so darker than any before...

Kirk suddenly wanted to be out in that dismal street, as unappetizing as it might look. He wanted to breathe the polluted London air.

"We were architects of the unknown, oblivious ourselves to what doors we might be opening... Our earlier music, as naïve and cartoonish as some have claimed, paved the way for what we are, what we have become.

The odd note, or chord that seemed to strike through to something, or some place not in our experience."

If the words were ambiguous, James had done his best to excavate their meaning: *"...each album a stepping stone to a higher truth, to a threshold the door of which was opening ever so steadily wider. To the initiated, their catalog of music is a causeway to a beautiful terror. A highway to Hell indeed. And what a glorious hell it is. The pure Apocalypse of their latest oeuvre. Goodbye rock 'n' roll, you fatuous, strutting comfort blanket, you have found your nemesis. Here is the Real Unplugged. Here is the antithesis of Comfort. Here is the death of rock and all who sail in her. Here is Morrison's* The End, *if only he could have put down the whiskey and pierced the curtain. Here is* Sympathy for the Devil *with no pouting lip service. Here is Sid Vicious screaming out of the Abyss, playing a bass on fire with Dante's flames. Here is Art for the Damned. If Music be the Food of Hate, play on..."*

Kirk ran his hand through his spooky shock of hair and withdrew from the window. He found himself drawn to the two CD racks in one corner of the lounge. One for him, one for her. It was Rose's collection he was more interested in right now.

Alphabetically listed, as neat and organized as ever, she had Cat O' Nine's complete CD back catalog. He began to pull out the first album, then pushed it back into the rack. He knew that one by heart. If there were any clues or anomalies on there, he would have been aware of them.

He took the second album from the rack, studying the cartoonish metal shock imagery on the cover. A skeletal guitarist standing atop a tomb, the rest of the band grinning zombies playing to an audience of corpses rising from their graves. He popped open the case and took out the disc.

Soft drums were syncopated over a sedate, rather pleasant guitar riff. Keyboards insinuated between the vocals, which were operatic enough, and while flamboyant in falsetto terms, they were far too similar to many other rock vocalists of the time. The whole CD had a tameness to it, which made it stand out so markedly from the preceding album, which had been rude and unfettered and borne along on a tide of alcohol- and drug-fueled frenzy, courtesy of Ray Starling.

There was nothing here. He listened to the first few tracks with the usual intolerance he felt toward this most crowd-pleasing of metal bands. He sat in the armchair, his head aching from reading the lyric sheet with its mangled grammar and tortured metaphors. He was about to switch off the CD player when the fifth track commenced. The opening arrangement was a strange one and sounded unlike the rest of the album's content. The notes jarred as if the mannered conservatism he had listened to for the last quarter of an hour had been rudely interrupted by a spike of ir-rationality that shattered the sedate riffs. He rewound the track, listened to the opening chords again. There. Just a few seconds of Les Paul lunacy, as if Jez Tweed had momentarily lost his thread, and they'd recorded it just for the hell of it.

He jettisoned the CD and replaced it with the third album. This time it was right there in the second track. The same discordant notes, extended this time, as if the band relished their rediscovery, and then guiltily buried them beneath the subsequent welter of mediocrity. The disturbing chord was still brief, but it fingered the base of Kirk's spine regardless.

He placed the fourth CD in the tray. The cover of this one had WWI British soldiers fighting in the trenches with spike-helmeted Germans whose faces were livid and demonic, eyes burning holes in twisted flesh. The first five songs were jubilantly crafted pop metal, bubblegum horror for the masses. The sixth song contained a subtly uneasy chord change that reintroduced the sinister notes. Sinister? Wasn't he overreacting? No. The sound stirred a deep and inexplicable disquiet in him.

If someone were just playing one album, the notes would have been pretty much indiscernible; Rose played them all the time and had never commented on any musical anomalies. It was only after hearing several CDs in a row that the sounds took on an accumulated significance, and only then because he was purposefully listening for them. But was it by design, or just the band fumbling with something they didn't understand? *And what the hell was that "something?"* The concept of particular notes or chords that could evoke real fear was one entirely new to Kirk.

By the time he'd played the fifth album, the notes had formed an unsettling musical phrase, jammed into the bridge of an otherwise forgettable track. By the sixth, they formed a solo, spiraling into a frenzied peak before Tweed hastily shut it down as if he'd almost released something that scared him. It scared Kirk. *Art for the Damned.*

He was reaching for the seventh CD when Rose returned home.

"What the fuck?" she said as she took in the music. Her beautiful almond eyes were wide with surprise. "You're playing Cat O' Nine Tails. The same Cat O' Nine Tails that you openly despise. And you really do look as though I've just caught you wanking."

He got out of his armchair and hugged her tight. She responded stiffly at first, then more warmly. The CD finished, and the room went silent. She started to ask him something, presumably why the hell he was playing music he hated, but he silenced her questions with a hungry kiss. She returned it. He didn't ask where she'd been, whom she'd been with. He held her tight and kissed her.

Eventually, Kirk let her go.

Chapter Twelve

There was already a queue outside the flagship HMV on Oxford Street when Kirk and Rose got off the bus. Not massive by any means, not snaking all the way down London's most famous shopping street like it would have if the signing had been publicly announced. But word of mouth had obviously spread enough to accrue a good hundred and fifty hardcores. The queue disappeared inside the wide open entranceway, which was flanked by two security men who did not belong to HMV. The queue mostly consisted of men on the wrong side of thirty-five, thinning, long hair and well-worn leathers and denims designating their long service to the cause. There were a few girls, too, some young and attractive enough to remind Kirk of Rose.

He smiled at her as they walked up to the doors. She looked stoked; she was about to meet her all-time favorite band. He had laughed off her queries as to why he was listening to her Cat CDs and said nothing about the way the recurring notes had freaked him. She would just call him paranoid. And perhaps he was.

He recognized one of the security men. He was a regular Cat O' Nine roadie, a genial and very tall ex-Hawkwind crewman who had been with Cat for the last five years. Kirk had seen him knocking about at various gigs and bars and had always got on well with him. The tales he'd told Kirk about Lemmy had always made him chuckle.

"Hey Deuce," he greeted the roadie, who was wearing his usual battered denim jacket, jeans, and biker boots. A heavy-duty pair of shades blocked his eyes as the roadie stared at Kirk without answering. Deuce always had a smile ready. But not today.

Momentarily thrown, Kirk hesitated, then remembering Deuce followed the band everywhere, along with a hand-picked selection of road crew, he tried again. "Glad you and the band made it back, mate. Thought we'd lost you for good when that plane disappeared. What the hell happened?"

Again, no answer, no smile. The usually jovial roadie inclined his head to stare down at the shorter Kirk.

"Come on, Kirk," Rose said pointedly. "He's obviously not in the mood for a chat."

Feeling rejected and confused, Kirk allowed Rose to draw him into the shop. Cat O' Nine Tails greeted them, blaring from the store's sound system. Their previous release from the year before. Kirk realized he was listening for that particular arrangement of notes that for some reason disturbed him; he took hold of Rose's hand instinctively.

They walked up the queue, which wound through the ground floor New Releases section and all the way up to a long table positioned at the rear of the store. The table was empty.

Davey was waiting for them at the main till, motorcycle helmet clutched in one hand. His greasy dandelion of spikes was clearly undented from having worn it.

"Kirk, you prick," he greeted the singer. "Took yer fuckin' time." He glanced disapprovingly at Rose. "I see you brought your side-car along."

"Fuck you, too, Davey," Rose snapped back, her gorgeous lips twisting with disdain.

"Leave it out," Kirk told them both, raising his voice over the music. "So where's the band?"

"In the manager's office, signing shit. You wanna go in? Me mate's the Ass Man; he'll let us in."

"Yes!" Rose almost clapped her hands with glee.

"Fuck me, you're a sad bitch," Davey said.

Kirk was about to defend Rose (and at least Johnny wasn't there to do the job for him) when Davey patted him on the arm urgently. "Filth's here."

Kirk turned to follow Davey's gaze. An impossibly young-looking copper, whose vocation was obvious despite his plain clothes disguise, was following a predatory-looking woman through the shop.

"Better leave it for a moment then," Kirk said as the two officers made their way to the till and spoke to a harassed-looking staff member.

"What the hell do they want?" Rose asked, disappointment making her peevish.

The staff member had dandruff on the collar of his black polo shirt, Detective Sergeant Louisa Gull noticed as the man punched in the code to the manager's door and let her and DC Trimble through. She resisted the urge to brush at it with her hand. She hated sloppiness and lack of personal hygiene.

The manager's office was medium sized and functional and was probably normally tidy, but right now the main desk and another smaller one facing a blank wall (for the less-important Assistant Manager, Gull assumed) was cluttered with CDs, t-shirts, and posters. Four men in leather jackets and fairly dilapidated denims sat stiffly with their backs to the door in front of the desk, behind which sat a more formally dressed man Gull recognized as Doug Roscoe, the band's manager. The band did not look around as she entered.

She hesitated for a moment, taking it all in. There was no sign of the store manager she had expected to find and whom she had expected to have to mollify for her uninvited visit. Perhaps he was making tea somewhere.

Except, as she stepped further into the room and the four musicians finally began to turn around to look at her, she had the sudden conviction that these men didn't drink a whole lot of tea.

The manager stared at the two police officers without speaking. The band remained silent, too. Even though they were inside, they all wore thick, black wraparound shades. Roscoe's were a bit more conservative, as befitting his more-advanced age. Except he didn't look as old as Gull remembered from her research…

"Detective Sergeant Gull, Detective Constable Trimble," she announced briskly, advancing across the room. "Mind if I have a brief word with you boys?"

Roscoe spoke for them. His voice was a gravelly slur. Was he drunk? He didn't look it. "I don't see…any necessity for a police interview…"

"This isn't a formal interview, sir. Just a quick chat. And I can see you're busy, so I'll make it short." *But not sweet by the looks of things.*

The manager said nothing. If he was annoyed, he barely showed it. The four musicians watched her from behind their sunglasses. She felt a trickle of unease, and that pissed her off just a little. She didn't like being intimidated. Never had. She always knew how to treat men who tried (and there had been plenty in the Met). But she realized she really didn't know how to react to these five men. It was something to do with their immobility, their uniform silence, their…*otherness?* And what the fuck did *that* mean?

She looked around for a chair and found one next to the Ass Man's desk. She carried it over to the group around the main desk, positioning it so she could face the band and forcing Roscoe to turn his own so he could see her.

"Nick James," she began, pausing as DC Trimble stumbled over Baz Cropper's chair leg as he made his way round to follow her. She breathed in deeply and continued. "Are you aware that you were the last people to see him alive?"

Silence for a beat. Then Roscoe said in his dirt tones, "I am not sure that is…correct, Inspector. Or relevant."

"Detective Sergeant," she said automatically…and a little defensively? Fuck Roscoe, he wouldn't unnerve her. "And according to our records, he visited you roughly three hours before going on a violent rampage in which six people were killed. He was writing a piece on your band for a rock magazine, as I'm sure you're aware. So apart from the people he butchered with a hatchet at Camden Lock, you were the last people he had social interaction with that day. I'd say that was pretty relevant." Her tone sounded harder than she had intended. Mustn't let their tacky rock 'n' roll star bollocks throw her.

It was Phil Carter's turn to join in. Gull recognized him, too, but again, he looked younger, less ravaged than in any of the photographs she had seen.

"We spoke to him…he left. What he did…after that, we can have no…responsibility for."

What was it with the dramatic pauses and the Hammer Horror deep voices? It was beginning to get on her tits. And on her spine, too, if she admitted it. Carter's voice was creepier than Roscoe's, like his vocal cords were smothered in dust and coffin dirt. *Trying to spook you, that's all. Typical rock 'n' roll bullshit.*

"Did he seem normal to you?"

There was a pause, then Baz Cropper cut in, his voice slow and buried, just like his bezzy mate on the bass. "What is normal, Detective Sergeant?"

His black sunglasses reflected her triangular face right back at Gull. She looked swallowed by blackness in those lenses. Her voice felt tight as she responded. "Did he seem agitated to you?"

Nobody answered. Gull felt more than uncomfortable. She was used to belittling men to assert herself over them. She was used to flirting with them and using her sexuality to disarm them. She could do none of those things here. And that made her angry.

"You know he hated Cat O' Nine Tails, don't you? So why did you choose him to interview you?"

Roscoe almost smiled. "We wanted to change his mind…"

"Oh, you did that, alright…" She leaned forward in her chair, determined to attain some authority over the situation. "But how did you manage it exactly?"

Baz Cropper stood up slowly. For a moment, DS Gull was convinced he was going to make a threatening move against her and turned instinctively to Trimble for back up. Trimble was pale and useless looking, staring at the band like a naughty boy dragged in front of the headmaster.

"I think this interview…is over," the singer said.

"As you can see, Detective Sergeant," Roscoe added slowly, "We are very busy…"

She felt helpless, and that infuriated her. She stood up, too, bristling with dissatisfaction. "I may need to speak to you again."

They were all standing up now, and she realized she really wanted to be away from this room, from these five men with the hollow voices and expressionless faces. Away from those black sunglasses that sucked her in and drowned her.

She jerked her head at Trimble, and he snapped out of his trance, followed her like a boy tripping after his mum.

They were still staring at her silently as she opened the door and left the room.

"They're cool," Trimble twittered as they emerged onto the shop floor again.

"Cool? Fuck me, Trimble. As cool as five corpses at an embalmment party. If creepy is the new chic, then they're the most happening dudes in town." Gull twisted her face at the continual barrage of Cat O' Nine Tails on the sound system. "They're certainly creepier than their shit music would suggest. Come on, Trimble, you hipster." She led him past the queue of metal fans waiting patiently for their heroes to emerge.

Rose nudged Kirk as he checked out the Damned CDs for the tenth time, just in case the band had finally got up off their fat, old asses and sneaked out a new album. "Police are going. We can go in now." He put down a new edition of the *Black Album*, which didn't have any variant tracks on it, and turned to face her.

The sassy-looking female cop and her stooge were striding purposefully toward them. For a moment, Kirk was sure they were homing in on him, and he met the woman's green eyes defensively. They lingered on his for a moment as she summed him up, almost flirtatiously, then she was sashaying past, and Rose was pulling at his arm.

"Come on, before they come out and we miss our chance."

He allowed himself to be dragged toward the manager's door. He signaled to Davey, who was chatting with his friend, the assistant manager.

He joined them at the door looking smug.

"The Ass Man told us to be quick, and not to be rude. Frankly, I'm fuckin' hurt," the bassist said as he thumbed in the code his friend had given him.

He led them inside. Kirk glanced at Rose as they stepped into the room beyond. Her face was flushed, her eyes shining. Maybe she had looked at him like that once upon a fairy time.

Kirk was surprised to see all four members of the band standing up, facing them as the heavy door slammed behind them. They were still and unresponsive, expressions neutral. Rose halted inside the room, and her hand sought Kirk's involuntarily, then released it just as quickly as she prepared herself to meet her heroes.

Kirk felt himself stiffen. Goosebumps? Fuck's sake. But they were undeniably there. There was something about the way all five men stood rigid, facing this latest interruption to their solitude, like the Earp brothers at the OK Corral, which put Kirk and his friends firmly on the losing side. It was not to be the only time he'd feel this way. But who would draw first? Now he was confronting the object of his apprehension, Kirk found himself without a word to pull.

Roscoe beat him down. "Who?" One syllable, but laden with hostility.

Davey moved forward. "Hey, your biggest fans, that's who," he cracked, his voice thick with sarcasm. "This sad chick wanted to tickle your testicles so we'd see if you could oblige."

"Davey, you *prick!*" Rose was scarlet with fury and embarrassment. The musicians and their manager made no move. Five pairs of sunglasses leveled on Kirk and his companions like cold, black gun barrels.

Kirk found his voice. "He's joking. But she *is* a huge fan." The room, big as it was, felt suddenly way too small; the musicians filled it with their coldness. Kirk felt insignificant and wanted the hell out of here. He plucked at Rose's sleeve, but she pulled forward and advanced on them before he could stop her. The five men watched her come like she was a fly landing on the desk before them. As she got nearer, her bravery drained, and she stopped, face pale. Kirk wanted to join her, to protect her, but his body failed him, too. The air between Kirk and the musicians felt like an open fridge door had released it. Davey giggled, though whether through sudden nervousness or at something else that tickled his twisted sense of humor, Kirk wasn't sure.

Rose mastered her nerves and pulled a CD from her handbag. It was Cat O' Nine's previous release, *The Ninth Circle*, and she held it out as if it were an appeasement offering. "I...wondered if you could..." Her voice trailed off. The five men stared at her. Not a flicker of emotion on any of their faces. Rose tried again as Kirk's heart died inside him. He felt so much love for her in that moment and so much despair at his own weakness. But he could not move or speak. Fear, irrational and by all appearances groundless, had turned him into a weak boyfriend. *Where was Johnny when she needed him?*

"I've always loved the band," Rose said almost pitifully, still holding out the CD. Not one of them made a move to take it from her. "Could you..." She singled out Baz Cropper. "...sign it?" When the singer failed to answer, she swung her arm toward Phil Carter, with the same response.

Kirk shrugged off his cowardly cramps. He was stepping forward to take Rose away, to end the embarrassing scene, when Carter finally moved. The bass player slapped the CD from Rose's grasp, sending it clattering across the floor.

Rose stepped back, mouth a shocked O.

Kirk froze again. It was Davey Crooked who was first to react. He pushed past the four musicians, right up to the table, and swept the CDs and t-shirts onto the floor. "How'd you like them apples, you twats?" He barked at them. "It's like being back at school, ain't it? Chuckin' food around at lunchtime." He laughed, clearly enjoying the unpleasantness of the situation, and rapped his motorcycle helmet on the tabletop as he spoke. "Always thought you was a bunch of fake pussies, playin' at being badass while drinking hot chocolate and wanking over Country File in your slippers. Glad to see you've got some real spite in you. I'd respect your attitude if you could actually crack out a decent tune to match it."

Baz Cropper moved this time. The table flew against the near wall as he smashed it aside with one swipe of his leather-jacketed arm. His other hand took Davey by the throat before the bassist had time to stagger back in surprise. Davey was off his feet, choking, helmet dropping to the floor as he vainly clawed at the grip on his neck. Baz fixed his other hand on Davey's throat as well, lifting him higher.

Rose screamed, "Kirk!!!"

It snapped him out of his inertia. He was rushing forward to help when Carter and Tweed moved faster than anyone had the right to, seizing him by each arm and lifting him up like they were deifying him. Or going to tear his limbs from his sockets.

The sudden rattle of the door code being punched in was loud in the silence that had accompanied the violence. Even as the door swung open, Kirk and Davey were being dropped unceremoniously, like sacks of garbage left out by the bins.

The store manager stood in the open doorway, his face a mask of incredulity at the sight before him.

A pause, then Roscoe stepped forward as if nothing had happened. "Is it time to meet our...fans?" he said slowly.

The store manager's mouth flapped in a fishy way. As Kirk stumbled to his feet, winded, he saw the assistant manager enter behind his immediate boss. "I told you not to be rude, Davey!" he wailed.

Kirk grasped Rose firmly and pulled her past the two staff members, not even waiting to see if Davey was following. The silly twat had nearly got them killed.

The door slammed behind them, and they were assaulted by another track from *The Ninth Circle* as they emerged onto the shop floor. Davey had made it through, too, and he had even remembered to collect his helmet from the floor.

Kirk rounded on him. "What the fuck were you playing at?"

"Defending me for once, I think," Rose said. Her face was still pale and shocked, but her eyes were strangely alive...and excited. "That was... fucking extreme!"

"What?" Kirk couldn't take it all in. His blood was still pounding in his ears, and the fear in his belly was still curled up in there like a still-born baby. "You look like you almost enjoyed it!!"

She suddenly pulled him to her and kissed him, wildly, passionately.

Bewildered, he gave in to her desires, but it was short-lived. She was pushing him away again and staring at the queue of fans who had watched them emerge from the office. "They're coming!" she shouted above the wailing guitars. "Cat O' Nine are back, and they're *bad*!!" Her face was elated. He hadn't seen her this excited in a long time.

The metal fans in the queue eyed her with a mixture of jealousy and curiosity. A couple of them gave her the devil's horn salute, and she laughed and returned the gesture, thumb and little finger sticking out provocatively.

"You can cut that clichéd bollocks," Davey hissed at her. "You're a fuckin' embarrassment."

A wave of anticipation rippled through the queue: the door was opening again. Had they reacted like this every time the door moved, Kirk wondered, only to be disappointed when a cop or members of an unknown, struggling band emerged?

The excitement turned to euphoria. A huge cheer broke out.

The band was emerging. Still wearing their sunglasses, they spread out as they strode through the empty area where racks of CDs had been moved aside to give room for the signing table, Roscoe hanging back, and again Kirk was reminded of badass gunfighters.

Suddenly, a woman who had been hovering around the head of the queue and whom Kirk had not really paid attention to before broke away and began hurrying toward the musicians. A road crew security man came out of nowhere and cut her off. He held her back as she railed against him, and Kirk recognized her from a newspaper photo. Baz Cropper's wife. An attractive blonde in her late thirties or early forties, she looked close to tears as she struggled with the roadie.

"Let me through! I'm Sheila Cropper!!" She caught sight of Baz as he approached across the shop floor. "Baz!" she shrieked. "*Baz!!*"

Kirk stepped forward to witness the scene more closely, Rose at his side. He felt somehow included in this most private human drama that was unfolding in public and wasn't sure why. He had failed to act quickly in the manager's office, but now he wanted to be in the thick of it. He needed to be involved. Why? This felt personal now. He had seen the band let their mask slip, and he wanted all the fans to witness it, too.

Baz stopped in front of the roadie still holding his wife. He stared at her through the dark shades as if he was reading a train timetable.

Kirk waited for Cropper to order the roadie to release his wife. He didn't. Sheila Cropper stopped struggling and stared at him aghast. The constant assault of the music suddenly abated. The manager had turned it off. Kirk heard a fumble of a microphone being adjusted over the speakers. He was about to make an announcement.

"Baz?" Sheila's face was drained and exhausted. She clearly hadn't slept in a while. "Where have you *been??* I've been trying to talk to you for nearly two weeks. *Why won't you return my calls??*"

"Take your place in the queue," Baz said slowly, dismissively. He turned away.

The manager's voice boomed across the store: "Cat O' Nine Tails apologizes that they will be unable to proceed with the signing. All those disappointed can claim a ten-percent discount voucher for use exclusively against the purchase of their forthcoming new album."

A huge cry of dismay rose from the queue. The band was already moving past the table, ignoring the queue, sunglasses focused straight ahead toward the entrance where a black limousine waited at the curb. Road crew security flanked them, pushing back fans who broke against them in disappointed waves.

Kirk felt like a cold well had opened inside him. His veins froze. Here was proof, if he'd needed anymore. Cat O' Nine was back. But it wasn't the same band anymore. The line-up hadn't changed, but their personalities had. These were four different men wearing their bodies. After six months of being missing, they'd been found alright. They'd just lost their souls along the way.

Chapter Thirteen

"Give me your helmet," Kirk snapped at Davey. "Quick! And where's your bike parked?"

"What the fuck you on? You ain't borrowing my Suzuki…"

"Just tell me. I've got to do this." He'd already snatched the helmet from the bass player and was frisking him for keys.

"Get the fuck off me, gay boy!" He pushed Kirk away and then relented, handing over the keys. "You're going after them, aren't you? What the fuck for? They've made it clear they don't do autographs no more."

"Kirk?" Rose was suddenly all ears. She clawed at his sleeve.

"Where's the bike, Davey!"

"Round the back, down a little alley. But—"

Kirk shook off Rose and bolted for the main entrance. Just as the four musicians and their manager were escorted into the back of the limousine, he saw two girls he vaguely recognized from the queue climb in with them, assisted by Deuce, and presumably picked by the roadie. They looked ecstatic.

Kirk stopped outside, blinking under the glare of the sun. Which side street? He hadn't asked Davey. Fuck. He took off to the right, heading westwards up Oxford Street before remembering there was nothing that way. He doubled back. There. Had to be Hanway Street.

He saw the red Suzuki straight away. Parked at a meter a hundred yards down the narrow alley.

He'd only ever ridden a small 100 CC before, and this was a squat 250. He would have to learn on the road. He straddled the bike, strapped on the helmet, and inserted the keys. The engine fired up, a heavy bass thrum vibrating his entire body. He released the clutch, and the Suzuki wobbled away from the curb, heading for a Jag parked opposite. Kirk almost toppled the bike as he maneuvered around in a U-turn, missing the flank of the Jag by inches, pushing himself along with his right foot for balance.

His wobbling decreased a little as he approached the Oxford Street junction. He peered west up the busy road, a double-decker obscuring the outside of HMV momentarily before trundling off. The limo was gone.

He peered further up the street but couldn't see any sign of the black car. Buses buffeted along, the pavements thronged with bustling shoppers. He swung his helmet eastward. And there it was, drifting past Tottenham Court Tube station. He accelerated and pulled out into the slow-moving stream of traffic.

The shiny limo was three cars ahead, crawling behind a lumbering double-decker. Kirk changed up to third, cruised behind a Focus saloon, wondering what the hell he was doing.

Impulse. He had always been a slave to it. But wasn't this just a tad absurd, following the band through London to God knows where?

To their lair, of course. Like chasing some mythological monster from Greek legend, he was riding a metal horse to their abode, Perseus with a crash helmet instead of a sword. And what then? Slay the beasts? Or insist they sign the fucking CD they'd callously flung on the floor?

Truth was, he didn't have a clear idea why he felt compelled to follow them. It had seemed a good idea at the time. No, more than an idea: a necessity. Now that he had seen them for what they were, he had to track them down and get to the heart of the mystery. So did that make him a motorbike-riding Miss Marple instead of a Greek hero? Whatever. All that was clear to him was that for some very strange reason he knew he would never be able to sleep again if he didn't chase down this frightening enigma.

The Focus was gone, peeled off at Holborn, and that left two cars, a Mini Cooper and a Jimny between him and the limo. He could see heads in the back window, the profiles of the two girls Deuce had plucked from the queue, their blonde hair shining in the mid-morning sunlight. He couldn't see how excited their faces were from this distance, but he could guess.

The limo kept on heading east. Over the Holborn viaduct, gliding along Newgate Street, dawdling in traffic by St. Pauls, the dome shining gaily in the bright light.

The Mini Cooper was gone, but another car eased in front of him at the crossroads by the Royal exchange, eliciting a honk from a black cab turning right from Bishopsgate.

Kirk slowed to allow the cab in, too, and now there were again three vehicles between him and the limo. The traffic was a slow-moving sludge as lunchtime approached. Kirk checked the fuel gauge and was gratified to see it was a third full. But what if the band was heading out of the city? He didn't think that was likely. Surely they were either heading back to a hotel for a post-signing party or…

He realized he had no earthly clue where they might be going. The band (at least in their new incarnation) certainly didn't strike him as party goers. Presumably, they wanted to take the two groupies somewhere for their carnal pleasures though… His broodings were interrupted by a Hackney Cab that almost took him off his saddle at Aldgate. He managed to right the machine and suffered a wanker gesture from the Taxi driver through his rolled-down window. Kirk winked back to infuriate the driver even more and accelerated past him. The cab in front turned left at Goulston St, but the limo kept on, sliding up Whitechapel High Street before hanging a left up Commercial Street. They were deep in Ripper territory now, a fact that did not go unnoticed by Kirk. He had penned a Ripper song for Lucifer Sam and intended to play it for the first time at their gig with The Men That Will Not Be Blamed For Nothing the following week. The fact the limo was traversing these history-soaked streets seemed strangely apt, considering the way they made him feel.

And what was he going to do when they finally pulled up? Again, he had no idea. Just an abiding compulsion to discover as much about the band as he could.

The limo hung a left at Wentworth Street. Kirk followed, allowing a white Nissan to precede him. Then a right up Toynbee Street; losing the Nissan, Kirk dropping back now that he had no vehicle cover to hide behind. At the junction with White's Row, the limo indicated right. Kirk hovered at the junction, watching the limo slow a little way down White's Row before finally stopping outside a dilapidated-looking building that didn't look like it had changed much since the nineteenth century. Right next to it, a modern NCP car park was an uncaring memorial to the site of the Ripper's fifth murder victim, Mary Jane Kelly, back in 1888.

The band was disembarking. The four musicians approached the doorway of the building, followed by Deuce and a couple of other roadies; the two girls were helped out of the vehicle by a solemn Roscoe. Kirk changed down and drifted slowly left and up to the other end of the street, stopping halfway down on a single yellow line. He switched off the ignition and eased himself off the seat, flipping down the kickstand and heaving the machine into position on it.

When he turned to face the other way, the door was closing behind Roscoe and the girls. Deuce remained on guard outside.

So how was he going to play this? The direct approach? Foolish. But that had always been his way.

He made his way along the pavement toward the detached building. It looked like a warehouse, cracked red brick, with a tiny side alley leading to a backyard overgrown with buddleia bushes. Strange place for a band to hole up.

Deuce didn't turn to face him as Kirk approached. He took off the helmet, tense and not a little freaked. After his previous encounter with the usually amicable roadie, he wasn't looking forward to this. And what the hell was he going to say? The tall biker would know he had followed them from Oxford Street. He had a plan, but it was a really shit one.

He stopped just short of the roadie.

"Deuce?" He tried for casual, but couldn't keep the wariness from his voice.

The roadie turned his head slowly, fixed Kirk with his Ray Bans.

"You remember me, right? Kirk, singer from Lucifer Sam."

Nothing. The roadie didn't even move an eyebrow.

"I wanted to speak to the band, Deuce. Need to find out if we can support them on their next tour." He realized exactly just how lame that sounded. Never mind. He was neck deep now. Push on, son. He was certainly making up for his momentary act of cowardice when Cropper smashed the CD out of Rose's hand and he had frozen instead of rushing to help her. So that was why he was here, was it? To make up for not standing up for her like Johnny always did? And had it really been cowardice? He had been shocked into immobility, but... Well, here he was, bottle firmly back in place.

"You...need...to fuck off," said Deuce slowly. He lifted a huge stub of a forefinger and prodded Kirk in the chest of his cherry red leather jacket. "Right now."

There was no emotion in the threat. Just a factual statement that should not be ignored. But Kirk must have expected this if his lack of surprise was anything to go by. He backed off a step.

"Can you at least buzz Roscoe for me, let him know my request? We could really do with the gig, mate. C'mon, for old time's sake. You always tell the best Lemmy anecdotes in town." As he spoke, he was checking out the lone bell at the side of the door, though no name plaques were present.

The finger rested on Kirk's chest for a second, then was replaced instantly by one huge plate of a hand that slammed into Kirk and sent him on his ass over the curb. He dropped the motorcycle helmet, which clattered off into the middle of the road.

Deuce resumed his immobile position outside the door. Kirk was forgotten. A fly swatted.

Kirk got up slowly, wiping the backside of his jeans, then stooped to retrieve his helmet. He straightened, nodded at the roadie and gave him a sardonic thumbs-up.

"Nice work, Deuce. That's one I owe ya."

It was like the roadie didn't really give a shit whether he was there or not, Kirk was that unimportant. Kirk turned and headed back down the pavement; then, making sure Deuce was still staring ahead and taking no further notice of him, he slipped surreptitiously down the alley next to the building.

He fought through the tangle of buddleia until he reached the rear of the warehouse, where he found what he had hoped for: a rusting metal fire escape that clung to the red brickwork. It looked anything but safe, but he'd come this far and wasn't about to quit now. *Quit what? What are you doing, you dick-head?*

He peered up at the three-story warehouse. Most of the windows were shuttered on the first two floors and those that weren't were dark. He thought he saw a flicker of movement behind the glass of a window on the top floor—or was it the reflection of a passing cloud? He heard a female squeal of delight emanating from the same room. Score. The fire escape snaked up to the window and stopped at a small metal balcony below the sill. It was like it was inviting him to do it.

Should he? Fuck yeah. In for a penny, in for a pounding.

He planted his foot carefully on the first flaky step. It seemed firm enough. He clung to the metal banister with his right hand, balancing himself against the cold brick of the wall with his left. He started upward.

A third of the way up, one of the steps tilted under his foot, and he lurched backward, pulling hard on the rail as he did. The rail lurched, too, loose in its moorings. His breath stopped, and giddiness almost peeled him off the fire escape. He leaned in against the wall, grasping the rough brick for dear life until his heart rate settled and he felt brave enough to continue.

He passed the first-floor balcony with its shuttered window and crept on, the steps dropping dandruff rust below him with every footfall. Up past the second floor, the distance to the ground below weighing heavily on his mind and his body.

When he reached the third-floor balcony, he froze, unsure what to do next. Stepping out too far onto it would leave him in plain sight of whoever was inside. So he pressed against the wall, took one ginger step onto the metal struts that formed the floor of the balcony, and slowly leaned his head around the side of the window.

Baz Cropper was staring straight back at him.

Chapter Fourteen

The other three musicians were staring at Kirk, too.

Their sunglasses were gone, and all four pairs of eyes were set on Kirk.

He froze in position and was just about to jerk his head back when he noticed that the musicians were not moving or reacting as if they had seen him at all. He stiffened against the brick wall, ready to hurtle back down the fire escape if they got up from the tatty chairs they were sitting in.

Kirk found himself unwilling to move, though, no matter how freaked he was. Those eyes held him, black and empty in a room that was almost as dark, even though outside the sun shone on an early summer afternoon. It was like they were draining the light from the room...or darkness was seeping from them. *Freakin' yourself out, Kirky boy.* Yet the room continued to darken almost imperceptibly until soon he could barely detect their forms sitting in a semi-circle. He could still just about make out the walls festooned with cobwebs, though the dust that furred the window panes through which he peered didn't help. There was barely any furniture, just the four old, wooden, high-backed chairs and a table before the musicians on which a device like a sound recorder rested. As Kirk stared, a door opened behind the band and a figure he could just about identify as Roscoe entered, ushering the two groupies into the room.

* * *

Monique giggled nervously as she and Gaby followed the manager up three flights of stairs. There was no carpet, and the bare walls were streaked with dirt and cobwebs. Roscoe had kept them in the lobby of the old warehouse at first while the musicians walked stiffly off into the darkness that filled the ground floor, the windows all being shuttered. Daylight had filtered through the cracks in the boards and from around the door, but it was a while before Monique made out the staircase ascending into deeper gloom, and by then Roscoe was ushering them toward it. The two roadies followed. Monique wondered if they were hoping for some female flesh, as well. If so, they were going to be disappointed; Monique and Gaby only shagged stars.

Just before he led them up the staircase, Roscoe told them in his weird Vincent Price-on-a-bad-trip voice that the band was "preparing themselves for entertainment," and Monique deduced that probably meant they were washing their dicks before giving Monique and Gaby a right good going over. Proper fuckin' gents, eh? She certainly had no problem with that; Cat O' Nine was her favorite band, and Baz and the boys certainly wouldn't be the first musicians she had fucked.

But what *did* unnerve her a little was the weird way the band was reacting. They hadn't said a word in the limo. The girls had been sandwiched in between the roadies while the band sat in the seats facing them, their backs to the driver. Every approach she and Gaby made to them had been met with silence until one of the roadies told them the band was tired and it was best they keep quiet. She and Gaby had exchanged puzzled glances but assumed the band would lighten up as soon as they reached wherever they were going and the girls showed them how to have a good time.

"No lights in this gaffe?" Gaby asked Roscoe as they tottered blindly up the stairs on their stacked-heeled Goth boots (Monique's sported a lurid green zombie design, the jagged teeth circling her open toes; Gaby's were black, studded, and thigh length). It was a miracle they didn't break their bleedin' ankles in the dark.

Roscoe didn't reply. Monique decided it was fair to get a little pissed off now. They had driven for an hour through central London and not only had they not been treated with the respect and flirtation they usually received from the rock stars they targeted, but they were hungry, too. And thirsty. Monique really hoped this party was going to get a whole lot better than it had started. And this place really gave her the creeps, as well. Dark and abandoned as fuck—she could barely see Roscoe's back ahead of her as he moved slowly upwards. Why the fuck had they brought them here? UK Decay Chic? Maybe they wanted a publicity photo sesh? Monique had hoped for a swanky hotel. Things were not going to plan, so she suddenly stopped on the stairs in the dark and waited for Roscoe to notice her little act of resistance. One of the roadies behind them pushed at her back, albeit not roughly. Beside her, Gaby stopped, too, staring at her friend with wide eyes.

"Wait just one minute, geezer," she told the roadie who had nudged her. "I ain't going another step until you tell us what's going on. No lights, no chat. This is a bit fuckin' weird, mate." Her last remark was addressed to Roscoe, who had stopped on the stairs and turned back to face her. In the thick gloom, Gaby's face was pale, and she was biting her lip in nervous expectancy.

"The band does not like too much illumination," Roscoe said by way of explanation. "And you girls should feel...honored. This is...where they are recording their new album. They need to add some extra sound effects...which is where you girls come in."

Monique grinned through the dark at Gaby, then faced Roscoe again. "Is that right? What a score. Okay. But what sound effects they wanna record? Shagging? We'll give 'em their money's worth, that's for sure." She let out a dirty whinny. Gaby chuckled along, but Roscoe turned and continued up the stairs.

They reached the third-floor landing. It was a bit lighter up here as some of the rooms they passed had open doors through which daylight filtered from unshuttered windows. Their boots left prints in thick dust covering the bare boards as they followed their guide. They reached a door halfway along, and Roscoe preceded them into the room. Monique stopped on the threshold, glancing at Gaby. She still had some serious misgivings, but the fangirl, as well as the groupie, wanted to take away an experience to remember, and she was determined not only to fuck Baz

Cropper like he'd never been fucked before (certainly not the way his staid wife would fuck him), but also to get the bastard to speak. That was a challenge she was not going to walk away from. Her pride and vanity wouldn't let her. He would be screaming her name by the time she was through with him.

The four musicians didn't react when the girls entered the room. Kirk drew his head back a centimeter or so, afraid the groupies might spot him even though the band seemed incapable of peering through the grime that smeared the panes.

The dirt prevented Kirk from seeing clearly, too, and the darkness that had gradually stolen into the room didn't help. But now he could see the taller blonde remonstrating with Roscoe and the manager nodding to one of the roadies, who responded by switching on a cobwebbed table lamp set on the floorboards in one corner of the room. It didn't provide much illumination, but the girls evidently seemed a little more satisfied, as they advanced toward the band and stood before them with their backs to the window, presumably chatting to the musicians. Kirk could still see Phil Carter and half of Barney Smolt from where he was watching, and judging from their lack of expressions and closed mouths, it was pretty much a one-way conversation.

Kirk couldn't help feeling a little excited despite his unease. The two blondes were gorgeous. The tallest was easily six foot, wearing tight jeans and a black Cat O' Nine t-shirt that clung to her small breasts. Her hair was piled up on top, and he could see from her profile when she turned to her friend that she had an eloquent, sex-goddess face. Perfect groupie material. Her friend was shorter, more curvy, with a short leather skirt and fishnets. A low-cut, leopard print top strained to contain the hefty contents of the bra beneath. Her hair was a perfect bob, not a hair out of place.

He suddenly felt guilty. It was obvious what the girls were there for. Was he really going to stay here and watch like a voyeuristic old perv? He'd satisfied his desire to follow the band to their lair, and even though his quest had resulted in more mysteries, at least he had an angle on them now. They might be creepy as fuck, but at least they remained conventional enough to bang groupies, something that made them almost comfortingly predictable.

He decided it was time he returned Davey's bike and got back to Rose. She would be fuming at being left so unceremoniously, and he had felt his phone constantly vibrating in his pocket on the way here. He glanced into the room one last time. The tall girl was kneeling now, and Kirk could see Baz Cropper's face as she unzipped his fly. The rocker was not smiling. And his eyes remained fixed straight ahead, maybe looking at Kirk, maybe not, his eyes black and empty as a dead seal's.

Kirk withdrew his head slowly, feeling a mixture of unnatural fear and revulsion, and made his way slowly down the rusting fire escape.

The band was still not talking. They hadn't said a word since the two girls entered the room. Just sat there like stiff kings on thrift-store thrones.

Monique gave up trying to get them to open their mouths and decided the best approach was to open hers, but not for talking.

She knelt in front of Baz, pushing the table back with her bottom. She glanced at the recording device on the table. "You gonna record us now?" she asked.

Nobody answered. Roscoe remained in the doorway, watching incuriously. The two roadies flanked him. Monique shrugged at Gaby and winked. Gaby giggled nervously. She always waited for Monique to make the first move. Today, that first move would be to free the singer of Cat O' Nine's cock from his rather grubby jeans.

She stroked his leg with her left hand while teasing down the zipper with her other. She grinned in satisfaction as the bulge behind the jeans grew larger. She snaked her hand through the gap of his fly, and the hardness pushed back at her. She freed his cock from the unexpectedly dirty boxers, suddenly recoiling from the stink that greeted her. And the sight... The shaft of his penis was mottled and slimy, like a toadstool past its prime. Monique had seen a lot of penises in her time, but this was the worst. And the stink wasn't just a whiff of bad hygiene, but something more, something she couldn't place, but which made her gag. But what the fuck… It was Baz Cropper's cock. You didn't get to suck that every day.

She stroked the unpleasant shaft, releasing his helmet from its foreskin, and the stink worsened. Now she could identify it: an aroma of pure trash. It reminded her of when she'd once stuck her head in the back of a refuse collection truck when she was a kid. A ripe mixture of things old and rotting, of vile mulch and liquid decay. A tear of black ooze trickled from the eye of Baz's cock, and that was enough. More than fucking enough. Choking, Monique stumbled to her feet, her senses spinning, only able to concentrate on the urge to vomit.

"Monique?" Gaby was staring at her in confusion.

Monique coughed until her eyes ran, dimly aware that Cropper was smiling for the first time, a reptilian shark smile while he massaged his swollen toadstool cock. She reached out for Gaby. She should have followed her first instincts when they first got in the limo. This lot was somehow very wrong, and very *bad*…

The roadies were moving forward now, one of them taking Monique's outstretched hand roughly in his, forcing her back down to her knees, the other stepping up to the device on the table and pressing the record button.

"Monique!??" Gaby sounded really scared now. But Monique couldn't answer her. The roadie had forced her face down into Cropper's crotch again, and the singer was thrusting his revolting member into her mouth, ramming it right to the back of her throat so she could barely breathe. The roadie held her head in position, and through her panic, Monique was aware the room had become even darker around them, though the weak light from the lamp still shone from one corner. Or was that just the effects of terror? She could hear her own gagging sounds and inarticulate cries stifled by the monstrous cock that invaded her mouth, now beginning to pump a trickle of cold sludge inside her. Summoning every reserve of energy, she suddenly yanked her head backward and freed herself of the vile organ. She saw thick, black fluid seeping from its head, felt it slick on her lips and tongue. She let out a scream that hit out hard and loud before the roadie forced her down onto the instrument of her torture again.

"We can use that..." she heard Cropper say, and her brain struggled to comprehend his words even as the vile thing thrust brutally down her throat again. She struggled to breathe through her nose, but the roadie was closing his other hand over her face now, crushing against her nostrils. She thrashed against his grip, but Cropper had released his cock and was gripping her breasts with both hands, crushing them fiercely, twisting, tearing at them, ripping holes in her t-shirt in his ferocious desire to get at them.

She could dimly hear Gaby shrieking. From the corner of one wildly rolling eye, she saw her friend sinking into the deepening shadows filling the room. Monique could see just enough to realize the other roadie was holding her in front of Carter. The bass player, along with the other musicians, sat at the very core of the dark, and in her fear frenzy, Monique was convinced it was emanating from them. Now Carter had pulled an old carving knife from inside his jacket. The blade was red with rust. Monique stopped watching as the blade was forced up her friend's skirt and between her thighs. Gaby's shrieks became fiercer, harder, tipping over the edge of hell, taking Gaby's mind with it. Monique ceased taking notice of anything around her then, as the breath that had filled her body for twenty-five years was denied her. Her last conscious thought was a quote from an old movie, which seemed so very, very apt now, and she could hear her disgusted Mum castigating her with it when she had discovered what her daughter got up to with those dirty rock bands. *"You'll end up sucking cocks in hell!"*

Her lovely, old Mum, with her cockney crudeness. And Monique clung to her image for comfort in the midst of her terror and agony as the room faded forever, the accusing words following her into darkness like a promise.

Chapter Fifteen

It was supposed to be a great honor. And when Jeff Stacks had first accepted the job, he'd certainly perceived it as such; Cat O' Nine Tails was the biggest rock band on the planet after all, and since returning from their mystery absence, they had become the hottest news item, as well.

He'd never engineered one of their albums before, but that didn't faze him. He'd worked on two Motörhead albums and mixed the Damned's last offering, which was obviously the pedigree that attracted the band to him in the first place. If he could make Lemmy's wall of noise sound like an album of distinct tracks and flavors, then he should have no trouble accentuating the Cat's sounds.

When Roscoe had offered him the job, he'd been initially puzzled, as he'd heard another engineer, Matt Faulkner, had been recruited for the task. Roscoe, however, had gruffly (the man sounded as if he were in the first stages of throat cancer) informed Stacks that while Faulkner had been adequate in the recording process, he hadn't been up to the job of the final mastering, which certainly surprised him: Faulkner had mixed and engineered CONT's three previous discs.

There was one stipulation to the job: the album had to be mastered after midnight as the band had been flat out all the preceding night recording and needed to recuperate. There was a timescale urgency, too, as Cat O' Nine wanted the album in the stores ASAP. The band was producing it themselves with Faulkner's assistance and had finally finished recording. Roscoe had not been given much more info, just that he should make his way to the studio the following night and basically work his ass off.

"Studio." That was a laugh. Slum would have summed it up better. Stacks paid the cab fare and ambled over to the rusted bell plate beside the door, craning his neck up at the grim, red-brick building.

The door popped open soon after he pushed the relevant bell marked "Nine," and a roadie escorted him through the dark lobby to a large room that ran the length of the building's rear. It looked like it had been a slaughterhouse in a previous time; there were still rusting hooks embedded in the sagging ceiling, and stone runnels and troughs traversed the ground. At the far end, the recording booth and mixing desk looked decidedly out of place. Moonlight shone through the tall, arched windows, somehow finding its way through the grime and buddleia branches that fought to block the panes. Stacks could just make out the set of drums in the booth. Beside them, a Fender bass and a Gibson SG, along with the skeletal shadow of a mic stand.

"Where's the lights?" Stacks asked the roadie. The tall man said nothing for a second as if this was an irrelevance, then crossed to the wall and flicked a switch. A single fluorescent hanging from loose wires in the center of the ceiling blinked, went out, then flicked into poor light again.

"That all you got?"

The roadie didn't reply.

Stacks sighed. This was going to be a tough job. "Why they recording in a dump like this?" The roadie started walking away.

"Wait!"

The tall roadie hesitated, his back to Stacks.

"That it? You not gonna show me the mix, or the deck, or at least make me a fucking coffee?"

The roadie carried on walking. The fluorescent dipped again as he closed the door behind him.

"Wanker," Stacks muttered, then made his way over the rough stone ground to the mixing desk set a few yards from the recording booth. If he had expected a bottle of wine or a welcome note from the band, he was going to be disappointed. The desk was uncluttered and clean, however, and it didn't take Stacks long to locate the mixtape. The half-inch master reel tape was ready in its spools. And that had been one of Roscoe's stipulations: the mastering would be done on analog tape to preserve the primitive sound the band wanted to achieve with their latest offering. Well, that wouldn't be a problem, and Stacks guessed this was probably another contributory factor in selecting him for the job; he was a dab hand at analog.

He stretched, feeling the muscles in his shoulders clench and relax. Despite the warmth of the June day, it was now damn chilly in the slaughterhouse-cum studio. He would have liked a tot of single malt, or hell, even a beer, to warm his insides, but the bastards hadn't even left him with a kettle. Yes, he got how they wanted the job done fast—in one fucking night, even—but the odd comfort wouldn't have slowed him down.

Fuck it. Best get the job done, and then he could sleep all the next day. And it would definitely take him all night to finish the job—and that would be working at a faster pace than he had ever had before. Normally, it took him a day or two, but then he was extremely meticulous.

He picked up the battered-looking headphones (no expense spared, CAT) and placed them gingerly on his head. The cold pressed against his back as he sat down at the mixing desk. The inadequate puddle of orange light from the fluorescent barely reached the controls. He sighed again and wished he still smoked. At least it would take his mind off the weirdness of it all. But he supposed this was the effect the band was striving for: recording and mastering the album in an old slaughterhouse in the dead of night. That would form part of the publicity drive. Still, it would have been nice to meet the band at least.

He ran his fingers over the keys and switches on the deck in front of him, feeling the usual rush of muted excitement. He was in his element despite the strangeness of the environment. He felt like a conductor hovering in front of his orchestra of knobs, ready to perform, to *transform*.

Best crack on then, see whether CONT had changed their tried-and-tested formula for safe, melodic metal at all.

He leaned forward over the deck and pressed PLAY.

His headphones filled with a hiss at first, which would have to be reduced by NR, until he realized it was an intentional part of the opening track, a sibilant snake sound that formed more clearly into intelligible whispers.

The fluorescent dipped out again, and for a moment the studio was plunged in total darkness. Even the moonlight beyond the windows took its time picking out details for Stacks. He shifted uncomfortably in his seat as the whispers continued in the dark and waited for the light to flick on again.

When it did, coinciding with the beginning of Track 1, it seemed a lot dimmer than before. But Stacks barely had time to register that; his mind was too preoccupied with the all-out battery of good taste that Cat O' Nine Tails had dished up as their opening song. Song? Fuck that. This was a vile contortion of their old melodic style, slathered over by unwholesome guitar sounds, bullied by monstrous drum thunder, kicked in the organs by a ramming, malevolent bass line. The track was a nightmare express train to Hell, and tonight, Stacks was its sole passenger. When the vocals kicked in, he wrenched the headphones off instinctively, repulsed.

He held the phones away from him. The "music" poured from the earpieces, spilling out in an excrescence of sound, subdued only by distance.

He was sweating. He glanced around and behind him at the dark, cavernous room. He felt colder than ever.

What the fuck were they thinking of??

Nobody would buy this foul shit. Nobody could listen to *this!*

Convinced the creepy slaughterhouse atmosphere must be playing with his perception a little, he decided to give the tape another listen, lifting the phones over his head with some trepidation, sliding the volume knob down as he did so.

The track had changed. Slower, equally insistent and sinister, the vocals were drawn-out supplications to join in a communal sin Stacks thankfully could not identify without a lyric sheet. Baz Cropper's voice had certainly undergone a transformation since Stacks had last heard it. Gone were the clean, operatic falsettos and melodic harmonies. Now he sounded like a wolf howling through a snootful of blood, spitting out gristle and grue with every syllable. It was a truly demonic sound, genuinely hellish in a way a thousand death metal bands had aspired to attain and failed miserably, falling into cartoonish melodrama. There was no drama here. This was sheer, abnormal spite.

Likewise, the scintillating solos and pleasing riffs that were Jez Tweed's stock-in-trade had been abandoned. His guitar sounded like it was chugging through flesh like a bloodied buzz saw. Phil Carter, highly praised for elevating his bass lines into melodies themselves, had submerged them in filth, a throbbing, muscled pounding of the senses. Barney Smolt's drumming no longer bounced the tunes along with teenage glee; now they were Triceratops feet stamping skulls in a human mire.

He snatched off the phones again. He was gasping for air now, his jaw locked where his teeth were ground so tightly together. Sweat had slicked his hair down over his forehead, and his glasses were beaded with moisture.

There was nothing he could do with this cacophonous mess. No wonder Faulkner had "not been up to the task." He started to get out of his seat. They would have to find some other sucker to shine a light on this obscene filth.

That's when the fluorescent went out again.

And this time it did not flick back on.

Stacks eased himself carefully back into his seat, waiting for his eyes to adjust to the dark. The moon beyond the panes was gone for the moment, hiding its face behind clouds as if it too wanted to distance itself from the music Stacks had unleashed.

Stacks peered around, trying to pierce the blackness.

Was someone in the far-left corner, opposite the door? The darkness was a wriggling knot as his eyes sought to register detail. Something pale hung against the wall there. Four reflections from the window at head height, moonlight finally emerging to paint silvery pools that could have been dim faces.

The music was still trickling from the headphones on the desk. It seemed to be calling to him, tempting him to put the phones back on, continue the job he hadn't even started. The track had changed again, a lulling, almost fairytale quality in the crooning vocals and tickling acoustic guitars. It crackled with intense evil captured on magnetic tape. It was an achievement, he conceded, feeling sick. He pictured the band recording here in the dark, in this disused house of death, right next to another, long-demolished house of death (oh yes, Stacks was well aware of the lady who had been systematically disassembled in her room in 1888 where an NCP car park stood right now). He imagined the band riding that death vibe, owning it, feeding it through their instruments. He imagined Faulkner mixing the result (and did he feel the same terror Stacks was feeling now? Stacks was sure he did), adding more bass here, tweaking the treble or the vocal there. That Faulkner had completed the job was a miracle in itself. That he had completed it with his sanity intact was extremely hard to conceive. And Stacks? Would he complete the job? And what would be left of him? He thought of his wife and two teenage sons at home. They'd long since lost interest in what he did, in *him*. He was a middle-aged man with a bald patch and bad breath who just happened to have a knack for mastering.

Stacks stared at the phones. A finger of moonlight lay across the desk, fondling them as if urging him to pick them up again.

A cold pool was spreading up his back. His nape was electric. He didn't want to pick up those phones, didn't want to hear any more of Cat O' Nine Tails' sonic blasphemy. In the end, he wasn't sure if it was his professional pride, the promise of £500,000 or something indescribably seductive in the evil pouring from the earpieces that made him do so.

The moon faces remained hanging on the wall as he settled the phones on his head for the third time. He paid them no attention now; they were reflections, and he had a job to do.

A new track had started, trembling guitar echoes filled his ears, then a distorted female scream of undiluted, abject terror that had him scrambling for the phones again, and resisting, as the music sucked him into its spell. Another shriek, then horrible gagging sounds, muffled, choking.

Then the song proper began, and an onlooker might have said that Stacks was adjusting to his task, acclimatizing to the horror, as his hands began to fly over the keys and knobs as the professional process began to take the place of terror and outrage. In truth, Stacks was sliding into a darkness far deeper even than that in the studio, the music creeping into his synapses and burrowing down into his psyche, while all the time his fingers guided and corrected, on autopilot as his sanity began to fade.

From time to time, as one hand worked on equalization and compression dials or applied leveling and pre-gapping to the tracks, his other would ineffectually claw at the phones on his head, which remained static over his ears as if glued. When blood began to trickle from his nostrils, spilling over his lips, he barely noticed it. His ears were in agony as atrocity vibes forced their way into his cochlea, but the fading and mastering continued, blood caking the mixing desk. More blood was seeping from underneath the big, spongy phones now, pattering the collar of his suede jacket, pooling on the floor.

When the last track was mastered, the pain began to reduce in intensity, the grip of the phones lessened. With a sucking rip, he managed to wrench them from his head. They fell to the ground. His job here was done.

He rose stiffly from the chair and turned. Mathew Faulkner was hanging from one of the rusted butcher hooks in the center of the room.

If Stacks was surprised to see him, the ebbing tide of sanity prevented him from showing it. He tottered forward as if to greet his predecessor. Faulkner twisted slowly in the moonlight. The hook emerged from his neck, blood mixing with rust. His eyes were fixed on Stacks as if warning him, but Stacks knew the engineer was far too late. He knew he'd mastered his last album. He wondered how the public would remember him. Would this be his greatest achievement?

"Who the fuck cares about the engineer?" Faulkner answered his silent query, his bluing lips unmoving as he turned slowly on the hook. "It's the band that takes all the glory..."

Stacks took another step toward the dead man, but when he reached the hook, it was empty. The four splashes of moonlight watched him from the far corner. Or had they moved? The reflections seemed nearer the central windows now.

Outside, a storm was picking up. The buddleia branches scraped and scratched at the window panes while scurrying clouds filled the runnels and troughs in the ground with shadows. More shadows frolicked on the walls. Wind buffeted the window frames, but the continued hiss from the headphones on the floor was louder.

The moonlight faces slid closer along the wall toward him. Stacks stopped. They had bodies of shadow, he realized, tall and thin. They stretched their fingers toward him as the clouds slipped past the windows, bullied by the wind. The faces loomed over him, blank as pillowcases, slit by shadow mouths, eyes full of night. Their hair fell long and spider-like, made of darkness.

The shadows detached from the wall and stalked him.

It's only a trick of the night... He was adamant of this. As adamant as a man who had lost his mind on a torrent of sound could be. He'd gone over the rapids for sure.

I've done a good job, you know that! Don't. Please don't make me like Faulkner.

The spindly shadows ringed him. Four distorted tricks of moon and wind with clutching fingers of darkness. Night lips opened to silently mock, then closed as the wind scattered its shadow play across the disused slaughterhouse.

He was on his knees now.

"Help me," he said quietly, far too quietly for anyone to hear and answer. His only reply was the gasp of the wind and the death rattle of the window panes and a sibilant hiss from the headphones lying on the floor.

CD 3

THE DARK SIDE OF THE TUNE

Chapter Sixteen

If the sound check had been bad enough, the actual gig was worse.

Two songs in and Kirk really wasn't feeling it.

It should have been a roaring success: the venue was respectable, the new Bridge House, a few streets away from the legendary original, demolished in 2002; the headlining act, The Men That Will Not Be Blamed For Nothing, was extremely credible, and a real crowd-puller, without being too big; and Lucifer Sam even had a handful of new songs Kirk wanted to try out. It all should have added up to a great platform for the band.

Maybe Kirk's heart just wasn't in it. Since spying on Cat O' Nine Tails a few days ago, he'd not been sleeping well. He couldn't get the image out of his mind: the four seated band members sinking into darkness in the top-floor room of the warehouse while outside the sun shone strongly. He couldn't forget their vacant stares, even when the two attractive groupies came in to service them. And he certainly couldn't forget the cold, off-hand way they had treated Rose at the signing, and the callous disregard Cropper had shown his wife.

He knew he wasn't performing to his best, and the songs fell flat as a result. Johnny glanced at him more than once as they played to the sixty-strong crowd—most of whom were there for the MTWNBBFN, of course, he had no delusions otherwise—giving him a visual crit he really didn't need. After finishing the second song, when Johnny turned to him with a frown, Kirk told him to fuck off. Johnny shrugged and began the intro to "Sundel Bolong," a new song Kirk had insisted they showcase tonight. The riff was good, sparse and spine-tingly. Davey was strutting his sinister bass line, which matched the creepy slow-burner perfectly, and Ned was on time with the drums for once. What sank the song was Kirk himself. His vocals sounded parched and lacking self-confidence. Kirk stared at Rose, who was standing with a few other friends of the band at the front of the crowd, as if waiting for her to encourage him, but he realized with a jolt she was watching Johnny instead.

He stopped the song halfway through when his voice slipped out of key on the chorus. The rest of the band looked at him in confusion.

Fuck this.

"This is our last song," he announced to the indifferent crowd.

Davey whirled on him. "What the fuck d'ya mean? We've got another five numbers in the set." He had been enjoying himself, despite Kirk's shit vocals.

"Not anymore," Kirk told him, off mic. He turned to Ned, who was seated behind his drum stool with a quizzical expression on his plump face. The drummer held out his sticks to either side in an enquiring gesture.

Kirk faced the crowd again, deliberately not looking at Rose. "'Yours Truly, Jack the Ripper,'" he announced and waited for the rhythm section to fall in with the intro. This was their best song; a catchy up-tempo, but decidedly macabre tune that encapsulated Kirk's vision for the band perfectly: Lucifer Sam was Voodoo Punk, and this was their signature opus.

It was supposed to skip jauntily through a musical hall East End with a cheeky cockney relish, but tonight the song limped and skulked and finally hid away down a back alley. Kirk had chased it there with his dour delivery, his nerves stifling the one true jewel they had in their crown.

Ned got up from his drum stool after it was all over and leaped off the stage, pushing through the bored crowd toward the bar. Johnny shrugged again and took off his guitar. Davey rounded on Kirk, his bristly face full of fury.

"Fuck's wrong with you, ya twat! This was our big chance, with a good support slot and you shat on it. Wanker!" He followed Ned in the direction of the bar, elbowing Rose aside as he did so.

Kirk sat down on the edge of the stage in dismay. He had never seen Davey so animated about anything before and was surprised to see that the bassist *did* care about the band after all. And Davey was right: Kirk had screwed up their one shot at reaching out to a new audience.

Rose approached him carefully. Was her diffidence caused by embarrassment over the gig, or something else? He had nothing to say to her tonight. He stared at her, and she had never looked more gorgeous: her hair looked shiny and healthy, the red stripe resplendent under the venue lights. The curved nose and slight pout of her lips made him ache to seize her. Instead, he jumped down from the stage and headed for the toilet to take a piss.

When he came back, Rose was talking with Johnny near the bar. He left them to it and went to watch the main act.

The Men That Will Not Be Blamed For Nothing was everything tonight that Lucifer Sam was not. The band was tight and focused, the songs performed briskly with a professional sheen and a sprinkling of off-kilter humor that captured the audience's imagination immediately. They played unabashed Steampunk, full throttle Oi ballads and ironic metal that mixed comedy with social venom. The singer, Andy Heintz, looked like a pink-bearded Victorian tramp as he strangled the mic stand during "Miner." Andrew O'Neill's guitar chords were clogged with coal dust and ire. Burrows pummeled his bass like he was digging from the rock face, and Jez Miller showcased his glorious Lords of The New Church pedigree by hammering the drums into submission. "Cthulhu Ftagn" had the audience in rapture, seaside whimsy and hardcore blissfully wed.

Kirk couldn't take any more. He should have stayed out of a sense of kinship with the band who had kindly offered them this slot as a helping hand up, but when the Men slammed into "The Gin Song," complete with Theremin and a chorus catchy enough to hook all the eels in Gravesend, he had to go. A huge cheer from the audience followed him out the door.

Chapter Seventeen

Sheila Cropper listened to the CD-R in the bath.

Baz had sent it to her. The note inside the package was very brief, and he hadn't even bothered to sign it, but she recognized his handwriting immediately, even if it had acquired a slightly crooked slant.

Sheila,
For You. Demo of New Album.
Welcome your thoughts.

That was it. After not seeing or speaking to him for seven months (apart from the horrible confrontation at HMV the week before), this was the first word she'd had. Their twenty-year-long marriage was only worth this?

Her first response was to toss the CD in the bin.

It took her all day to decide that she would listen to it. She sat in her dressing gown and stared at the TV, its constant babble her only companion. They had never had any kids, something which had given her the occasional pang when they were happy together but which now tormented her even more with loneliness now that her husband had seemingly abandoned her. Seemingly? She laughed humorlessly over her third Vodka and tonic, only dimly aware of the game show contestants competing with each other on the screen in front of her. She could have called a friend; there'd been no shortage of those comforting her while Baz and the band were missing. Now he was back and ignoring her, they didn't quite know how to respond. Nobody did, and that included herself. She could have called on her neighbor, a lovely woman disabled by early MS who had retained her good humor and warmth. But right now, Sheila just needed the companionship vodka offered her, that and her memories.

Her memories followed her to the bath she poured herself. She lay down in the hot bubbles, silent tears coursing down her cheeks, and reached out to press play on the portable CD player on the chair beside the bath. She knew why it had taken her all day to listen to the demo. She was hoping there was a coded message amongst the songs somewhere, just for her, and was scared to play it in case there wasn't. She hated herself for that little act of desperation.

She hated herself.

DS Louisa Gull had her thighs clamped around the young man's head, his face buried in her pussy, when the call came through.

The handsome young man was handcuffed to the bedposts, of course. If her conquests didn't elect to spend most of the night going down on her, then they weren't much use to her, and this way left them no real choice in the matter.

His tongue must be aching by now, poor lamb. He stopped for a breather, turning his head aside on the pillow. She ground her crotch against his lips and nose more forcefully until he got the hint and returned his attention to her pussy. She gasped as he went to work again.

Her mobile shrilled on the bedside table, spinning around in its urgency.

She peered at it as she knelt astride the naked young man (Pete? Paul? Fuck knows.) and cursed when she saw the caller's ID. Balls.

Still pressing her deliciously tingling crotch into the young man's face, she leaned sideways to collect the phone.

"Sir?" She continued to ride the boy's face, jolts of pleasure making her back arc as she held the cell to her ear.

She listened to her superior officer for a minute, biting her lips to prevent herself from moaning into the mouthpiece as her orgasm shuddered through her.

When she trusted herself to speak, she swallowed and said carefully, "On it, guv," and cut the connection.

She tapped Pete, Paul, Fuck Knows on the cheek with her phone. "Good boy. I might have to arrest you again if you carry on behaving badly like that." She slid off him, leaving him shackled and naked while she headed for the shower.

"DS Gull? Could you unlock me? My arms are aching. DS Gull??" She had forbidden the junior officer to call her by her first name, but as it was, her official title fell on deaf ears, too; DS Gull was far too busy in the shower to hear.

She collected Trimble from the Bethnal Green station where they were based and drove toward the Cropper's family house in Chiswick. As they wove through the midnight traffic, Gull's thoughts dwelled more on the satisfying sex she'd just been enjoying than on the case at hand. While the big-eared policeman drove, she turned her cat-got-the-cream smile on him, deciding it was time to wind the reticent constable up a little more.

"I don't think you ever told me, Trimble—or if you did I forget. Are you married?"

"No, Ma'am." Trimble concentrated on the traffic as they passed through Shepherds Bush.

"Gay?"

"*No*, Ma'am!!"

"Truncheon not working, is that it?"

Trimble had turned the habitual red color he always seemed to sport in Gull's company. "Er, no… I mean, yes!" He narrowly missed a couple of drunk youths trying to cross Goldhawk Road.

"Careful, constable," she chided him. "We want to get there in one piece." She smiled at him again, wondering what the awkward twenty-five-year-old would be like between her legs. He wouldn't know where to put his tongue. She shuddered at the thought. "You're not still a virgin, are you?"

His mouth flapped open and his color intensified. "No, Ma'am!! Can I just focus on the road, please."

"That means yes. Glorious." She settled back into her seat with a chuckle.

"It does not!" He sounded like an offended school boy. "Shagged loads, I have."

"Imaginary ones don't count. Nor does knocking one off over web-cam girls when your Mum's gone to bed. And that's 'shagged loads, *Ma'am.*' Eyes on the road, detective constable Trimble."

Some uniforms were waiting for them at the Croppers' house. Gull got out of the Merc and sighed. A CSI team was already busy on the property, a pleasant two million pound villa on a leaf-lined street.

"What you got?" she asked the female police constable who approached them.

The officer was cute and younger than Gull, which put her back up a little, along with the fact she looked like she had as much sense of humor as a wasp. When she spoke, her Canning Town accent grated, too. "Nuffin' suspicious, Ma'am. Neighbor called us about 22.30. 'Eard screams comin' from next door. Said she'd been worried abaht Missus Cropper's 'ealth of late, on account of 'er bein' distraught over 'er 'usband an' all. Looks like suicide."

"Yeah, well let's leave the deductions to the experts, shall we?" The female officer blinked but showed no other sign that she was concerned by the rebuke. She led them under the police tape and into the house.

White-suited CSI officers were examining every room in the detached building but were concentrating mostly on the bathroom. Gull stared down at the naked woman lying in a cold bath of her own blood and sighed again. She accepted the blue forensic gloves a CSI officer gave her and leaned over the body.

Sheila Cropper had been an attractive lady in her early forties. Clear, blue, intelligent eyes, now wide with mercifully ended agony; mousey blonde hair streaked and tousled by blood. Her body was in fine shape, no breast sag or overt roundness of the hips. Gull couldn't help comparing it to her own. Pretty similar, though Gull preferred the shaven look. She grimaced at Sheila's thick tuft of pubic hair, which floated on the surface of the filthy water. One hand clutched a CD-R next to the gently stirring pubes, the disc held just under the mix of cold bath water and blood. The other clutched a pair of nail scissors, the tip, caked in blood, sticking up from the water. One of Sheila's ears floated next to it. The other, half-severed, hung from the side of her head.

She mentally thanked her superior for sending her on this little trip. Bastard. She could have been riding her second or third orgasm by this point. She wondered if the young officer had fallen asleep back at her flat. His arms must be aching like fuck by now. Guilt? Nah. Men were there to be abused. Just like they thought women were. He could complain to her superior about her treatment, but she knew he wouldn't. The sex was too good, and besides, every male officer on the Met knew not to fuck with Gull.

She pursed her lips and concentrated on the body.

Reaching forward, she pried the CD from the stiffening fingers, trying to avert her eyes from the reproach she imagined in those blue eyes, the locked grimace of her mouth.

She examined it briefly before handing it to the chief CSI next to her. He dropped the CD-R in an evidence bag and sealed it. She didn't need to tell him what to do with it; he knew better than to not keep DS Gull informed of any findings.

He was gone from her mind, a walking job in a crinkly teletubby suit: a man. She turned back to the pretty copper. "Any sign of anyone else in the house?"

"No, Ma'am..." She looked like she was going to add something, and then thought better of it.

"Go on..."

"Why would you do that, Ma'am?"

"What?"

"Why would you cut off your own ears?"

Gull was about to rebuke her for jumping to conclusions again, but let her have that one; all the evidence pointed to that being the case. She stooped over the nail scissors, gently removed them from the death grip, too. They looked sharp enough, but it would have taken a lot of effort and determination to use them to—

"'Ow could she do that?"

Gull glanced at the policewoman.

"Slice off your own lugs like that. Wiv a pair of nail clippers. That takes guts, Ma'am. She musta been proper upset."

"Yes, thank you for your psychological insights, constable." She turned as another CSI moved out of her way and she saw the CD player on the chair beside the bath. Her attention had fallen on the hand-written note folded next to it.

She picked it up carefully, unfolded it, read the words quickly.

"What a delightful man," she quipped and showed the note to Trimble.

"Proper romantic, that one," the DC muttered.

"Yes, DC Trimble. A shining example to the male species." She handed it to the nearest CSI, returned her attention to the uniformed officer.

"We'll need to talk to the neighbor. You can get all the prelim info, though. Whether she heard any voices, sounds of an intruder, the usual. I've got someone else to see. Trimble?" She turned, left the room, was already halfway down the stairs, not waiting for her fellow officer to keep up.

She sat in the Merc and waited for him. She inserted Snoop Dogg's *Doggystyle* and turned the volume down while she thought. The rapper summed up everything about men she hated, but that didn't stop her from loving his music. Trimble climbed in beside her and started the car.

"Where to, Ma'am?"

"Home. I've got another orgasm waiting for me." She smiled thinly as the color rose in his flaccid cheeks again. "And then tomorrow we're going to pay another visit to a certain Rock God..."

Baz Cropper had abandoned his lovely villa in Chiswick, along with his lovely wife. His new abode was a disused slaughterhouse in White-chapel. *No accounting for taste*, thought Gull as she and Trimble waited for a response from the door buzzer. The band had obviously tired of the plush EMI premises from which they had conducted their business with Nick James. The only way she had been able to contact Cropper had been through the manager, and Roscoe had reluctantly agreed to another police interview (not that the bastard had much choice). Cropper had not been told of his wife's death yet. That pleasure was all Gull's. She figured he could wait until the morning, seeing as he hadn't even bothered to speak to her since returning from his little jaunt to nowhere.

She recognized the roadie who eventually opened the door. Deuce Chambers. She had busted him a few times for possession. Nothing heavy.

"Top of the morning, Deuce, you gorgeous specimen of male loveliness," she greeted him cynically.

To her surprise, the tall biker didn't bite. In fact, his expression didn't move at all.

"Baz Cropper," she announced, dismissing the roadie's uncharacteristic reticence for the moment.

Deuce let them into the gloomy lobby. Roscoe appeared from a door off to the right.

"Where's Mister Cropper?" she asked him, skipping the formalities.

"What's this all about?" The manager retrieved his sunglasses from inside his suit jacket.

FFS, Gull thought. She felt like snatching the shades from his hands and stamping on them. She hadn't had a good sleep. After returning from the crime scene, the manacled officer had been far too exhausted to service her, so she had reluctantly let the wimp go. By then, it had been 2:00 a.m. It was now 8:30. That didn't equate to a good shift in the arms of Morpheus.

"I need to speak to Mister Cropper over a private matter, as I explained to you on the phone."

"I'm their manager. I am here to look after them." His voice was still deep and distant, although the annoying pauses seemed to have cleared up. *Maybe he was finally recovering from his six-month jet lag,* she thought wryly. "If you need to—"

"Thank you, sir. I'll speak to Mister Cropper now, please."

If he was annoyed, he didn't show it. "Very well. Follow me, please."

He ushered her through the door from which he'd come. The room beyond was large and featureless and might one time have acted as the warehouse office. The only furniture was a single chair. No desk, no chest of drawers, no concessions to comfort or industry or anything.

Cropper was there, though.

The tall singer was standing in the center of the uncarpeted room, his sunglasses on. The room was dark, apart from chinks of light from the shutters.

Gull hesitated for a moment, then turned to Roscoe. "Lights, please."

The manager almost smiled as he flicked a wall panel. A fluorescent buzzed into life above her head. It didn't help much. "You can leave us now," she told him.

The manager paused as though ready to argue, then left, closing the door.

"Mister Cropper..." She moved toward the singer, Trimble at her heel. "I'm afraid I have some bad news."

The singer started walking toward her, slowly, heavily. Despite her self-confidence, accrued through twelve hard years on the force successfully dealing with men with Neanderthal attitudes, Gull still felt a little intimidated.

Cropper stopped a couple of feet in front of her. He towered a good six inches above her. "All news is indifferent to me," he intoned gravely.

She stretched out her chin and let him have it. "Your wife was found dead at her home last night, sir."

His expression didn't change. It was like looking at a Madame Tussauds' figure of Baz Cropper.

"Did you hear me, sir?"

"I heard, officer. That is unfortunate." His vocals, like Roscoe's, seemed to have overcome their long-distance slur a little, although they were still clotted with gravel. There was no hint of emotion whatsoever.

"That's one word for it." She glanced at Trimble, who looked uncomfortable as usual. She pressed on. "You not interested in hearing how she died?"

Nothing. The wraparound sunglasses tilted down at her.

"Okayyy…" she coughed, her nerves plucking at her now. She hadn't felt this uncomfortable in a man's presence since…since last time she had interviewed these bastards. She steeled herself. "You sent her a CD… asking for her thoughts on it."

The singer remained impassive.

"Along with a note," Gull continued, "asking her to listen to your new album. I believe that was the first time you'd been in touch with her since you returned from your, ah, absence."

The singer nodded slowly.

"Can I ask why you haven't visited her?"

No answer. It was like talking to a corpse. She found herself looking at his chest to see if it was rising and falling and pulled herself together. "Had your wife tried to hurt herself before to your knowledge?"

The sunglasses continued to stare at her.

"We can make this more official if you want." The threat was clear.

"My wife was prone to theatrics."

Not true, according to the neighbor's statement, who was also her best friend, it seemed. According to the officer on duty's report, the neighbor had attested to Sheila being strong-minded and fundamentally sensible.

"Would you say it's in her character to do something like this?"

"Something like what? You have not told me how she…died."

True that. Okay, fuck face, I'll tell you. "She cut off her own ears with a pair of nail scissors." She remembered the police woman's words from the previous night: *That takes guts, Ma'am. She musta been proper upset.*

Baz Cropper turned away as if deep in thought. With his back to her, he said, "That's rather a damning indictment of our music…" He turned around again and damn if there wasn't a little smile on his lips. "Wouldn't you say so, officer?"

Cunt. She almost said it. She had her mouth open to do just that.

Instead, she controlled herself and said abruptly, "Where were you last night, Mister Cropper?"

The singer spread his hands expansively. "This is my new home. I was here all night long…" He made it sound like he was going to burst into horrible song. She turned to Trimble, unable to stomach much more. She thought of the pretty, intelligent, blue eyes staring up at her from the bath, the pubic hair floating in bloody scum water.

"I expect Mister Roscoe can confirm your statement as to your whereabouts?"

The singer nodded slowly again.

Gull cleared her throat as if about to say something more, then changed her mind. She felt sick. And a little scared. Not a little: a lot. This cruel cadaver of a man freaked the fuck out of her. There was still one last thing to clear up before she could go and breathe clean air again, however. "Do the names Monique Glass and Gabrielle Evans mean anything to you?"

Silence.

"Maybe you don't remember the names of all the girls who follow you around, but these two were seen leaving HMV with your band the other day and have not been heard from. DC Trimble?"

Trimble jerked to attention and rummaged in his pockets for what seemed like an hour before pulling out the photographs of two pretty blondes he'd printed off at Bethnal Green that morning.

"Like you say, we have so many girls… interested in us."

"Is that a no?"

"It's whatever you would like it to be. I do not recall them." He stepped an inch or two closer. His aura crushed her self-confidence. He was a solid wall of hostile indifference. She felt queasy to the core of her soul. "We could get a warrant to search this place if you refuse to co-operate."

Now he smiled. For a moment, she was sure his teeth looked like gray chips of stone in the dim light. Then the white shine beloved by a million teenage (not to mention middle-aged) girls was back. "Knock yourself out…" Was that a threat disguised as sarcastic helpfulness?

Drawing in a quick breath, she said, "We'll probably need to speak to you again, Mister Cropper. And I'll need to be informed of your whereabouts."

"We are going nowhere, officer. We have been nowhere, and we're going...nowhere. We will always be here." And that definitely sounded like a threat.

She led Trimble over to the door and opened it. She was not surprised to find Roscoe waiting outside in the gloomy lobby. Her eyes rose to the staircase winding up to darker floors above, but Roscoe drew her attention back to him. He was holding something out for her.

"With our compliments," he said tonelessly.

He was holding a CD-R in a plastic jewel case in his hand.

"What's that?"

"Cat O' Nine Tails' new album, officer." He paused. "It's a killer," he added and waited until she took it from him.

Outside again, Gull breathed deeply. She noticed Trimble looked decidedly relieved as well.

"Something about them, Trimble," she said after she had calmed herself a little.

"Yes, Ma'am," he said with conviction. "Something not right."

They crossed to the Merc and climbed in. "First, Nick James, then these two missing girls, and now Sheila Cropper," Gull said, scanning the building through the passenger window. "I think we should keep an eye on them for sure."

"Or an ear?"

"Hmmm?" She glanced at him as he started the engine.

He nodded at the disc still clamped in her hand.

"Oh. Yes." She looked at the blank CD-R for a moment, then tossed it in the back of the car. "Fuck that shit," she said and played Snoop Dogg instead.

Chapter Eighteen

"Whatever you think, I do love him…"

Johnny paused as he undressed, watched her lying in matching red bra and panties on the bed in the long mirror on the wall.

He thought about that for a second, then: "I do, too."

"No, you don't, or you wouldn't be doing this."

He turned to her and pulled off his t-shirt. He shook his head by way of answer and grinned at her sardonically.

She flushed. "Yes, I know. We're both as bad as each other. But don't you feel guilty?"

"Deliciously so," he said and began to unzip his jeans.

"Bastard. It's not funny."

"I never said it was." He threw his jeans over a chair. "I grew up with Kirk. I *do* love him. We always had each other's backs at school."

"So how can you—"

He leaned forward over the foot of the bed in just his briefs. "Don't lecture me, Rose. I do feel bad, but this ain't helping. You wanna know how I can do this to my best bud? Two reasons. You, first of all. I fancied you from the first moment Kirk showed you off in the pub that night… When was it? Shit, five years ago? You were the hottest girl I'd ever seen, with your crimped hair and fishnets. But it was those honey brown eyes that got me the most…"

He paused. She was listening now. Of course, she was. Girls always listened when they were being flattered. But it was all true. He had always been jealous of Kirk. And not just for his girlfriend…

"Thanks. That's cute. But still indefensible, as are my own reasons for doing this. And what's excuse number two?"

"Huh?" He stood up straight, brushed a hand through his quiff.

"You said there were two reasons you were doing this."

"Yeah. You're hot."

"That was reason number one."

"It's number two as well. You got any objection."

She smiled. Her guilt momentarily forgotten. Her eyes were fixed on his briefs now, at the bulge pushing out, increasing as he looked at her lying on the bed. Fact is, he would never tell her about the real Reason Number Two. How though he loved Kirk like a brother, he hated him, too. Hated the way he wrote songs so effortlessly without having a musical note in his body; songs that were so powerful, eerie, and darkly beautiful that Johnny almost resented having to play them. Next to Kirk, Johnny's attempts at songwriting were like a clumsy child's. He knew Kirk's songs were genius; that if the band could only get the right platform, the right showcase to deliver them, then the band could be, *would* be huge. Of course, he would never tell Kirk any of this. The way he made Johnny feel like a session guitarist backing a star. Not through the way he acted, of course; Kirk was a true gent, modest and unassuming. But by being a fucking genius when Johnny was a second-rate troubadour. A strummer who shagged his best mate's girlfriend. Johnny had the looks and the girls, but he didn't have the talent. And that made him feel empty. A rock music mannequin, with his perfect cheekbones and his plastic heart. He was almost grateful that they were still heading nowhere. If they made it, Johnny would be spotlighted for what he was: second rate.

If he couldn't have Kirk's talent, he would have the next best thing. The one thing Kirk cherished even above the music, even though Rose was too self-obsessed to realize it.

Did that make Johnny a cunt?

Oh yes. And they all thought Davey was the bad boy in the band.

Davey was a lamb in comparison…

Looking at Rose now, with her long, sleek limbs spread out on the bedspread, her skin a light honeyed brown from all the holidays she'd spent in the Med as a child with her rich parents, Johnny could forgive himself his petty jealousies, his mean-minded insecurities. But could he forgive himself for this? It would destroy Kirk. Was that what he *really* wanted? Of course not. He loved Kirk as a—

You keep telling yourself that.

Fuck it. He peeled off his briefs and knelt on the bed beside her. She was smoldering. And he hadn't been BS'ing: she was the most sensuous girl he'd ever met. She drove him mad. Every inch of her.

He kissed her. "Forget Kirk," he breathed, his passions escalating as he stroked the lacy cup of her bra. "Just for a few stolen minutes."

She responded to his kiss, her tongue snaking into his mouth, soft, full lips molding against his.

He unclasped her bra and moved his lips to her right breast, nursing the nipple erect with his tongue, kissing it, teasing it, then moving on to her left breast, small but perfectly formed, caramel brown with the darker aureole that drove him insane. His right hand smoothed down her flat stomach, rested on her panties. He let his fingers play with her through the lace, feeling the moistness that was waiting for him.

He knelt up on the bed and pulled her panties down slowly, enjoying the sound of the fabric riding down her smooth thighs. He tossed them aside, still kneeling, looking down at her. She parted her legs for him to enjoy the sight, one hand straying down to tease her pussy. Johnny could have stayed there forever, staring at her fingers idly toying, spreading the folds of her lips to reveal the lighter pinkness inside, wet and waiting for him. Fuck, she was beautiful. Could any man blame him for this? If Kirk didn't know how to look after her right, then…

He stooped and kissed her pussy lips, nuzzling gently at the hood above the moist entrance, his erection the only thing driving him now.

Rose's mobile killed the moment.

It was lying on the floor on top of her discarded jeans, and the familiar Cat O' Nine Tails ringtone was shattering the mood.

"Sorry." She sat up on the bed and retrieved the mobile. Johnny could see the caller ID over her shoulder.

"Don't answer it," he said.

She looked up at him, guilt twisting her gorgeous features, and thumbed the eject button. He almost loved her then.

"I've got to go," she said, reaching down for her panties.

"Kidding me." He indicated his erection. "Seriously gonna leave me with this?"

"Play with it yourself. In front of that mirror. I'm sure it won't be the first time."

"Fuck off then." He got off the bed and put his briefs back on.

She dressed hurriedly and left without another word.

Johnny stood in his stripy briefs in front of the mirror. "Loser," he said.

Rose caught the bus home, chewing her lip most of the way.

She was a real bitch. But that was the last time. One-hundred percent. She would be there for Kirk now. She loved him, and he needed her.

He was still seriously depressed after the gig the other night, feeling the band was a failure, and he was the biggest failure of all. If he hadn't kept insisting Cat O' Nine had contributed to his lackluster performance, she would have had more sympathy for him. That was probably what drove her to Johnny this time. He wouldn't shut up about it. But if he hadn't pissed her off so much by leaving her standing in HMV in the first place and tooling off to stalk *her* favorite band like the biggest, saddest fan of all, she might have been able to forgive him. That still rankled. But it wasn't the reason she had ended up sleeping with Johnny again. She couldn't kid herself.

She had fallen for Johnny's charms because she could still see the desire in his eyes. She hadn't seen that look in Kirk's for a long time. They hadn't had sex for over a month, and that last time had been perfunctory. Boring and safe, going through the motions. Johnny made her feel like the hottest girl on the planet. But she would never love him, the way she had loved Kirk—*still* loved Kirk?

Of course, she did. That was why she was running away from her good-looking lothario to go back to her man. He had something he needed to talk to her about, or so he'd said in the text that followed his abortive call.

Sounded ominous. She checked her phone as the bus took her toward Stoke Newington. A new email caught her attention: CAT O'NINE ANNOUNCES MONSTER GIG AT WEMBLEY ARENA.

She clicked on the message and read the entire article. The email had been sent to her as she had signed up to CONT's fan club. She'd already received news of the imminent release of the new album, and now this.

Cat O' Nine Tails will be showcasing material from their new album, Crimson, *on July 5th at Wembley Arena. Tickets go on sale tomorrow, available in advance for CONT fans. The album drops at stores and will be available online from June 25th. But maybe even more exciting for Cat fans is the revelation that the band will be performing a secret show in London next week to trial their new songs. This gig will not be announced to the general public, and only a select number of lucky subscribers to the CONT fan club will be eligible to attend. E-tickets will be drawn from a lottery and dispensed over the next few days.*

Rose switched off her data and stared out at the London streets as the bus chugged along. She'd forgotten all about Johnny, her secret shame, and even Kirk for the moment. The child in her responded to the email. It felt like Christmas in June. She could never explain to Kirk why Cat O' Nine meant so much to her. They'd been there for her right through her passage from child to womanhood, through the traumatic death of her father, through a string of failed relationships, and there for her on the day she met Kirk. She remembered listening to their newest release as she put on her makeup to get ready to go out. The *Fear Me* album would always be synonymous in her mind with meeting Kirk.

The band made her feel safe. They were something she had always depended on at key points in her life. And now here they were again, ready to see her through the next stage. Whatever that would be.

Shame that Kirk just didn't get it.

She got off the bus at the stop around the corner from their flat and wondered what he had to say to her. It couldn't be about Johnny. She'd already dismissed that idea. There was no way he could know. But that was just one more reason to end her affair; she really couldn't bear the thought of what it would do to him if he did find out. The one thing Rose was proud of in herself was her steadfastness. Once she made up her mind, there was no going back. She and Johnny were dust.

She let herself in through the main door of the terraced house and up the stairs to the second floor. The interior of the building had certainly seen better days. The landlord didn't really give a fuck about maintenance, and this was all they could afford, what with the small wages she got as a secretary and Kirk's redundancy package from the music magazine he'd once written for rapidly dwindling.

Kirk was waiting for her in front of the TV. He turned to face her when she entered, his bushy hair even more disheveled than usual, although his gaunt face was set and determined. She felt a flush of guilt mixed with treacherous love for him when he jumped up and offered to make her a coffee. Relief, too. For all her certainty, it was good to have her suspicions that he was ignorant of her crimes confirmed.

He put the kettle on and hurried back to her as she sat down in the small, rather drab lounge.

"Two things," he said, as the kettle began to whistle from the kitchen. "First, Lucifer Sam has a gig booked for Monday night at The Ten Bells in Whitechapel. It'll be our last. I'm scrapping the band."

She sighed. "Is this supposed to be good news? You know how much the band means to you."

"Not as much as you do. I've been neglecting you, Rose. Letting the band be my priority instead of the most beautiful girl in the world. I'm so sorry. Lucifer Sam is done. But I want us to be forever."

Rose burst into tears.

Kirk looked confused. "What's the matter? Don't you want that?"

She smiled through her tears and her awful, relentless guilt. "Of course I do, you idiot!"

He smiled with relief. "Then why—"

"Because I love you, that's why. Now shut up and make me a coffee."

"Don't you want to hear my second bit of news?"

She nodded, wiping her nose and feeling so very bad about herself.

"Cat O' Nine Tails are playing a gig at Wembley. And there's no way on fucking earth you're going."

She sniffed, stopped crying. Blinked up at him as he stood over her, his expression more serious than she had ever seen it.

"Now you sound like my fucking Dad! You've got to stop this, Kirk. This obsession with Cat being dangerous. It's all in your head."

"You're *not*…going. Do you want me to tell you why?"

She shrugged.

"Those two girls I saw at Cat O' Nine's gaffe in the East End?"

"What about them…?"

He crossed to the moth-eaten sofa and picked up a copy of *The Sun*, held up the front page for her to see. Black-and-white photos showed two glamorous rock chicks. Rose gawped at the tactless headline and read the article below it:

THE GORE GROUPIES

The butchered bodies of two blonde Cat O' Nine fans missing for five days were found by a dog walker in a popular picnic area on Hampstead Heath. Police have questioned the members of the band who were the last to see them alive at an impromptu party in their East End studio following their public appearance at HMV on Oxford Street last week. The band's manager expressed his 'sadness over such tragic circumstances.' Other members of the band declined to comment. The discovery of the bodies follows hot on the heels of the revelation that Sheila Cropper, 39, of 12 Belvedere Close, Chiswick, the estranged wife of Cat O' Nine Tails singer Baz, reportedly committed suicide on the 16th June. Police are not linking the 'biggest band on the planet' with the girls' murders and are asking the public for any clues that might lead to the perpetrators of these Jack the Ripper-esque crimes.

As usual for the tabloid, the story milked sensation at the expense of sober detail and was more than likely factually inaccurate. The paper was obviously reveling in tying the awful story of the groupies' disappearance and subsequent discovery of their mutilated bodies to the band to maximize shock and sales, profiting nicely from the current interest afforded Cat O' Nine since their miraculous return. And practically any murder perpetrated on a female in London was inevitably painted as a Ripper-style killing if *The Sun* got the slightest opportunity.

"This is…ridiculous," Rose said, throwing the paper back onto the sofa. "I know you hate them, but this is going too far. Never thought you'd believe anything that rag says."

"Last time they're seen alive, they're in a room giving the band blow jobs. Next, they're found ripped up on a common. That's not coincidence. You remember how they were with us in HMV. They're not…not—"

"Human? Fuck's sake, give it a rest, Kirk. I've heard it one time too bloody many. You're pissing me off now." She sighed, her guilt driven away. "Those girls were obviously out of their skulls on something. Their sort don't give a fuck who they service or how many. They've obviously been around the block. Who knows how many rock stars they've been partying with since they left Cat O' Nine. They obviously got in with a bad lot…"

Kirk shook his head, staring at her reproachfully. "'Their sort?' That doesn't sound like you, Rose. Have some respect. They were happy, excited rock fans who got butchered. Really not like you to be so callous."

"I'm callous cos you're pissing me off! It wasn't Cat O' Nine who did that to them. How could it be?"

He left her and went to make the coffee. When he returned, he was quiet.

"If you're that paranoid about them, why don't you tell the police?"

Kirk sipped his coffee before answering. "What, admit I was stalking the band and playing peeping tom at the same time? Besides, it's not news that the girls left with the band. They've admitted it and released an official statement that the girls were alive and well when they left the band's studio."

"Well, there you are."

"You're not going, Rose. There's something evil about that band, and I can't risk—"

"You've gone from sounding like my Dad to bleating like a South Carolina preacher. I thought you were cool!" She laughed humorlessly. "The new album's released in three days, Kirk. I've got a feeling it's going to be their masterpiece. Maybe then you'll finally realize you're wrong, that you've always been wrong about them."

Kirk stood up and wandered over to the window. She watched him for a while, resentment at his attitude mingling with genuine affection and remorse at her own treatment of him, and said, "I love you, Kirk. But I love Cat O' Nine, too. Don't make me choose."

He turned slowly. His thin face was genuinely worried. "Can't believe you just said that."

She looked down at her cup.

"You say I'm the one obsessed, but to me it sounds like you're the crazy fan. Wake up, Rose. Cat O' Nine is back alright, but this time they're bad. I feel it in every part of me. Very, *very* bad. If you love me like you say, don't do this."

Rose got up and went to the bedroom. She lay on the bed and plugged in her earphones to her mobile, searched for an album in the music app, and pressed PLAY.

Fear Me, track one. She closed her eyes and waited until the cozy riffs and melodies lulled her to sleep.

Chapter Nineteen

Sally gave Jacko a little pout as she dropped the Royal Mail package on his desk.

She was in her early forties with a good figure. Married. But what the fuck did that matter? She'd made it plain enough she liked Jacko. One of these days he'd take her over his desk when the rest of the *Rock!!* staff had gone home for the night. He was sure of that.

"Cheers, Sall. What is it?" He tossed his long hair over his shoulders and leaned back in his swivel chair to look at her.

"Dunno love. Looks like a CD." She giggled and pushed her wonder bra out at him, straining the nylon top she wore. This was a little comedy routine between them; Jacko received hundreds of CDs a week, ranging from hopeful wannabes desperate for the Reviews Editor to check out their stuff, to the latest releases from established bands seeking a *Rock!!* endorsement.

"Well, dash me, my dear, you appear to be correct in that assumption!" He picked up the package absentmindedly, his attention diverted by her not inconsiderable breasts. "Top button's undone," he said with a leery grin.

"Oh goodness me, so it is," she trilled coquettishly. "What should I do about that?"

"Undo another one, of course!" He gave her a wide grin, careful not to reveal the silver crown on the lower left side of his mouth that he was all too conscious of since having it put in the month before. It made him feel tarnished somehow.

"Jacko!" The bellow came from Ticer, who was glaring at them from his desk with all the placidity of a bull locked in a very small crockery shop with red-painted walls. "How many fucking times?"

This was also a daily routine, though not one Jacko was so fond of.

"If you wanna stare at the receptionist's tits, do it on your fuckin' day off. Sally, lower your weapons and get your curvy ass over to your own desk, try answering some calls for a change. In other words, *pretend* to be a receptionist. Fuck's sake."

Jacko waved cheerily at Sally as she gave him a wistful look and did as she was told. Then he glanced at the package still in his hand. It was addressed to him in thick, handwritten felt pen. He turned it over. No return address. He was just about to toss it into the tray beside his desk that was already piled up with similar packages when something stopped him. An impulse. It was like a little voice had spoken inside his skull: *Open me.*

He didn't rationalize the voice but acted on it immediately. He tore the paper away to reveal a CD-R in a transparent plastic jewel case. A sharp pain jabbed through his chest as he read the felt-tipped words on the CD: CAT O' NINE TAILS NEW ALBUM DEMO.

He let out a little whoop that drew Ticer's glance from across the room.

"Fuck's wrong with you?"

"Nothing! Abso-lutely nothing…" Jacko felt elation spread through him. The album was due to hit stores in a week, and he'd been pestering the EMI publicity department responsible for the band for days to get hold of a review copy. And now, at last… He felt like an eight-year-old waking up on his birthday.

"What's that you got?" Ticer didn't bother to get up, and Jacko could tell he wasn't that interested.

"Nothing much. Just a new album demo." His voice shook a little with his own excitement.

"Fuckin' poof," Ticer barked. "I don't pay you to *enjoy* your fuckin' job. Might have to consider making you voluntary."

Jacko ignored him. He was already scrambling for his headphones and inserting the CD into the drive on his PC.

He settled the 'phones on his head and leaned back in his chair. There was no note in the package, no tracklist. That would make his review harder, but then, he could always email EMI for a proper tracklist later.

The first track was heralded by a hiss that Jacko at first took for tape leader. Then it occurred to him that it could be a reptile hiss. It reminded him of the sinister gasp a Komodo dragon had made in a natural history doc he'd watched not long ago.

Then the music began.

After the first few notes, he wrenched the 'phones off his head. Sweat beaded his upper lip. He was tempted to eject the CD-R to check the name scribbled on the shiny surface because this sure as hell didn't sound like the cozy old Cat he knew and loved.

His breathing regulated a little and the initial panic the music had kicked up in him began to abate. He was being a tit. They were experimenting with new sounds, that was all. He could hear the music bubbling out of the 'phones on his desk, the sound indistinct, but even in its subdued volume, it was still somehow sinister enough to make Jacko reluctant to listen again. Reluctant to listen to a new album by his favorite band?? Ridiculous.

He placed the headphones over his ears and sat back.

The music took him away. It held him by the hand and led him to a dark place. A very dark, and very bad place inside himself. Jacko didn't like it there. No, not at all. But he had to stay now. You see, he'd forgotten the way back. He was lost in the dark.

Things were all around him. Vicious, nasty things. He couldn't see them. But he could hear them. The bass was the shuffle and stomp of their deformed feet, the lead guitar the screech of their lunatic laughter, sometimes the rending of their claws through arteries and skin; the drum thunder the sound of their pounding as they demolished flesh and bone in the blackness; the vocals a dark spring of undiluted Evil, on the rocks. All the freaks of Insanity were crowding him, waiting to tear him down.

He curled into a ball, and his sobbing was lost in the dark, in the storm of cruelty that lashed around him. They'd taken him away to the Loneliest Place.

He knew that Place.

He hadn't been there since he was a child.

The other boys, the older boys had taken him There that first night in the Orphanage, that institution in the Ninth Circle of Hell that had been his home since his parents died in a car crash.

They'd taken him to that Place in the cellar and locked him in with the Dark and the boiler sounds and the creeping sounds and the whispers.

They'd taken him there every night, you see.

They'd taken him there every night for what seemed like a year, or more.

And now they'd taken him there again.

Except this time the boiler sounds were louder, a gurgle and hiss that he knew (as he'd known back then) could not be the sound of water in pipes but something so much more sinister. His imagination knew what the sounds belonged to, but he had never given shape to the horrors with words.

The creeping sounds were back, too. Stealthy padding and scuffing of naked feet circling him. And there were the whispers. Now (as then) they sighed about the depraved things they must do to him.

Jacko was back in the Place.

This time, nobody was coming to let him out.

"Would you like a coffee, hun?"

Sally held out the steaming mug for Jacko. She'd made it in his favorite Cat O' Nine Tails mug. She'd even undone another button on her top, just for him. It was just their little flirty game, of course. She would never actually *do* anything with him. Her husband would kill her.

Jacko didn't respond. He was sitting back in his chair with his head-phones clamped to his ears, his eyes staring ahead without seeing.

In a daydream, poor love. He often did that when he was lost in music, bless him. He looked rather handsome, apart from the little bald clearing cruelly encroaching on the wilderness of heavy metal hair that tumbled down to his shoulders. *The little dribble stretching from lip to chin kind of spoiled the nobility of his features as well,* she thought. Still, if it hadn't been for her husband, Jerry, big and red-faced with his drink and anger, working on the building sites all day and too tired to get it up all night, she would probably have done him. His flirting made her feel female again.

"Jacko, dear..." She nudged his shoulder with her free hand and placed the coffee mug down on an old, scratched CD he used for a coaster.

He looked up at her.

She blinked at him. He seemed different. No longer gazing at her with amorous eyes and a lecherous smile. His expression was vacant. Like he was staring at a blank wall. He certainly didn't see that the second button of her top was undone. His eyes were wide, locked open like trauma had lodged there. His mouth was working more saliva out and over his chin.

"You alright, hun?" She backed away a step, not liking that manic stare one bit. Was he having a stroke?

Now his hand was twitching to life, reaching out to take the coffee mug. He held it up in front of him, not looking at it, still fixing her with that empty stare (cold and empty as the beady eyes of a dead crow she'd seen on the roadside one morning).

"I made it in your favorite mug, honey. See?" She pointed at the picture of the band on the curved ceramic surface. They looked happy and carefree, basking in their early-nineties youth.

Jacko flicked the contents of the mug at Sally's face, launching himself up from his chair as she tottered back, yelping in pain and surprise.

The headphones lead popped free of the PC jack as he threw himself on her, forcing her backward onto the floor of the office. He was straddling her, the 'phones off his head now, wrapping the lead around her throat until she stopped squealing. He watched the tautness of her throat, so pale, so tender as he garroted her with the cable, watched her tongue

148

pop out of her mouth like a pale frog emerging from a moist cave.

Even though the headphones were disconnected from the CD drive, he could still hear the music snarling from the earpieces as they rested upon Sally's breasts. He pulled on both ends of the plastic cable, watching the coils bite deep into her throat. She had gone King Crimson now. Quite apt. She was rapidly going Deep Purple. Soon she would be Black Sabbath, and his job here would be done.

He felt the others trying to pull him free, but they were weak and afraid. They didn't have power chords for energy. Solos to die for did not rip through their synapses. He shrugged them off easily until he had completed the color palette on Sally's features.

Then he rose from the corpse, proud in all his Rock God majesty, and faced them.

His grin was a stadium salute of welcome to an adoring crowd. Jacko was no longer in the Lonely Place. He was amongst fans now...

Bill Ticer was backing away. Jacko saw Jeremy, the prick in charge of Advertising, babbling urgently into his cell phone. Jacko had never liked Jeremy; the tosser's idea of Rock Greatness began and ended with The Darkness. Jacko pounced, snatched the cell off Jeremy, and battered it into the *Rock!!* staffer's face until he had bashed out several incisors and a molar or two. He left Jeremy on the floor, choking on the teeth lodged in his throat, and went after Ticer.

The editor was making for the door, along with the three other staffers. Jacko let the others go and caught up with Ticer, snatched at the trails of his collar-length hair, snapping his head back and yanking him onto his ass. Ticer began wailing, clawing at Jacko's grip on his hair. But Jacko wasn't going to relinquish his hold easily. He had Jez Tweed Riffs for muscles.

Jacko dragged Ticer over to his desk, over the rubble of his shattered Cat mug. Releasing Ticer's hair, Jacko snaked his left arm around Ticer's throat and hoisted him into a sitting position. With his other hand, he pressed EJECT on the CD drive.

He retrieved the Cat CD-R and held it in front of Bill Ticer's terrified face for a second or two, displaying its greatness.

"Who the fuck said Cat wasn't 'cutting edge' enough?" he said, and using the disc like a trowel, dug into Ticer's forehead.

Ticer screamed. Blood flowed down his forehead, masked his pugnacious features. Jacko was merciless; he had a gig to finish. He pounded the edge of the disc repeatedly into the editor's face, chopping through the jelly of Ticer's left eye in the process. "D'ya see it now, Bill ol' buddy?" he panted as he sawed through his right retina with the CD-R. "D'ya see how truly great Cat O' Nine is at last?"

He released Ticer after a while and stood breathing heavily over the corpse, the red disc still in his hand.

Encore?

But there was nobody left to play to.

He lifted the disc, leaned back against his desk, and began sawing at the thick power chord of his own artery. The applause began to fade, the lights to dim.

The Lonely Place was waiting.

Chapter Twenty

"Rock 'n' roll, eh?"

DS Gull was standing in the middle of a mess. A mess of bodies and blood. She didn't like it.

"Bad for you," DC Trimble said sullenly.

Gull turned to face him, hands on her pinstriped hips. "You don't fucking say. Any other pearls of wisdom?"

The CSI team was finishing up. Surfaces were dusted, the positions of the bodies photographed, every forensic clue covered. Not that there was much need for all that, of course; they had three live witnesses who had already told them exactly what had happened. But it didn't hurt to be thorough.

She stared at Jack Wiley, the apparent perp. He was sitting with his back to his desk, the compact disc he'd used to slice his own artery now tucked safely away in a bag. It had reminded Gull of one of those gimmicky red vinyl singles they used to release, with the playing surface a garish crimson. She was sure she had one at home, or was it her older brother's? The Damned's *Smash It Up*. Yes, definitely her brother's. She wouldn't listen to that crap.

Shame they probably wouldn't be able to play the offending CD-R. The fact it was caked in blood and its edge was jagged and broken after being used to cut through Jacko's neck and Ticer's face kind of precluded that possibility.

But she'd seen the felt pen scribble through the red coating.

"All roads lead to Roscoe and his boys, eh, Trimble?"

Trimble scratched his head and did his best to look thick. He didn't have to try very hard.

"You want to see them again, Ma'am?"

"Hell no!" If she was a tad too vehement, nobody could blame her. She really *didn't* want to see that band ever again, and if she had her way—

She strode carefully over the patches of dried blood to the bodies of the three victims: Jeremy Blythe, cause of death, suffocation due to broken teeth blocking his air pipe; Bill Ticer, blinded and sliced to death by a CD; and finally, Sally Barrows, strangled by the headphones' cord.

A CSI was waiting patiently for her to signal the removal of the bodies. After a few more moments she gave it, stepping back to watch the white coverall-clad investigators stretcher first one, then the other two bodies away.

If she had her way, oh yes, if she had her way…

She glanced up at Trimble, who was flicking one of his large ears pensively.

"Come on, handsome. Nothing more to be gained here."

"So what do you think, Ma'am?"

"I think there's nothing more to be gained here, Trimble. That's pretty much all I think. Apart from we should be running that band out of town in tar and feathers, but that ain't gonna happen, is it?"

Trimble squinted at her. "Because of what the Super said?"

"Because of what the Super said, Einstein." She watched as Jacko's body was carefully placed on a stretcher and carried from the office.

"So let's review the facts, shall we?" She sat down in Jacko's swivel chair, which had miraculously managed to avoid the splatter of his life fluids. "First off, rock journalist Nick James goes postal after interviewing the lovely Cat O' Nine Tails and finally kills himself at Camden Lock. We then have two girls missing after attending a private party with the band. Their bodies later turn up butchered on a heath. We have the singer's wife commit suicide after receiving a demo CD of the band's latest album..." She picked a pen out of a pot on the desk and tapped the CD drive on the PC with it. "We then have a missing persons file opened on one Jeffrey Stacks, music engineer, last reported as having been commissioned to work on Cat O' Nine Tails' latest album and not seen or heard from by his wife for over a week. Now we have another apparent suicide and murder rampage committed after our friend Jack Wiley receives a review copy of the same album. So what do all these cases have in common, Watson?"

Trimble gaped at her. "But the Super said—"

"I know what the fucking Super said. We can't touch 'em. We could search their studio, we could check under their beds, even shake out their pajamas... We could empty out their pockets while we're at it. I think we might find more than conkers and bubble gum. And then face a massive legal challenge for our efforts. Like the Super says, the evidence is all circum-fucking-stantial. Tenuous with a fucking capital T. That doesn't make it any the less..." She searched for the right word. Obvious? Glaringly so. But her hands were tied. She'd already called for a boycott on the band. The Super had gone pale when she mentioned the Wembley Gig should be canceled and all tickets refunded. His lip had trembled at her suggestion of a search of the band's studio. He'd lost a few hairs from his crown when she posited they bring them in to the station for questioning. *Where's your proof, Gull? Where's your damned evidence? Their legal team would crucify us. Get out there and find me something concrete to pin on 'em instead of this comic strip conjecture!*

"The Super wants us to chase down the drugs angle, Ma'am."

"You can chase it as far as your chubby little legs will carry you, son. That way's a dead end, despite what our esteemed superior believes. I've never encountered a drug yet that can lead two different men to commit such separate and hideous crimes, even if they did both work in the same office. No, Trimble, you spectacular example of manhood, it's safe to say it wasn't a virulent strain of Skunk Jacko and Nicko were indulging in, financed by the office's petty cash, that led to this current trend in rock-related violence. As I said, there's absolutely nothing more to be gained here."

So she curbed the comic strip conjecture, tucked the pen back in its pot, stood up, and took Trimble by the hand.

"Come on, dear, let's go and have a pint."

"Ma'am?"

"A beer, Detective Constable. Is that such an unreasonable suggestion?"

After all, there was fuck all else she could do.

And it certainly beat the hell out of confronting that creepy band again.

Chapter Twenty-One

Rose looked positively smug.

Kirk knew what she'd done before she pulled the little square HMV bag out of her coat pocket.

He turned away from her. He felt anger and frustration boiling under the surface, directionless, futile. Of course, she hadn't bought it just to spite him—on the very day of its UK release—but it certainly felt like that. A slap in the face, as stinging as every rejection in bed over the last month had been. If he stayed here with her in the flat, he knew he would blow...

Still with his back to her, he said, "I hope it's worth it..."

She dropped the bag on the sofa and shrugged out of her coat, almost indecently eager to play her new acquisition, like a teenager all over again. *Had she ever stopped being one,* he wondered? *Grow the fuck up,* he felt like saying, but decided to leave the flat instead.

Fresh air would do him good.

And besides, he really didn't want to hear that band ever again.

His cell vibrated in the pocket of his jeans before he'd made the end of Clissold Crescent.

"Ned," he answered, not really in the mood.

"Tonight's gig still going ahead?"

"You know it is."

"And is it still going to be our last ever...?"

If the drummer felt any sadness, he disguised it well.

"You know it is."

He sensed Ned's shrug and felt one of his own answering it. His fist tightened on the cell as he waited for Ned to say something else.

"Johnny Deathshadow from Hamburg..."

"What about them?" Kirk felt his irritation increase.

"Wanker! Sorry. Tourette's. No, fuck it, I don't need to apologize to you. You know I'm not calling you a wanker. Twat! But yeah, I did just call you that. Johnny D: They're supporting us."

"What the fuck? We can't be headlining..."

"Not really, but it sounds good, don't it? Equal billing, obviously. Cheer up, ya prick. See ya tonight."

Yeah, can't fuckin' wait.

He put the phone back in his pocket and stopped beside a bright red Royal Mail pillar box. He remembered once when he'd been out of his head on magic mushrooms and the post box had been the most vibrant, reddest thing in the universe. Now it looked dull and tarnished, the red paint flaking away.

Abruptly he turned on his heel and paced back to the flat. He couldn't walk out on her like this. If he was losing his band today, he didn't want to lose her along with it. He loved her. He fucking needed her (Was *that* love?).

He tramped back up the dingy, carpeted stairs to their second-floor flat and fumbled his key into the lock. He could hear the thump of music through the walls and tensed.

He pushed the door open and stepped inside.

She had it on loud. He winced, and not just from the volume.

Whatever he had been expecting, it wasn't this.

This didn't sound like the Cat O' Nine Tails he was familiar with from Rose's CD collection.

They sounded so much heavier, more hostile, menacing.

He felt the music working on him as soon as he entered the flat. It picked at his mind, crawled under his skin, raised his bumps, and pinched his scalp. It tightened his ball sack and left him with an urge to both vomit and defecate all at the same time. It also gave him one hell of an erection.

He stood behind the door to the lounge for a good five minutes, listening, his cock stiffening in his trousers, peering through the gap between door and jamb, peering at his girlfriend as she lay on the sofa masturbating.

He heard two tracks before he pushed the lounge door wide and announced his presence. Two dirty, filthy tracks that slithered into his skull, battering his ears and mind, while cupping his balls with lascivious sonic lust.

Rose looked up, busy as she was. She looked up, and the smile she gave him was her slinkiest ever. He couldn't remember her ever smiling at him like that. It made him harder.

Her panties and skirt were around her ankles, one arm thrown back behind her head, the other hand busy between her thighs.

She waited for the lull between tracks before asking him, "You want to watch?" She showed absolutely no trace of embarrassment at having been caught out. If anything, it was turning her on even more. Her mouth was parted, her lips glistening. He felt shame for being a voyeur (second time in two weeks no less) mixing with unbridled lust. He had never seen her like this before. His normally reserved and prim girlfriend was taking wanton to a whole new level. Her dirty brown eyes held his. Was she mocking him? The next track on Cat O' Nine's new album kicked in, a dark, sibilant number, a slow-beat eulogy to depravity. It pumped his fear, pumped his cock, too.

With her free hand, she hiked up her top, revealing the dark blue lace of her bra. She reached behind herself, arching her back, her other hand still busy, the fingers stroking her petal-like lips, probing, thrusting inside. She undid her bra as he continued to stand over her, his jeans bulging. She squeezed and molded her breasts, tweaking the nipples awake, the brown aureoles drawing Kirk in.

She paused in her masturbating, held out juice-sticky fingers for him to lick. The music seduced him, oozing sinister temptation. He sucked her fingers, staring into her eyes in a way he would have thought impossible an hour before. She withdrew her hand from his mouth, seized his instead and pulled him to the sofa.

The music pounded, urging him on. It was the soundtrack to the filthiest, most degenerate orgy he could imagine, and he wanted to be its star. He felt the urge to indulge in sleaze he had previously laughed at, to explore sadism he'd always felt nothing but contempt for... Would she let him piss in her mouth? What would it be like to cut her, to slice those gorgeous breasts?

Any revulsion he would have normally felt at these thoughts failed to launch. The basest of fantasies seemed eminently desirable now rather than shameful. He felt the music groom him, and he welcomed it. At last, he could share Rose's excitement for a band he had long disdained. But they had never been like this before. They could never make him—or Rose—behave like *this* before...

He unbuckled his belt, dropped his boxers and jeans, and kicked them away. He leaned down to kiss her parted lips, and her tongue was a brutal invasion of his mouth. He withdrew for air, and her hand came up to caress his right cheek before tracing a line down it with a sharp fingernail. He didn't notice when the tracing became a tearing, so powerful was his lust. Nothing mattered but his animal need and pain was a spur to his desire. He seized her head in both hands and speared her mouth with his monster cock. He wasn't sure he had seen it quite so defiantly, brutally erect. She planted her sensuous lips around the shaft eagerly, let them ride up and down him, pausing at his tip to unfurl her delicious tongue and tease him to hell and back before closing over him again, her mouth warm, moist, velvet. As she sucked, she stared up at him with animal eyes.

There were no words (not that she could have spoken anyway). There was just bestial sex. One of her hands cupped his balls while the other pawed at herself furiously. When Kirk felt the tremors of ejaculation, he pulled free of her mouth, then used his hand to aim over her waiting, upturned face. He jetted thick, pearly semen over her outstretched tongue, her lips, and her delicious cheekbones. After he had done, she closed her mouth and swallowed hungrily, all the time working herself into a frenzy until she too was finished, sagging back against the cushions, completely sated.

Kirk found his pants and jeans and put them back on. Neither of them said a word. The music swelled and seethed from the speakers. No longer cajoling, it seemed mocking, cruel. It jeered his shameful desires now. He moved to turn it off but her voice cut at him like a whip. "No!" She was turned away from him on the sofa, eyes closed. He noticed she had begun to caress herself again.

Full of a deep self-disgust (the sex had felt inexplicably *unhealthy*, no matter how erotic it had been) and feeling more distant from her than ever, Kirk headed for the bathroom, pausing only to gingerly touch the red line she had scratched in his cheek before hitting the shower.

The hot water cleansed his body, but the sense of despoilment remained. He had somehow felt coerced into the act, egged on as if by detestable onlookers at a gang rape. He wondered if he could look her in the eye after this.

But fuck, it had felt *goooood*...

He scrubbed at himself even more furiously. Through the thin walls, he could still hear the music.

Rose didn't accompany him to the gig.

It would be the first one without her there. He was not sorry this time, however. As he had predicted, conversation between them after he emerged from the shower had been cold, distant. She was still lying where he had left her, listening to the album for the second time, though she had stopped masturbating. He had turned the volume down as he searched for his Black Sabbath Converse boots, which he had kicked into one corner of the room in his impatient lust. Surprisingly, she had not argued the point, and he concluded that she was too weak from her own exertions.

When he was sure she was asleep, he switched off the CD altogether.

He resisted the urge to kiss her forehead. His mess was still drying on her face. He fetched a kitchen towel and gently mopped at her beautiful features, careful not to wake her. Then he left. It was time for the sound check.

The pub in which Lucifer Sam was to play their final gig was auspicious for many reasons. It had a hell of a history, for one. The Ten Bells in Whitechapel was notorious for being at the very epicenter of the Jack-the-Ripper horror. That the killer had drunk in there while he eyed potential victims was a matter of conjecture, though almost certainly true; that the destitute women he ripped had supped gin in its dingy saloon bar before venturing out to meet their fate in the foggy, cobbled streets was indisputable.

It hadn't been Kirk's choice. This one was down to Davey. He seemed to know every dodgy landlord in London, along with every dodgy musician. He secured the deal over a pint, and for added value, he got the proprietor to book German rockers Johnny Deathshadow as a final leg of their British tour.

When Kirk asked Davey why the Ten Bells, Davey simply shrugged. "If Lucifer Sam is gonna be consigned to history, then we might as well do it in a place steeped in the stuff." It was probably the most eloquent thing he'd ever said. And, as Kirk stepped off the bus at Commercial Street, he had to admit the bassist had a point.

The equipment was already set up when he arrived at the pub, all cozy on a street corner right next to the imposing, ghostly white structure that was Christ Church. Davey had borrowed a mate's Transit van and, along with Ned, had lugged all the gear here an hour before, and even moved some of the tables and chairs in the rather small bar to make room for their impromptu stage—a raised corner of the saloon. *Good of them*, thought Kirk with a twinge of guilt. A lot of effort considering they knew he wanted to bin the band. He should have been helping instead of pumping semen over his (sweet) girlfriend's face.

He greeted Davey and Ned somewhat sheepishly. "You been forcing yourself on unwilling women again," was Davey's comment upon seeing the badly disguised scratch on Kirk's cheek. The landlord shook his hand

and offered him a beer, which he drank almost in one. The second one he had to pay for.

Johnny arrived half an hour late for the sound check. He glanced at Kirk's scratched face with what Kirk felt was more than casual interest, a frown on his good-looking face. Kirk was tempted to ball him out for being late, then remembered sheepishly this was the end anyway. The thought left him with a deepening sense of futility. After Rose, the band was the most important thing in his life. Now he felt estranged from his girlfriend; the last thing he really needed was to rid himself of his other source of pleasure and pride as well. Except it wasn't anymore, was it? Especially after that last gig with the Men That Will Not Be Blamed For Nothing, which left him feeling useless and insecure. What was it the late Bill Ticer (his as-yet-motiveless murder had been all over the papers over the last few days) had said? *Second-rate singer in a third-rate band. Don't hold back, fella. No wonder his office colleague had finally done for him,* Kirk thought. The guy had needed lessons in tact. But he hadn't deserved to die…

With Mr. Diesel in place, they completed the sound check in time for their fellow headliners, Johnny Deathshadow, to follow with theirs. The German band seemed a decent enough bunch. Younger than the members of Lucifer Sam—mid-twenties instead of mid-thirties—they seemed as committed and enthusiastic about their craft as Kirk's band had been in the early days. He felt even more depressed watching them re-hearse. He hit the bar for his third pint, thinking about Rose, wondering what she was doing now…and whether she was listening to that vile album again.

And it had been vile. A complete change of direction for the once-cozy rock band. No longer treading the grooves of formula, they had broken through the walls of rock convention at last. Something Kirk had always despised them for resisting doing and now wished fervently that they hadn't. Fervently? Why exactly did he care?

He pictured Rose on the sofa. So decadent, abandoned in her lust. That wasn't his girlfriend. And why did he feel ashamed for hoping she would still be like that when he returned?

Ned, Davey, and Johnny were their usual ridiculous selves as they drank at the bar and waited for the evening to settle around the small, old pub. Kirk sat a little away from them and did not join in their banter. When he got up to take a leak, nobody seemed to notice him leave, like they had already gotten used to him not being a part of their scene anymore.

Kirk made his way down the old spiral staircase to the cellars, where the toilets were located. He didn't glance at the crude etchings of the Ripper slayings reproduced from the front pages of Victorian newspapers framed on the stained stone walls. He'd seen them all before. Often, he was forced to push past gore tourists poised before the pictures, snapping away with their mobile phones.

The cellar was cold and grimy. He kicked up a toilet seat splashed with piss and emptied his own bladder, wrapped in dark thoughts. It seemed like Johnny and the other two were indifferent to the band's demise. But it was difficult to tell with them. They were always looking for the next thing, with the attention span of bored twelve-year-olds. Perhaps they'd already found the next thing. Perhaps they'd already formed a new band without him. Kirk found he didn't care. He stared at the crumbling bricks of the wall in front of him but saw only Rose's face, dirty brown eyes and mouth wide, tongue extended to collect his jizz.

Johnny Deathshadow played first as the punters began to fill the small pub.

Kirk leaned against the bar and watched.

They were good. And they had made a real effort. They wore matching black boiler suits, and each of them had spent time on perfecting their makeup, their faces transformed diligently into skull faces, Misfits style. Programmed keyboards complimented the hard rock riffs perfectly. The tunes were strong and clean, the vocals upbeat despite the dark lyrics. The bassist looked like a demented, undead version of Elvis' original bass player, Bill Black. The guitarist emanated menace, tall and skeletal.

Kirk found himself applauding with more than polite courtesy. He finished his beer and asked for another. His head was beginning to spin a little, but the image of defilement remained. Rose's, and his own.

Then it was time for Lucifer Sam to play.

Chapter Twenty-Two

"Here ya go." The landlord tapped Kirk on the shoulder just as he got up to move onto the makeshift stage. He glanced down at the battered Victorian undertaker's hat the large man held in his hand.

"What's that?"

"Can't let you go on without it. Seems like it would suit you, mate. See it as a gift from the Ten Bells."

Kirk shrugged and placed it on his head, glancing at himself in the mirror behind the bar. It was perfect, matching his sleep-blackened eyes and gaunt expression. He nodded and strode onto the stage.

He felt nothing.

What was he supposed to feel? Excitement, sadness, resignation? This was Lucifer Sam's last gig, and he felt none of those things. He felt empty, like a vessel waiting to be filled.

Johnny was tuning his guitar next to him, Ned settling down at his drum stool and fiddling with his cymbals. Davey sauntered on, all badass in his ripped leathers and wolfish appearance, wraparound shades in place.

Kirk held the mic stand and stared at the small crowd that nevertheless filled the pub. Thirty or forty people. Most of them were probably fans of Deathshadow, he reasoned. They certainly couldn't be following The Sam after their disastrous gig from the other week in The Bridge

House.

He didn't recognize any of the punters. A lot of Goths, understandably enough, thanks to the Death Rockers from Hamburg's presence; some older blokes come along for the crack, bored of their wives on a Monday night probably; a couple of chavs in their tracksuits and baseball caps. And one girl who had jostled herself to the front of the crowd. He'd noticed her earlier while she danced to Deathshadow. You couldn't fail to notice her; she wore a skimpy leather mini dress and a skimpier leather halter top that allowed her considerable charms to explode from the bra beneath. Her limbs swathed in colorful gothic tattoos, her long dark hair was twisted up and backcombed. She held Kirk in a steadfast gaze, eyes kohled with purple allurement, lips strawberry bliss. Kirk had watched her distractedly as she writhed to the riffs, but his mind had been on Rose. He had seen the way Johnny's gaze was fixed on her though.

But for once Johnny's rock-'n'-roll good looks weren't winning the day, and Kirk could have taken a small satisfaction from that if it hadn't been for the fact he no longer gave a fuck. This rock chick was obviously a frontman-only fan.

They started fast and hard with "Curse of the Screaming Dead." If Kirk was surprised at the tightness of the band, then he didn't let it show. His vocals were in time, his tone deep and raunchy. He knew immediately that the band had been looking to him to set the tone of the gig, and here he was doing just that. The frontman doing what he did best. Johnny's solo was precise and played with undeniable gusto. Davey stalked the small space in front of the audience, a Werewolf Sid Vicious, head cocked to one side, sneer cutting through his bristles. Ned let hell loose on his drums.

After the first song, Kirk threw a look behind him. Ned nodded, lips pouting in surprised approval. Johnny flicked him a razor-blade smile. Kirk nodded slowly, aware that the rock chick's eyes had never left him. Her lips were pouted like Ned's, but rather more suggestively, and a hell of a lot more attractively.

And Kirk felt something.

Maybe it had been there all along. Maybe it just needed some coaxing. He felt a flame flicker in his heart. A wildness sprang up, fueling his tired muscles, his flagging spirit. He thought of Rose, masturbating on the sofa, and the same rampant excitement he felt earlier flooded him again. His blood filled with the music.

But *what* music? Lucifer Sam's or...

He didn't care. If Rose's new album had given him the kick up the ass he needed, then he would run with it, thank you very much. He suddenly felt so fucking alive...

When they launched into "Electric Chair Blues," it was the best they'd ever played, the best *he* had ever performed. There was a vibe in the air, and he snatched it down and made it his own. He felt elated with the darkness of that vibe (of course it was dark, it had to be) and let it despoil his mind and body with its glorious filth. He would take from it and throw it back when he was done. He would take from *them*, borrow some of the evil in a jar he'd unscrewed with Rose earlier that afternoon, and then he'd slam the lid back on and close it tight. Rock music had been called evil a million times before, but Kirk knew that had always been a fundamentalist, bible-belt reaction, the resistance to unbridled youth and all the challenges to conformity that brought with it. But right here in this shitty little boozer in Spittalfields, Kirk recognized the stark Bacchanalian delights to be found in unfettered sonic Evil and reveled in its cruelty and chaos. For one night only, of course.

And the crowd was loving it. Kirk stared at them as he prowled the front of the small stage. He scanned their excited, eager faces. They wanted this. They *needed* it. It felt like his gift to them. The gift of release. From all the tribulations and mundanities of their day-to-day existence.

"Sundel Bolong," a ten-minute exercise in spider-guitar dread, packing a chorus that lifted the crowd's hair and tickled their spines. Then "Bones of Dreams," lilting, whimsy horror, absurd lyrics of prostitute skulls bobbing in the lake and all.

Kirk had them.

Lucifer Sam had them.

The slinky girl in the leather two-piece was gyrating madly. Her breasts were practically popping from their cups now, her head thrown back in ecstasy. Kirk sang the next song, "Under a Java Moon," to her, but he saw Rose dancing in her place.

By the time they crashed into their finale, "Yours Truly, Jack the Ripper," Kirk was sure the small pub would collapse around their ears. The entire crowd was leaping and writhing, sweat running down their faces and bare arms. Johnny chopped out rhythms with a gleeful crack of a smile. Davey pounded his bass, stomping back and forth like a furious bear. Ned demolished his drum kit, eyes wide and delirious. And Kirk garroted the vocals, imitating a Vaudevillian version of Jack as he spewed forth the lyrics.

Come with me to London Town
A hundred years ago
Meet the Whitechapel Romeo
Likes a quickie down Buck's Row

Kirk looked around wildly at the period wainscoting and old stone walls as he sang. Beyond the windows with their niter-stained mullions, he could see a woman leaning against an alley wall leading off Commercial Street. She was dressed in a short skirt and leopard-print top, fishnets and high heels. She looked patient. The more things change, the more they stay the same… Kirk smirked at the appropriateness of it all and finished the final chorus to a massive cheer.

"That was our final gig," he announced.

A moment's silence, a blank, collective stare of disbelief, then a wild disavowal. A rejection of his words.

Kirk smiled at the reaction. For it was good.

"That was the final gig…" he repeated, glancing around at his fellow band members as they froze, looking for their cues from him as ever, "…of the Old Lucifer Sam. The new one is just beginning."

The girl in the black leather halter was staring at him in open adulation.

He bowed to her, to them all, and walked offstage to get a drink.

Chapter Twenty-Three

Her name was Jessica, and she wanted him.

She cornered him against the bar as he sat on a stool that felt suddenly like a throne. She told him he was the best singer, and Lucifer Sam was the best band. She told him his music had transformed her as the rest of the crowd pushed forward to talk to Kirk and the rest of the band, who were leaning against the bar accepting free drinks with a general sense of amazement.

Kirk didn't argue with her. He didn't know what had happened, but he had felt transformed himself. The band had fallen into line with his new-found zeal. Lucifer Sam had truly found itself, whether for one night only or not.

When she tried to kiss him, he gently held her back. He thanked her for all her enthusiasm and told her she was beautiful (she was), but he had someone already (did he? Did he really?).

"Melons! Squeeze those juicy tits!" Perfect. Ned had noticed Kirk's new friend and had interjected at the most sensitive moment. "Sorry, nothing personal," the drummer grinned disarmingly at Jessica. He was still buzzing from the gig, and his Tourette's didn't know what to do with itself. She smiled back, equally disarmingly.

When Johnny tried to move in to take up the baton, she thanked Kirk for being a gentleman and left the pub. Johnny watched her go in amazement.

"You turned her down?" He seemed genuinely confused. "How the fuck could you do that?"

Kirk turned to him, the elation of the gig still coursing through his veins. "Because I'm in love with someone. And because I'm not you, Johnny."

Ned interrupted their conversation impatiently, his face still infused with disbelief. "What the fuck happened tonight?" He stared at Kirk like he didn't recognize him anymore.

Kirk stared back, shrugged, and grinned wildly. "I don't know, Nedders. If you find out, pass it along to me."

"You were fuckin' good tonight." Davey had pushed through the throng of well-wishers. He gave Kirk a playful slap on the cheek. "What was it? Coke? Speed? Pills?"

Kirk shook his head silently in answer. He didn't…know. He didn't know what had happened.

And he didn't want to analyze it too closely just in case he found out.

That Lucifer Sam would continue was something of a no-brainer. They could all agree on that. The band was rejuvenated, *recreated* in a blitz of almost evangelical rock 'n' roll fire in the old Ten Bells that night. Kirk felt the flames of new-found zeal still burning in his blood the next day as he set about promoting a new set of gigs in venues he wouldn't have dreamed of approaching the day before. And with the help of Archie, the Ten Bells landlord, who acted as an invaluable and enthusiastic reference, he secured most of them.

And now here he was on the way to Johnny's flat after a long, tiring, but fulfilling day of negotiating, mostly by phone, but also on foot. You could never underestimate the power of footwork, of personal approaches. He had some great photos of the gig the night before, too, courtesy of his new Facebook friend, Jessica, who had forwarded a plethora of snaps of an enraptured audience and a wild-looking performance that didn't hurt Kirk's negotiating efforts. But beyond all that, he felt empowered, more confident than he had in a long, long time. The zeal showed in his face. Not many promoters turned him down.

So, all in all, he was in a damned good mood when he thumbed Johnny's bell and waited for an answer. He wanted to share the good news in person. Lucifer Sam was a legitimate project again.

Johnny didn't answer the door, but Kirk saw a shadow move away from the ground-floor flat window.

"What you hiding for, you pillock," he barked into the grille as he pushed the bell again. "Got good news…"

The buzzer sounded, and the door popped open.

Johnny opened his own door in a dressing gown, looking disheveled. Behind him, his flat was dark.

"Not hiding," he announced, averting Kirk's gaze. "Just not feeling too good. Been in bed all day." He led Kirk through to the kitchen, glancing quickly at the closed door of his bedroom as he passed.

"So what's the good news?" Johnny said, trying to sound bright. As he turned to fill the kettle from the kitchen tap, the late-afternoon sunlight fell through the window onto his chiseled face. Kirk looked at the long, ragged scratch that ran along one cheekbone, fresh, the groove still smudged with blood.

Kirk's hand rose unconsciously to his own scratch even as the music started up from Johnny's bedroom. He recognized the dark, nasty vibe immediately.

"Someone's playing the new Cat CD, Johnny. In *your* bedroom."

Johnny looked at his toes, shrugged, started to raise his gaze, then dropped it again.

Kirk raised both hands in a shrugging gesture. He stepped back into the hallway just as someone pushed open the bedroom door.

Kirk stared at her, and his world fell away. He was dropping with it, and there was no soft landing.

She was smiling at him. She leaned against the door jamb provocatively, completely naked.

"Hello, Kirky…"

Inarticulate, Kirk sagged back against a wall.

"I brought my CD 'round for darling Johnny to hear…" She stuck out her breasts as she said his name. "I think he likes it. Even more than you did."

Johnny had moved into the hall now, looking sick. "Put some clothes on, Rosie," he said weakly, still looking down. "Have a bit of decency."

"Decency?" Rose repeated it like it was an obscenity, her mouth twisted. She moved up to the guitarist, her hand exploring under his dressing gown. "You didn't want me to be *decent* before…"

A wave of darkness swirled over Kirk. It all felt unreal, like he'd blundered into somebody else's nightmare, not his own. He felt distanced from it. He watched Johnny push her away like he was watching a film. He saw Rose lift her hand to Johnny's face as if to stroke it, and saw the fingers curl into claws to scratch again. Johnny yelped at this new affront to his good looks, but the damage was already done. Rose pushed past him into the kitchen, her buttocks still shiny with her previous bedroom exertions.

Johnny's cry of pain roused Kirk a little. He pushed himself from the wall, Cat O' Nine Tails pounding his ears, his brain, and Rose, his Rosie, was out of the kitchen now, a wicked blade clasped in her hand.

"Peer through an open window to hell," she said as she advanced on the two men, kitchen knife clutched in front of her, eyes wide, and at first Kirk thought she was talking to him before he realized her words matched those spewed forth by Baz Cropper from the CD player in the bedroom.

"Love is an abyss, death is your friend. Peer through a window to hell, then down to Hades we'll wend." She laughed raucously, as if reading Kirk's thoughts. *Yes, you pedantic prick. They might be a very, very different band now, truly the Devil's Minstrels, but their lyrics are still just as shit as ever.*

"Did you know they're putting on a secret show?" she trilled with laughter. "A secret show just for me…" She lunged without warning, her knife cutting through Johnny's dressing gown and just missing the skin of his chest. Then she was through the door of Johnny's flat and across the lobby and out the main exit.

Kirk froze for one second more. Johnny stared directly at him for the first time since his unexpected arrival. "She's gone insane, mate! I—"

Kirk wasn't listening. He spun and ran from the flat, following his girlfriend. Following Rose.

She was running down Bethnal Green Road, completely naked and waving a kitchen knife. People were getting the fuck out of her way. Even some of the men who were stopping to gaze in amazed appreciation of this rare sight made no move to intercept her. Why should they?

She pushed a gaggle of women in burkhas out of the way, slashed at the white-bearded Muslim man who remonstrated with her until he cowered in a vegetable shop doorway. The women scattered across the street and Rose pounded on. And she was still singing.

Kirk was barely ten yards behind her now. She didn't look back as she hacked at a couple of young Asian men who were whooping in derision and delight at her nakedness. They soon stopped whooping and ducked behind a parked Mazda. Rose ran on, reaching the end of the road and, without hesitating, hurled herself down the steps to Bethnal Green Tube Station.

Kirk lost her for a second as he swung around the rail and down the steps, but he heard screams ahead, and someone pushed into him, clawing him out of the way frantically, knocking him down on the steps.

Kirk disentangled himself from the elderly man and leaped down the rest of the stairs just in time to see Rose skip past a London Underground security man and over the barrier. The man shouted after her but seemed more intent on watching her pert, naked arse than making any real moves to prevent her.

Kirk passed the man who was now barking into his RT. He copied Rose's action, hurtling over the gate without bothering to grope for his Oyster card.

He heard the man shouting after him, but Kirk was more intent on Rose as she threw herself onto the downward-moving escalator, her knife jabbing and hacking at anyone in her way.

Kirk followed relentlessly. People were shrieking and attempting to stumble back up the escalator to escape Rose, preventing Kirk from making much progress. He squeezed past the panicking commuters as the escalator bore him to the lower concourse. Rose was already streaking away again.

She opted for the Eastbound platform. He saw her dance through a knot of confused and instantly terrified people and out onto the platform just as a train hissed into view. Kirk came after, pushing through the people eager to avoid the naked madwoman.

"Mind the gap." Rose slashed her own gap through those remaining few people still unaware of her presence as the train doors parted to release new victims for her blade.

Most of them crowded back inside the carriage, instantly thinking better of any plan to emerge, but one big black man hopped off, a big grin plastered on his face as he took in Rose's naked delights, seemingly oblivious to the knife she was also sporting.

She lunged, shrieking at him, and made his grin wider as the tip of the sharp knife took him inside the mouth and peeled away a portion of his lip. His screams drowned out hers as he collapsed onto the platform. Rose leaped over him and onto the train. Kirk followed. The train lurched into motion again, the station drifting away past the windows. Rose had gripped one of the ceiling handles and was swinging on it one handed now, still singing to herself, the blade flashing around her. Some passengers huddled back in their seats, terrified. Still more pushed toward the rear of the carriage, opening the door to flee to the next.

Surely security had contacted the driver by now? The train would be stopped soon. Armed police would be on their way. That thought was even more terrifying than seeing Rose like this. He remembered the incident with the Brazilian gunned down by police in the wake of the July 2007 Underground bombings. They wouldn't hesitate to put her down.

He grabbed a handle not far from her and regained his breath. She seemed oblivious to him. She was leaning down to stare at an old woman cowering in a corner seat, her knitting unraveling in her lap.

"Rose…" he called, still panting.

Her head twitched to one side. He saw her beautiful eyes stretched in madness. Her mouth worked saliva as she hissed out the lyrics.

"Love you in the mourning, love you to death. Be mine, in your hearse of lust, be mine in the twilight time." She threw her head back, reveling in the music still in her head. Reveling? No. Pleasure was one thing she was not deriving from the silent tune in her head. Kirk could see that in the empty horror of her irises, the agonized tautness of her cheekbones.

"Rose…"

She turned to face him then. Her mouth was slack. She held the knife out, warning him off.

"It's me, Rosie. It's Kirk." He felt a sob coming and forced it back. His eyes brimmed with tears. She looked confused, tilted her head birdlike.

"I can help you, Rosie..." The tears were tracking down his cheeks.

She narrowed her eyes and released the ceiling handle, falling back against the old woman, who wailed in terror. Rose held both hands over her ears as she rocked against the pensioner, the knife clutched against the side of her face. "I can't..." she whispered hoarsely, her voice barely audible over the tumult from the frightened passengers. But Kirk heard it. "I can't...get it out...of my head... I can't get it *out!!*" She looked up at him, her face twisted with desolation and pain. "It'll never come out. *Never!!*" She opened her mouth wide, and her last words were a full-throttle scream that silenced the babble from the carriage. "I CAN'T GET IT OUTTTTTT!!!!!"

The knife dropped from her hand. Kirk was about to leap forward and seize her, but he was too slow. Always too slow. Too slow to prevent his girlfriend from sleeping with his one-time best friend, too slow to stop her following the course that had led her to this. Too slow in protecting her from the Devil's Minstrels. Certainly too slow to stop her from snatching the sharp knitting needles from the old lady's lap and jamming them repeatedly into her own ears as if in time to a rabid riff.

By the time he'd managed to wrestle her to the floor and tear them away from her, the needles were slick with her blood. She lay passively beneath him now, eyes fixed in a stare that stretched along all the corridors of time but would never reach him again. She lay naked beneath him in a parody of lovemaking on the dirty carriage floor as the tube came to a halt at last, blood gluing her cheek to Kirk's own as he clutched her tightly, so tightly, her lips moving silently against his ear as she continued to mouth the lyrics of the damned.

CD 4

THE SECOND COMING

Chapter Twenty-Four

Kirk was staring numbly at the bland pictures on the hospital refectory wall while he waited for Gull to return from the counter.

She had left Trimble outside. She needed to be delicate, tactful even, and the detective constable didn't understand those concepts. She glanced over at the young man as she waited for the two lattes the café assistant was taking her time making. He looked like a little boy trapped in a disheveled man's body. Cooked up quite a thousand-yard stare there. Just like his girlfriend.

Gull thought of Rose Amberley now alone again in her secure ward upstairs. The sight of her had rattled her. Yes, even the Bitch of Bethnal Green had her weak points. Seeing the vacant-eyed beauty with the mutilated eardrums had pressed all of them.

Of course, she would be consigned to a mental facility for the foreseeable future. But it could have been a lot worse, Gull reflected. There had been many injuries suffered from Rose's madly swinging blade, but fortunately no fatalities. Except one. Staring into Rose's bottomless eyes had unnerved the policewoman more than she could explain.

When the call came into the station about a naked mad woman slashing up commuters, Gull's first reaction was to leave it to the uniform boys. It wasn't until she happened to glance at the name of the boyfriend involved on the incident report that she'd suddenly taken an interest. The name had been familiar, and it had taken her a moment or two to remember why. Kirk Stammers. An odd name. Which is probably why it had stuck in her mind after Bill Ticer mentioned it to Gull when she spoke to him in the offices of *Rock!!* The singer of a struggling rock band, Ticer had quoted his paranoid theories regarding Cat O' Nine Tails and suggested she should speak to him. It had taken her a while, but now she was doing just that. Call it a police woman's gut instinct, or whatever, but she felt he had a wider story to tell than just a domestic case of insanity.

She took the two mugs from the assistant and carried them over to Kirk.

He said nothing when Gull placed the cup in front of him.

"I'm sorry," she said. And she meant it. Kirk barely blinked.

"I'm sorry about your girlfriend. I really am."

For a moment she thought he wasn't going to say anything.

"How sorry?"

"Beg your pardon?" He was still staring at the wall.

"Exactly how sorry are you? Sorry enough to actually *do* something about it?" Slowly, he turned his deep gaze on her. Although it wasn't the first time she'd looked into his eyes that day, it still carried a live-wire shock. Yes, this man had a tale to tell alright. Or was that a Tail? The pieces of the jigsaw were coming together in a way she didn't like. He was about to add some more to the frame, and she wasn't at all sure she wanted him to.

"You tell me exactly what it is you want me to do…"

His eyes didn't waver. "I think you already know."

"Do I?" This could go on all day. "Why don't you make it nice and simple and explain exactly how you think Cat O' Nine Tails are involved in your girlfriend's unfortunate circumstances." That had been the first thing he'd said when the Firearms Unit had arrived, along with the Paramedics. *"It's them,"* he'd babbled as they had loaded him aboard the ambulance outside the station, together with his now-restrained girlfriend. She'd read the report comprehensively: *"Cat O' Nine. They did this. They're gonna do it to a lot more if you don't stop them."*

For an answer, he pushed a tabloid newspaper along the table toward her.

She glanced down at the front page.

RASH OF HOMICIDES AND SELF-HARM INCIDENTS ROCK THE UK

She didn't bother to read the entire article. She'd already seen a similar report in another paper that morning.

She nodded and looked up at him. "And you think this band is responsible for all this?"

He didn't answer. His level gaze bored into her head. She shrugged. "Maybe it's the time of month. Nutters like a full moon, you know."

No reaction to that, not that it deserved one. Last time she'd looked out the window at night, there had been a half moon floating above London, and that had only been two days ago. "Okay, so there have been an unprecedented number of cases recently. It doesn't mean—and after all, how could it?—that the band is responsible for that. You'll be blaming them for the weather next."

He ignored her flippancy. Like he knew she almost believed him and was doing everything she could to prevent herself. Which was silly, of course. Wasn't it? She remembered interviewing Cropper. The fear he had aroused in her. She pictured his wife's corpse in the bath.

He tapped the newspaper. "Notice the pattern? Incidents of rape, murder, and self-harm have tripled since the start of the month, which was only just over a week ago, and it just happens to coincide with the release of their new album. Believe it." The way he was watching her, she somehow knew he suspected she already did.

"This is just paranoia, honey," she said brusquely. "Music doesn't influence people." Even as she said it, she knew it was possibly the lamest thing she'd ever uttered. Usually, she was the commanding presence in any interview. Recently (and she could pinpoint exactly when that started happening), she'd felt like she was the one being interrogated, with no rug left to place her high heels on.

"Try telling that to Charlie's family," he said.

She laughed to hide her discomfort at this role reversal. "I think Manson used more than his guitar to sway his disciples."

"You think so? Maybe. But they grooved to his nasty little tunes nevertheless. And look what they did."

She shook her head. If Trimble were here, maybe she could have asserted a bit more authority. He was her signpost to rationality. Her mundane rock. She took a big gulp of her latte. "So how's the band doing it, in your opinion? I mean, for the sake of argument, let's say they *are* bent on civil unrest, or whatever the hell it is you're suggesting. How the hell does that work? Listening to a band's music can't send you mad…" She thought again of Sheila Cropper in the tub, the scissors that had cut off her own ears still clutched in one hand, the CD-R in the other.

She could tell Kirk had noticed her sudden uncertainty. He leaned forward.

"Nobody else has joined the dots yet. Even these rags haven't seized on the sensational possibilities. But I'm one-hundred percent certain that if you checked on every incident in here…" He jabbed the front page again. "…you would find a copy of a brand-new CD lying around in the home of those involved." He raised his eyebrows to emphasize his point.

Gull stifled the dubious laugh. She felt suddenly cold and bereft not just of authority but confidence.

"You need to do that check. Then you'll see I'm right. You need to do it, and then stop this CD from being pressed, stop it from being released. Get it out of the fucking shops."

This time she couldn't stop an indignant snort. "You think I have the power to prevent an enormously powerful company like EMI from releasing products? If I even suggested it, I would end up directing traffic quicker than you cut your toenails, sonny." She was back on safer ground now. If there was one thing DS Gull was very sure of, that was her relatively lowly position in the hierarchical edifice that was Modern British Society.

He shook his head dismissively. He pushed the untouched coffee away from him and stood up. "Then you're wasting my time, as well as yours. Gonna have to do it my way."

"Hold it right there, Frank," she barked. He glared down at her in obvious contempt. "I said I was sorry about your girl, and I meant it. And if there's anything to what you say, it *will* come out, believe me. But I can't have you playing vigilante. What you gonna do, bust into every record store and confiscate the stock?"

Kirk fixed her with his deep stare for a moment longer and then turned away. She watched him wait by the lift, thumbing the button for the second floor where he had left Rose half an hour before. When the doors closed on him, DS Gull put her cold coffee down and picked up the newspaper.

Fuck this bollocks. She got up to join Trimble in the Merc outside.

Chapter Twenty-Five

The boozer was the same, but now things were very different.

For a start, the last time Kirk and the rest of Lucifer Sam had a band meeting in the Three Lamps, Rose had been here with them.

Kirk was very much aware of this absence. And it fueled his cold, contained fury. And fury was strength.

The others sat around the table in dismal silence. They had all expressed their condolences, their hopes that Rose would recover some day...and Kirk had winced more with each good intention. Recover? If they had looked into her eyes as he had done, they would realize how ineffectual that word was. If they had looked at the scabbed wounds of her ears, they would have drunk their beer and shut up.

Johnny, of course, looked the most uncomfortable of all. He had not been able to meet Kirk's gaze once, although he had attempted to express how sincerely sorry he was over everything that had happened. Kirk's contempt for him was boundless. The first time he'd tried, when he turned up at the hospital in the vain hope that he would be received with something other than overt hostility, Kirk had slammed him up against the corridor wall outside Rose's ward. He hadn't said anything. He could see by Johnny's face that the guitarist regretted everything, but what did regret matter to Kirk? How would remorse fix Rose's mind?

Over the last two days, Kirk had grown to accept the fact he couldn't blame the guitarist for that, of course. But it didn't stop him from loathing him deeply.

He stared at Johnny, now pale and furtive-looking, his gaze lowered to the table top like social inadequacy was his last claim to style. How could Rose have fallen for *that?*

He forced himself to focus. He needed all their attention, all their suspension of disbelief if he was going to succeed in convincing them.

They would listen, of course; maybe even pretend to go along with his theories. They wouldn't want to upset him even more after what he had gone through. But would they really accept his claims?

If his plan of action was going to succeed, he needed them to not only accept what he had to say but commit one-hundred percent to help him achieve it.

Plan of action? The desperate, delusional schemes of a madman, more like. And who was to say *he* hadn't been contaminated, too, albeit to a lesser degree than Rose? Had he not been exposed to the CD himself as he cavorted with Rose on the sofa?

He took a long gulp of beer and suppressed the thought. He was still rational. Barely, maybe, but he had not succumbed yet. And, of course, he hadn't listened to the hellish CD as many times as Rose...

He put down his pint and picked up the tabloid, held out today's front page for them all to see.

The headline declared an increase in the inexplicable, wholesale outrages, homicides, and mutilations.

"It's spreading," he said, watching their expressions carefully. "Every day there's more."

They knew about his dark obsession with Cat O' Nine, of course; Rose had passed it on. *Probably to Johnny as they slept together.* Ned and Davey were all too aware already because of Kirk's previous declamations against the "dubious nature" of the band since they had returned from their long Flight to Nowhere. And then there were his voyeuristic activities on the fire escape in Whitechapel. They were aware of that, too, and it wouldn't help his cause. They would see it as more paranoia. They would give him a sympathy fuck, so to speak, but they wouldn't truly embrace his aims.

He pressed on. "Let's agree for the sake of—for Rose's sake, for *my* sake—that these incidents are all related and that Cat O' Nine are the cause. Let's just accept that for now. I'll get you your proof—or maybe you'll see it for yourself. But for now you just have to take my word for it. Even the police are listening..." Was that true? Gull had looked uncomfortable, like she definitely had her own suspicions, but she certainly hadn't gone anywhere near conceding his point of view.

"But even though they might suspect the band of something—and God knows there's enough reason for them to do so, what with dead groupies, dead engineers, dead wives, and dead journalists all with the same band in common—despite all this, they still won't act. They *can't* act. Not without proof. Cat O' Nine are too powerful, too embedded in the system. They've got EMI's lawyers behind them, their financial gears nicely oiled from releasing the CD nationwide."

Ned chose that moment to interrupt, the only one to really sound as though he was paying proper attention to Kirk's possibly grief-induced ramblings. "Nationwide? Did they not release the CD all around the world, then? And if they did, is this pattern of homicides repeated globally?" His right shoulder rose in a Tourette's tic as if to emphasize the question.

Kirk dropped the paper. "I checked this. The CD was premiered exclusively in a limited UK release. For one week before going worldwide. Which would be the day after the Wembley gig."

"Why do that? Doesn't make commercial sense."

Kirk nodded. "Could be to trial it," he said gravely. "Evaluate the results here first. See how effective the CD is..."

"Pretty much so, if your theory about these deaths being connected is true..."

Davey couldn't restrain himself any longer. He'd been good; he'd lasted ten minutes out of respect to Kirk and Rose. "For fuck's sake! Listen to yourselves. This is so much hog bollocks! I'm sorry, Kirk. I love you, man, and I'm so fucking gutted about what happened to Rose, but you cannot be fuckin' serious. You make the twats who bang on about Hollywood being the only fuckers to land on the moon sound rational."

He sighed in evident frustration.

If he had expected Kirk to act defensively, he was to be surprised. "I know that, Davey," the singer said slowly, patiently, but with a cold trace to his words that carried conviction. "I know exactly how this all sounds. You either go with me on this or you don't. I'm not forcing this down anyone's throat. But I'll tell you this: Cat O' Nine Tails is evil. I'm not talking in a God and Devil religious sort of evil. I'm talking about evil in a way I don't think we can ever understand…a pure essence of malignance. And if that sounds like I've been reading too much H.P. Lovecraft, then there's nothing more I can say. So I'll need to *show* you. I'll get visual evidence of what they are capable of. A record of the harm they do. Then you have to act with me, or this whole fucking country is going down the pan. Anarchy in the UK is coming, and we ain't gonna want to pogo to it."

He paused. He could see his words, so calmly spoken, yet carrying all the icy fury that had lodged in his heart over the last few days, had impressed them.

"And how you gonna do that? Get evidence, I mean?" Ned's face held no disbelief, only grave concern, which a sudden twitch of his Tourette's did nothing to lessen.

Kirk paused. "I'll get to that in a moment. First, I need you to understand how important it is we stop these fuckers. And to do that, I also need you to understand how dangerous their music is. It's not just a case of stopping people from listening to the CD. They've also lined up a massive gig at Wembley Arena next week. Tickets are already sold out."

Ned looked confused. He tapped the table top idly as he tried to keep up with Kirk. He looked as if he was genuinely trying to grasp the singer's mad theories. "So if the music on the CD is as deadly as you say," he began, choosing his words carefully, "then why the need to perform a concert? Surely everyone who attends will already have listened to the CD? And if you're right, they'll already have been…" He looked uncomfortable, obviously thinking of Rose, "…affected."

Kirk was ready for him. He leaned forward, anxious to hammer this point home. "My idea is the CD isn't powerful enough to affect everyone who listens to it, or at least not all in the same way and not all in the same time period. Some might only be subliminally affected, like..." He grimaced sardonically. "...like me, when Rose played it in our flat. Yet I can't honestly say I didn't feel weird afterward. In fact, I could even go so far as to lay the success of that whole bloody Ten Bells gig down to being fired up by their shit. It was in my blood, contaminating me. I can still feel it, but now it's turned to anger. And I only heard a couple of tracks. Johnny..." He suddenly turned his gaze on the guitarist. "...maybe you heard more when Rose came to call..." His voice had collected shards of ice.

Johnny shook his head quickly, slammed his empty glass down. "No. I-she... No. Couple of tracks, too. Maybe. Same as you." He had gone very pale. His eyes suddenly looked haunted. Kirk was glad of that. He hoped he would feel some of the self-doubt and fear he was going through himself. The bastard.

Kirk let it go. "Then there's the variation psychiatrically," he continued. "Some people might be able to resist the CD to a certain extent. Maybe those with certain mental traits, those with less or more vivid imaginations, perhaps, have differing reactions. Or maybe hormones or individual brain waves can be a factor. And then, as I just said, there's the amount of exposure, of course." He thought of Rose listening to the CD for hours, lying on that sofa. And how many other times had she let its venom pour into her ears when he wasn't around? He braced himself to carry on. "And the question of delayed reaction... Rose didn't... She wasn't..." He stopped, looked down, then up at them again, forcing himself through this. "She didn't lose it all straight away. It was a more gradual corruption in her case, over a day or two." He dared them to comment. Nobody did. "A live gig will be a whole different proposition, in my mind. A platform for the band to deliver unadulterated evil in sonic form. There will be no defense for the unprepared."

Davey cleared his throat. "That's the biggest fucking speech I've ever heard you make. I'm fuckin' impressed, mate. And if what you're saying is true, we're all fucked. But listen, I'm far from sold, man. *Far* from sold. If I didn't love you, if I didn't feel for you and Rose, I would say..."

"What would you say, Davey?" Kirk leveled his gaze on the scruffy bassist.

"I would cry, 'Acid casualty.' I would say all those 'shrooms you took back in the day have finally caught up with you, Kirk, my friend. There's a delayed reaction I can believe in."

"Fair comment. And we're back to the matter of proof." He rummaged in his jacket pocket and pulled out Rose's mobile.

"I've never gone through her phone before." They didn't question him on that point. It seemed so trivial now. "But after what she told us at Johnny's flat..." He let his eyes settle coldly on the guitarist, who promptly grabbed his Jack Daniels and took a long sip. "...I decided to drop my principles."

"She said they're putting on a secret gig... a 'secret show just for me.' And I couldn't figure out what she meant until I went through her messages." This time he didn't even bother looking at Johnny. "There was one recent text that I found pretty interesting..."

He hesitated. "Interesting" wasn't really the appropriate word. "It turns out the secret show wasn't for her after all. Actually, her friend Sarah was going to be one of the special guests for that little party. Seems like there was a lottery drawn for lucky Cat fans to attend an unadvertised, pre-Wembley gig at the 100 Club this Thursday. That's two days' time. Only members of the online fan club were eligible. Lucky for Rose, she didn't win." He could hear the hard, bitter edge in his own voice. The others were listening attentively now.

"But Sarah did. And Sarah, being a good friend, decided to give up her ticket to Rose, seeing as she knew how much the band meant to her."

He had to stop now and take a long, deep drink. It took him a while to cool the rage, and the alcohol was only partially successful.

"My spin on the secret show is this: it's another trial, like the CD, this time presumably to test out the power of the music live. The 100 Club is ideal for their purpose: small, intimate, a showcase in front of a 'selected' fan group. A nice little warm-up, you might say, and I'm sure they could find a way to put a lid on the results. Remember, they belong to a massive record company with limitless resources. They could spin the incident anyway they wanted. Blame any aftermath on drugs, gangs, whatever. Of course, it would be ridiculously dangerous for one of us to crash this gig with Sarah's ticket. But maybe if we used the proper pro-tection…"

"Protection?" Davey was beginning to sneer but thought better of it.

"Earplugs. Yes, it sounds crazy. And they might not be enough to stop whatever the band throws at the brave fucker who tries it. But some-one has to get the proof. So I thought if *I* go, earplugs in place, and film the gig on my phone… "

"You're right," Ned interrupted. "It does sound crazy. Which is why you ain't doing it."

"I'm the obvious choice," Kirk replied.

"They'd recognize you. They'll remember you from the HMV signing you went to with Davey. And they might know about Rose… It made the papers, remember. They could guess you're after them. No, there's only one obvious choice."

"You think I would allow that?"

"You think you got a choice?"

Johnny stood up. He paused, then said, "I'll go."

Kirk said nothing. Ned looked unsure. One arm rose in a salute-like tic.

"Then it's decided," the guitarist said. And for the first time in two days, he met Kirk's gaze.

Chapter Twenty-Six

Kirk was on the bus to Canning Town when he got the first text from Johnny.

At the 100 Club. Forgot my earplugs.

Kirk cursed out loud. A young mother with a child looked around at him in disgust. Kirk ignored her. He texted back immediately: *Abort. Get out of there and find some plugs.*

He sighed. He knew the stubborn guitarist would do no such thing. Of course, he wouldn't; not for the first time, the realization that the rest of Lucifer Sam was just playing lip service to his mad-sounding theories passed through his mind. Additionally, Johnny was too damn lazy to go home again just to get plugs. But then, wouldn't Kirk have done the same in his position?

Yeah, sure, came the unconvincing reply text.

His thumbs went to work: *I'm not fucking joking. Do NOT expose yourself to their sound unprotected!* Kirk's text sounded concerned, but didn't a part of him exult at the thought of Johnny sailing into danger? He would be lying if he said no. He would never forgive the guitarist. Never.

Johnny's next text injected a note of banter that belied the guilt he must still be feeling: *You've won first prize in both the double entendre and mixed metaphor comps. Well done.*

Kirk realized he was wasting his time. He considered changing buses and making his way to the 100 Club despite Ned's misgivings about his presence being too obvious at the gig. But was he being too paranoid? There would be at least a hundred people at the gig. He might not be spotted.

Except he knew he would. There was no doubt their roadie of choice would be there. Deuce had already prevented him from gaining access to the band's premises once, after seeing him at the HMV signing where he, Davey, and Rose had clashed with Cat O' Nine; Deuce knew him of old and would throw him out in an instant.

So he would just have to let Johnny go through with it, plugs or no plugs. He considered calling Ned and getting him to haul his ass up to Oxford Street with a spare pair but dismissed that idea, too. The band was already stretching their credulity and patience with him this far; he couldn't expect Ned to jump at his every whim. And there would be questions, too…like why couldn't Kirk take them himself?

And the answer to that was something he didn't really want to go into just yet…at least not until tonight's mission was over and he could share with the band how successful it had been. Or not.

It wasn't going to be easy. It might take a few days to accomplish his goal. But he knew he had to start now.

So he stayed where he was on the 276 bus from Stoke Newington to Canning Town. If he managed to find the person he was looking for, it was going to be a *very* interesting night.

Johnny nursed his pint, reading Kirk's latest text with a shake of the head. *Don't be a wanker as well as a cunt. Last warning: leave.*

Prick! Johnny didn't bother replying, shoving the phone back in his pocket. The dude had serious issues. Okay, things were bad for him at the moment; his missus got fucked by his supposed best mate and was now losing her mind through stress. Major guilt for Johnny. Big anxiety for Kirk. Yeah, get that. But this delusion about Cat O' Nine… Fuck's sake, drop me out.

Johnny was standing just behind one of the pillars that supported the ceiling of the small club. He wondered whether it was the same one Sid Vicious threw a pint against in 1977, aiming for Dave Vanian, the Damned's singer who had been on stage at the time. A girl had been blinded in the process by a shard of glass. Clever Sid.

The band would be on in a minute. The sense of excitement in the club was building. The audience consisted of more women than Johnny would have guessed; he'd always assumed Cat O' Nine Tails was followed by the usual battalion of denim- and leather-clad males that were to be found in attendance at most metal gigs, although there were plenty of those, too. The small club was full to capacity.

He took another sip and glanced around, hoping to catch the eye of some of the more attractive females in the crush. If he was being sent on this fool's errand, then he preferred it not to be a total waste of time.

Rose resurfaced in his mind. He felt another smart of guilt and slurped at his beer hurriedly, washing away her face. His mood darkened. Although he hadn't seen her in her traumatized state at the hospital (Kirk had been emphatic about preventing that), he had heard how bad she was. What did it take to drive knitting needles through your own eardrums? Maybe there *was* something to what Kirk was saying about this band...

Bollocks. Kirk was just looking for someone to blame for his girlfriend's instability. Kirk had been playing second fiddle to Cat O' Nine Tails in his relationship with Rose all along. Or was that third fiddle, since Johnny came a-playin'?

Fuck this. He finished his pint and was deciding whether to buy himself another when the roadie Kirk knew (Ace, Deuce, whatever?) ambled on stage and began sound-checking the mics.

Ah well, might as well see it through. Pander to Kirk's fantasies. Because he supposed he owed him that at least.

By the time he'd bought another lager and just started up a conversation with a pretty blonde who just happened to have the best ass in the club, the band came on.

The four musicians prowled on stage, panther-lithe despite their age (and Kirk was right about something, at least; they did look ten or so years younger than they should). They took their positions, Carter over to stage left as usual, Tweed to the right, Barney Smolt settling behind his drums, Cropper unhitching the mic. They were dressed in battered leathers, grubby jeans. *Rock 'n' roll, man*, Johnny thought with a sneer. No fuckin' imagination. The musicians were silent as they fine-tuned their instruments, ready to begin.

Johnny leaned against a pillar next to the blonde, casually taking out his mobile. Might as well film the first song just to prove Kirk was full of shit, and then maybe he could fuck off early, hopefully with the blonde in tow.

Kirk was nearly at Canning Town when Johnny's next text came through some ten minutes later.

I think it's all going tits-up. This is fucked fucked fucked.

That was it. No embellishment. Kirk thumbed the call button and waited. No reply. He reached voicemail after ten seconds of ringing. He tried again. Same result. He texted back. *What do you mean? What's happening?*

Then a photo sent by text. Kirk squinted at the blurry shot, trying to make it out. A close-up of a contorted face, smeared with blood, an agonized, silent scream. Blood smeared the camera lens as well as the face, making it impossible to recognize. Was it a selfie from Johnny or of somebody else? He prodded the stop bell on the bus and was jumping out onto the pavement when he got Johnny's final text: *In Hell. You'll like it. Cum visit.*

Again, no answer when Kirk rang Johnny's number.

He wasted no more time. He waved down the first taxi to come along and was soon in the back, frantically texting the guitarist as the cab bustled through the evening streets.

It took him just over half an hour to get to Oxford Street.

He paid the driver and trotted over to the entrance to the 100 Club.

There was nobody on the door, first surprise. The second was the absolute silence from within. He entered the small foyer and paused at the top of the short flight of steps that led down into the club. Darkness waited for him below. The only light came from the bulb in the foyer.

Every inch of his body crawled. Nothing about this was right. If the gig had ended, then why were the doors open? And if it *had* ended, why so soon? It was barely 9:00 p.m.

He strained his ears and eyes downwards. He could make out vague details: a silhouetted pillar, a dull glow of optics from behind the bar over to the right. The stage and the rest of the club were completely dark.

He had no choice. He sent Johnny here. He would have to go find him. Maybe he was backstage…with the band…

His fear left no room for clear thinking; it barely allowed him to breathe. But he had to go down those steps.

By the time he'd reached the bottom step, he had reached the limit of light from the foyer, too. He waited, scanning the darkness. And now, at last, away from the illumination upstairs, his eyes adjusted, and he could begin to see what awaited him.

Bodies.

Piles of corpses littered the floor of the club.

He couldn't make out any detail, just vague forms sprawled in contorted positions, two, three bodies thick in some places.

Every instinct was pushing him to run. Terror surged in his mind. He took a step back, put one foot on the stairs. And stopped. No. Johnny was down there somewhere. Among the corpses. He had to find him, at least check whether he was too late to help him.

And then he realized not everybody was lying on the floor.

Kirk's heart bucked. His slowly improving night vision showed him one vague figure standing in the midst of the corpses.

He fumbled his phone out of his pocket and activated it, using it as a torch. No proper torch on his outdated relic.

The illumination was dim and did not reach far, but it gave him enough light to see the figure standing facing him was Johnny.

Chapter Twenty-Seven

The light faded on Kirk's phone, and he re-activated it, heart rocking.

"Johnny?" His voice was a croak, loud in the silence of the club. There could be no doubt. The figure had been wearing Johnny's unique Theatre of Hate varsity jacket. He'd know it anywhere.

This time when his phone lit up, it showed him another figure he had not spotted before, also standing, but further back and taller than Johnny. As if in response to Kirk spotting him, the second figure began moving slowly around the side of the pile of corpses, toward Kirk. The light died. Kirk thumbed it back on, taking another step back up the stairs as he did so.

Deuce was smiling at him as he neared the foot of the steps. In one hand he carried a mobile, in the other a can of petrol. He held up the phone so Kirk could recognize the Clash logo on the case. Johnny's. Had Deuce sent the final text then? To lure him here?

The roadie was grinning maniacally. "Caught your friend filming the gig," he said in a thick, nasty tone. "Very naughty. We don't want our exclusive party ruined by some prick showing it on the net, do we?" He tossed the phone into the midst of the mounds of corpses that looked increasingly like they had been heaped purposefully. Deuce was unscrewing the cap of the petrol can now.

Kirk's phone died again, but not before he had seen Johnny making his way through the indistinguishable corpses toward him, pushing and kicking bodies out of his way as he came.

"Johnny?" It was even more of a croak this time.

Johnny didn't answer. His shadowy form leaped over a small pile of the dead, their faces lost in darkness, and came at Kirk in a run. Deuce got out of Johnny's way, began making his way methodically around the club, pouring petrol over the corpses.

Kirk didn't move. The light from upstairs finally picked out the guitarist's face as he approached. Kirk dropped his phone then, his bowels plummeting, too. Johnny hurtled up the couple of steps still separating him from Kirk and seized him in an embrace. "Love ya, Kirk," the guitarist hissed. "Kiss old Johnny..."

Johnny had lost several teeth. Those that remained were snaggled, rotten. His face was lopsided, pushed out of sync. His right eye had fallen down to the level of his nostrils, giving him a Quasimodo look that would not see him win the hearts of many girls in the future. The cheekbones that were his pride and joy were misaligned. His neatly coiffed, rockabilly haircut was punk wild. Despite all this, Kirk knew instinctively it was still Johnny. The band had fucked him up.

Kirk tried to push the guitarist away, the bear hug embrace squeezing tighter. Johnny had acquired manic strength along with his new bad looks. He hefted Kirk off the step, spun, and hurled him back into the club.

Kirk landed amongst the cadavers, feeling petrol-slick flesh beneath him, and scrambled to free himself. The fumes burned in his nostrils, along with the stench of blood. A hand clawed at his belt. Something was moving beneath him. Another survivor like Johnny, although it was too dark to see if the form struggling to rear up under Kirk was as horrifically altered as the guitarist had been.

Johnny was wading after him through the corpse surf.

The hand released his belt as Kirk ripped himself free from the pile, almost toppling again as he stood on an unseen face. He felt something crunch under his heel. He was sliding off the pile as Johnny caught him in a rush. Another embrace. This time Deformed Johnny's hands found his throat.

A spark of light over to the side of the club, near the bar, and Kirk realized Deuce was using his lighter on the human compost heaps.

Johnny's mutilated mouth puckered at him as he squeezed. "Kiss ol' Johnny..." His breath was sewer-foul.

Kirk felt himself bent over backward, forced down into the human debris again. Another hand clutched at him. Then two more, seizing his leg as the flames began to roll around the room.

"Kiss me, you fucker. Like Rose did..." Johnny pressed his monstrous face toward Kirk's, his grip tightening.

The flames were not lighting up Kirk's world; his senses were being blotted out as his former friend throttled him. Dimly, he saw Deuce empty the rest of the contents of the tank over himself, grinning as he applied the lighter. Then Johnny's close-up hogged the camera, and the sparks were behind Kirk's eyes.

"Fuck me... Fuck me like Rose did..."

The words crawled into Kirk's brain. A hand was snatching at his hair as he was pushed backward into the pile of dead that no longer seemed so dead.

The bodies were wriggling now as if some unspoken command had activated them. Sucking in a breath through his constricted lungs, Kirk had the vaguest impression of mass deformity, a sea of abnormality wriggling and rising to greet the flames that licked at them, consumed them. He saw Deuce standing, Jesus-like, arms spread as the flames rolled along them.

His strength was going. The hand beneath pulled his hair, and his head went down.

And then the grip on his throat was lessening.

Someone was pulling Johnny off him.

He sucked in air and tore himself free from the grip below, falling sideways into the wriggling bodies, like a stage diver reveling in the contact with his fellow fans.

Heat blasted at him. He scrabbled to his feet, kicking away at the groping claws. Stumbled away from the knot of humanity as the flames took the pile he'd been lying in seconds before. He turned away from the glare, the ferocious heat, and the twisted, freakish forms melting rapidly in the inferno.

Johnny was grappling with somebody near the steps.

Kirk staggered toward them, seeing Deuce topple and fall in a burst of incendiary heat. The roadie had been so convinced Kirk would be taken out by the suspect device he had left for him in the shape of Johnny, he had proceeded to burn himself and all the evidence before making entirely sure. Big mistake, fella. Kirk halted to regain his breath, then lunged toward the two figures fighting at the foot of the stairs.

Ned slammed Johnny against the banister. Johnny tore a chunk out of Ned's hoody as his unnaturally distorted fingers clawed to get at the drummer's face.

Ned was holding one of his drumsticks, thrusting it at Johnny's throat. Black bile welled from the entry wound. There was another stick in his hoody pocket. Kirk pulled it free, spun to face Johnny, rammed the drumstick into one glaring blue eye. He pushed it in deeper, putting his weight behind it until they both fell back against the wall of the stairwell. He pushed harder until the drumstick would go no further, sheathed deep, felt the savage joy burst inside him. And the hate was gooood...

"For Rose," he hissed.

Johnny was sliding sideways down the wall. Kirk helped him with a kick, and the guitarist's body rolled back into the club. Flames crawled along the floor to greet him.

Kirk fell backward into a sitting position on one of the steps, barely aware of the lump of his phone beneath him or of Ned's hand shaking his shoulder. He blinked up at the drummer, then rose dumbly, collecting the cell without thinking as he did so, as if it could possibly be important, as if it could possibly make a difference on a night of insanity like this. Yet it felt reassuring in his grip, and that was something. That was something...

The heat beat against their backs as Kirk and Ned clambered up the stairs and into the cool of the night.

Chapter Twenty-Eight

Detective Sergeant Gull was wearing a strap-on and was giving it all she could. Kirk was lying face down on his bed as the dominatrix detective pumped away at him from on top. He turned his face on the pillow, and Johnny was lying next to him, distorted face still pushed out of true, snaggle teeth grinning at him.

The doorbell pulled him out of the nightmare. He lifted his head from the wet pillow, tried to focus. The bell trilled again. Then a third time, demanding he answer.

He groped for his phone on the bedside table, momentarily confused at finding the screen shattered. That would be because he had dropped it in the 100 Club the night before, and the memories came stomping back, a wave of nausea and terror riding through him.

He rushed to the toilet to be sick, the doorbell a continuous background.

Finally, after a succession of heaving breaths but no actual vomit, he staggered to the intercom phone next to the door and picked it up, convinced it would be Ned. Ned, the unlikely Tourette's Syndrome hero, who had turned up to save the day after getting no replies from either Kirk's or Johnny's phones and had instinctively assumed the worst. They had both been too shocked by events to handle a rational discussion the night before and had promised to meet today to try to make sense of nightmare.

Kirk couldn't form any words to welcome him, however, but Gull must have heard the phone lift because her voice buzzed through the intercom: "I need to speak to you. Now."

He squeezed the phone in his hands, assailed by a vision of Gull from his dream, studded leather bra and panties, strap-on…

"Mister Stammers?"

"I-I'm not feeling—"

"I know what you did last night."

His mind reeled. He felt sick again. Panic jump-started his mind. But he buzzed her through the main door, then staggered away from the hall to splash water in his face and search for some clothes.

She was knocking on the door of his flat while he was still struggling into a pair of jeans.

He let her in, pulling a t-shirt over his head.

She pushed past him, alone.

"You look like you've had a bad night. Did you get burned at all?" She sniffed the air and glanced at him sharply before striding into the lounge.

He followed, lamely. "You've…you've lost me."

"Have I?" She screwed him with those hard emerald eyes. "Have I really?"

She sat down in the armchair and beckoned him to the sofa. She surveyed the room carefully, taking in the framed movie poster of *Rawhead Rex* before her eyes alighted finally on the rack of CDs.

"Cat O' Nine Tails," she said. "Quite a collection. Their entire catalog?"

"It's…Rose's…" he said. His guts were swimming with nausea and horror. Images of the night before tilted his mind. He was finding it difficult to breathe. "Not feeling good. Can you come another time?"

"No." Her eyes were boring through his crazy mind like she could see the images, too.

"You were there, weren't you?"

"Where?" He couldn't look at those all-knowing eyes, so he found the view from the window to fix his gaze on instead.

"The 100 Club. I know you were there."

"Do you?"

"I can't prove it. But I'm sure you had something to do with the fire."

He steeled himself and looked her right in her gorgeous green eyes. Was she going to fuck him up the ass while he was awake, too?

"So now you're accusing me of arson. Are you really that blind?"

She pursed her lips, judging his reaction. Then, "A coffee would be nice. Looks like you could use one."

He was about to answer, then changed his mind and got up to go to the kitchen. He didn't bother asking her preference. He reached for a mug from the cupboard, then put it back when he realized it was Rose's. His hand was shaking when he pulled another one down, and the first sobs were heaving up from his chest.

He hadn't heard Gull slip up quietly behind him. She took the mug from him and put it on the kitchen counter. "It's alright, son. I'll make it."

He snatched at his tears furiously, but they would not stop. Tears for Rose, tears for Johnny, for himself. Tears for the ordinary life he had once enjoyed. He went back to the lounge and slumped on the sofa.

She brought through two steaming mugs, and he took one of them gratefully.

"Any change in Miss Amberley?"

He shook his head, eyes scoured by terrors as well as tears.

"Tell me about it."

He drank a gulp of coffee. Then another. It helped restore a little meaning to the day.

"Just don't bother lying. About last night, I mean. If you weren't there, then you know something about what happened." She picked up the shirt he was wearing the night before, which he had thrown on the floor in his distraught state before going to bed.

"I smelled fire as soon as I entered the flat. But I sensed you had something to do with what happened as soon as I heard at the station. Call it cop's intuition. Or the fact that last time I saw you, you said you were going to sort the band out."

He stared into his cup.

"Whatever you say stays between us."

He laughed. "Am I supposed to believe that?"

"I left Trimble downstairs in the car." She fixed him with that hard, sexy glare. "I mean it. I'm beginning to think you were right about this band. Trouble follows them around. I checked on the victims of the recent rash of homicides and cases of mania like you suggested...and guess what? You were right. Ninety percent of homes involved had a copy of Cat O' Nine's latest album. Since we spoke, cases have more than doubled." She paused, took a sip from her mug, and leveled her gaze on him again. "If you were there last night, I need to know everything if I'm ever to put a stop to this madness."

He snorted bitterly. "Like you said, you don't have the power."

She let that go. "Would you like to tell me what happened?"

"Everybody died, that's what happened. Everybody except the band, of course."

She watched him carefully. "What did you see?"

He turned away, gazing at the houses across the street again. "I saw Hell."

"Did you see the band?"

"No. They were gone by the time I got there. And everybody else was dead." Not quite true, was it? He thought of Johnny—or the thing that Johnny had become—waiting for him in the dark. "I saw the fire and ran."

"Why did you go?"

"I needed proof. You didn't believe me when I said they were evil. Do you now?"

She ignored that. "Did you get your proof?"

He shook his head. He had his phone, of course, with its text picture of blood and death on it, but he knew its inconclusive blur would not sway Gull. "I'm sure you'll find proof amongst the ashes if you look hard enough."

"That'll be tough; everybody who attended the gig is burned beyond recognition. Except you."

"Are you accusing me again?"

She was silent, weighing him up.

"Why don't you check security camera footage of the gig. That'll tell you exactly what happened. Or better yet, ask the band..."

She gave the tiniest of smiles at his bitter sarcasm. "All CC evidence went up with the flames, of course. We've had a statement from the band in which they claim to have no idea how the blaze started but were able to get out through a fire escape at the back as soon as it did. They called the fire department immediately, but, of course, it was too late. Oh, you'll be gratified to hear they've sent out a press release declaring their huge sorrow and grief at the loss of life. They're blaming it on inadequate health and safety regs at the club." Her thin lips tightened again. "Why did you arrive late?"

He paused, unsure whether to involve Johnny or not. But Gull was reading his face, saw the hesitation. He was committed. "Johnny went to see them. Our guitarist..." A shudder rippled through him. A drop of coffee spilled on the knee of his jeans. "He sent me a text so I came as quick as I could."

"What did the text say?"

He didn't pause at all this time. He looked her straight in the eyes. "It said: 'In Hell. Come quick.'"

She nodded briefly. "I should be taking you down the station really. You're my only witness."

"So why aren't you?"

"I don't honestly know. Maybe it's because I think you're more useful left to your own devices."

His eyes widened. She was reading his mind again.

"I think you know something we don't. Something that might be helpful in stopping them doing...whatever it is they're hell-bent on doing. I don't know what that is, and I'm not entirely sure you're wholly convinced of it yourself. But I think you have an idea. And right now an idea is all we have. So I'm going to stick my neck out a bit here and cut you some slack. But..." She leaned forward on the chair. "...only for one week. Until after the Wembley gig, and if things haven't been sorted by then, I just might have to pin it all on you."

"After the Wembley gig will be too late. You know that, don't you?"

She wrinkled her sharp nose a little. "You've got a week to get me some proof, or at least some answers. Then I'm going to have to reveal that you were the last person alive at the 100 Club. My Super would love it. Open and shut case: you torched the 100 Club out of revenge because you blamed Cat O' Nine for what happened to your girlfriend. A case of psychopathic delusion. Sorry, but that's the way any sensible copper would look at it." She winked at him. "Maybe I'm going crazy, too…"

"No, I don't think you are." He fixed her with an interrogative glare in return. "What made you change your mind?"

Now it was her turn to look out of the window. "Let's just say, something about our favorite band didn't smell right…" Was there a touch of fear in her face? She had seen something, knew something herself that she wasn't sharing. He thought of wading in deep, telling her about what had happened to Johnny but stopped himself just before his mouth began to form the words. He would simply smash the iota of confidence she had in him.

"What you were saying about the CD… Like I said, in ninety percent of the cases, you were right. Speaking to witnesses, it seemed those affected were slow burners. They didn't flip out straight away. Loved ones, colleagues, neighbors noticed a gradual worsening of their condition until insanity kicked in fully." She turned to face him again. "Is that what happened with your Rose?"

He didn't want to think about that again. Hadn't he been over this enough times with his friends, with himself? Rose had certainly been increasingly more erratic and moody over the last few months, but that was because she was shagging Johnny, but she hadn't turned nasty until she bought the Cat CD. He remembered their violent, bitter lovemaking as they listened to the music.

"It might have happened faster with her. She was a devoted fan. Listened to the CD a lot. But yeah, it took a couple of days for her to…" He didn't finish.

Gull nodded again. "Whereas the *Rock it!!* journalists and Missus Cropper lost it pretty quickly, almost immediately after being exposed to the band's music—if everything you say is true, of course." She gave him an ironic look.

"So why do you think that is?"

He could tell she'd already worked out the answer, and he realized he was the only one she could trust to share her theories with. She would have been on traffic duty or removed from the force altogether if she broached these suspicions with a colleague.

"Jack Wiley and Sheila Cropper received CD-Rs of the album through the post. I haven't played them, of course..." She arched her brows.

"Unmastered demos," he cut in immediately. "A more potent, undiluted mix than the widely available commercial disc. Its effect was more immediate."

She shrugged. "It's a theory, I suppose."

And one you're beginning to believe, aren't you, Detective Sergeant Gull? Maybe he had an ally of sorts after all.

"But that isn't consistent with Nick James. We haven't been able to track down a copy of the CD-R amongst his possessions."

"He interviewed them, didn't he? They probably subjected him to a purer form of the music, too."

She frowned but said nothing. She looked scared again. What he said next deepened the unease on her face.

"You know Wembley is going to be their musical Last Supper, don't you? Cat O' Nine's farewell feast. But it's their dedicated fans who will be the ones to get crucified. You see, if you believe in something too much, it screws you over..."

Her eyes narrowed. "I've leveled with you. Now it's your turn. Stop getting biblical on my sweet ass and tell me what you really expect to happen."

"The Apocalypse. That's what I expect to happen, Detective Sergeant Gull." He could feel himself shaking again. "Are you going to help me stop it?"

"I told you to drop the religious crap. It's screwing with my atheistic copper's belief in simple right and wrong." She sighed. "What do you seriously expect me to do? Get my Super to speak to the Commissioner of Police to have a word in Mayor Boris's ear hole? Tell the fat, blond-haired Tory twat that he needs to shut down an extremely lucrative gig by the biggest rock band in history because some nut job says they're the Devil's

Own?"

"Something like that."

Gull rose from her chair and handed him the empty cup. "I'll see myself out, honey. Remember, one week."

Kirk remained in his armchair for a moment after she left. The shaking had stopped. Gull had believed in him.

And that was a start.

Now it was time to see if he believed in himself. Gull had read his mind, all right. He *did* have an idea. Yes, it was a crazy one. Yes, it would probably never work. But in seven days' time, it really wouldn't matter anyway if it failed.

They were all on the Highway to Hell, but one Bon Scott had certainly never dreamed about.

Chapter Twenty-Nine

The other two were already waiting for him.

Ned looked as if he hadn't slept at all, which was hardly surprising. Davey looked confused, his natural belligerence held in check. Kirk ordered a double Jack Daniels and sat down at the table.

Nobody said anything for a moment. Finally, Davey could restrain his impatience no longer. "Is this bollocks real?"

Kirk nodded, his gaze level with Davey's. He knew he looked as ravaged as Ned. Davey could read the truth in the newly minted lines on Kirk's face; he certainly didn't need to read between them. It was all there to see, five-mile stare, bags, the complete haunted survivor make-over.

"And Johnny?"

Kirk nodded again. He wondered exactly how much Ned had told the bass player.

"I've had the cops 'round this morning. Gull. She knows I was at the 100 Club." Ned's eyes widened. "Relax. She's not going to do anything."

"And you believed her?" Ned's shoulder rose in a twitch. A tic pulled his mouth into a sneer.

"I think she believes *me*, more importantly. She's given me a week to provide proof before busting my ass." He took a gulp of JD. The hand holding the glass was steady. His whole world might be shaking, ready to fall, but he could feel a harder resolve being born from the ashes of his old fears.

"Never mind that shit!" Davey was way out of his depth. "What the fuck happened to Johnny? Is everyone really dead, like this rag says?" He tapped a copy of *The Sun* underneath his pint.

Kirk nodded again. "Except for the band, of course."

Kirk lifted Davey's pint to read the front page. There was a picture of the burned-out interior of the legendary club and a shot of Cat from earlier days, all smiles and perms. The headline ran:

CATASTOPHE O' NINE

Kirk scanned the lurid article. Bodies burned beyond recognition. It would take several days to identify the charred remains. The band's official statement revealed how they had only just escaped in time thanks to the heroic efforts of the roadie, who got them out through the rear fire exit and perished in the attempt. There was a formal expression of sympathy to the hundred and twenty fans who died in the fire, the cause of which had not yet been ascertained, although the owner of the club was being investigated on suspicion of inadequate fire safety precautions.

"Deuce was left behind to burn all the evidence." Kirk's voice was grim and hard. It didn't sound like his at all. Was this how the new Kirk sounded? Was *this* the new Kirk? He felt a cool rage bolster him as he read the article. He had changed, he knew that. And that was good. He would have to be cold and strong to see this through. Adapt and survive. He rolled the whiskey glass between his fingers and continued. "They presumably gave him enough time to burn everyone before contacting the fire brigade, although they didn't realize he'd self-immolated himself for nothing."

"Immo-fuckin'- what?" Davey's aggression was returning, amplified by his bewilderment and, yes, fear. Kirk could see the fear in those small, bear-like eyes. Good. Fear was good. It meant belief was dawning. "And what evidence? Dead bodies?"

"Fucked-up dead bodies," Ned corrected him.

"You still giving me that shit about the bodies havin' changed? How the fuck can that be? Do I look like some kind of Twatfish, with me gob flappin' waiting for a hook? I ain't gullible. No Horror Show bollocks. No more fuckin' with my mind just cos I ain't as intellectual as you two wankers. Give me the truth! What the fuck happened in there? What the fuck happened to *Johnny!?*"

Kirk waited for him to calm a little before answering. "Cat O' Nine did something to them with their music. It didn't just drive them insane, like...like Rose..." He dashed off the JD. It didn't even touch the sides. "This time it was physical, too. A little warm-up gig to see how lethal their live sound was. I'd say it was *very* lethal."

Davey was struggling to take it all in. "Physical? What d'you mean?"

"Changed them. In horrible ways. I didn't look too closely, and it was dark, but I saw what it did to Johnny..." He fumbled with the empty glass, really needing another drink but not wanting to waste any more time. "DS Gull thinks I've got a plan to stop them, even though I didn't tell her what it is. She's a smart one, all right."

Davey snorted. "What you gonna do, criticize their lyrics?"

"Not quite." He reached inside his jacket pocket and pulled out a CD he'd found in the bin back at the flat. The other two stared at it in disbelief. Ned sighed and put his head in his hands. Davey shook his head.

"Brilliant. You're gonna play 'em their back catalog."

"Again, not quite. But warmer." He tapped the CD cover. It was a still from an old horror movie depicting a witch tied to a tree having an iron mask hammered onto her face. It was Cat O' Nine' Tails' first album. He turned the CD round to show them the black-and-white band photo on the back. The musicians looked impossibly young, and all were smiling. Ray Starling had the cheekiest grin of all.

"It's the fact Rose had thrown it deliberately in the bin. It was like a statement from her, influenced by whatever Cat has become. I got to wondering why she would turn her back so completely on that first CD..." He tapped one of the figures in the photo with his forefinger. "The answer was, of course, Ray..."

The two men across the table stared at him as if he had finally lost the plot. Davey's jaw hung open. Before they could start swearing at him, he bulled on.

"The first album had a wildness that made it stand out. It was unique, so different from the rest of their formulaic crap—apart from the latest album, of course, which is a *whole* new fish altogether." He thought of the tracks he'd heard with Rose, of wanting to cut her, and how good that had felt. He swallowed and continued. "But Ray brought a vital, no-bollocks approach to their debut that was entirely his own. There was undeniable power there, and the rest of the band turned their backs on it, on Ray, and went searching for something else. I think eventually they found it, but it probably wasn't anything like they were dreaming of…"

Ned was interested again. He'd seen Johnny the night before and was obviously more inclined to suspend his disbelief. "Meaning?"

Kirk shrugged. "I don't know. But I think they were probably just playing around at first, exploring ideas in the confines of their more commercial sound after kicking Ray out. Experimenting with certain chords, certain notes that they developed further on each new album. I went through their back catalog after spying on them in their studio. You see, I knew there was something very wrong about them after that. If you'd seen them sitting up there in the dark…"

"You told me they were getting blowies off groupies," Davey chipped in. "Sounds perfectly acceptable to me."

"Groupies who were later found mutilated."

"Fair point."

"I think maybe they experimented too far. Maybe they let something in they shouldn't have. Don't ask me to explain it. Obviously, I'm just guessing. And my guess is they found a certain note, or vibe, that resonated with something very nasty out there somewhere…"

"Out where?" Davey was being facetious now. Feeling out of his depth always made him that way.

"I don't fucking know. Another dimension, a musical Bermuda Triangle they flew into after hitting upon the right sonic key to open the door. I can't describe it any better than that."

"A musical Bermuda Triangle? Do you realize what a twat you

sound?"

Kirk cocked an eyebrow. "Oh yes. Believe me, I do. But if you'd seen what happened to Johnny..."

Ned took the CD off Kirk, examined it briefly before dropping it gently on the table. "But what's all this got to do with Ray?"

Kirk looked even more uncomfortable. "This is where you're really gonna have to trust me, boys..."

He told them his idea. How he thought the debut CD from Cat O' Nine was boiling with rock-'n'-roll fury, and that maybe by recruiting the author of that fury to their cause, they could harness it and use it against his former band. He explained how he'd checked online, and the first album was now virtually impossible to get, apart from through second-hand auctions and used outlets, a real rarity.

"Rose didn't chuck the first album away until she started getting hooked on the new one," he persisted in the face of blank bewilderment from his two friends. "And why delete it from their catalog? What threat did that particular work, and maybe Ray, in particular, pose for them? That's what I was on my way to discover when I got Johnny's text from the 100 Club. I was gonna track down the original Beast of Rock and enlist him to fight for us. We're gonna crash the Wembley gig with Ray as our special weapon and shut these evil bastards down."

When he finished speaking, they stared at him, speechless. Ned looked faintly embarrassed for him. Davey looked like he needed to defecate. When Kirk pulled out four tickets from his wallet with Cat O' Nine Tails emblazoned on the front, their expressions barely changed. Kirk put the tickets and the CD back in his pocket and went to the bar.

When he came back, they were still silent.

"Two of those tickets were a present from Rose," he said, and saying her name aloud emboldened him against their lack of response. "I found them hidden in one of her drawers. A present to me. Maybe she wanted to convert me once and for all..." He refused to let the sudden stab of grief deter him now. Stay cold. Stay strong. His gaze was steady as he continued. "The other two I bought on the way here. Lucky to get them, I suppose, or that's what the silly sod in TicketZ told me. He also told me sales had slowed a bit this morning after the news of the fire. Funny that…" He took a sip from his JD, and then passed the ball for them to do what the hell they liked with it.

"I know. I *know* how mad I sound. But is my idea any madder than what you saw last night, Ned? So what's it gonna be? You with me?"

Ned looked down at the pint Kirk had just bought him. He was looking for words in the amber depths, but his tic got there first, raising his right arm in a mockery of a Nazi salute.

Davey sat back. "Well, if this is all you got, we really *are* fucked."

Kirk had to agree that maybe he had a point.

Chapter Thirty

He watched the Rejects play from the back of the Bridge House. The last time he'd been here, playing with Lucifer Sam, Rose had been with him. How long ago? Three weeks, a month? His life had flipped on its head in so short a time.

The band was playing their anthem, "Bad Man." He watched Jeff Turner performing knee jumps on stage, the singer at fifty as fit as any teenager. His brother, Mickey Geggus, powered gut-raw solos and riffs into the appreciative audience, and if things had been different, Kirk would have been as stoked as the rest of the crowd of aging punks and herberts.

But things weren't different. He was here on a mission. Mickey had stuck him on the guest list after Kirk gave him some bullshit about Ray Starling over the phone. Of course, he hadn't explained the exact reason why he wanted to track down the elusive singer; Mickey had done plenty of boxing in his time and didn't treat fools with anything less than an uppercut.

Mickey came off the stage to enthusiastic back slaps and handshakes as he wove through the crowd toward the dressing room with the rest of the band. He nodded at Kirk and took his hand, his grip slick with sweat.

Kirk followed the guitarist through to the small backstage area and sat on a leather seat, waiting patiently while Mickey toweled himself off. Kirk had worked as a roadie for the Rejects a couple of years back, little imagining he would be calling on them for help in saving the world one day. And no matter how ludicrous that sounded, Kirk was under no illusion the stakes really *were* that high, once Cat O' Nine released their IED of a record across the globe in just over a week.

Mickey was a big, stocky Docker's son from Custom House, shaved head and a cheeky black goatee—the cockniest cockney you could imagine. His chainsaw-through-metal tones mixed aggression and bonhomie. Loyal and huge-hearted, he took no shit...from *anyone*. In his time, he had chinned BBC Top of the Pops producers and fellow musicians alike for slighting him and had once famously kicked Billy Idol up the ass for not returning his greeting. You didn't fuck with him or his brother. Mickey was the real deal.

"So what the fack's this all abaht, then, Kirky?" Mickey chucked the sodden towel and helped himself to a can of Stella, tossing one over to Kirk. "Why d'ya wanna see Ray so fackin' much?"

This was the difficult part. Kirk peeled open his can and took a gulp. To get the info he needed, he really had to play this down, so he told Mickey Lucifer Sam wanted Ray to collaborate on a song Kirk had written and was hoping they could recruit him to sing with them, too.

"Good fackin' luck wiv that, son," Mickey grunted and sat opposite him. The rest of the band was unwinding with beer and cigarettes at the other end of the room, still on a high from the gig. "Right fackin' loose cannon. Ya must know that, right? Not 'eard all the stories? Geezer went right off the rails arter he got his arse kicked aht of Cat O' Nine. Surprised he's still alive t' be honest, mate."

Kirk knew all that. And yes, he'd heard all the wild-man stories. But he wasn't here for those. There wasn't time for anecdotes. "Yeah, the guy's got issues, I heard all the stories. But I'm hoping we can calm him down enough to help us. You never know, he might jump at the chance to 'come out of retirement'..."

Mickey laughed hoarsely. "Jump all over yer 'ead, more fackin' like! You got balls, I'll give ya that."

Kirk tried not to let his impatience show. "So do you have any idea where he lives, Mickey? Or have you got his number? I know he used to be a mate of yours back in the day."

Mickey paused and stared hard at him, his t-shirt revealing heavily muscled, tattooed arms still glistening with sweat. "You gonna be straight wiv me? You look...well, fuckin' twitchy. Don't give me no bollocks abaht needin' Ray for a duet. What's this really abaht? An' don't give me no shit, Kirky boy."

Kirk had feared this. He sighed. He knew the guitarist was too shrewd to fall for his flannel. He met Mickey's gaze full on, his jaw set and firm. "Can't tell you that, Mickey. I really can't. But you have to know this: it's fuckin' *vital* I find him, for reasons I'll tell you all about if this insane, fucked-up plan of mine actually works. Believe me, if I told you, you'd kick my ass right out of here, so you're just gonna have to trust me on this. I *have* to find him."

Mickey stared at him for a moment longer, doubt, suspicion and finally stoicism flicking across his hardened face. "Awright. I'll fackin' believe ya if youse say it's that urgent. Fack's sake. This had better be good, though, son. You know I don't like ta be facked abaht."

Kirk nodded. "And before you ask, yeah, I've tried googling him. Nothing. He's buried his traces pretty well. Which is why I came to you. He's from your manor. If anyone knows where he's gone to ground, it's you..."

"Google my fackin' arsehole. I coulda told you you wouldn't find the cunt that way. But the truf is, mate, I ain't got a fackin' clue where he's holed up these days, either, though I have seen 'im dahn the boozer a few times over the years. All I know is I 'eard he's still on the manor somewhere, but keepin' his 'ead well dahn, apart from the odd pub scrap— always was a scrapper, was Ray." Mickey grinned affectionately. "You tried tracin' his family? Got a feelin' his old dear still lives in Canning Town somewhere, but I very much doubt he'd be livin' with her."

"I tried that, too. There's over a hundred Starlings listed in the East End. I don't have time to check them all for his Mum's address. And he's bound to be ex-directory. So I thought you might know where he hangs around. You mentioned some pubs."

Mickey gave him the names of four or five pubs in Custom House and Canning Town where he'd either bumped into Ray over the years or heard he'd been spotted. "Like I said, good fackin' luck wiv it mate. I know he's always out on the piss, but he tries to shun the limelight these days, so I reckon ya got a right fackin' quest on yer 'ands..." He finished off his beer, then added, "But ya gotta be careful if ya do find 'im, Kirky. Last time I bumped inta him, he was so off his fackin' rocker he 'ardly recognized me. Bin through a lot, that boy. He's as likely to fackin' slap ya as shake yer 'and. Buy 'im a fackin' drink, that's my advice. And don't fackin' mention Cat O' Nine Tails, whatever the fack ya do..."

Kirk nodded wryly, shook Mickey's hand, promised he'd get back to him if it all went to plan, and left the Bridge House.

The first pub on Mickey's list was only three streets away. It was a typical East End corner boozer, and when Kirk pushed the door, he was assailed by raucous chat and laughter. The pub was half full. Nobody gave him a second glance as he searched the bar before ordering a pint of London Pride and sitting at an empty table by the window.

He scanned the customers as he sipped his beer. They were the average crowd of working-class Eastenders you'd find in a hundred-and-one similar pubs in this part of the city, hard-bitten faces, tatts, wife-beaters. A football game was in progress on a screen in one corner, although being a Liverpool V Man Utd game, it didn't attract the devotion it would have done if a couple of local teams had been playing.

Of course, there was no sign of Ray. Had he really believed he would find him that easily? He checked the time on the shattered screen of his cell phone. 10:05 p.m. He didn't have long before the pubs shut. A proper fool's errand, this.

He drank up and decided to try his luck with two more pubs on Mickey's list, the first of which he found after half a mile's walk through the quiet streets. It was dark, and the lateness of the day, combined with the lonely burden of his quest and the trauma he had suffered recently, played heavily on him. Mickey must have seen it in his eyes, as the Reject genuinely looked concerned, though being the diamond geezer he was, he hadn't pushed for answers.

The Shakespeare was emptier than the first pub. Decidedly more down-at-heel as well, Kirk knew as soon as he entered that it was more the sort of boozer Ray would frequent. There was even a Black Sabbath riff blaring from the jukebox. *Fairies Wear Boots.* Kirk bought a beer and sat on a bar stool, surreptitiously glancing around at the punters. Mostly a sullen metal crowd, long hair, leather jackets. Laughs and jokes were not on the menu with this bunch. They looked tense, almost expectant, but they couldn't have been waiting for him, Kirk reasoned. Some of them glanced at him with hostile indifference.

Of course, Ray was noticeable by his absence. The crowd was too young, Kirk supposed. The ex-Cat Singer would probably feel too exposed in here, especially if, as Mickey had pointed out, he wanted to hide from his past these days.

He stared gloomily into his pint, thinking of Rose. He had visited her again this morning, and as he had expected, there had been absolutely no change in her catatonic condition. He had left a fresh bunch of flowers, which a nurse had kindly placed in a jar, kissed her pale forehead while she stared through him with her bottomless gaze, and left, chest heaving with sobs.

He gripped the glass in his hand until it almost shattered, heaved out a deep breath.

And then some idiot put Cat O' Nine on the jukebox.

He recognized the hideous bass intro immediately. It slithered from the speakers overhead before giving way to frenzied percussion that put the barely contained ferocity of *Killing Joke* to shame. He glanced up from his pint. He'd heard it before on the new album while having sex with Rose. His hackles lifted even as his innards churned. The gang of metal fans stiffened as this offering from their Gods called to them. It was as if they had been waiting for it, waiting for someone brave enough to put it on. A nightly ritual? A rite of manhood? They looked as equally vapid and vicious for that to be a possibility.

Cropper's vocals sprang free, sadistic, cajoling, while Tweed's guitar slashed out from the speakers. Kirk couldn't remember the name of the song, and didn't want to; he had seen it advertised in Kerrang. The proud, new single. Whatever it was called, he didn't want to be anywhere near it. He got up from his stool as the first argument began between the rockers.

There seemed no rhyme nor reason behind the row, but the result was fast and furious, and ugly as only a bar fight truly is: one teenager smashed his glass on the table top and buried the broken half in his friend's face. Kirk saw a shard pop the young rocker's left eye.

Kirk left the rest of his beer and strode out quickly as the bar exploded into mass violence.

He shivered as he walked the streets. It certainly wasn't cold, and the fight in the bar had no real power to shake him anymore. He felt as tense and ready for violence as the rockers had been when he entered the bar. He had his own role to play, and in his own way, he was just as primed to react as they had been.

But right now he had no more stomach for the quest. Passing a bus stop, he gave up the fight for the night and jumped on the first number 270 that pulled up.

The following evening he started early.

He reached the next pub on Mickey's list by seven. He'd decided to try Custom House this time. The Duke of Cumberland certainly didn't look very inviting as he approached it. A dirty, white exterior that reminded Kirk of toilet décor, England flags strung beneath one window sill, two battered old men smoking by the entrance way glowering at him over their fags. Certainly looked like the sort of place he'd find Ray.

But again, it wasn't.

Nor did he find him at The Fox, the last pub on Mickey's list. When he asked a group of men roughly Ray's age chatting by the bar if they knew of the singer, they acted as if he were coming onto them, glaring at him like he was filth. He left pretty quickly.

He found himself walking along Barking Road as the midsummer night began to fall. His ridiculous plan had failed before it had even started. While Davey and Ned were still far from convinced about the efficacy of his solution to the Cat problem, they at least had some faith in him to pull this particular rabbit out of the hat, no matter how drunken and unfit for the purpose he turned out to be.

Approaching The Princess Alexandria, which looked even rougher and disheveled than the Duke, he paused as it became apparent he was walking toward another argument, this time between three middle-aged men who were standing outside, smoking.

It sounded like the conversation was turning increasingly violent, so Kirk pulled up short of the doorway where the altercation was taking place. Slurred cockney expletives were mounting in ferocity to the point where blows would ensue imminently. Kirk made to cross the road instead.

He had to wait for a bus to pass, and so clearly heard the voice of one of the men raised in outrage.

"You wanna watch yer fackin' mouth, ya cunt! You ain't nobody no more. You're fackin' nuthin'. So don't play the fackin' rock star round 'ere, ya washed-up loser. Headin' fer a slap, fer fuckin' sure!"

Even over the drone of the accelerating bus, Kirk heard a fist meet flesh.

Kirk turned, and he was there.

The hero he had spent two evenings searching for. The savior of the world.

The scrapper.

Chapter Thirty-One

Ray followed through on the punch with a knee to his aggressor's groin. The man, a thickset skinhead somewhere in his late forties, folded, grunting.

"Don't fuck with me, ya cunts!" Ray was in classic fighter stance, legs slightly bent and braced for attack and defense, fists clenched at the ready. Even though Kirk had seen fairly recent photos of him on various websites when he'd been caught unawares by some chancer with a camera, those shots hadn't prepared him at all for the degraded mess that was Ray Starling in the flesh.

He had put on about seventy pounds, and his face was ravaged with drink and despair. His bald head glistened under the street light, his goatee was black as Mickey's, albeit thicker, twice as fierce-looking, and Kirk could see how closely they were cut from the same street-fighting East End cloth. Ray's eyes, always large and expressive, bugged with violent urges and a will for self-destruction. He looked like a Rum-soaked buccaneer at the end of his pirating career. "I can still kick your asses all over Canning Town, ya wankers…"

The other man still standing, short, tufty gray hair like a used paint-brush, face as bruised as a Dockers' fist, swung at Ray and connected. Ray tumbled into a wheelie bin beside the pub entrance, scattering banana peels, old coffee jars, and baked bean cans as he fell.

"You fackin' *cunt*!" Paint Brush Hair croaked, stomping in to deliver a kick to the face that would surely put Ray down for good. From the corner of his eye, Kirk saw the skinhead begin to rise again.

Kirk was no fighter, as his scuffle with the deformed Johnny proved. He had tried his best to avoid violence whenever he could. It was ugly, pointless, and a poor way to handle situations. Kirk preferred to argue his way through an opposing point of view rather than throw a punch at it. But here on this East End street, seeing someone he'd admired ever since that long-distant festival in Frankfurt being bushwhacked by two envious thugs, Kirk acted in a way that was most unlike him. He threw himself at Paint Brush, tackling him around his waist and propelling him backward into the brick wall of the pub.

The man's eyes widened at this new attack, but the collision with the wall didn't seem to have winded him at all. His head shot forward and butted Kirk's nose. Kirk dropped, sparklers fizzing up his vision.

Through the pain and confusion as he rolled on the pavement, Kirk noticed Paint Brush coming to finish him off while Ray wrestled with the skinhead who was back on his boots.

"Who the fuck are you, ya skinny cunt? Starling's cum bum?" He was bending over Kirk, face etched with a thousand pub fights, a Millwall tattoo adorning his stanchion-thick neck.

Kirk scrabbled backward, trying to gain his feet. A boot came at him, caught him in his right kidney. The pain curled him into the fetal position. Through the tears of pain, he saw Paint Brush stumble forward as something shattered over his head from behind. He staggered like a drunken bull, started to turn, and Ray took him clear off his feet with a right hook that would have done Mike Tyson proud.

The skinhead was down, too, groaning in a pool of tea bags and leftover spaghetti sauce oozing from the mouth of the overturned bin.

Then Ray was helping Kirk up, dropping the broken remains of the wine bottle he'd smashed over Paint Brush's head.

Kirk tottered as he stood again, his vision blurred. His nose felt broken, and he could feel blood waterfalling over his chin. His kidney felt like someone had driven a truck into it.

"Don't know who the fack you are, but cheers for the help, mate." Ray was crouched over, hands on knees now, panting heavily after his exertions. He watched Kirk curiously as he struggled to regain his breath.

"I'm Kirk," he said through a fresh wave of pain that caused Ray to swim in and out of focus. "And I need you to save the world..."

Of course, Ray had to take him home after that. As it turned out, his house wasn't far from The Princess Alexandria, and soon Ray was inserting a key into the door of a terraced Victorian house in a shabby residential street. They hadn't spoken much on the brief walk, Kirk insisting he would explain after he got a bandage and a glass of water. Ray had grunted and told him he'd better not turn out to be a journalist after a story or he'd "need more than *one* fackin' plaster..."

Kirk glanced at the tatty front gardens of the houses on Ray's street, many of them cluttered with cheap prams, plastic slides, and other accouterments of family life on the cheap, and wondered what Ray had done with all his money. His front door was badly in need of a fresh lick of paint for a start. *As if he really gave a fuck about that right now.* The door opened, and Ray ushered him into a short hallway.

The contrast between the interior and exterior of the house was striking; the clean, freshly vacuumed carpet and a fresh bunch of flowers in a bowl on a side table immediately spoke to Kirk of a woman's touch.

And there she was: Ray led him into a small, neat living room to meet the pretty, neat woman in her early forties sitting on the sofa in front of the TV.

She looked up at Kirk with eyes dulled by years of resignation. He smiled at her through the blood on his lip, and she stood up immediately.

"What have you done now, Ray? And who's this?"

"Fack knows. He helped me out in a ruck down the Alexandria. Says he's got summat important to tell me..." He frowned at Kirk as if his hospitality was all done and it was time to get down to business.

"That looks nasty... Come into the kitchen, I'll wash it for you." He followed the attractive blonde out of the living room and down the hallway to an equally clean and bright kitchen. Ray stalked after them, his face surly with impatience.

"Don't fackin' mamby pamby him too much, Michelle, I still don't know what the fack he's after."

"Oh, be quiet, Ray..." Michelle had moistened a pad of cotton and was dabbing Kirk's face. He couldn't help wincing. Ray let out an exasperated sigh. "That looks nasty," Michelle said. "Perhaps you should go to A&E." Kirk shook his head, winced again at the pain the movement caused him. She dried his face with a kitchen towel and applied a plaster across the bridge of his nose. "Honestly, Ray, can't you go anywhere without causing trouble?"

"Leave it out, Michelle." He looked at Kirk. "Let's have it, then..." He gestured with his head in the direction of the lounge and strode off down the hall, not waiting to check if Kirk was following or not.

"I'll make you both a coffee," Michelle said, her pretty features strained by habitual disappointment. He thanked her and went after his host.

Ray was already pouring out two glasses of Jack Daniels. He handed one to Kirk, gestured for him to sit in an armchair by the gas fire. He switched off the TV with a remote, sat back in the sofa, and looked long and hard at Kirk.

"Okay, sunshine: You're on..."

Kirk sipped his JD. The pain in his kidney was just a dull ache now, but his nose throbbed hellishly. This was the moment he'd been preparing himself for mentally over the last few days, ever since this whole ridiculous, crazy idea popped into his head. Except, when it came to it, he realized he hadn't prepared much of anything, because he hadn't actually really believed he would find Starling. And now that he had, how the hell was he going to explain why he needed him? How was he going to convince this mad, drunken ex-rocker that he might just be able to save them all?

The answer was, of course, he couldn't. He didn't even know where to begin.

Ray knocked the JD down in one, refilled his own glass, ignoring

Kirk's, and placed the bottle on the table again. "Right. This is what I think: you ain't a journalist, cos if you was, you woulda done a runner at the first sign of aggro. And you don't look like one neither..." He appraised Kirk's slightly battered leather jacket, his Damned t-shirt, and army boots. "Apart from maybe one of them music journo cunts... You ain't one of them, are ya? Fackin' twats. Can't fackin' join a band so they *write* about 'em instead. Wankers. Had some proper hatchet jobs from them talentless cunts in my time..." Ray's face knotted with contempt.

Kirk was about to put him right when Ray continued. "Nah, my guess is you're in a band and want me to work on a track wiv ya... Am I right? Well, I can tell ya now, I've jacked all that bollocks in. Michelle will tell ya. So I'm sorry you wasted your time an' all that bollocks, an' thanks for helpin' me out—not that you really fackin' did, you ain't exactly tasty wiv yer mitts, are ya, but—"

"I'm here about Cat O' Nine Tails..."

Kirk waited for his words to sink in. He was tired, his nose hurt like hell, and he was pretty sure he had trailed all the way out here for nothing, so there was no longer any point trying to beat about the bush. So he charged in and said the one thing he'd been expressly warned not to.

The contempt on Ray's face darkened into a cold rage.

"You can get the fuck outta my house right now while you can still fackin' walk..." Ray's voice had deepened threateningly. He finished his second glass of whiskey, and his big, wild eyes bored into Kirk's.

Kirk finished his own drink in one gulp. Then he stared hard right back at the ex-Cat frontman, and he felt the anger building. No, more than anger: it was a cold, determined fury that had been boiling under the surface ever since Rose mutilated herself and took a permanent stay in a mental ward. It was righteous rage, only just controlled, ready to lash out in a frenzy of hate at any moment. It was vengeance. And he knew Ray saw it in his eyes...

The big man's attitude changed in that instant. Now Kirk knew the older man could see a fellow victim in the battered visitor sitting in his armchair. He saw real hurt, *real* pain, and the need to fight back against an injustice that put Ray losing his position as a singer in a rock band very much into perspective. Kirk saw all this register on Ray's face as the bitter words of truth spilled forth:

"They fucked up my girl, and they put her in hospital. They fucked up my best mate. Put *him* in the morgue. And they're going to do a whole lot worse to all of us unless you stop feeling fuckin' sorry for yourself and listen to what I have to say..."

Ray was quiet for a moment. This time he refilled both their glasses.

So Kirk told him.

He didn't spare anything. There was no longer any point obfuscating, and certainly not enough time. He started with the disappearance of the band, their miraculous reappearance, the way they had all changed, become colder, impossibly younger (and at this point Ray grunted, snapped his third JD down, and groped for the bottle again); how they had reacted at HMV, sitting in the dark of their studio room like four corpses; the dead groupies, the rash of homicides and cases of murderous insanity relating to the band's music and the release of their new CD. When he came to Rose, he spared no detail, even down to Rose's infidelity with Johnny. If Ray noticed his voice become harder still, like a knife cutting out crazy words, then he said nothing. In fact, he said nothing all the way through Kirk's narrative, his bugging eyes locking onto Kirk's, listening with an intensity the younger man could never have expected. Kirk got to the 100 Club incident, the mass burnings inside, and finished with the band's scheduled appearance at Wembley in three days' time.

After he was done, Kirk sat back in the armchair, exhausted at reliving every painful, horrific detail. Still Ray said nothing, watching him without expression now. But was that a fleck of fear Kirk saw in his eyes?

Finally, after a long pause, Ray finished his drink and poured the last of the JD into both their glasses. "That's some story ya got there, fella," he said eventually. There was a quiver in Ray's voice that Kirk recognized. It was in his own.

"You tell me the band members are some kind of fackin' demons..." he said, attempting an ironic smile that looked ghastly. "Have to tell you, I got plenty of those already..." He took a long drink, put down the empty glass on the table, and sighed long and hard, the sigh breaking up before it finished. "If all this is true..." he said, eyes unmistakably haunted, "...and I ain't sayin' it is, then there's only one thing I gotta ask you..."

Kirk waited. The fear in Ray's eyes was good. For some reason known only to himself, the singer believed Kirk's story. Believed every fucking word of it.

"Why me?"

Kirk told him that, too. Every mad word of it. Again, Ray listened carefully. When Kirk finished with, "It would be the Mother of all Comebacks," he actually smiled a grim smile and gave Kirk a slow hand clap.

"Nice pitch, son. What are ya gonna tell me next? That I'm gonna get a whole new record deal out of it? Surely, that's the least I can expect, for saving the whole fackin' world..."

"Can't promise you that, Ray," Kirk said resignedly. The fear was entrenched in Ray's features; it had been there all along, for the last twenty-five years. Kirk had just brought it swimming back up to the surface again. Fear of failure, fear of rejection...most of all, fear of this band...

"Not gonna lie to you," Kirk continued. "If you do come and help us, you're more likely to end up in a mortuary than a recording studio. And that goes for me, too, and the rest of my Godforsaken band..."

Ray turned away, stared at the opposite wall, at the framed portrait of Michelle he had commissioned. Without looking at Kirk, he said, "What's the name of your band, son?"

"Lucifer..." Kirk said. "Lucifer Sam."

"Ray..."

He hadn't realized Michelle was standing in the doorway until she spoke, her voice grave. He wondered how much she had heard. He saw the fear in her face, too. And the deeply etched resignation. She'd built up a good few years of that as well, he guessed.

He got slowly to his feet, his kidney aching, his nose flaring. "I've said what I came to say. That's it as far as I'm concerned. We're meeting in the Green Man near the Wembley Arena at five. If you're there, you're there, and that's that. If not..."

"If not, then that is certainly not facking that, eh?"

Kirk reached out to shake Ray's hand. Ray hesitated, then slowly offered his own. But he was watching Michelle as he said, "I never really left Cat O' Nine, you know that, right?"

Michelle's eyes were filling.

Kirk nodded and let himself out onto the quiet street.

CD 5

THE LAST GIG

Chapter Thirty-Two

"So where is he then?"

Davey sat back in his seat in the lounge of the Green Man and held out his hands. "Where's our great Savior?"

It was obvious Ray had bottled out. Had Kirk only imagined the conviction in the older man's face the other night? His fear had been real enough, though, as if he believed everything Kirk had told him. But that fear could be exactly the reason Ray hadn't shown up, not because he didn't buy Kirk's admittedly fantastic-sounding story.

"Give him another half hour," he said, sipping his ale.

"And then what?" Davey put one boot up on an empty chair next to him, affecting a nonchalance he surely couldn't feel. He picked up his bottle of Newcastle Brown, took a loud slurp.

Kirk didn't answer. He glanced at Ned, who twitched once in sympathy but remained silent.

So they gave Ray another half hour. At the end of it, Kirk looked at his two friends, finished his beer, said, "Let's go..."

Davey stood up slowly, a big grin splitting his stubbly face. A wild relish was in his eyes before he whipped out his wraparound shades and covered them. "Why not?"

Ned looked up at them both, nodded, rose to join them.

* * *

There was a hub of excited activity in Arena Square. Throngs of people were enjoying the July sunshine, milling around the Arena concessions and shops, so blithely oblivious to the impending evil that Kirk would surely have begun to question his own sanity if it weren't for the fact two of his gang were missing. Rose and Johnny's absences provided a strong wake-up call for every time he began to be lulled by the sense of normality prevailing around him.

They proceeded to the main gate, Kirk refusing to be daunted by the impossibility of his mission, which seemed intensified by the grandeur of the venue. Kirk had never been one for stadiums; he preferred the intimate atmosphere of a sweaty pub gig to the detached formality of a 12,000 seater like the SSE Arena. He gazed up at the huge arc of interlaced steel that rose above the humped back of the venue, at the impressive glass face of the entrance, resembling a neo-postmodern twist on the pillared gateway to some Grecian Temple of the Gods, and felt his insignificance amplified tenfold.

Davey spat into one of the numerous fountains that sprouted near the entranceway, a gesture as futile as any of Kirk's plans, and symbolizing the same impotence. They were three misfit Davids entering the arena without so much as a slingshot.

They produced their tickets and made their way into the massive vestibule. Above their heads, a bustling balcony restaurant competed with the lower floor in terms of noise volume. The interior décor was silver-gray, functional with a touch of futuristic to the aesthetic. By nightfall, Kirk imagined neon would imbue the venue with a whole new layer of magic.

If Kirk was supposed to be reassured by the sight of the fairly significant police presence, he certainly didn't feel it; and there was DS Gull herself, a stone's throw away through the crowd, watching everyone arrive. It wasn't long before her hawk eyes spotted Kirk. He made his way through the eager pushing fans toward her, Davey and Ned following, Davey in particular not too happy about being seen chatting to the "filth."

Gull didn't smile as Kirk approached. Beside her, the ever-reliable Trimble chatted to some uniformed coppers, but he ignored the messy-haired singer of Lucifer Sam. Gull moved away from her colleagues to greet Kirk, an act of confidentiality not lost on him.

"So here we are," Gull said, her green eyes electric. "Ready to play?"

Kirk ignored her levity. She knew the dangers. Like Ray Starling, Kirk knew she believed the band presented a threat. But unlike the former singer of Cat O' Nine Tails, she had the balls to see it through.

"You going to tell me what you have in mind?" she said, just loud enough for Kirk to hear over the hubbub of excited fans milling around the concourse. "You know I can't condone any violence." An ironic wink. "How's the grand plan for love and peace proceeding?"

He looked away for a minute.

"Oh," she said. She arched her brows. "You don't have one. Does that mean I have to bust your cute backside after all..."

He shrugged, glanced at Davey and Ned. They looked distinctly uncomfortable being in the vicinity of the detective.

"Don't worry," she said brightly. She glanced at the seat numbers on Kirk's ticket. "I know where you are and will try not to make a stranger of myself throughout the performance."

"Gee, thanks, Miss," Davey quipped. "You can sit next to me and hold my hand if you want. I'd like that."

Gull turned her piercing, unassailable gaze on the bass player. "I might just do that, handsome."

Kirk pushed Davey ahead of him, and followed by Ned, they made their way around the massive building, past the numerous merchandise stalls flogging Cat O' Nine t-shirts, wristbands, posters, and patches, following the signs to C block through the hordes of metal fans, young, old, male, and female. "Nice day for it," Ned said as they located their seats in C4.

Kirk said nothing. He was staring at the sound desk situated at the front of the next block of seats to his right, the position of which had driven him to purchase these particular tickets. He nudged Ned and pointed, but the drummer had already spotted the booth. He nodded tersely. Kirk saw the indecision on his square face and felt even more despair gnaw at him. He was expecting too much of everybody, let alone himself. The sound desk was protected by a low wall, but the two security men guarding it looked pretty insurmountable, while the two engineers inside doubled the odds against them. This was where he could have done with Gull's assistance but knew that was impossible; she could not be seen assisting in sabotage. Now that Starling had abandoned them, it was down to Ned and himself—and he just hoped Ned's skills on a mixing desk were up to the job.

"I need a piss," Davey announced. "And a beer."

It was still early, barely 6:30 p.m. The support band would not be on for at least another hour, although it didn't specify who they were on the tickets, or on the net when Kirk had surfed it the night before, looking for anything in connection with the gig or venue that might help him in any way.

"I'll come with you," said Ned. "Kirk?"

He shook his head. He'd already drunk two pints at the Green Man. He needed to keep his head clear, even if he couldn't exactly insist the other two did the same. If they were all going to die, what did a few beers too many matter?

The seats were filling up. A significant group of Hells Angels, verging on middle-age and beyond, were congregating in the seats in front of Kirk. Many of them bore rockers on their leather jackets announcing the club they belonged to. Strangely, Kirk felt a little comforted by their presence. He had seen more than one t-shirt bearing the artwork taken from Cat's first album, but whatever solace that might bring him, a t-shirt was not going to be of much help today.

Kirk realized he was not the only one to have noticed the bikers. Gull was patrolling down a side aisle with a clutch of uniformed men, as well as the ubiquitous Trimble. She turned her attention from the twenty-something-strong bunch of Angels and locked eyes with Kirk. She nodded, walked on.

Kirk's attention was drawn inexorably to the stage. From his seat, the figures on it would be the size of the little, plastic Airfix soldiers he used to play with, but that didn't bother him unduly. He was more interested in how difficult it would be to access the stage itself. Not far from the front row in A block, an interlocking waist-high fence blocked off the mosh pit, and several yards beyond that was the raised stage itself, with steps on both sides leading up to it. Certainly not impregnable by any standards. But once the gig commenced, the wall of security provided by the band (and Kirk had no illusions they would be the same roadies that had followed them on their ill-fated flight) would be a major obstacle indeed.

The drum kit, PA, and guitar stands were already in position on the stage. What should have looked like an innocent set up of musical apparatus attained a sinister nature for Kirk. He tried not to think what terrifying notes might emerge into this huge hall and what impact they might have on the thousands of excited fans packing the rows and tiers. But he couldn't turn his mind away from the glimpse into Hell he'd snatched at the 100 Club, the human shambles piled up on the floor, the twist of deformity that had consumed Johnny. Had it not been for these dark intrusions on his reveries, he might even have been able to fall into the notion he was at a conventional stadium gig, sitting with twelve thousand other fans ready to enjoy a pleasant evening of contrived, mainstream rock.

His forebodings increased in correlation to the excited expectations of the crowd as the evening pushed on. Davey and Ned had returned with their drinks, not looking any more relaxed from their refreshments. Kirk's phone told him it was seven fifteen, but time held as much meaning for him now as it had when he had attempted to check it on a digital clock in the midst of an acid trip a few years before. The same remorseless absence of all mental control he had experienced then assailed him now, too. He was here, he was now, but none of it made any sense. Was he losing his mind?

He fingered the industrial-strength earplugs in the pockets of his jeans and desperately wished he not only had a better plan, but better props to go with it, and his feeling of unreality intensified.

He thought of Ray and the scared look on the old rocker's face. What the hell had possessed him to place all his faith, all his hopes for defeating these bastards in one pathetic, washed-up alcoholic? He could almost have felt ashamed at the utter futility and ludicrousness of his grand plan, were it not for the fact that within a few hours nothing would matter anymore.

He thought of Rose, and she immediately pulled him out of his morbid self-pity. Her face admonished him with its blank, empty stare, the horror implicit in that gaze snapping him into a new determination that whatever happened, he would not just sit here and wait for it to take him down. Her image was his badge of honor. She gave him strength, and looking back over their time together, he realized she always had. He remembered once joking to her in a pub on their second date, telling her drunkenly how he would slay giants, dragons, and ogres for her if she ever needed it. She had laughed and kissed him, pleased with the silly talk, and never believing he would ever have to come true on the idle boast.

Ned, sitting to his right, inclined his head toward Kirk as a roadie emerged onto the stage and began checking the mics. Two more that Kirk recognized from Cat's closest entourage ambled out to stand behind the fence, guarding the stage. "If we get through this, we're going to play the motherfucker of all celebratory gigs at the Bridge House," Ned said. "And it's going to be the finest gig we've ever played." He held Kirk's gaze, and not a single tic spoiled his moment.

Kirk nodded and even let out a little smile. To his left, Davey chuckled darkly, slurped his beer…and said nothing at all.

Chapter Thirty-Three

But before the excited audience could enjoy the headline act, there was the support group.

They came on about 7:40 p.m. Kirk knew that because he'd just told Ned the time a couple of minutes before, and a couple of minutes before that, and so on. Ned was taking considerable interest in time, but it really didn't matter to Kirk anymore. He supposed the drummer was freaking out in his own quiet, controlled way (apart from the tics, of course—they were anything but controlled, a dead giveaway of Ned's inner turmoil.)

They didn't so much strut on stage as shamble. They certainly silenced the eager hubbub of anticipation from the 12,000-strong crowd. Even from two-hundred yards away, Kirk could see there was something wrong with them. He needn't have worried about missing out on detail, though, as the giant screen behind the figures blinked into life to show obliging close-ups for those unlucky ones at the back. With the musicians' faces now twenty feet tall, the "wrongness" became startlingly evident.

For a start, they were all in varying stages of decomposition, although maybe not as much as could have been expected considering how long most of them had been in their graves. Come to think of it, Kirk was pretty sure the singer had never been buried at all. Hadn't he read somewhere Stiv Bators' girlfriend had snorted some of his ashes in tribute? And surely Brian

Jones would be more bone and worm than flesh by now, no matter how mottled and flaky it was? The ex-Stones guitarist could almost have been described as fashionably wasted as he tuned up his guitar with mold-blue fingers if it hadn't been for the patch of skin flapping loose from one cheek and the bald spot of skull showing through the bell of blond hair.

"Fuck me, it's Sid," said Davey as his hero stumbled up to the bass mic, swinging his instrument at his hips like a weapon. It was the first thing Davey had said in ages. And Sidney it was, indeed; albeit a Vicious with only one eye, the other socket brimming with twisting worms.

Kirk didn't buy it. He was about to say as much, but the proof was there right in front of them. Philthy Animal was taking his place at the drum kit, his spiky quiff gray, his skin grayer.

Ned, ever the musical technician amongst them, was concentrating on the finer details. "They're using Cat's instruments…" But there was panic in his eyes, and his banal words were surely trying to anchor it.

Was that significant? Kirk didn't know, and in the dazed shock of it all, he didn't really care. Did it matter that an undead Brian Jones was tuning up Jez Tweed's guitar, or that a zombie Sid Vicious was fucking about with Phil Carter's bass? Kirk could verify that this was indeed the case; he recognized the distinctive tattered gravestone sticker on the Fender bass from interviews and video clips.

Kirk couldn't take his eyes off the stage. There were shouts and growing sounds of confusion, not to mention unease from the audience. If these were nameless musicians made up to resemble the dead rockers, then the make-up artists had done a bang-up job. Some of the younger teenage girls in Blocks A and B began to scream. Kirk saw one of the bikers two rows in front of him stand up to get a better view. One of his mates pulled him back down.

Then things got more bizarre. The band began to engage in what Kirk realized was a gruesome form of stage banter.

Stiv started it. He clenched the mic with one hand, peeling back his t-shirt to show his left flank and a congealed bruise shaped like a tire mark through which nubs of rib protruded. "Fuckin' taxis these days, man," he said in a voice choked by grave dirt. "Run ya over sooner than pull in for ya…" If this was an act, it was a wholly tasteless one, Kirk thought, even though his distaste was pretty ridiculous itself in the face of everything he'd experienced. Of course, it wasn't an act; this Supergroup from the Grave was real—fashioning a corpse for Stiv to inhabit and re-dressing the others in less worm-ravaged stage gear was just one more part of the grand performance Cat O' Nine was putting on for their lucky fans to-night. This was merely the first course in the supernatural feast they planned to dish out.

As Stiv posed campily at the mic stand, one spindly leg bent, his bony body didn't look that much thinner than when he was alive. His wild bush of hair was midnight black, apart from the white flecks that coiled and burrowed to get at the skull beneath. Kirk dragged his gaze from the huge screen to concentrate on the live figures themselves. Sid was in his familiar stance now, long legs spread out defiantly, Elvis sneer joining with a rent in his cheekbone. The black swastika on his red t-shirt was punctured in places, revealing glimpses of white skin and the even whiter skeleton be-neath. His hair still looked good, though.

Kirk had to confess, this support act knew how to work their au-dience…

Sid addressed the bewildered and disquieted crowd, who were still ob-viously under the illusion this resurrection of icons was an elaborate and wholly artificial—even if remarkably tasteless—ingredient of the show. Sid's vocal cords were challenged by the worms that tenanted his throat, but he managed to get the words out regardless.

"We wanted fuckin' Brian James on guitar, but he ain't dead yet—or not quite—so we got this cunt instead…" He jerked a thumb at Jones, and a close-up on the screen showed Kirk the tip—along with the ends of his other fingers—was pure white bone, like he was wearing flesh mittens.

Brian swung his golden bounce of hair to face his antagonist, smiled a once-perfect smile that was now a grimace of yellow stubs soiled by cemetery dirt. "Thank fuck I died before Punk," he enunciated in his Chel-sea tones, degraded somewhat by his forty-five-year sojourn under the ground.

"Posh wanker!" Sid retorted, gobbing in his direction.

A hellish cartoon…that's what I'm watching, Kirk thought, his fists clenched, waiting for something horrible to happen. He wouldn't have to wait long; the banter was nearly worked out.

Brian swung away from the punk, the fur-lined collar of his psychedelic tunic almost, but not quite, covering the base of his neck, where the spinal column emerged from broken flesh. "At least I can play my instrument, man…"

Sid retorted by strumming his bass. The notes bellowed through the speaker system, hushing the growing rumble of the crowd as they continued to voice their confusion. Some were even getting up to leave, this display of bad taste just too much. They had obviously expected middle-of-the-road metal, the way Cat normally served it to 'em. *Had they even listened to the new album,* Kirk wondered? He suspected not. Or at least, certainly not as assiduously as Rose and the other victims had done. Otherwise they would be in a hospital or morgue right now instead of enjoying the show.

Sid's bass rumble was the cue. The Support Act from Hell launched into their first number.

It was "God Save the Queen," and Stiv did a reasonable enough impersonation of Rotten, chucking in his own Noo Yawk inflections, which somehow detracted from the lyrical content a little bit—not that Kirk gave a shit about that right now. The chords emanating from Sid and Brian's guitars were interlocking with the frenzied drumming from Philthy, creating a perfect storm of sonic malevolence. Kirk was forced to acknowledge its power: it pulverized all dissent and pushed those about to leave back in their seats. Kirk could feel it tickling at his mind with skeletal fingers, plucking at his cortex like the membranes were guitar strings. Before he could be lulled further, he groped for his earplugs and forced them down snug against his drums, urging his two friends to do likewise. It was almost too late for Davey; the bass player was already hypnotized, mouth open, eyes wide with shock and hero worship. Kirk slapped him hard, the action managing to wake himself up more in the bargain.

The song was over, and the audience was shell-shocked. Nobody applauded. Nobody moved. Kirk could see Gull with her officers half-way down one side aisle, staring at the stage in astonishment. She would be the first to succumb, Kirk guessed. Her discipline was just an illusion; the more regimented and conventional the mind, the easier it was to subvert. He could tell that by the way the officers were rooted in disbelief, their faces vacant, their radios abandoned.

But Kirk was wrong.

Gull wasn't going to succumb to the spell cast by the band that easily.

She had earplugs, too.

Yet the power blasting out from the dead Supergroup was so insidious that she could feel it kicking down her barriers regardless. But she would fight it.

As soon as she saw Sid Vicious swagger on stage, followed by the rest of his rotting peers, she knew this was no game. So Kirk had been right all along, just as she had suspected he was. The Cat O' Nine Tails show was more than just a concert; it was an opening to the Inferno, and this was the first Act.

But despite the ear plugs, she could still feel the music the band was playing tugging at her thoughts and instincts. When the band smashed in-to their second number, the ode to gun murder and desecrated love called "Ain't It Fun," she didn't need to know that this was one of Stiv's songs from the Dead Boys, or that Guns N' Roses had covered it so impeccably on *The Spaghetti Incident*. All that mattered was she was beginning to fall.

She leaned against the wall next to her, shook her head. She felt a surge of nausea and swallowed it down hard. She checked to make certain her earplugs were in place, and then almost forgot why she was doing it, and what she was going to do about this public disorder she was supposed to be policing. Disorder? Yes, of course, it was. It couldn't be right, could it? To allow rock stars to leave their graves and upset the public in such a foul show of public indecency... Especially not ones as obnoxious as Sid-fucking-Vicious.

Wasn't that why she was here...? To protect the peace...?

Peace... Peace and love. She'd never bought any of that shit. Give her sex and violence any day. Any night. She would rather be fucking some young stud up the ass with a strap-on, or whipping strips off his back than sniffing flowers and smoking a joint. Fuck that. She could even begin to appreciate Sid now. Almost. Even that fucking twat of a hippy, Brian Jones, looked pretty cool, grinning his death grimace—hell, even his huge purple flairs weren't too objectionable, muddied as they were from the grave.

When the song finished—and it seemed to stretch into eternity—she felt like she'd lost something. A lover, a connection, a passion. She couldn't remember what she had felt exactly while the music flowed from those ghostly fingers and out through the instruments, but she knew she wanted to feel it again.

She watched in awe as Stiv Bators regaled the prettiest females in the audience to come join them, ordering the two roadies to kick down the fencing blocking access to the stage. "I don't need fuckin' fences between me and the chicks," Stiv postulated, cheekbones like shovel blades, emaciated beyond the point of no return.

The roadies responded readily enough, dismantling the interlocking fence and allowing access to anyone who fancied sharing a stage with four dead guys.

Apparently, some females did. Quite a number, in fact. The roadies had to hold most of them back, there were so many females willing to invade the stage.

If the girls' eyes looked as blank as their minds must be, it no longer seemed a concern to DS Gull. Her clitoris ached as the band played the intro to "Sympathy for the Devil."

Oh yeah, she wanted to get on stage, too. She would quite happily have fucked the Devil right now, not just feel sorry for him.

The girls on stage were moving to the music, entranced, discarding their clothes with mechanical abandon. Absently, DS Gull wondered why her officers weren't reacting to this latest breach of the peace, but she didn't need to look at their faces to know they were far more gone than she was. She had her earplugs, didn't she? She could enjoy the show without losing her mind...

Stiv was snogging one of the girls. Gull could clearly see long, gritty worms coiling from his mouth and into the newly recruited groupie's, a lithe rock chick with sleeve tattoos and effulgent red-dyed hair.

Another girl, stripped down to leather bra and panties, a skull tattoo on her perfect right ass cheek, had got entangled with Brian, who stopped strumming his guitar and played her instead. Her raven-dark hair was thrown back, allowing him to drool his grave teeth over her arched neck. Gull longed to be up there now. Her fingers were unbuttoning her blouse, her head swirling with lust.

When Brian locked his decayed lips onto the girl's, Gull saw the rock chick's cheeks bulge as though something was emptying into her mouth. When she saw the trickles of dank-looking water dribbling from the groupie's mouth as Jones emptied his drowned lungs of its swimming pool contents, Gull imagined she could even smell the chlorine. But that was ridiculous, wasn't it? Mind playing tricks.

Her fingers continued to unbutton her blouse…

Kirk couldn't smell any chlorine. Not from this distance. But he saw the girl choke and fall and the flood of stagnant liquid gush from Jones's mouth. Like Gull, he had ceased to register its meaning or its context. He let the music lap him along and felt serene for the first time in…

But now Sid was destroying the serenity, or trying to, just as he always did. He was punctuating the chorus of "Woo-woos" by battering the female fans with his bass, swinging it by the neck and dealing out death blows.

Just as every cop is a criminal
And all the sinners saints
As heads is tails
Just call me Lucifer
Cause I'm in need of some restraint

Blood and teeth spilled onto the stage floor, and Kirk smiled. *Just call me Lucifer…*

Lucifer Sam…

Sounded familiar. And he couldn't…quite…remember why.

And then the mayhem stopped. Sid dropped his bass unceremoniously on the ground and stalked away. The bass continued to boom out a long, indignant note that filled the auditorium. Brian leaned his guitar dutifully against a monitor and followed Sid, who took up a rebellious stance at the rear of the stage. Philthy and Stiv left their positions, too, and joined their band members in a line as if waiting for the next part of the show to begin.

They didn't have to wait long. The roadies wasted no time clearing away the victims' bodies, tipping them into the mosh pit before resuming their positions in front of the stage, ready for their masters to arrive.

If the audience hadn't been so stoned on terror tunes, they would have erupted right then, as their adored heroes finally emerged from the wings…

…and Cat O' Nine Tails took the stage at last.

Chapter Thirty-Four

Or at least three of them took to the stage.

Jez Tweed, Phil Carter, and Barney Smolt assumed their habitual positions, Phil picking up the bass discarded by Sid and silencing its reverbs.

Kirk felt a new excitement steal through his crazed brainwash. It was the elation he used to feel years before at gigs when any of his musical heroes finally stepped out on stage after seeming eons of prevarication.

They were finally here.

Cat O' Nine Tails...

The trio began to play. Kirk remembered the track from the new CD—although he couldn't remember when he had heard it, or with whom. Some girl, maybe? It was a long, mostly instrumental track, which explained the delayed appearance of Baz Cropper, of course. The melodramatic singer wanted maximum build up for his entrance...

The music began to escalate, coiling rhythms as deadly as nightshade tangling the auditorium, the same chord playing over and over repeatedly. It was a chord Kirk had heard before, but that seemed long ago. And what did it matter? Kirk was mesmerized, earplugs useless against the drums, mind a slate wiped clean of missions, of vengeance, of...of somebody whose face continued to hover just off screen in his mind as the music took its hold and the band played on.

To either side of him, Ned and Davey followed the groove, eyes trained on the three unsmiling figures on stage. The musicians were clad in battered leathers and worn jeans that were the antithesis of theatrical. Their faces were as grim as tombstones, their eyes hollow places where maybe nothing dwelled.

The three members of Lucifer Sam copied their new idols, even down to the new chic—the soulless eyes that would surely catch on in any fashion-conscious youth demographic.

And then someone ruined it all by calling Kirk's mobile.

He ignored it at first. So what if he had forgotten to mute the ringtone? It hardly mattered here. The music drowned it out completely, and he wouldn't have noticed it at all if it hadn't been for the vibration in his pocket that accompanied it. Still, he ignored it. More interesting things were happening on stage. The singer had made his grand entrance for one.

Cropper was wearing the bronze demon mask prop from the Mario Bava flick *Black Sunday,* just as he always did at the start of every show. He would discard it after a song or two. The singer stood at the lip of the stage like a statue. Kirk felt the intoxicated hysteria of the crowd rise, though they were all too stoned from the music to make a sound. Cat O' Nine had the entire 12,000-plus audience in their paws. Enrapt. Kirk, too…apart from that bloody, incessant buzzing in his pocket. He could ignore it; it was a bothersome fly, hardly worth swatting…

Except…except it butted into his trip. It was raining on his parade.

He could switch it off completely, and then he could go back to enjoying the music as it ascended in layer after layer of powerful and intense rhythm, building around the same demented chord, a cabalistic symphony for the Devil. It was an orgasm of sound…and how could he ever have thought it *evil?*

Now Cropper was raising his hands to either side, like Jesus on the cross. And why did that seem strangely familiar? Like Kirk had seen the exact same thing on another day, another stage.

Cropper froze in his crucified position, masked head tilted back, arms outstretched, soaking in the waves of silent adulation from his fans. The music continued to build in power and volume, transcendent.

The buzzing stopped in Kirk's pocket, and Cropper took off the Mask of Satan.

Only it wasn't Baz Cropper's features that were revealed.

This was a face that had not had its lines magically erased; the bags around the prominent eyes had not been smoothed by supernatural means, nor the hair restored to its thick, prior glory.

This head was bald, the eyes bloodshot, the ravages of time and alcohol only too evident.

Ray Starling plucked the mic from the stand. The music faltered and began to fade as the other members of the band became aware of his identity, those staggering structures of sound crumbling, toppling, crashing into a resounding stillness.

"That's enough of this bollocks. I'm Ray Starling, and I'll fackin' take it from here…"

At first, silence. Then…

Chapter Thirty-Five

At first silence... Then...

Applause? The crowd looked completely wasted to Ray, and every-thing Kirk told him was seemingly true then; Cat's music was fucking them all up good and proper. There was a moment of total silence when he revealed himself, as the band stopped playing, momentarily thrown by the unmasking. The audience stirred slightly in their catatonia, some of them realizing exactly who it was standing at the lip of the stage with his arms outstretched.

A smattering of muted applause at first. Hardcore fans were shaking off the spell, however momentarily, the shock of seeing the original singer back in his old position after over twenty-five years jarring their dulled senses.

The clapping began to increase, Ray's oldest fans in the Angel Chapter leading the way, which was only to be expected, as he'd kitted them out with plugs before the gig and prepped them to expect a whole shit-load of trouble. Others were beginning to pick up on the apprecia-tion, the applause spreading slowly across the auditorium. Some were even standing, albeit in a shaky, befuddled fashion, responding uncon-sciously to this phenomenon, to this rare event...

Ray Starling was back.

The applause was building rapidly now. Escalating, just as the band's music had done minutes before. The crowd moved from stupefaction to amazement, to rapturous recognition.

The response to this Mother of All Comebacks filled the venue.

And Ray smiled.

"I'm back, and I'm mad as *hell!*" he shouted, his hands still outstretched.

The resulting applause drowned out his next words, and it didn't matter. After all the lost years of self-hate, self-doubt, of self-destruction and despair, Ray Starling was back, fronting the band he had once loved more than life itself. The ovation filled him, lifted him. Top of the World, Ma.

This was momentous. The audience was roaring for more, and distinct above the colossal noise, Ray could hear his name in a rising chant. He felt electrified.

He felt joy and total excitement orgasm through his body. He spread his arms, tilted his head to one side to take in the adoration of the crowd. His name was a massive chant that would shame the rest of the band: "Starling, *Starling*... STARLING!!!"

Ray was staring at 12,000 upturned faces. And they were all staring at *him.*

Ray had known exactly how to gain access to the dressing room area. Down through the underground lorry and coach park and over to the guarded doorway. It wasn't hard if you had the connections. Not only did he have a ticket, but he was Ray fuckin' Starling, and that might just count for something still...

It did. He even showed the security men (the arena's own security men, not Cat O' Nine flunkies) the special sword of honor his fan club had forged for him all those years ago when he was first kicked out of the band. They let him through, no problem.

Locating the band's dressing room was not too difficult either, although it was one dressing room in particular that he wanted. He knew the band insisted on separate rooms. It had been the same when he was with them, and he didn't anticipate it changing now. As long as he didn't get seen by the others before he found the room he wanted.

Arena security passed him in the corridors. One or two of them even half smiled at him as if there was a touch of recognition. Once, he turned a corner and two Cat roadies were making their way toward the wings for the sound check. He ducked back and let them go, crossed another corridor, came to a central restroom complete with bar, ping pong table, arcade video games, and other forms of entertainment for musicians. One geezer in a whistle was sitting on a chair talking into a phone. Ray didn't recognize him. Probably some hot shot from EMI come to watch the band. Well, if half of what young Kirk said was true, the plum was in for one hell of a shock.

He passed the suit casually as if he had a perfect right to be there. The man didn't look up from his call.

Ray moved on. So…did he believe all the shit Kirk had said? That was easy enough to answer. He had seen them change, even if the signs of that transformation had only been witnessed over the removed media of television interviews. One look at their rejuvenated appearance, their altered characters, the evil behind the emotionless faces had been enough for him. As soon as he'd heard their aircraft had been discovered in the same airspace, Ray had known there was trouble afoot.

They'd found what they were looking for then.

He had never understood their search until now. They had played at being comic strip Satanists, reading Aleister Crowley books and pretending to be bad. They'd done that shit when he was still with them of course, even though Ray was having none of that bollocks. Probably another reason they sacked his arse. But he didn't give a fuck about their musical quest to find the perfect note, the sonic key to open doors to new dimensions, or whatever bollocks Tweed and Carter, in particular, had discussed back in the old days. He'd been happy to leave them to the Holy Grail they would devote their careers to discovering.

And what exactly was to be found through this special door they had kicked open with their clumsy, naïve gropings? Ray hadn't wanted to know then; he wanted to know even less now. Whether the secret of eternal youth, a really fucking good anti-aging make-over, or all kinds of dark, horror show fuckery: it meant less than nothing to Ray. Back then, all he gave a shit about was drugs, booze, and tits. He hadn't really changed much in his philosophy. But those Crazy Cats had really gone and done it…whatever the fuck "it" was. They'd found *something*, and it had fucked them over good and proper, far more drastically than the way they'd fucked over Ray. That much was clear from the evidence of his own eyes seeing them on TV, reading the newspaper reports about missing girls, the fire at the 100 Club, and Sheila's self-mutilation. And especially after hearing Kirk's story, he had no doubt the band was responsible for *all* of it. He believed the younger man without question; he'd just been waiting for someone to come along and say it out loud.

And maybe the reason Ray didn't want to know about what they were chasing was because he was so damn afraid. Oh yes. More scared than he'd ever been in his whole fucking life. Which was why he'd almost not turned up at all. Michelle had seen the fear, and she had done her best to stop him, too.

So what made him decide to come then, on a death or glory mission to—if you believed the Lucifer Sam singer—save the fucking world?

It wasn't even as if he'd get to shag any groupies on this one-stop tour.

So what was it, Ray? What made you put yourself through all this bollocks again to join a band that didn't fucking want you back then and certainly didn't want you now?

He came to a final corridor, and there were the names on the temporary plaques: Good ol' Barney Smolt, lovable Jezzer Tweed, gorgeous Phil Carter… and bubbly Baz…

The fear was strong in this one, Yoda.

He paused for one final second outside Baz's door. He thought of Michelle, the one good thing in his whole fucked-up life, and then he pushed the door open.

249

For Michelle.

That's why he was here.

For the only girl he'd ever cared about. For her to look at him with admiration instead of disappointment just one last time...

For her, he'd fuck with the Devil.

Baz was sitting in his dressing room as if waiting for him.

There he was, the one man Ray had focused twenty-five years of resentment upon: his replacement.

Baz watched him enter without any sign of surprise.

"Looking good, Baz," Ray said, closing the door behind him.

Baz didn't answer for a moment, though Ray could see his cold slug eyes were taking him in.

"Ray Starling... I'd like to say it was a pleasant surprise, but we both know you're here to kill me..."

Baz's voice was sepulchral and gritty, like it was dragging itself along a very dirty highway to get here.

"What ya bin up to, Baz?" Ray was keeping it light, though his blood was bolting around his body and the fear was BIG. "You gonna tell me what the fuck happened to you and your pals?"

Baz's head didn't move. The dark, luxuriant hair and smooth face made him look like he'd barely edged into his thirties. Just his eyes let him down; they belonged to a forty-five-thousand-year-old.

"The Darkness happened," Cropper said slowly. It was the first honest interview reply he'd given since returning from Flight 757.

Ray smirked. "What, as in 'I Believe in a Thing Called Love'? You gonna cover their Christmas hit or somethin'?" He seized on the face-tiousness. It felt better than the fear.

Cropper ignored him, still unmoving. "It was waiting for us...in the airspace, a dead pocket over the Indian Ocean. Easy to lose a few things in that lonely vastness... It dragged us through a crack between what's here and what's there. We blindly sought it out for years without understanding its nature, Starling. Rather like you hunting for the ultimate high or the ultimate in forgetfulness in your case." An ironic twist of the mouth, which must pass for humor with Cat O' Nine Tails these days. Yet Cropper's eyes remained mirthless as cold, black stone. "Such brave voyagers into the unknown, with music as our guide… And at last we found it. What that Darkness was, we don't know or remember. We went to a dark place, and we are this now."

Ray waited. He waited for the right moment to make his move; he waited for his breathing to slow, for the fear to *let* him move. Face to face with the evil, and now he didn't quite know what to do. Keep it talking while he waited for his bravery to come rescue him? "You're gonna fuck things up badly, ain't ya, Baz?"

"You have no idea, Raymond. No idea…"

They could have been bantering at a pub table. The unreality of it kicked around in Ray's head for a bit. Had he snorted too much coke over the years? Had he decked too many E's? Smoked too much weed, swallowed too many tabs? Was that what all this was? One Mother of a trip with no stops along the route to a rusty, old terminus in the Asylum?

But Baz was continuing in his gravelly monotone as if warming to his theme, though there was no warmth at all in his voice, tunneling up from the dark as it was. "You want to ask why? You want motivation? You're in the wrong place, my friend. No reason for what we do. No explanation to satisfy you, no lyric you can understand or relate to here. It just is. It's a different kind of nature we're offering. Reality upturned, Black Art for Black Art's sake. If music be the food of love? Not any more… Are we providing a radical statement on the nauseating blandness of the industry? Write that down, Ray, it's a good one… But if you're looking for answers, you won't find them on the back of our new record sleeve…" And now Baz actually grinned. It was the first time since his return from wherever that Ray had seen him smile. His voice took on a nasty, sarcastic twist. "Maybe we just want to change the world… Our music is *killer.* That's it. Move on and die with the rest."

While Cropper was talking (talking? Exhaling evil would be a more accurate description), Ray was glancing around the room looking for objects to help him. There wasn't much, and he couldn't exactly have tried to smuggle a machete past security. He saw Baz's Mask of Satan on the dressing table behind the singer, all ready to be picked up. Hardly a weapon, creepy though it might be. His eyes moved on, found nothing, returned to Cropper as the singer finished his little hate speech.

"All done? You waitin' for me to get my dick out for you to sign, is that it?" He looked at Baz squatting there, master of metal, God of all he had stolen from Ray, and realized he had all he needed. He could feel it inside. Building. His old friend: The Rage...

"We gonna tussle now?" Ray said brightly, his right hand fingering the sword around his neck. His head was beginning to buzz the way it always did when the Beast was coming out. The Beast didn't understand fear. "You know I like a good scrap..."

Even as he finished speaking, he was leaping across the room, the five-inch sword unclasped in his hand.

Cropper didn't even try to get up from his seat.

Ray crashed into him, spilled them both onto the floor.

Ray felt Cropper's arms clasp around him like two leather-sleeved pythons. The pythons constricted. Ray's back began to creak, began to go...

"Got this...for ya, Baz," he wheezed as the breath was squeezed from his body. "From...my fans... I bet they...never..." He worked his right arm out from beneath the crushing grip, slammed the miniature steel sword home in Baz's right eye.

"...made... you one...ya cunt!" He leaned on the sword with all his sixteen stone, pushing the object into the black bubble until all that protruded was the three-inch hilt.

The pythons released their pressure. Ray rolled free, coughing, gasping.

Baz lay still on the dressing room floor. Then slowly began to sit up.

"Oh, fuck *off!*" Ray said and kicked him in the head with his Doc Martens boot. Once, twice. Baz lay down again. Ray continued to kick the singer's head until it was quite out of shape, although no blood ran free. He stood back for a moment, surveying his handiwork. "Pussy!"

He gingerly retrieved his sword from the burst black eye, then rammed it into Baz's forehead just for luck, raising his boot to slam it down on top of the blade until it dug in a few inches. Ray left it there like a flag, picked up the mask, and went to meet his fans.

Chapter Thirty-Six

Good ol' Ray…

Kirk watched the singer work the audience, and a part of him—the part that wasn't still detached and mind-fucked by the music—drifted back to that festival in Germany twenty-five years before.

Knew he wouldn't let me down…

He clapped along with the others, not really one-hundred percent sure why he was clapping, or even where he was. The rest of Cat O' Nine was ignoring their erstwhile singer, picking up where they'd left off, and their music soon began to build again, the repetitive three notes escalating in volume and urgency.

Kirk watched Jez Tweed's fingers creep up and down the fretboard of his Gibson as he played the chord. It seemed the most important thing in the world right now. Phil Carter's bass was rumbling out the same notes, too. Sounded like Apocalypse Blues to Kirk. He kinda liked it. Shame about the singer…Baz? No, not Baz, Rich, Rob…Ray! That was it. Shame he was being dragged from the mic by the roadies. Why wouldn't they let him sing? It had been a long while after all.

Ray was shouting into the audience as he wrestled with the three roadies. He'd already slapped one of them down—what a scrapper! He was calling names, a list of names. Already some of the bikers in the rows in front of Kirk were stirring sleepily, dazedly, some of them stumbling to their feet in response to the call, but unsure what it meant. One of them hollered in response: "Got your back, Ray. Always!" But his shout was drowned under Cat's music, and then he stroked his head and sat down again.

Ray was shouting for his fans to rally. Kirk dimly realized that, but it didn't look like they were doing much rallying. The hypnotic monster note was boring a tunnel through Kirk's mind. It looked awful dark at the other end of that tunnel.

It was obviously beginning to affect his vision, too; things were happening all around the auditorium. Dreadful things. People had stopped applauding Ray when the music started again and were sitting peacefully in their rows like the most submissive audience ever, watching the singer fight the roadies. But now their submissiveness was rippling, their bodies responding to the sound in violent, surreal ways. Kirk saw flesh buckle and burst; faces distort. Large portions of the crowd were raising their hands high in the air, forefingers and pinkies extended in a parody of the metal salute, the other digits rotted away. Ears were falling, too, blood geysers ripping out from the holes. Kirk watched in fascination as the transformation chord worked the crowd into a horror frenzy. A dim thought in his mental recesses: *Thank fuck we've got our plugs.*

Faces were shivering from the effects of the music, sliding like melted butter. Bodies contorted nightmarishly, heads stretched into deformed sculptures made by a lunatic artist. Twisted abominations were reclining in the seats once held by rock fans, but they weren't reclining for long. They were rockin' and rollin' in their positions, and then up and out of them to cavort in the rows, in the aisles.

And yet not all were changing, Kirk noticed as he sat enjoying the show. Roughly sixty percent at a guess. He remembered his earlier theories and even nodded to himself, or it could have been to the rhythm. *It's only rocking those more easily susceptible to influence for the moment—and of course those without plugs.*

Kirk was pretty sure that wouldn't be the case for long, though—

he could feel his own mind plucked by the tune, and that tunnel to no-where in his head opened wider.

Ray was on his knees, though he still had the mic in his hand. Two roadies were forcing him down, twisting his other arm behind his back. Ray was still calling in increasing desperation, but it was just one name he was shouting now. A strange name. It sounded familiar to Kirk, though.

"Lucifer Sam! Lucifer Sam!! LUCIFER SAM!!!"

And right then, as if on cue, Kirk's phone rang again.

Kirk thought about answering it in his dream. But what was the point? He was drifting, drifting. Nobody could bother him if he went down that dark rabbit hole in his mind.

The phone wouldn't let him drift. He was sure he could hear the ringtone even over the sonic crescendo from the stage. The vibration in his pocket was nagging at him, too. Ned turned to him with a zombie stare and said in a tone that suggested he didn't give a shit either way, "Aren't you gonna answer that?"

So Kirk took it out of his pocket and answered it.

He saw the caller ID even as he thumbed the answer button.

Rose.

He put the phone to his ear and her scream cut through his drum, spiking into his brain. The scream was long; it would never end.

He dropped the phone and stood up.

Rose.

Rose!

He was back in the room. Rose's farewell scream was an adrena-line shot that jerked him awake. He looked around, saw horror and madness. Took in the stage, with Cat using it for their own twisted in-cantation. He saw Ray.

A roadie's arm was around the singer's throat now, crushing the life out of him. Ray's eyes were locked on Kirk's.

Lucifer Sam…

Kirk moved.

He slapped Ned hard, shook him until the drummer's eyes swam back into focus. "We've got a job to do, Nedders," he said almost calm-ly. He wasn't so subtle with Davey; he punched him hard on the jaw. Davey came up and out of his dream ready for a fight. Which was good…

Without a word, he led them along the row toward the aisle. Most of the punters between them and the last seat were catatonic but had remained blissfully human. A couple right near the end spoiled things, however. Kirk remembered them snogging earlier in the afternoon when they first took their seats; now they wanted to snog everyone, but with mouths sealed up like stitched wounds in the featureless blanks of their faces and claws that raped and pillaged those in the seats next to them. Kirk had no time for their freakery, however, and slammed the male out of his way. He turned back to see the female attempting to press its stitch mouth against Ned's, but Davey punched it down, trashed its featureless head with stomps of his boot, and then they were through into the aisle between blocks C3 and C4.

Two roadies were guarding the sound desk. They were watching the metamorphoses around them with indifference. But they came to attention when they saw the three members of Lucifer Sam heading their way down the aisle.

Rock fan mutations were freaking out all around them. One of them with a face flicking between the monstrous and the normal, as if undecided which was more horrific, cavorted into Kirk's path, a hand like a nub of cactus swinging at his face. Kirk ducked it just as one of the roadies came for him. The cactus spines raked out the stooge's throat instead, and that was one down.

The other roadie was advancing on them. Past his shoulder, Kirk saw one of the mixing engineers behind the desk standing in a daze while his colleague underwent a change detrimental to his or anyone's sanity. The two techs danced a death tango to Cat's offbeat tempo, abandoning the controls as they did so.

"This fucker's mine," Davey roared as he overtook them to face off with the roadie. "Get to the mixing desk!"

Kirk and Ned let him carry on. They reached the low wall separating the desk from the rows of seats behind and hesitated. The untainted engineer was being dismantled, blood spraying the mixing knobs. The horror that was unbinding him swiveled to face them, its head a gash into another realm. Kirk peeked in there once, and that was more than enough.

He vaulted over the wall and charged, head down, ramming into the former engineer with his shoulder, slamming the freak against the farther wall. Ned was with him, but Kirk saw him slide on a streak of blood from the dead tech, and Ned was down. Kirk risked a quick glance behind him. Beyond the booth, Davey was on his back, the roadie about to stomp his face. A shambling corrosion of normality took the roadie from behind, unraveled Cat's slave like a child breaking down a fly, musical anarchy recognizing no masters.

The engineer Kirk had barged away was wearing a ripped Cat O' Nine t-shirt and weaving like a giant worm, tentacle arms unspooling from the short sleeves to embrace Kirk swiftly before he could move. He looked up at the face as he fought and the hole there was widening, a black wind tunnel that promised...nothing.

And then the music died.

Not fading this time, but an abrupt silence. Choked, like someone had killed it.

The abomination wrestling with Kirk gave up the ghost and hit the floor along with Cat's music.

Down on his knees, panting, Kirk saw Ned at the controls.

His fingers glided over knobs and dials, silencing the hellish orchestra that was Cat O' Nine Tails. Then he was inserting a download he pulled from his pocket and flicking up the sound levels.

Kirk leaned against the desk, covered in scratches and blood.

DS Gull had never cared much for rock music. Give her rap any day. But she'd kinda grooved on this shit. It made her hot as fuck. Especially for the three sexy bastards pummeling their instruments on stage.

She didn't care much for the fat, bald fuck who was trying to up-stage them though. She didn't rate him at all. So why was he getting so much applause?

Strange that. Could never work out these rock retards, that was for sure.

He was ugly, he looked drug-addled, and his belly swung over his studded belt. Looked like he was more handy with his fists than a mic—he'd already decked one of the big roadies the band had sicked on him, but now the music was stopping.

No, no… It was starting again… Or was it different music? Yeah, definitely different this time. And Jesus fucking cobblers, the fat fuck was singing along to it…

And fuck it all if he wasn't actually pretty good…

Better than good… The fat bastard with the alco-complexion could really fucking sing!

Beside her, Trimble was shaking off his trance like he'd had a bad case of night sweats. Gull felt an ache in her head and another in her groin. The latter was fading fast, regrettably. She wasn't exactly sure what the hell had just happened, but it felt like the Queen of all Mi-graines was ripping through her, blurring her vision. Making her see freaky stuff, there one minute, gone the next. But bodies… She could still definitely see lots of bodies in the aisles and rows of the auditorium as her consciousness flicked back in.

And the ugly bastard continued to sing.

Ray was ready.

The familiar opening drum beat, the guitars crashing in, Phil Car-ter's twenty-five-year-old bass line hammering the song forward, waiting for the vocals to answer the call…

That was all he needed. He was up off his knees, shaking the roadies away like fleas, picking up the mic stand, slamming the end into the face of one of them as he came at Ray again, snapping his nose, shattering teeth, putting him down. As the other lunged for him, Ray cracked his skull with the pole, dropping him next to his mate, and continued to rain blows on both 'til they lay obediently still at his feet. Then he was spinning with an agility that belied his figure, tossing away the stand, holding the mic to his lips. All in time for the first verse.

And Lucifer Sam did not let him down. They'd faded down the original vocal track just for him to sing live. So he did.

While the three members of Cat O' Nine paused at their stilled instruments, Ray took it away from them, like they'd done to him so long before.

It was the opening track of the first album. Ray had written it himself. It was Ray's song. The lyrics were all about overpowering personal demons, and that was funny as fuck to revisit twenty-five years on. He ran with the irony, embraced it. Revitalized by it. He could feel the power, surging from the audience, surging from within himself. It had been hidden—fucking well hidden—but now it was back. The fury. The wildness. Flushing all the freakery Carter, Tweed, and Smolt had summoned back into the spider hole it had crawled from. Best singer this band ever had? He surveyed his audience, or what was left of them. And sang for the survivors. For the corpses, too, for all those who had fallen for Cat's bollocks over the last few weeks; he sang for those who had disowned him, too. Ray sang for his life and theirs.

And now he had a new band...of sorts. Sid Vicious was lumbering toward Phil Carter, intent on winning back the bass. Brian, Stiv, and Philthy had snapped out of their inertia and were planning on an encore. Rage from the Grave carried them on, incensed over their rude awakening and spiritual abuse at the hands of Cat O' Nine Tails.

But Cat didn't want to relinquish their instruments a second time, and Ray knew why. The zombie Supergroup was playing for him this time.

Carter swung his bass at Sid, flattened that perfect head of spikes as well as half his face, which crumbled into a fall of maggots, soil, and skull fragments. Sid fell to his knees, still groping for the bass as the rest of his head slid away to shatter on the floor. Carter casually kicked the rotting punk's body over. Always a lousy scrapper, Sidney, Ray admonished him as he bellowed out a falsetto that must surely have curdled Baz Cropper's toes in hell.

Ray's audience was starting to abandon him now that he had freed them. Maybe they just didn't care for his backing band...

The survivors were clogging up the aisles, trying to escape, screams vying with the ex-barrow boy's vocals for supremacy. Ray sang them out and searched for his fans amongst the exodus. There they were: his loyal troops. They were buffeted by the evacuees, but standing their ground, waiting for Ray to call.

He turned to see Jez Tweed had reduced Stiv to ashes once more with a desultory wave of his guitar—just like it was an electric Gibson wand—and was now battering Brian Jones backward with the instrument. Barney Smolt decided to help out, climbing down from his stool to spike a drumstick through the hippy's heart. Brian smiled through his tomb teeth and gave up the ghost, stretched out on the floor at peace with himself again. Philthy's last stand didn't last long. Those who had summoned him reversed their offer. He sat down on the drum kit Barney had vacated, laid his head to rest on a cymbal. The *tissssshhhh* almost drowned out Ray's vocals in an extended, sibilant clash.

Ray could see that he'd won a partial victory, but not the war. Carter was advancing on him now, tossing his guitar aside to take him with his hands. Ray dropped the mic and took a stance, ready to enjoy the thing in life he was second best at...

"It's not enough!" Kirk hissed. He watched Ray give up his vocals and take up scrapping again, launching himself on his old enemy in a crash of bodies that took them both to the floor.

"What the fuck you on about?" Davey panted, stumbling into the mixing desk. "The freaks are all gone. Just corpses now. Half the fuckin' fans are out the door! That's a result, ain't it?"

"Not if you're the corpses' families," Ned snapped back with whiplash anger. "Kirk's right. Cat is too strong. Even with Ray, the old music's not enough."

"Fuckin' turn it up then, ya daft cunts." Before they could stop him, Davey had lunged inexpertly at the controls. One hand settled on the volume switch, more by accident than design, and slammed it up, while his other, not so fortuitously in its frantic scrabbling across the desk, hit PLAY. Immediately, the reel-to-reel tape the techs had been using to record the gig whirled into action. Ray's song was cut off in its stride, and the live recording blasted through the auditorium speakers again. The same three notes were back, like very unwelcome friends, and they were louder than ever.

Chapter Thirty-Seven

"You clumsy fuck!" Kirk snatched at the controls, managed to hit REWIND instead of the OFF switch, and the tape began to re-spool.

And then something interesting happened.

As the magnetic tape rewound, the transformation chord played backward through the auditorium speakers, and Phil suddenly let go of Ray and lay still.

Ray got up on his knees, blinking at the bass player. Phil blinked right back at him, eyes no longer black, but soft brown and confused. Lines cascaded across his face. His hair was dipped in a tide of encroaching gray.

"What the fuck?" Ray croaked.

"Ray?" Phil sat up dazedly. "*Ray!*" He got unsteadily to his feet. Ray copied him, crouching, wary.

"You back with us, Ray?" he said, sounding like an old man losing his memory.

Ray looked around him, at the exits choked with people screaming to escape, at the piles of dead and dying. The tape was still rewinding, the three notes reversed. Then the speakers were silent again. Had one of the Lucifer Sam boys switched off the tape altogether?

"Killer gig," Phil said, trying to get a fix on it all. "Helluva comeback, son." Then he turned to Ray, remorse twisting his face. "I'm so sorry... Ray. What we did to you. I'm so fucking sorry, man..." He reached out a hand to take Ray's. As he did so, his other hand came out from inside his leather jacket. Phil slid the knife blade comfortably into Ray's heart as his eyes bugged black again and his hair darkened.

"Sorry, Ray, old buddy, but you were never right for us..." His voice was a deep bass, his flesh picked clean of the ravages of time.

Ray was on his knees again, mouth open as if about to argue. Nothing came. He'd run out of resentment. He stared up at the bass player and thought of Michelle, lying naked in a Holiday Inn bed with a brunette by her side. He'd had some good times on tour.

Had some good times...

Michelle...?

Michelle...

The scrapper was done.

Kirk saw him fall.

"What did you switch it off for?!" Ned shrieked at Davey. "Rewind it again!" Davey managed to look aghast and stupid all at the same time. "I didn't fucking touch it!"

Kirk pressed rewind, but the tape wouldn't move. "It's stuck." He wiped at some of the engineer's blood that still washed the mixing deck. "Tape's got blood on it..."

Ned thumbed the buttons and switches dementedly, but he had to concede Kirk was right.

"I've got a better idea," Kirk said slowly, as if not sure what he was saying or how ridiculous he might sound. He looked at them with a mad glint in his eyes.

Then he was out from behind the desk in a rush, heading down the aisle.

Toward the stage.

"The fuck?" Ned hesitated, but it was a moment only, then he punched Davey in the arm and followed the singer.

They had to battle through a stream of those panicking rock fans still fighting to get out of their blocked rows, having finally woken up to the fact this was a *really* bad gig now the music was no longer thinking for them. But even with the exodus going the other way, Kirk, Ned, and Davey weren't the first to reach the stage.

The bikers got there first.

They had seen Ray's betrayal, too. They'd shaken away all vestiges of Cat's music from their ears and synapses, and now they were fully amped up for vengeance.

They took the stage in a denim- and leather-clad tide, all graying goatees, tattoos, and big muscles. They tore into the band and the remaining roadies like they were prison guards blocking their exit.

But again, it wasn't enough.

As Kirk made it to the fallen fence and hurled himself up the side steps, he saw the supernatural musicians deal with the stage invasion far more effectively than any bouncers. Heads were twisted backward, intestines spooled out, limbs cracked, bodies hurled back into the mosh pit.

Still, the bikers did not give up. They had always loved Ray. And he was right on the mark: they would never have made a sword of metal for Baz Cropper...

The stage battle raged around them as Kirk rushed to the guitar dropped by Jez Tweed, forced as he was into hand-to-hand combat. He pointed Ned in the direction of the drum kit, where Philthy still sat, head down on the hi-hat. He could see Ned understood now what was in his mind. Davey would need more persuading.

"The notes!" he shouted at the bass player. "We've got to play them backward."

"What the fuck?" Davey shouted through the screams of the battle. "That makes it worse, don't it? Didn't ya learn nuthin' from Judas fuckin' Priest?"

"Just *do* it!" Kirk called back, but his voice was lost under the chaos. He plucked at a string, searching for the right note. He was crap on guitar, always had been. But surely he could manage three notes, one measly chord?

He plucked again, twanging the E string disconsolately. No. Wrong. He was shoved violently sideways by a biker tossed like a bag of shopping across the stage by Carter. Kirk stumbled, tried again.

Through the turmoil of battling bodies, Kirk could see Davey strumming Carter's bass. A hollow note boomed out across the auditorium. Two more followed. Davey had it. For once, the idiot had sussed it and was playing Cat O' Nine's transformation notes in perfect reverse order. Ned was lifting Philthy clear of the drum kit reverentially. He turned to shout something at Kirk, but a death shriek in his ear blocked it as some poor member of the Ray Fan Club bought it. Ned cupped his hands, but the pummeling thunder from Davey's bass took away the words.

Then someone was taking the guitar firmly away from him. Kirk stared into a familiar face. Or almost familiar. One of the bikers, handsome, piercing blue eyes, jagged black fringe. He nodded at Kirk, threw the strap over his head and shoulders, began to play the three notes.

Ned had found a beat to complement the backward chord. Kirk wasted no time racing to pick up the mic, which lay not far from Ray's outstretched hand.

"I'll take it from here, Ray," he whispered.

He wasn't sure what to sing, so he made it up. The words were nonsense, but they fitted the rhythm of the three notes, so he kept on singing. Like Ray, it was what he did best, after all.

Trimble was shaking like a junior officer who had never seen action. Which was pretty much what he was, the poor lamb. Gull had to grab him and shake the pussy into the present day.

Then she rounded on the other officers who were all standing around in a shocked daze waiting for someone to tell them what to do. That would be her, then.

The bikers were fighting a losing battle on the stage, and Kirk and his boys were doing some weird shit with Cat's instruments, kicking up an unholy racket in the process. That left her in charge of the sensible stuff. She was the long (splendidly finger-nailed) arm of the Law, and it was about time she stopped watching the show with a throbbing clitoris and a vacant mind and got on with exercising it.

She led the five officers toward the stage at a run. Another party of policemen deployed to patrol the other side of the auditorium jerked into action, too, following her example. She was on the radio as she ran, calling for back up.

They reached the steps up to the stage, and Gull didn't hesitate; she had a taser in one hand and a pepper spray in the other. Lucifer Sam was playing the repetitive chord more urgently, faster, faster, but couldn't they see they were wasting their time? Not to mention giving her a right proper headache. And what the hell was that cat-strangling choon the singer was coughing out? Thank God she still had the plugs. It didn't look like the band would be able to sustain the noise for long, though; Jez Tweed had already broken apart the biker who had detained him and was striding purposefully toward the handsome devil in Hells Angels gear playing his guitar. The young usurper wasn't aware of the danger stalking him, but Gull had enough on her plate. The hottie would have to look after himself.

She could see Carter lifting a huge biker in the air like he was made of straw. The bass player locked eyes with her as she came, and she gave him more to look at than he bargained for, pumping spray into those bugging orbs. No effect. He strained to hurl the biker at her, and she ducked aside in a roll as the heavy body flew past, skittling two officers behind her. She came up on one knee, firing the taser as Carter advanced. He performed a dance, came on, face dissolving into a black whirlpool.

Gull lowered the taser, gazing into the swirling absence that had been a face. She felt herself floating, floating, going out with the tide...

And then Carter's features were re-appearing in the midst of the sucking pit, brown eyes pouched in a crow's nest of wrinkles, slightly bent nose, mouth guarded by deep worry lines. He faltered, held out a hand, then fell backward in a sitting position. His graying head slumped forward.

Gull got up, still clutching the taser.

The surviving bikers were climbing to their feet, too, checking their not-so-fortunate friends. Barney Smolt lay under a pile of dead rockers. One of the drummer's hands was outstretched from beneath the scrum, unmoving.

Jez Tweed was still moving implacably toward the imposter playing his guitar, his perm losing its luxuriance and color as he went. Finally, Tweed stopped and surrendered all rights to his instrument for good. The Cat guitarist staggered, then took a stage dive into the empty mosh pit.

Gull watched him twitch for a second and then not move at all.

Kirk stopped singing.

Davey strummed his last note.

Ned put down his sticks.

The young biker that looked so familiar dropped his hands to either side.

Kirk nodded at him. "You did great."

Davey wandered over, bass still slung over his shoulders. He wouldn't let it go now. Not ever. He pulled out his shades, popped them over his freaked-out eyes. "Anyone ever tell you you look just like fuckin' Brian James," he said to the biker.

"Who?" Ned joined them, still carrying Barney's drumsticks. He was breathing heavily from his exertions and looked like he didn't believe he was still alive.

"Ex-Damned geetarist," Davey told him. He turned back to the biker. "You his son or somethin'?"

"Who knows?" the guitarist said. He wasn't going to let go of his Gibson either. Not ever.

Davey wiped his pale face with the back of a hand, surveyed the carnage all around them, let out a long, slow breath. Then he turned to his friends, patted Ned's sweaty shoulder almost affectionately. "That gig's done you some good, I reckon, mate. Not seen you twitch since the band came on. Reckon Cat O' Nine scared the Tourette's right outta ya."

Ned nodded slowly, pondering Davey's words. "Reckon you could be right...ya big-nosed, pig-eyed wanker." His arm rose toward Davey in a final tic, a grand British, two-fingered gesture that Sid would have been proud of.

"Good enough," Kirk said. He was looking into the wings, past all the human debris littering the stage. DS Gull was ahead of him, cuffing an elderly looking man who had been sitting watching the show. She led him out under the floodlights.

Doug Roscoe stared at Kirk without seeing him. His mouth worked endlessly, but only drool emerged.

Gull handed him over to some officers, who led him away to the steps. They could already hear sirens cutting through the night, reminding them for the first time that there was a world outside this auditorium, and it would go on. It would go on.

"Good enough," Kirk said again and nodded at the members of Lucifer Sam.

OUT-TAKE

Good enough?

I reckon. I reckon we did our job. Got a new backline and a new band member, too. The bikers were the only ones to pay us our due that day, mind; they loved us after that Wembley gig alright, even though it was us that got their beloved Ray Starling involved in the first place. They helped us pack all of Cat's gear in the back of a truck in the basement car park and away. Guitar, bass, most of the drum kit, and the PA. Davey's idea, if I recall. Thought he was fuckin' Steve Jones from the Pistols, didn't he—nicking gear from bigger acts. Too much chaos going on for anyone to notice, y'see, though I reckon that sexy DS spotted it and turned a blind eye. She knew what we'd done for the whole fuckin' world, even if no bastard ever thanked us for it. And we certainly paid for it all in other ways; we lost a few along the way... But that's life, ain't it? That time we lost Johnny, Ray, and...

Rose.

I said I couldn't talk about her, didn't I? But I still think about her. Even after all these years. She's still there, in that ward. I visit her now and then, but she never recognizes me. Her eyes are far away. Best not think about that now, eh? Got a gig to perform. Best zip up, get the hell out of this stinky lav, and join the rest of the lads.

I'm starting to turn away from the stained mirror above the wash basins and I see him again. Just a brief glimpse, like. I look again, and the old geezer's gone, thankfully. Bin happenin' a lot that, lately. Losin' my grip. Reality's a funny thing; I know that more than anyone.

I see the old fella sometimes, but I don't look too closely. Don't want him around. I'm only thirty-seven, for fuck's sake—ten years older than the 27 Club, so I outlasted those old wasters.

Right, let's do this. Get out and face my public. Time to climb that crappy, little stage in the corner of this godforsaken boozer and do my stuff.

Where's the rest of the bastards? We're due on in five minutes, and nobody's even set the gear up on stage yet. Lazy fucks. They must be outside takin' a smoke. Davey, Ned, Johnny... no, that's not right, is it? I forget who's in the line-up these days, we've bin through so many...

I'll just take a pew here at this grubby table, finish my beer.

Weren't we supposed to be playing a gig shortly? I'm pretty sure we were... or was that another day? One day slips into another, don't it?

But there's nobody here in this shabby bar who'd appreciate us, that's for sure... just a few old drunks, pissing away the afternoon, and those young bastards laughing at me from over by the jukebox. They say they never heard of Lucifer Sam. What do they know?

I can see my reflection in my pint glass. I can see the wrinkles and sagging pouches, the white hair. But fuck it... I can see the dark pupils of my eyes, too, and in them, I can see *me*, and I'm young...

And I'm singing for Lucifer Sam.

ABOUT THE AUTHOR

Leo Darke was once famous for being sacked as a scary actor from the York Dungeon in England. His thespian efforts were so chilling as he menaced the public in between hanging Dick Turpin and describing the drawing and quartering of Guy Fawkes that girls shrieked and indignant parents wrote furious letters… His subsequent dismissal was plastered all over the newspapers shortly after. "Is this the most terrifying man in Britain?" screamed one headline. Well, he may not really be all that scary in person, without the make-up and costume, but he certainly hopes his novels are. He is also the author of *Mr. Nasty* and *Pandemonium*.

Press
Presents

THE FEAR IS GROWING

From the moment he saw the ancient castle rising out of the picturesque Scottish countryside, filmmaker Dan Martin knew he'd found the ideal location for his vampire horror movie. And nothing could make him leave. Not the eerie legends of soul-stealing beasts of the night…nor a bizarre series of freak accidents. Not even his pregnant wife's tragic miscarriage.

THE TERROR IS BORN

Except that now there is another fetus growing in Vicki's womb. But little Darian is not going to be a normal baby. The Martins' adopted ten-year-old son Marty will soon find that out. In fact, Marty will soon know exactly what his new brother really is.

Shrouded in Mystery

The locals call it Isla de los Perdidos.
Island of the Lost.
According to the legends, those who venture onto the shores of this cursed
island never return.

Abandoned

Valarie DeNola and her sister Julie have chosen to ignore the legends and the
warnings. They have been selected to lead a team of explorers to the island to
discover the mystery surrounding it. But once ashore, they become cut off from
the outside world, and what they discover is something they could never have
prepared for.

Inhabited by Death

Now they must fight against an unknown presence that is picking them off one
by one. No one can be trusted, and when even nature rises up against them, all
seems lost. Their one hope is the extraction team they know is coming.

But will any of them survive to see it arrive?

It all started with the sibilant, unintelligible whispering and the movement of shadows within shadows. For Dennis Parkes, it was a sign of his worsening mental health. That is, until the day it spoke clearly and told him what it wanted.

Swanhilde

When amateur ghost hunters Jake Maxfield and Elton Hoggarth discovered the stone with the letters G and J engraved into it, they suspected they might have made a significant find, but because of the worsening weather, they are forced to abandon their amateur dig. They send their photos to a university contact, who confirms that they have indeed discovered something important.

Gjallarbru

Can this bridge be behind Dennis's situation? And does it explain the strange darkness that has settled over Ottmor Wood and the surrounding area? Or is something more sinister at work? And are Dennis's motley group of friends enough to beat back the darkness and save their hometown — and the world?

SUFFER THE LITTLE CHILDREN TO COME UNTO ME...
AND BE LIKE GOATS IN MY PARADE

The city of Portland, Maine, is preparing for a parade to end all parades, one that will usher in a thousand years of darkness. The only thing is, they don't know it.

Four strangers will engage each other on the Devil's battlefield and fight not only for the future of the city, but for the entire world.

Warren Pembroke, Satan's Chosen One. He has been charged with making sure everything goes according to the Dark Lord's plan.

Svetlana Barnyk, a gypsy street performer cursed with the Gift of Sight. She lives in fear of the day when *Zee Doctor* will return to reclaim the gift he bestowed on her.

"Tobacco Joe" Walton, an ex-con who served a 43-year term for committing a savage crime in the name of Justice. He is seeking redemption, but Ol' Scratch has other plans for him.

Erik Marsh, a crime beat reporter driven to the edge by the atrocities man has committed against his fellow man. All he wants is to preserve his sanity and spend time with his son.

Will they be able to defeat the Devil and stop the Goat Parade, or will the world be plunged into an age of darkness and endless suffering?

Printed in Great Britain
by Amazon